Praise for the Novels of the Nine Kingdoms

A Tapestry of Spells

"Charming, romantic, and verging on the wistfully sweet . . . Kurland deftly mixes innocent romance with adventure in a tale that will leave readers eager for the next installment."
—*Publishers Weekly*

"Lynn Kurland has created a rich fantasy world beyond compare . . . I am always surprised by Ms. Kurland's ability to spin out the story with so much imagination. One can only wonder what her dreams are actually like." —*The Romance Readers Connection*

"[Kurland] truly shines in the Nine Kingdom books."
—*Night Owl Romance*

"Fans will feel the author magically transported them to her realm as Ruith now fights against what his father wrought while concealing secrets from his new ally who does likewise."
—*The Best Reviews*

Princess of the Sword

"Packed with enchantment, adventure, terrifying battles, and a love so strong that no wizard or mage can affect it . . . Beautifully written, with an intricately detailed society born of Ms. Kurland's remarkable imagination, this is an extraordinary tale for fantasy readers as well as those who just want to read a good love story."
—*Romance Reviews Today*

"Over the course of this splendid trilogy, Kurland has provided an action-packed fantasy as well as a beautiful love story between characters who respect each other's talents." —*Romantic Times*

"An excellent finish to a great romantic quest fantasy . . . readers will relish Ms. Kurland's superb trilogy."
—*Genre Go Round Reviews*

"An intelligent, involving tale full of love and adventure . . . If you enjoy vast worlds, quiet love stories, and especially fantasy, I would suggest you give this trilogy a try." —*All About Romance*

continued . . .

The Mage's Daughter

"Lynn Kurland has become one of my favorite fantasy authors; I can hardly wait to see what happens next." —*Huntress Reviews*

"The fantasy world, drawn so beautifully, is too wonderful to miss any of it. Brilliant!" —*ParaNormal Romance Reviews*

"A fabulous . . . tale that sets the stage for an incredible finish." —*Midwest Book Review*

More Praise for the Novels of Lynn Kurland

Dreams of Stardust

"A masterful storyteller . . . [a] mesmerizing novel." —*Romance Junkies*

"Each new book is cause for celebration!" —*Fresh Fiction*

A Garden in the Rain

"Kurland laces her exquisitely romantic, utterly bewitching blend of contemporary romance and time travel with a delectable touch of tart wit." —*Booklist*

"[Kurland] consistently delivers the kind of stories readers dream about." —*The Oakland (MI) Press*

"Kurland out-writes romance fiction's top authors by a mile." —*Publishers Weekly*

From This Moment On

"A disarming blend of romance, suspense, and heartwarming humor, this book is romantic comedy at its best." —*Publishers Weekly*

"A deftly plotted delight." —*Booklist*

My Heart Stood Still

"The essence of pure romance. Sweet, poignant, and truly magical, this is a rare treat."
—*Booklist*

If I Had You

"Kurland brings history to life . . . in this tender medieval romance."
—*Booklist*

The More I See You

"Blends history with spellbinding passion and impressive characterization, not to mention a magnificent plot."
—*Rendezvous*

Another Chance to Dream

"Kurland creates a special romance."
—*Publishers Weekly*

The Very Thought of You

"[A] masterpiece . . . this fabulous tale will enchant anyone who reads it."
—*Painted Rock Reviews*

This Is All I Ask

"Both powerful and sensitive . . . A wonderfully rich and rewarding book."
—Susan Wiggs

A Dance Through Time

"An irresistibly fast and funny romp across time."
—Stella Cameron

Lynn Kurland

Star of the Morning

BERKLEY SENSATION, NEW YORK

THE BERKLEY PUBLISHING GROUP
Published by the Penguin Group
Penguin Group (USA) Inc.
375 Hudson Street, New York, New York 10014, USA
Penguin Group (Canada), 90 Eglinton Avenue East, Suite 700, Toronto, Ontario M4P 2Y3, Canada
(a division of Pearson Penguin Canada Inc.)
Penguin Books Ltd., 80 Strand, London WC2R 0RL, England
Penguin Group Ireland, 25 St. Stephen's Green, Dublin 2, Ireland (a division of Penguin Books Ltd.)
Penguin Group (Australia), 250 Camberwell Road, Camberwell, Victoria 3124, Australia
(a division of Pearson Australia Group Pty. Ltd.)
Penguin Books India Pvt. Ltd., 11 Community Centre, Panchsheel Park, New Delhi—110 017, India
Penguin Group (NZ), 67 Apollo Drive, Rosedale, North Shore 0632, New Zealand
(a division of Pearson New Zealand Ltd.)
Penguin Books (South Africa) (Pty.) Ltd., 24 Sturdee Avenue, Rosebank, Johannesburg 2196, South Africa

Penguin Books Ltd., Registered Offices: 80 Strand, London WC2R 0RL, England

This is a work of fiction. Names, characters, places, and incidents either are the product of the author's imagination or are used fictitiously, and any resemblance to actual persons, living or dead, business establishments, events, or locales is entirely coincidental. The publisher does not have any control over and does not assume any responsibility for author or third-party websites or their content.

STAR OF THE MORNING

A Berkley Sensation Book / published by arrangement with the author

PRINTING HISTORY
Berkley Sensation trade edition / December 2006
Berkley Sensation mass-market edition / December 2010

Copyright © 2008 by Lynn Curland.
Excerpt from *Spellweaver* copyright © by Lynn Curland.
Cover art by One by Two.
Cover design by George Long.
Interior text design by Kristin del Rosario.

ISBN: 978-0-425-23822-6

BERKLEY® SENSATION
Berkley Sensation Books are published by The Berkley Publishing Group,
a division of Penguin Group (USA) Inc.,
375 Hudson Street, New York, New York 10014.
BERKLEY® SENSATION and the "B" design are trademarks of Penguin Group (USA) Inc.

PRINTED IN THE UNITED STATES OF AMERICA

10 9 8 7 6 5 4 3 2 1

Prologue

❧

It was a splendid day to be dealing out death. Adhémar, king of Neroche, nodded to himself over the thought, though he suspected that nothing so exciting would actually come to pass. He was out for a simple jaunt along his northern borders, not a pitched battle. Indeed, it had been so long since he'd encountered any trouble that it seemed that the only thing he did with his sword these days was prop it up at his elbow at supper.

It was a pity, truly. He came from a long line of superior warriors. And he had to admit, quite modestly, that he had inherited more than his fair share of prowess. It wasn't something he made mention of overmuch; his reign spoke for itself. No disasters since he'd taken the crown fourteen years earlier, no wars with neighboring kingdoms, no real trouble with the menace in the north. That sort of peace was a fine accomplishment, though it had robbed him of as many exploits to brag of as he would have liked. At least there was nothing of a disastrous nature for some bold-tongued bard to use to entertain those less respectful of a king's burden.

Aye, it was a good life. Adhémar looked about him in satisfaction. He was surrounded by his most elite guardsmen, each of them equal to an entire garrison of a lesser king. His castle, Tor Neroche, hovered on the sheer side of a mountain behind him like a fearsome bird of prey. Even kings of other lands shivered a bit when they rode beneath the shadows of those battlements. And who could blame them? It was impressive in the extreme.

And there were the more personal particulars to consider. Adhémar turned to those with a decent amount of enthusiasm. He examined himself, looking for flaws. It was difficult to find many, though he was surely more critical of himself than he was of anyone else. He was young, for a king of Neroche; he was handsome, based on reports by others he knew to be perfectly impartial; and his entire life had been full of might, magic, and many other kings wishing they could be him.

And now to be out and about, savoring the first days of what promised to be a glorious autumn, knowing that the seasons would stretch out ahead of him in as fine a manner as they trailed off behind him. He listened to the jingle of tack and the low conversings of his men and knew deep in his heart that today would be yet another day that would pass peacefully and quietly into the splendor that was his reign.

And then, quite suddenly, things changed.

There was the sound of a slap. Adhémar turned around in his saddle to find the man behind him looking quite surprised to see an arrow sticking out of his chest. The man met Adhémar's eyes.

"My liege," he said before he slid off his horse and fell to the ground. He did not move again.

Adhémar turned to face the assault. It came, somewhat surprisingly, from a bit of forest to the north of the road. Adhémar cursed as he spurred his horse forward. Surely someone could have warned him about this. There were mages aplenty in his kingdom and one in particular whose duty it was to see that their northern borders were secure. There would be words later, to be sure.

But for now he would do what he did best, and that would be to intimidate and terrify his foes with his sheer presence alone. That and the Sword of Neroche, the king's sword that had struck fear into the hearts of innumerable enemies in the past. Adhémar drew his sword with a flourish. It blazed with a bloodred magelight that sent his enemies scattering.

Adhémar bellowed his war cry and followed, with his men

hard on his heels. They cut through the enemy easily, soon leaving the ground littered with the bodies of the fallen. Adhémar paused on the far side of the glade and examined the corpses from his vantage point atop his horse. The lads before him weren't precisely of the sort he was accustomed to encountering. Indeed, he suspected that they weren't precisely human. He found himself hoping, with a desperation that never found home in his breast, that he was imagining what he was seeing.

He watched his men finish up their work, then resheathed his sword and nodded to his captain to move on. The men made their way up the small hillock to the road, looking over their shoulders uneasily. Adhémar normally wouldn't have admitted that he understood such looks, but he could not lie and say he did not. There was something fell about these creatures, fell and foul and not of this world. And here he'd thought that pesky black mage to the north had been contained.

Obviously not.

He looked over his shoulder for one last quick count of the dead. He counted two score.

But apparently that wasn't all.

Adhémar watched, openmouthed, as from those trees stepped one last something that was definitely not a man.

Adhémar's captain checked his horse and started back toward the creature. Adhémar called him off. If this spoil belonged to anyone, it was to the king. Adhémar wheeled his horse around and urged it forward, but despite its training, the horse reared with fear. Adhémar, despite his training, lost his seat and landed on the ground in an undignified sprawl. He scrambled back up to his feet with a curse. He twitched aside his finely wrought cloak and drew his sword. The magelight shone forth brilliantly.

Then it went out.

A blinding headache struck him at the same time. Adhémar reeled, but managed to shake his head hard enough to clear it. He took a minute to look at his sword in astonishment. This was beginning to smell like a disaster. He drew his sleeve across his eyes, trying to wipe away the sudden sweat. Damnation, would the indignities never end this day? He resheathed the sword with a curse, then drew it forth again with a flourish.

Nothing. Not even a flicker.

He took the sword and banged it with enthusiasm against its scabbard.

Dull as stone.

He spat out a spell or two, but before he could wait to see if they were going to take effect, his enemy had taken him by a gnarled, four-fingered hand and flung him across the clearing.

Adhémar narrowly missed landing in a very unyielding clutch of rocks. He sat up, looked around blearily, then realized that he was no longer holding on to his sword. He looked around frantically for it, then saw a shadow fall over him. The creature who had thrown him across the clearing was standing above him with its sword raised, preparing to plunge it through Adhémar's chest.

Then the creature paused. His face, gnarled in the same manner as his hands, wore what might have been termed a look of surprise. Then he slowly began to tip forward. Adhémar rolled out of the way before the creature crashed to the ground. There was a sword hilt sticking out of his back.

A hand pulled him to his feet and shoved his blade back at him. Adhémar nodded his thanks and resheathed his useless sword. The headache and that unsettling weakness were receding so quickly, he almost wondered if he'd imagined both. It was with an unwholesome sense of relief that he put the whole episode behind him.

Well, except for the discovery that his sword was now apparently quite useless for anything more than carving enemies in twain.

He walked swiftly back to his horse. All was not well in the kingdom and he knew just whom to blame.

He swung up onto his horse's back, then nodded for his company to return to the keep. Someone would need to come back to see to the corpses. Perhaps then he would have answers as to what sort of creatures they had been and who had spawned them.

He looked around him to make certain no one was watching him, then drew his sword halfway from its scabbard. Still nothing but a sword. He waited for it to speak to him, to answer to the kingship in his blood.

The sword was silent.

He, on the other hand, was certainly not. He cursed as he led his company swiftly back to the castle. He swore as he thundered through the gates, dismounted at the front doors, and strode angrily through the hallways, up and down flights of stairs, and finally up the long circular stairway that led to the tower chamber where his youngest brother was supposed to be diligently working on affairs of the realm.

Adhémar suspected that he might instead be working his way through the king's collection of fine, sour wine.

Adhémar burst into the chamber without knocking. He allowed himself a cursory glance about for piles of empty wine bottles, but to his disappointment found none. What he did find, though, was the sort of semi-organized clutter he'd come to expect from his brother. There was an enormous hearth to Adhémar's right with two chairs in front of it, straining to bear up under the weight of books and clothing they'd been burdened with. Straight ahead was a long table, likewise littered with other kinds of wizardly things: papers, scrolls, pots of unidentifiable substances. Adhémar supposed they couldn't be helped, but it seemed all foolishness to him.

He found his brother standing behind the table, looking out the window. Adhémar cleared his throat loudly as he crossed the chamber, then slapped his hands on the table. His younger brother, Miach, turned around.

"Aye?"

Adhémar frowned. His brother looked enough like him that he should have been handsome. He had the same dark hair, the same enviable form, even the same flawless facial features. Today, however, Miach was just not attractive. His hair looked as if he'd been trying to pull it out by the roots, he hadn't shaved, and his eyes were almost crossed. And they were red. Adhémar scowled. "Miach, your eyes are so bloodshot, I can scarce determine their color. What have you been doing, perfecting a new spell to cause painful rashes on annoying ambassadors?"

"Nay," Miach said gravely. "Just the usual business."

Adhémar grunted. He had, quite honestly, little idea what the usual business was. Spells, puttering, muttering; who knew? His brother was archmage of the realm, which Adhémar had always suspected was something of a courtesy title. Indeed, if he were to be completely honest, he had begun to suspect that quite a few things were merely courtesy.

Or at least he had until that morning.

Adhémar drew his sword and threw it down upon Miach's worktable. "Fix that."

"I beg your pardon?"

"It doesn't work anymore," Adhémar said, irritated. He glared at his brother. "Did you see nothing of the battle this morning? Don't you have some sort of glass you peep in to see what transpires in the realm?"

"I might," Miach said, "but I was concentrating on other things."

Adhémar thrust out his finger and pointed at his sword. "Then perhaps you might take a moment and concentrate on this."

Miach looked at the sword, clearly puzzled. "Is there something amiss with it?"

"The magelight vanished!" Adhémar exclaimed. "Bloody hell, Miach, are you up here napping? Well, obviously not because you look terrible. But since you weren't watching me as you should have been, let me tell you what happened. We were assaulted by something. Many somethings, of a kind I've never seen before. My sword worked for a moment or two, then ceased."

"Ceased?" Miach echoed in surprise.

"It was as if it had never had any magic in it at all."

"Indeed?" Miach reached out to pick up the sword. "How did that—"

Adhémar snatched up the sword before his brother could touch it. "I'll keep it, thank you just the same."

Miach frowned. "Adhémar, I don't want your sword. I only wanted to see if it would speak to me."

"Well, it's not going to, so don't bother."

"I think—"

"Don't think," Adhémar said briskly. "Remedy. I can't guide the bloody realm without the power of this sword, and I can tell you with certainty that there is no power left in it."

"Adhémar," Miach said evenly, "let me see the damned sword. You can hold on to it, if you don't trust me."

"A king can never be too careful," Adhémar muttered as he held his sword out to his brother. Point first, of course. There were limits to his trust.

Miach looked at it, ran his fingers along the flat of the blade, then frowned. "I sense nothing."

"I told you so."

Miach raised his eyebrows briefly. "So you did." He looked at his brother. "What of you? Have you lost your magic as well?"

Adhémar thought back to the spells he'd cast as the creature had attacked him. He'd left the scene of battle too quickly to determine if they'd taken effect or not, but he wasn't about to admit as much. Who knew how closely and with what relish Miach might want to examine that? "I'm having an off day," Adhémar said stiffly. "Nothing more."

"Here," Miach said, taking a taper and putting it on his table. "Light that."

Adhémar drew himself up. "Too simple."

"Then it shouldn't be too hard for you."

Adhémar glared at his brother briefly, then spat out a spell. He waited.

There was nothing.

"Try it a different way," Miach suggested. "Call the fire instead."

Adhémar hadn't done the like since his sixth year, when his mother had taken him aside and begun to teach him the rudiments of magic. It had come easily to him, but that was to be expected. He had been the chosen heir to the throne, after all.

He now closed his eyes and blocked out the faint sounds of castle life, his brother's breathing, his own heartbeat. There, in the deepest, stillest part of his being, he called the fire. It came, a single flicker that he let grow until it filled his entire mind. He opened his eyes and willed it to come forth around the wick.

Nothing, not even a puff of smoke.

"An aberration," Adhémar said, but even he had to admit that this did not bode well.

"Let me understand this," Miach said slowly. "Your sword has no magic, you apparently have no magic, and you have no idea why either has happened."

"That would sum it up quite nicely," Adhémar said curtly. "Now, fix it all and come to me in the hall when you've managed it. I'm going to find a mug of ale." He turned, walked through the doorway, slammed the door behind him, and stomped down the steps.

Actually he suspected it might take several mugs of ale to erase the memories of the day he'd just had. Best to be about it before things became worse.

Miach looked at the closed door for a moment or two before he bowed his head and blew out his breath. This was an unexpected turn of events, but not an unanticipated one. He had been archmage of the realm for fourteen years now, having taken on those duties the same moment Adhémar had taken the throne, upon the deaths of their parents. In that fourteen years, he had constantly maintained the less visible defenses against the north, passing a great deal of his time and spending a great deal of his strength to keep Lothar, the black mage of Wychweald, at bay. Those defenses had been constantly tested, constantly under siege of one kind or another.

Until the previous year.

It was as if the world outside the realm of Neroche had suddenly fallen asleep. His spells of protection and defense had gone untouched, untested, untroubled. He'd known it could not last and was not meant to last.

Perhaps the assault had begun, and in a way he hadn't foreseen.

But what to do now? He was quite certain Adhémar's sword hadn't given up its magic on its own, and that Adhémar hadn't lost his just as a matter of course. If a spell had been cast upon the king, the king had magic enough to sense it. Or at least he should have.

Miach considered that for a moment or two. Adhémar was the king and as such possessed the mantle that went with such kingship. Yet perhaps he'd spent so many years not using his magic for anything more desperate than to hasten the souring of his favorite wine that he'd lost the ability of it, a bit like a man who lost his strength because he sat upon his backside with his feet up and never lifted anything heavier than a fork.

But to have had the sword lose its power as well?

Miach rose and began to pace. There had been no spell laid upon the blade that he could discern, but perhaps there was more at work than he could see. Perhaps Adhémar had been stripped of his magic in the same way. But why? And by whom? He was very familiar with the smell of Lothar's magic and this had no stench of that kind.

Miach paced until the chamber ceased to provide him with room enough to truly aid him in his thinking. He descended the stairs and began to wander about the castle. He tramped about restlessly until he found himself standing in the great hall. It was a place made to impress, with enormous hearths on three sides and a raised dais at the back. Countless kings of Neroche had sat at that table on that dais, comfortable in the magic they possessed.

In the beginning of the realm, the magic had been the king's and his alone. The first pair of kings of Neroche had guarded the realm by virtue of their own power. In time, the kings had either had enough power in and of themselves, or they had found other means to augment that power. The Sword of Neroche had been endowed with a bit of magic itself, but it had always been dependent on the king.

That had changed eventually. It had been the grandson of King Harold the Brave who had looked upon his posterity, considered the queen who had left him for one of Lothar's sons, and decided that the only way to assure the safety of the kingdom was to imbue his sword with all of his power. He did, chose his least objectionable son as king, and made his magically gifted nephew archmage as a balance. It had been the Sword of Neroche, from that time on, that had carried most of the king's magic, folded into the steel of its blade.

Miach looked down at the floor and rubbed the back of his neck. Of course, he had magic of his own, more than he had ever admitted to his brothers, more than even he had suspected when he'd become the archmage. But he knew, in a deep, uncompromising way that reached down into his bones, that it would take all the magic he could muster, as well as all the king could draw from the Sword of Neroche, to keep Lothar at bay should he mount an all-out attack.

Unless there was another way.

He heard the faint hint of a song. He looked around him, startled, but the great hall was empty. He frowned, then resumed his contemplation of the floor.

Again, he heard the whisper of a song.

He realized, quite suddenly, where the music was coming from. He looked up slowly until his eyes fastened on a sword, hanging above the enormous hearth at the end of the great hall.

The Sword of Angesand.

Miach crossed slowly over to the dais, stepped up, and walked around behind the king's high table. He looked up, finding that it was impossible not to do so. The sword was hanging well out of reach, so he was forced to fetch a chair. He pulled the sword down and looked at it.

The Sword of Angesand, fashioned by Mehar of Angesand, queen of Neroche, and laced with enough magic to make even the most strong-stomached of souls quake. Miach held the sword aloft, but saw nothing but firelight flickering along the polished steel, firelight that revealed the tracery of leaves and flowers along the blade. All the things that Queen Mehar loved . . .

It whispered the echo of the song he'd heard, then it fell silent.

Miach looked at the blade. If the Sword of Neroche was unresponsive, was it possible the Sword of Angesand might not be? Could not a soul be found to awaken its magic? If a wielder could be found, perhaps it would be enough to keep Lothar curbed until Miach could solve the mystery of Adhémar and his sword.

Perhaps.

Miach's hand shook as he replaced the sword—and that wasn't from the exertion. It might work. Indeed, he couldn't see why it wouldn't. He turned and walked out of the great hall, convinced that there was no other path to be taken. Neroche's king had lost his magic and the archmage could not win the battle on his own. The Sword of Angesand had power enough bound into its elegant steel to tip the scales in their favor.

Now, to find someone willing to go off and search for that wielder.

Miach made his way through the castle and back into the private family quarters. He found almost all his brothers gathered in their own, more modest hall, sipping or gulping ale as their particular circumstance warranted. He paused at the doorway to the chamber and looked them over. Was there a man there who might have the clearness of vision to recognize a wielder when he saw one?

Miach looked at Cathar, who sat to the right of the king's chair. He was a serious man of five and thirty winters, a scant year younger than Adhémar, who never would have thought to take an uninvited turn in his brother's seat to see how it felt.

Of course, that kind of testing was nothing to Rigaud, two years Cathar's junior and as light-minded as the rest of them were serious. He lounged comfortably in Adhémar's chair, dressed in his finest clothes. Miach looked pointedly at his green-eyed brother and only received a lazy wink in return. When Adhémar entered, he would be forced to bodily remove Rigaud from his seat, which Rigaud would enjoy immensely, though he would no doubt complain about the damage to his clothing.

Next came Nemed, a lean man of thirty-two years with soft gray eyes and a gentle smile. Miach shook his head. Cathar wouldn't have dared take on the task, Rigaud would have forgotten the task in his pursuit of fame and fortune, and Nemed would have found himself ripped to shreds by anyone with any ambition for power.

That left him with only his twin brothers, Mansourah and Turah. They were canny warriors, but with weaponry was where their allegiance lay. They likely would have spent their time fighting over which of *them* might have been more suited to wielding the Sword of Angesand than searching out someone else to do it.

Miach sighed heavily as he realized what he'd known from the start. There was only one to seek out the wielder, and that soul would not be happy to hear the news.

Adhémar suddenly entered the chamber. All stood except Rigaud, who apparently didn't want to give up his seat any sooner than necessary. Miach suppressed a smile at the squawking that ensued when the preening rooster was unceremoniously removed from his perch.

Adhémar sat, then looked at Miach. "Well?"

Miach shut the door behind him, then leaned back against it. No sense in letting anyone escape unnecessarily. "I believe I have found a solution."

"A solution?" Cathar echoed. "A solution to what?"

Miach folded his arms over his chest. He wasn't about to reveal the details of the king's current condition. Adhémar could do that himself.

Adhémar shot Miach a glare, then turned to Cathar. "I lost my magic," he said bluntly.

There were sounds of amazement from several quarters. Cathar frowned.

"This afternoon?" he asked.

"Aye."

"Is it permanent?" Rigaud asked promptly.

"Don't hope for it overmuch," Adhémar said shortly. "I'm sure it will return soon." He shot Miach a look. "Won't it?"

"I'm still working on that," Miach said. And he would be, no doubt, for quite some time to come.

Adhémar scowled, then looked back at the rest of his brothers. "It isn't permanent," he said confidently. "So, until I regain my magic, I'm sure our clever brother over there has a solution to our problems." He looked at Miach expectantly.

Miach didn't want to look as if he was gearing up for battle, so he tried a pleasant smile. "I do," he said pleasantly. "I suggest the Sword of Angesand."

"The Sword of Angesand," Adhémar mouthed. He choked, looked about in vain for something to drink, then pounded himself upon his chest in desperation. Cathar handed him his own cup of ale. He drank deeply. "The what?" he wheezed.

"You heard me."

"You cannot be serious!"

"Why not?" Miach asked.

"Because it is a woman's sword!" Adhémar exclaimed. "You can*not* expect me to carry a woman's sword!"

Miach suppressed the urge to roll his eyes. "It *isn't* a woman's sword. It was merely fashioned by a woman—"

"It has flowers all over it!"

"Think on them as nightshade, dealing a slow and painful death to those upon whom the sword falls," Miach said. "Many men have carried that sword in battle and been victorious with it, flowers aside." He paused. "Have you ever held it?"

Adhémar scowled at him. "I have and nay, it does not call my name. Fortunately," he muttered, "because I wouldn't carry it even if it did."

"I don't expect *you* to carry it," Miach said. "I expect you to find someone *else* to carry it."

Adhémar gaped at him. Miach noted that the rest of his brothers were wearing similar expressions. Except Rigaud, of course, who was calculatingly eyeing the throne.

"What kind of someone?" Cathar asked cautiously.

"I imagine it will need to be a mage," Miach said slowly. "After Queen Mehar last used it, it has only been wielded by those with magic."

"Why don't you take it up?" Adhémar asked. "Or don't you have the magic necessary to do so?"

Miach looked at his brother coolly. "I daresay I do, but the sword does not call to me."

"Have you asked it?"

"Adhémar, I am no longer a lad of eight summers. Even I can reach up far enough to pull the blade off the wall—which I have done a time or two while you were napping."

"I've seen him," Rigaud put in helpfully. "And more than twice."

Miach shot Rigaud a glare before he turned back to his king. "We need a sword to replace yours until we can determine what ails you."

Adhémar grunted. "Very well, I can see the sense in it. Where will you go to find this mage?"

Miach considered. He couldn't leave Adhémar guarding the borders without his magic. There were times he suspected it was dangerous to leave Adhémar in charge *with* his magic. But telling him as much was out of the question. This would require diplomacy, tact, and very probably a great deal of unwarranted flattery. Miach cleared his throat and frowned, pretending to give the matter much thought.

"I suppose I could go," he began, "but I have no way of recognizing who the man will be." That wasn't exactly true, but there was no point in telling Adhémar that either. "Unlike you, my liege."

"Bloody hell, Miach, I can't call enough magelight to keep myself from tripping down the stairs! You go find him."

"But no one else sees as clearly as you do," Miach said smoothly. "And it will take a special sort of vision, an eye that discerns far above what most mortal men can see, a sense of judgment that only a man of superior wit and wisdom possesses." He paused dramatically. "In short, my liege, it is a task that only you can possibly be considered equal to."

Adhémar opened his mouth to protest, then shut it suddenly. Miach supposed he was grappling with the unexpected flattery and weighing the potential glory of it being true against the trouble of actually leaving Tor Neroche to traipse over the Nine Kingdoms, looking for someone to wield a sword that wasn't his.

Miach saw Rigaud stir, no doubt to say something about keeping the throne warm for his brother while he was away. He shot Rigaud a look of warning. Rigaud made a rather rude gesture in return, but grinned as he did it. Miach pursed his lips and turned his attention back to Adhémar. His brother finally cursed.

A very good sign.

"I'll need to be back by mid-winter, at the latest," Adhémar announced.

"Why?" Miach asked carefully.

"I'm getting married."

"Finally," Cathar said, sounding rather relieved. "To whom?"

"Don't know yet," Adhémar said, finishing off Cathar's ale and handing his brother's cup back to him. "I'm still thinking on it."

Miach was set to suggest that perhaps Adhémar choose someone with a decent amount of magic to make up for his lack, but he forbore. For now, it was enough to have time to sort out what was truly going on in the palace without his brother underfoot, bellowing like a stuck pig about his sufferings.

Adhémar scowled. "I've little liking for this idea." He

looked at Miach narrowly. "I suspect this is a ruse so you can keep your toes warmed by the fire while I'm off looking for a fool ready to volunteer to take his life in his hands to protect us from the north."

Miach didn't offer any opinion on that.

Adhémar swore for quite some time in a very inventive fashion. Finally, he swept them all with a look. "Well, it appears I am off to find a wielder for the Sword of Angesand."

"Have a lovely journey," Rigaud said, edging closer to the throne.

Adhémar glared at him. "Turah will sit the Throne while I am gone—"

"What?" Rigaud shouted, leaping in front of his brother. "Adhémar, what of me! I know Nemed is worthless—"

Miach was unsurprised by either the volume of the complaints or Adhémar's choice. After all, it was well within Adhémar's right to choose any of his brothers to succeed him.

Adhémar held up his hand. "He is my choice and my choice is final. You will, of course, aid him as you would me."

Miach didn't need to look into the future to know what would happen in the king's absence. Mansourah would shadow Cathar, Nemed would stand unobtrusively behind Turah and steady him should he falter, and Rigaud would rage continuously about the injustice of it all. Adhémar looked at Miach.

"And you will do as you see fit, I suppose."

"As he bloody pleases, you mean," Rigaud grumbled.

"As I usually do," Miach said with a grave smile. "I have quite enough to do to keep me busy."

"You watch your back, Adhémar," Cathar rumbled. He wrapped his hands around his cup of ale. "I've no mind to crown Turah any time soon."

"Heaven preserve us," Rigaud gasped. "My liege, perhaps I should come and defend you."

"With what?" Cathar said, scowling. "One of your brightly colored tunics? Aye, blind the bloody buggers with your garb and hope they don't stick you in spite of it."

Rigaud, for all his preening, wasn't above defending his own honor and he launched himself at his elder brother with a curse. Adhémar moved his legs out of the fray and helped himself to Rigaud's ale. The king's respite was short. Soon he was pulled into the skirmish. Miach sighed. Things never changed, or so it seemed.

Or perhaps not.

Miach looked over the scene of skirmish and though things seemed the same, they were indeed not. Adhémar was powerless. His remaining brothers, even put together, did not have enough magic to keep the brooding darkness at bay. Nay, a wielder for the Sword of Angesand had to be found, and Adhémar was the one to do it.

"Miach!" Adhémar bellowed from the bottom of the pile. "Any thoughts on where I should go?"

"Probably to the most unlikely place possible," Miach offered.

"Ah, but there are so many choices," Adhémar said sourly. He shoved his brothers off him one by one, then sat up and sighed. "The kingdom of Ainneamh?"

"Only elves there," Miach said. "I wouldn't bother. I would turn my eye to a more humble place." He paused. "Perhaps the Island of Melksham."

"What!" Adhémar exclaimed. "The Island of Melksham? Have you lost all sense?"

"It was but a suggestion."

"And a poor one at that." He shook his head in disgust as he crawled to his feet. "Melksham. Ha! That will be the very *last* place I'll look." He glared at Miach one last time, then he strode from the room, his curses floating in the air behind him.

Miach watched as his remaining bothers untangled themselves, collected their empty cups, and made their way singly and with a good deal of commenting on the vagaries of the monarchy from the chamber.

Miach was left there, alone, staring at the empty place where his brothers had been. Unbidden, a vision came to him of the chamber before him, only it was abandoned, desolate, ruined, uninhabitable—

He shook his head sharply. That was no vision; it was a lie spawned by his own unease. All would be well. He was doing all he could. No doubt this was the worst of the disasters.

He reflected again on the places Adhémar might possibly go to find the wielder. Melksham Island was certainly the least likely, which would make it the most likely—but he wouldn't

tell Adhémar that. With any luck, he would make it there eventually on his own.

Miach turned and left the chamber, leaving the search
for the wielder in his brother's hands.

For the moment.

One

Morgan of Melksham walked along the road, cursing both autumn's chill and her journey that caused her to be traipsing out in that chill instead of hunkering down next to a warm fire. This was not what she had planned. Her life had been proceeding quite nicely until she'd received the missive in the middle of a particularly muddy campaign in which she'd been trying to pry one of Melksham's nobles from a keep that did not belong to him. The message from Lord Nicholas had been brief and pointed.

Come soon; time is short.

Morgan didn't want to speculate on what that might mean, but she couldn't help herself. Was the man suffering from life-threatening wounds? Was his home under siege from nobles he had exacted donations from once too often? Had he had a bountiful harvest and needed an extra pair of hands to bring that harvest to the cellar?

Was he dying?

She quickened her pace, forcing her thoughts away. She would know soon enough and then that uncomfortable, unwholesome pounding in her chest would cease and she actually might be able to eat again.

She reached the outer walls of the orphanage just as the sun was setting. Melksham Orphan's Home at Lismòr had begun

many years ago as a home for lads, but at some point it had
also become a place of study that had brought together a collection of the finest scholars from all over the Nine Kingdoms.
Nicholas, the lord of Lismòr, was the orphanage's undisputed
champion and the university's chief procurer of funds.

Over the years, it had become different things to those who
had experience with it. Many called it "the orphanage." Others referred to it as "the university." Nicholas simply called it
"home."

Morgan agreed with the latter, though she never would have
admitted it.

The outer walls of Lismòr soon rose up before her, forbid-
ding and unfriendly. It made her wonder, not for the first time,
why a university merited anything more than a sturdy gate. It
was rumored that Lismòr hid many things, including chests
of marvelous treasure. Morgan supposed those rumors could
have been referring to the offerings that appeared each night
on Lord Nicholas's supper table, but she couldn't have said for
certain.

There were rumors, though, of another sort that swirled
around Lord Nicholas. It was said that he never aged, that he
conversed with mysterious souls who slipped inside the gates
after dark and left well before dawn, and that he even possessed magic.

Morgan snorted. She had never seen any display of other-
worldliness at the orphanage, and she'd lived there for many
years. No doubt Nicholas's garden bloomed in the depth of winter because he was a damned fine gardener, not for any more
magical reason. He was a man of great intelligence, quick wit,
and an ability to convince others to fund his ventures. He possessed no magic beyond that.

Surely.

And surely his missive had nothing to do with his health.

She knocked on the heavy gate, then waited impatiently as
a single square of metal was slowly pulled back and a weath-
ered face appeared, looking out suspiciously.

"Hmmm," he said doubtfully.

Morgan pursed her lips. "Aye, hmmm."

The porthole was slammed shut and the gate opened without haste. Morgan tapped her foot impatiently until the moment she could slip inside. She shut the gate herself, then looked at the gatekeeper.

"Is he dying?"

"Morgan," the gatekeeper said pleasantly. "You've been away long."

"But I have returned, in haste, and my hope is that it is not to attend a wake. Master James, is he *dying*?"

"Who?"

"Lord Nicholas!"

Master James scratched his head. "Not that I know of. I think he's holding court with the lads in his solar. Best to seek him out there, aye?"

Morgan could hardly believe her ears. Nicholas was well?

She wasn't sure if she was relieved that he was apparently hale and hearty or furious that he'd tricked her into coming by means of such a cryptic, panic-inducing message. One thing was certain: they would have words about the wording of future missives.

What she wanted to do was sit down and catch the breath she realized she'd been holding for almost a se'nnight. Instead, she nodded to the gatekeeper and walked weakly away. She would sit when she reached Nicholas's solar. And then once she recovered, she just might put him to the sword for her trouble.

She made her way across a rather large expanse of flat ground that the students and lads used to play games on, then continued on toward the inner walls that enclosed the heart of the university. Now, these were walls that offered protection against a foe. Morgan walked through the gate, casting a surreptitious look up at the heavy spikes of the portcullis gleaming dimly above her as she did so. Perhaps Nicholas was more concerned about the safety of his scholarly texts than he appeared.

Or perhaps he was concerned about the safety of his lads. She suspected she understood why. He had only mentioned once, in passing, that he'd had sons of his own at one time who had been slain. She supposed that since he hadn't been able to protect them, he felt compelled to protect others who could not see to themselves. Whatever the true reason, there were many, many souls that had benefited from his altruism. She certainly counted herself as one of them.

She threaded her way through many buildings and along paths until she reached the heart of Lismòr. It was an enormous building, with chambers and apartments surrounding an inner courtyard. Nicholas's chambers took up one half side of the building, and his solar happily resided in one of the corners. Morgan had spent many a pleasant hour there, conversing with an exceptional man who had made an exception in her case, allowing her to remain at the orphanage in spite of her being a girl.

Which was no doubt why she found herself standing not fifty paces away from his chambers, instead of at a siege that had been destined, thanks to much effort on her part, to yield quite a tidy sum. Her comrades had thought her mad for walking away; she had agreed, yet still she had packed her gear and left.

All because of a message from a man who had been like a father to her.

Morgan pursed her lips and continued on toward Nicholas's private solar. She would contemplate her descent into madness later, perhaps when she was sitting before a hot fire with a mug of drinkable ale in her hand and Nicholas before her to answer a handful of very pointed questions.

She stopped in front of a heavy wooden door, turned the handle, and slipped inside. The chamber was an inviting one, luxuriously appointed yet not intimidating. A cheery fire burned in the hearth, fine tapestries lined the walls, and thick rugs were scattered over the floor to spare the lord's feet the chill of cold stone. Candles in abundance drove the shadows back into their corners and sweet music filled the air.

Until she closed the door behind her, that is. The music faltered. The young man who plied his lute averted his eyes when she looked at him.

"Continue, Peter," said a deep voice, roughened by the passage of many years. "Now, lads, I seem to remember one of you asking for a tale."

The dozen or so lads strewn about the floor like so many shapeless garments were successful in varying degrees at tearing their gazes from her. Morgan was acutely aware of the filth of her clothing and the poor condition of her cloak. She looked about her for a place to sit. She settled for a corner and sank down onto the stool that had been handily placed there for just such a need as hers. She pulled the edges of her cloak closer around her and did her best to become part of the shadows.

Then she glared at the man holding court, for Lord Nicholas looked fit and strong and certainly in no need of anything from her.

He only winked at her and turned his attention back to his lads. "What will it be tonight?" he asked. "Romance? Adventure? Perilous escapades that should result in disaster but do not?"

"Peril," Morgan said before she could stop herself. "Imminent death. Something that requires an immediate and drastic rescue. Something that might include missives sent and travels made when apparently there was no need."

The lads again turned to look at her briefly, many of them slack-jawed, the rest looking quite confused.

"Oh, nothing so frightening," Nicholas said smoothly. "Lads? Any suggestions?"

"The Tale of the Two Swords," a young lad piped up.

Half the lads groaned. Morgan groaned right along with them. Too much romance in that one. Unfortunately, it was one of Nicholas's favorites; he would never do the decent thing and refuse to retell it.

"The Two Swords," Nicholas agreed readily. "So it will be."

Morgan rolled her eyes and leaned back against the wall, preparing to completely ignore all she would hear. Obviously, she would have no answers out of the man before he was ready, and if he held true to form, his nightly tale-telling would last for at least an hour. It was his ritual, repeated as consistently as the sun rising and setting each day. It gave the lads a sense of security, or so he said.

Morgan closed her eyes, wondering if she might be able to snatch a bit of sleep and block out the romance that would ooze out of the tale Nicholas was beginning to spin. But, despite herself, she found herself listening. Gilraehen the Fey was bold, Mehar of Angesand was beautiful, and Lothar of Wychweald was evil enough to make the most hardened of listeners shiver.

In time, the romance in the tale increased. Morgan was quite certain there would be tender sentiments exchanged soon between Gilraehen and Mehar—things entirely too sugary to be inflicted upon the hapless lads in the chamber. Morgan shot Nicholas a warning look, but he blithely ignored it.

She gave up and turned her attentions to the condition of her own hands. As she listened to Mehar placing her hand in Gilraehen's and giving herself to him as his queen, she pursed her lips. She herself hardly had time for such pleasantries; it was just as well, for no man would look at her hands, scarred and rough, and ask her to do anything with them besides curry his horse. A mercenary's life was not an easy one.

It was especially hard on one's hands.

"What of the two swords?" a lad asked. "The king's sword, especially." He paused. "I hear it is very sharp."

Nicholas laughed. "Well, of course the king keeps the Sword of Neroche. But the other—" He paused and shrugged. "The Sword of Angesand hangs in the great hall at Tor Neroche."

"But," another asked, sounding quite worried, "isn't the king afraid someone might make off with it?"

"Nay, lad, I daresay not. Before she died, Queen Mehar, she who fashioned the blade, laid an enchantment of protection upon it, that it would never be stolen. She also prophesied about several special souls who would wield that blade at a time of particular peril, but that is a tale for another night."

The lads protested, but not heartily. They were secure in the knowledge that the following night would bring more of the same sort of pleasure. Morgan watched them file past her and understood precisely how they felt. She'd been orphaned at six, taken in by a company of mercenaries for several years until she'd begun her courses, then heartlessly deposited without a backward glance upon Nicholas's doorstep at the tender age of ten-and-two. She had had her own share of those long evenings passed in the comfort of Nicholas's solar, listening to him tell his stories. But she had never, for reasons she never examined if she could help it, allowed herself to luxuriate in that sensation of security.

There were times she suspected she should have.

An older lad, one who looked as if he spent far more time thinking about heroic tales than determining how he might become a part of them by some time spent in the lists, stopped by the door and turned back to Nicholas.

"I know the prophecy, my lord," he said quietly.

Nicholas remained seated in his chair, resting his chin on his steepled fingers. "The prophecy?"

"Queen Mehar's prophecy about the Sword of Angesand."

"I imagine you do, lad."

"I can recite it for you—"

Morgan was about to tell him not to bother, but Nicholas beat her to it.

"Not tonight, my son. I've a guest, don't you see, and you need to be abed."

"I could speculate," the lad offered.

Nicholas rose slowly and walked over to stand by the door. "In the end, my son, unless you are intimately involved in either the doing of the deeds or the making of the tales, it is naught but speculation. And since we are neither, we should leave the speculating to others and retire to our beds before our nerves are overworked." He held the door open pointedly. "Good night, Harding's son. Have a peaceful sleep."

"And to you, my lord," the lad said, then unwillingly made his way from the chamber.

Nicholas closed the door and turned to look at Morgan. "You came."

Morgan rose and looked at him narrowly. "Your missive said to hurry. I feared you were dying."

Nicholas laughed merrily and enveloped Morgan in a fatherly embrace. "Ah, Morgan," he said, pulling back, kissing her soundly on both cheeks, then drawing her across to sit upon his exceptionally comfortable settee, "I'm not dead yet. What a pleasure to see you."

Morgan scowled at him as she sat. "You asked me to come."

"Did I?" he said, sinking down into an equally comfortable chair.

"It sounded as if your trouble required my immediate attention."

"And so it does," he said with a smile. "But not tonight. Tonight you will eat, then go to your rest. We'll speak of other things tomorrow."

"My lord—"

"Tomorrow, my girl."

She frowned fiercely at him. "I made great haste away from a *very* lucrative bit of business, simply because you called. I've hardly slept in a se'nnight for worry that I might arrive too late and find you *dead*. I daresay I deserve to at least know why you wanted me here!"

He smiled. "Is it not enough for an old man to simply wish to see the daughter of his heart?"

Morgan felt a sudden and very uncomfortable burning begin behind her eyes. She rubbed them to ease the stinging and to give herself time to recapture her frown. She was better off in a pitched battle. She did not do well with these kinds of sentimental utterings.

"A pleasant visit does not seem a good reason to me," she managed finally.

"Doesn't it?" he asked kindly. "A pleasant visit, a se'nnight of comfort, a chance for me to make sure you're still alive?"

"I suppose," she conceded, but she wasn't sure she agreed. She did not need the luxurious surroundings she found herself in. She did not need the affection of a man who had taken her in as a scraggly, snarling, uncivilized lass who had been accustomed to sleeping with a dagger under her pillow and holding her own against men three times her age. She did not ever dwell with pleasure on those many years in Nicholas's care when he taught her of letters and numbers and the quiet beauty of the seasons changing from year to year.

She also did not think on him each time she drew the sword at her side, the glorious sword he'd had made for her and adorned with gems from his own personal treasury.

"Morgan?"

"Aye, my lord?"

"What were you thinking on?"

She sighed deeply. "I was contemplating my condition as an appallingly ungrateful wretch."

Nicholas laughed. "I daresay not. There is a chapel nearby, my dear, which you may use on the morrow for your penance. For now, fill this old man's ears with your adventures. We'll speak about other business tomorrow."

Morgan lifted her eyebrows. "Other business? Is that why you sent for me, in truth?"

"Tomorrow."

Morgan shot him a final, disgruntled look that he completely ignored, then she relented, and sat back against his dreadfully comfortable couch to give him the tales he wanted.

She told him of her travels, leaving out the more unsavory encounters. She told him of the places on the island she'd seen, the wonders she'd seen come in on ships at port, the tidy sums she'd earned.

"Obviously not of late," Nicholas said dryly, casting a look at her clothes. "A rough year so far, I'd say."

"Not the most profitable," Morgan agreed.

"I told you the last time you were here, my child, to marry one of Harding's sons, not fight the man's battles for him. He is notoriously stingy."

"Only because you've coerced so many donations out of him, my lord."

"Goodness," Nicholas said with a laugh, "you've been too many years out of polite company. Although it is all too true about the funds, we usually don't like to bring it up. Now you realize I have Harding's youngest here. He's a handsome lad."

"He's likely half my age."

"But he is rich."

"*Was* rich," she corrected. "I hazard a guess he will be less rich still once you're through with him—"

A discreet knock prevented her from discussing with Nicholas his extortionary techniques. Soon she found herself with a hearty repast sitting atop a table before her. Nicholas invited her to help herself, which she did without hesitation. It had been, after all, a rather lean autumn. Nicholas watched her thoughtfully as she ate.

"You know," he said casually, "there are richer prizes farther afield."

Morgan stopped chewing and looked at him. "What?"

"There are nine kingdoms, Morgan, my dear. The last time I checked, those nine kingdoms contained at least nine kings. I would imagine that any of them would be more than happy to pay you quite handsomely to raise your sword in his defense."

Morgan continued to chew. When she thought she could swallow successfully, she applied herself to her goblet of wine.

"I don't fancy traveling," she said with conviction—the conviction of one who truly did not enjoy traveling.

"A pity," Nicholas said, admiring his own wine in the hand-blown glass goblet. "Gold, silver, renown. Glorious deeds." He looked at her placidly. "Hard to resist."

"And yet I manage," she said. "What are you about in truth, old man? I've resigned myself to a decent meal and pleasant conversation, but I only find one of the two here."

Nicholas smiled. "Finish your meal, my dear, then get yourself to bed. We'll speak on other things tomorrow. You'll stay for a bit, won't you?"

"Perhaps," she said, but she knew she didn't dare. Too many nights with her head on a soft goose-feather pillow and the rest of her under an equally soft goose-feather duvet would completely ruin her for hard labor.

"However long you can manage will be long enough," he said enigmatically. "Eat some more, Morgan. You're too thin."

She ate her fill, ate a bit more just in case, then sat back with a cup of the orphanage's finest and savored polite conversation for a bit. She and Nicholas spoke of the weather, of the harvest, of his garden that still produced a very fine grape even past the hard frost. Morgan learned of new lads who had come to be sheltered and of older lads who had come to study, then gone on to make their way in the world. All of it perfectly normal; all of it unremarkable and secure. It eased her heart.

All but the part of her heart that knew such peace was not to be hers for long.

She thanked Nicholas for the meal, bid him a good night, and walked with him to the door. He put his hands on her shoulders, then kissed both her cheeks. "A good sleep to you, daughter. You'll need it before you start your next journey."

"My next journey?" she asked blankly.

"Aren't you going on a journey?"

Ah, so this was where it lay, apparently. "I don't know. Am I, my lord?"

"An assumption, my dear," Nicholas said easily. "Sleep in peace tonight."

Morgan wondered if he had lost his wits, or it was that a decent meal and promise of a gloriously comfortable bed had robbed her of hers. She frowned at him, thanked him again kindly for his hospitality, then escaped his chambers before he could say anything else unsettling.

She had hardly made it ten steps from his solar when she was accosted by a voice from the shadows.

"My lady."

Morgan stopped and sighed. "I'm not your lady. I'm just Morgan."

"My lady Morgan." The lad from Nicholas's solar stepped out from the shadows.

He stood there, Harding's youngest son, squirming uncomfortably until he finally gained control enough of his gangly limbs to stop and look at her. Morgan was not given to shifting, having earned her own measure of self-control on the other side of Melksham Island where self-control was a particularly important subject to learn, but there was something about the moment that left her with an almost uncontrollable urge to rub her arms.

She managed not to. "Aye, lad?" she asked.

"Lord Nicholas won't speak to me about it," the young man whispered, "but I've heard rumors."

"Rumors are dangerous."

Apparently not dangerous enough to deter him. He leaned closer to her. "I heard," he whispered conspiratorially, "that the king of Neroche has lost his power."

She felt her eyebrows go up of their own accord. "Indeed. And where did you hear that?"

"I eavesdropped on Lord Nicholas while he was discussing it."

Morgan waved aside his words. "He worries overmuch."

"I don't think so. 'Tis rumored the king also searches for a warrior of mighty stature to wield a sword for him." He paused, looked about him as if an enemy might be listening in, then leaned closer to her. "The Sword of Angesand," he whispered.

She blinked in surprise. "The what?"

"The Sword of Angesand. It was fashioned by Mehar of Angesand, who wove into it—"

"Aye, I know all about it," Morgan interrupted. That was all she needed, to have to listen to another of Nicholas's romantic and completely unsuitable tales while *outside* his solar. At least inside she had a warm fire to distract her. Here she only had a skinny, trembling lad who couldn't have been more than ten-and-two, who was making her cold just by looking at him.

"Go to bed," she ordered, "and forget what you've heard. The king is well. Indeed, all is well. I would say that listening to too many of Nicholas's stories has worked a foul work upon you."

The lad hesitated.

Morgan nodded firmly toward the dormitories. The lad nodded in unison with her, looking only slightly less miserable than before. He cast her one last desperate look before he turned and disappeared into the darkness.

Morgan snorted to herself. Rumor and hearsay. The lad was confusing fact with the stuff of Nicholas's evening's entertainment.

She put the matter out of her mind and sought her chamber, finding it just as she had left it two years earlier. Indeed, it looked just as it had for the six years she'd called it her own. She hadn't used it very often since going on to make her way to other places, but each time she'd returned, she had found it thusly prepared for her. She leaped into her bed with a guilty abandon she would regret in a se'nnight's time when she was reduced to rough blankets near a weak fire. She closed her eyes and promised herself a good, long march through bitter chill at some point in the future as penance.

But not tonight.

The king has lost his magic.

It couldn't be true. Morgan rolled over and pulled the covers up over her ears. The king of Neroche was as full of vile magic as ever, the Nine Kingdoms were safe, and she was indulging in a guilty pleasure she rarely allowed herself.

Surely all was well.

Two

The next morning found Morgan not in her warm, deliciously soft bed under an equally delightful goose-down duvet, nor banging on Nicholas's door demanding answers as she had briefly contemplated, but in a cold, drafty chamber of scrolls where a sharp-eyed, suspicious man made noises of disapproval each time she unrolled a scroll or turned a leaf. He complained even more bitterly each time she dared ask for something else.

And it was barely dawn.

After a terrible night's sleep passed dreaming of swords and darkness and skirmishes against things one did not normally find on the field of battle, she had descended into the bowels of the university where she had hoped to find something to ease her mind about the state of affairs in the kingdom of Neroche.

She realized, with a start, that she was resting her chin on her fist and staring at the shelves of manuscripts without really seeing them. She shook her head to clear it, then rose and wandered about the chamber until she found herself standing before a large book. It had been set in a place apparently built exactly for it, for it fit in its niche with neither too much nor too little room.

Morgan looked at the keeper of records. He was beginning

to wheeze, which she took as a sign she might be standing near something quite interesting. She raised one eyebrow in challenge.

"You cannot," he squawked, finally.

"Master Dominicus, I am only taking it over to the table to read it. I am not putting it in my pack to then sell off to the highest bidder the moment I can escape through the front gates."

He hopped down off his stool and strode over to her. He frowned fiercely. "I, at least, will carry it to your place. Have you washed your hands?"

"I haven't eaten anything to dirty them."

"Then perhaps you should—and return later."

"I'll manage without, thank you."

He frowned a bit more, then carefully and with great cere-mony removed the book from its place and carried it over to the table. He set it down reverently, then he spun around and glared at her.

"Do not tear the pages."

"I wouldn't dare."

He watched her as she sat, then hovered over her until she slowly drew a dagger from her belt and very carefully set it down next to her. Then she looked up at him pointedly. He scowled, but retreated to his seat with all the dignity he could likely mus-ter, under the circumstances.

Morgan looked at the book before her, then carefully and with a terrible sense of inevitability, opened the cover and turned over the first leaf.

The Tale of the Two Swords.

She should have known.

She sighed and began to read it again. But this time, how-ever, she found herself reading the tale of Queen Mehar and King Gilraehen with a new eye, ignoring the romance that seemed to be slathered all over the story at every opportunity, and finding that there were several details she had missed.

She'd known that Mehar had forged her sword with her own hands and laid upon it many enchantments. That the queen had possessed the wherewithal to make such a thing left Morgan with warm feelings toward her; that she apparently knew how to use it as well was another thing to like about her. Mehar had been rumored to be a spectacular horsewoman as well as a lover of all things bright and sharp. Morgan supposed she could even forgive the woman her dabblings in magic for those two things.

Morgan hadn't remembered, however, that Mehar had possessed the magic of Camanaë. Even she had heard enough of Nicholas's tales over the years to know that Camanaë was a powerful matriarchal magic—one that Lothar had been from the beginning determined to eradicate. If that was the magic that Mehar had bound into her sword, it was powerful indeed.

Morgan was half surprised that the blade still existed. One would have thought Lothar would have made a special effort to find that sword, or steal it or destroy it.

She mused about that possibility for several moments. What would happen, she wondered, if the sword were destroyed? Would Neroche cease to be or would it merely limp on in a crippled fashion?

She wasn't sure she wanted to know.

She continued to read about Harold the Brave, Uisdean the Wise, Edan the Fearless. She continued on through the years, finishing with King Anghmar and his lady wife Queen Desdhemar. It was his son, Adhémar, who sat the throne at present. The line of kings had always retained some bit of magic, some more, some less, but always enough to keep Lothar at bay.

Where the current king stood on matters of magic, she couldn't have said. She knew nothing of him save his name, and that only because she could not be in a battle where she did not either fight alongside or against half a dozen men whose parents had obviously thought his name to be a good one for their own sons. But of the king himself, she knew little. She had troubles enough of her own without adding to them things he should have been seeing to himself.

She sat back and sighed, wondering if she had the stomach to read through any more histories of any of the other kingdoms who were so dependent on the strength of Neroche. Watching the world unfold before her eyes was wearying.

She turned the leaves back toward the beginning, glancing

idly at pieces of history, wondering how it had been for those who had gone before and done such glorious deeds—

The Wielders of the Sword of Angesand will come, out of magic, out of obscurity, and out of darkness . . .

Morgan went still. That was part of Mehar's prophecy, but what could it mean? That there were three poor, unfortunate souls predestined to carry a sword so magical that all sensible souls would flee from it? She pitied any who found themselves so burdened. At least she would never find herself in such terrible straits.

She closed the manuscript before it could trouble her further, rose, and nodded politely to Master Dominicus. "I will be on my way now," she announced.

He looked no less relieved by that than by her arrival. He muttered indignantly as he gathered up what she'd been reading and continued to complain rather loudly as he put things away. Morgan thanked him politely and left the cellar. Perhaps he needed to be aboveground more often where he could at least see the sun. It might have improved his temperament.

She walked up the steps and paused at the doorway to let her eyes adjust to the brightness. It was obviously well past noon; that she hadn't noticed was proof enough of the distressing nature of what she'd read. She sighed and rubbed her hands over her face, wishing that so doing would wipe away her unease.

"Have you heard nothing about her?"

The whispered voice from just around the corner startled her back to herself. She would have continued on out of the shadowy stairwell, but there was something about the intensity of the whisper that kept her where she was. Besides, she would likely give the man fright enough to render him useless for the day if she popped out into the light. It was only altruism that motivated her.

"The lady Morgan?" said another man.

Morgan paused. When the gossip was about her, how could she not listen?

"Aye." The first voice lowered. "You know, she spent a handful of years on the *other* side of Melksham Island."

Morgan pursed her lips. She could just imagine where this was going. There were many sides of Melksham, but none containing anything so famous as the university.

Except Weger's tower, of course.

"It cannot be," the second voice whispered in astonishment. "At Gobhann?"

Morgan nodded her head in time to the first man's wheezing. "Aye, 'tis so."

"But rumor has it Weger trains assassins there!"

"Mercenaries," the first voice corrected, but he didn't sound any less troubled. "Or so 'tis said. Who knows what really happens behind those impenetrable walls?" He paused. "I've heard that he turns out men who will only take on tasks that are extremely dangerous or impossibly difficult. Ones that no simple soul would dare contemplate, and no seasoned soldier would dare attempt."

"In truth?" the second said reverently.

"So I've heard." He paused, perhaps to gather the courage to divulge even more appalling details. "He marks them, you know."

"Who?" the second breathed.

"Weger, you fool! He marks those who win their freedom from his tower."

"How?"

"None so marked will speak of it. But you can tell. The coldness in their eyes speaks for them."

Morgan snorted. These men would do better to attend to their lectures more and listen at doors less. She cleared her throat loudly and stepped out into the passageway. It was an open passageway that surrounded a courtyard full of flowers and a fountain. The passageway contained two wheezing scholars who gaped at her then sped away as quickly as if she stood to draw her sword and end their gossiping lives at the slightest provocation.

Morgan shrugged. There was truth to what they'd said about her, though she didn't think her eyes were all that cold.

"Good day to you, my dear."

Morgan pursed her lips as she turned around to find Nicholas behind her. He was leaning against a post, watching her with a smile.

Morgan scowled. "Eavesdropping, my lord?"

"It seems to have occupied your time well enough."

"Ha," she said with a snort. "Idle gossip might be interesting, but it never yields anything of substance."

"Hmmm," was his unsatisfactory response.

Morgan turned to face him.

"And what of you?" she asked. "Are you going to divulge your secrets now or will I need to pass another dreadful night on that horrible bed?"

He laughed and came over to draw her arm through his. "Dreadful indeed. Come, my dear, and let us find supper. I will tell you all you want to know after that."

She soon found herself yet again on that comfortable bench, with a hot fire nearby and the promise of a fine repast to come. But apparently Nicholas wasn't going to wait for victuals to arrive before he said his piece.

"I need a favor," he said, without preamble.

"Anything, of course," Morgan said, before she thought better of it. It wasn't in her nature to promise before determining the lay of the land, but how was she to deny this man any whim he might have? Besides, he wouldn't have sent for her if he hadn't needed her.

Nicholas studied her in silence for several moments, then rose. He walked to a table set against a wall, rummaged about through stacks of papers, and came up with a key. This he used to open a plain wooden box that sat on the windowsill, in the company of several other ordinary wooden boxes. He drew forth something wrapped in cloth and brought it back with him. Resuming his seat, he laid his burden on his knees.

"There is a history behind this," he said, "but the knowing of it will not aid you at present."

"If you say so," she said, looking with interest at what Nicholas held in his hands.

Nicholas smiled at her briefly, then pulled back several folds of cloth, finally revealing a slim dagger. The late-afternoon sunlight that streamed in through the window burned fiercely along the blade, as if the metal had been freshly forged. The hilt was studded with rubies and emeralds and surrounded by graceful swirls of gold and silver. The blade was a tracery of flowers and leaves, worked in a most elegant and pleasing fashion.

Morgan reached out toward it. Nicholas caught her hand before she touched the metal.

"It is not an ordinary blade," he warned.

"I've handled sharper, I'll warrant." After all, she was a connoisseur of all things deadly. She reached out and started to take the knife.

But she had scarce touched it before a faint hint of magic had already run up her arm. She jerked her hand back in revulsion.

" 'Tis a mage's blade," she choked out. She scrubbed her hand against her leg, but the feeling of magic was still on her skin. "It is covered with magic!"

"Is it?" he mused, fingering the hilt of the blade. "I suppose it might be."

"It is vile," she said in revulsion.

"Why are you so opposed to magic?" he asked. "I daresay it could be quite useful in the right situation."

"It's cheating," she said promptly. "And unmanly. I find it to be quite a prissy way to be about your business, muttering and waggling fingers when you could just be wielding a sword."

Nicholas smiled. "Now, that is Weger speaking through you."

"And he was perfectly correct," she said. "Never rely on magery was his first lesson." And it was one she had had no trouble learning. She trusted what she could see and what was solid under her hand. Anything else was suspect. "A sword," she repeated with a knowing nod. "There's something to rely on."

"I suppose so."

Morgan looked with disfavor upon the blade. "Why do you keep such a thing?"

"Because I am the keeper of many secrets," Nicholas said mildly.

"Well, if I were you, I would rid myself of that particular secret."

"I agree," he said. He patted the blade on his knees. "And that is the favor I need from you. I need you to take this blade to Neroche for me. To the king."

She opened her mouth, but no sound came out.

"You did say anything," he reminded her.

"I didn't mean *that* kind of anything!"

Nicholas only smiled. "The king will need it."

Morgan scrambled for something to say. She was almost certain she could not, for any price, touch that blade again. Carrying it all the way to the king was out of the question. "Why don't you take it to the king yourself?"

"Bad knees." He patted his knees gingerly, as if to convince her that they were indeed less than useful. "The cold makes them worse."

She snorted. "Scholars should not lie. It reflects poorly upon you as a group."

He coughed weakly. "Would you send an old man on a perilous journey and deny him his few meager comforts—oh, lads, just set that down here on the table near me where I don't need to reach too far for it."

The servants came inside with enough food to feed half a dozen people. They arranged everything, then bowed to Nicholas and left the chamber.

"Morgan, mulled wine? Delicacies from Ghermalt?"

Meager comforts, indeed. Morgan accepted what he gave her only because it allowed her more time to think on a good reason why she couldn't do what he asked. Unfortunately, the offensiveness of the blade aside, she was having a difficult time dredging one up. Nicholas had given her a home, a sword, and all the peaceable things in her life. How could she refuse him anything?

"So," Nicholas said, setting the blade beside his plate and tucking into his meal, "you will do this thing for me, won't you?"

"Ah—"

"I daresay it will be difficult," he continued, as if he hadn't heard her. That, or he wasn't listening, which she suspected was the case. "So difficult, that there are surely few who would dare attempt the quest. Fewer still who would succeed. Indeed, I daresay there is only one who could manage what needs to be done. That one is, of course, you."

Morgan glared at him, then buried her curses in her cup.

"In the end, taking this blade to the king might possibly mean the difference between victory and defeat," Nicholas said.

Morgan looked at him sharply. "Victory and defeat against whom, my lord?"

"Lothar," he said easily.

Morgan wanted to apply herself to her meal, but found that quite suddenly she could not. She sat back, not trusting herself with a goblet of wine either. "In truth?"

He looked at her seriously for the first time that day. "In truth, my girl."

She rubbed her hands over her face and sighed deeply. "Has the king lost his power?"

Nicholas paused, seemed to consider his words, then nodded. "So I've heard."

"How long ago?"

"Two months is what I understand."

She felt a little faint. "That long?"

"Aye. But again, it could be nothing but a rumor. I suppose when you take the king this blade, you'll find out the truth of it for yourself. You'll return and let me know?"

"Have you no shame, old man?" she said in exasperation. "I haven't agreed to go!"

"But you will," he said confidently. "How could you resist such a challenge?"

She wanted to say *easily*, but before she could get the word out, a servant broke into the solar.

"Your pardon, Your Lordship, but you are needed immediately," he said breathlessly. "A pitched battle in the buttery!"

"I must attend to this," Nicholas said, springing to his feet and striding spryly to the door. "Priorities, you know—"

The door shut firmly behind him. Morgan snorted. Bad knees, indeed. The man could likely outrun her. She turned her attentions back to the *meager* offerings before her and applied herself with single-mindedness to them. Soon, though, she found she could not eat anymore. She pushed the table away from her, then rose and began to pace about the solar.

She had absolutely no desire to go to Tor Neroche. It meant leaving Melksham and she had more than enough to do on her own poor island. Besides, she did not like to travel. Off the island, that was.

She glanced at the blade sitting next to Nicholas's plate.

She did not like the feel of it, though she could not help but admit that the blade itself was beautiful.

She turned away abruptly and found herself facing Nicholas's desk. There was a thick book open there beneath the window and she practically leaped toward it in an effort to keep herself from having to pay any more attention to that lovely bit of silver slathered with such vile things.

She turned the pages, perhaps a little desperately, wanting nothing more than a distraction from a journey she did not want to contemplate.

And then she found she could turn no more.

She stared down at the words swimming before her and wondered why it was they seemed so perilously cold and brittle.

Then came the black mage of Ceangail, Gair by name, who never aged and begat children after a thousand years . . .

A noise outside the door startled her and she jumped as if she'd been caught doing something she shouldn't have. She hastened away from the desk and went to stand near the fire before the door was fully opened. She shifted nervously, her face flaming, her heart racing. Nicholas shut the door behind him and returned to his seat. He sat with a gusty sigh.

"Bloodshed averted," he said happily. He looked over his shoulder. "Come and sit, my dear."

Morgan did, praying that he wouldn't notice her appalling condition. She reached for her goblet of wine, but her hand was shaking so badly, she could hardly hold it.

But why?

She knew nothing of mages or magecraft and she couldn't have cared less about the bloody black mage of Ceangail. Perhaps he had a tale that was so truly dreadful, even just the reading of his name was enough to make one unsettled. She drank deeply of her wine. No doubt she had heard his tale at some point, found it unbearable, and forgotten it, only to remember the horror and not the details . . .

Nicholas wrapped the blade back up in its velvets, then patted it meaningfully. "Now, let us seal this bargain. You will take this to the king for me, won't you?"

"Why me?" she asked, in one last attempt to escape what was beginning to feel like Fate.

"Because you are the only one I would trust," Nicholas said.

Well, if he was going to put it that way, she could protest no further. Besides, there was no point in arguing with Nicholas when he'd decided upon something. He would wear her down until she relented.

She sighed. "Stow it in the bottom of my pack where I need not touch it and I will do as you ask."

He looked at her for quite some time in silence, then he leaned over and brushed the hair back from her face. He hadn't made the gesture often, not after she was grown and needed no father's comfort. But he'd done it the morning she'd left the university for her trip across the island to Gobhann, and he'd done it the first night she'd returned after winning her liberty.

He ran a finger over the faint mark above her brow.

"I never can decide," he said quietly, "whose you are: mine or Weger's."

"You say that often."

"I think it often." He smiled and sat back. "You are your own, Morgan, my dear, and you carry in your heart the best of both worlds." He patted the knife. "Take this to your king and offer him your sword as well."

"I'll take him the dagger," she conceded, "but I will not stay. I have business here on the island. Important sieges." She said it firmly, but it sounded rather hollow to her ears, as if those sieges might not be so important after all.

"Is the island big enough for important sieges?" Nicholas asked.

Morgan glared at him. "It is full to the brim with bickering lords bent on mayhem and willing to pay for aid in perpetrating it. There is work enough here for me."

"If you say so," Nicholas said. "Perhaps you will change your mind when you reach Tor Neroche."

"I doubt it," she said grimly. "Very well. I'll go tomorrow."

"Tomorrow? Surely not. You'll need supplies. It will take me at least a se'nnight to see to them."

"A week, old man, will leave me too spoiled to make it across Melksham, never mind finding my way to the king's hall."

"Then sleep on the floor, Morgan, my dear."

She frowned. "The floor? And leave that bed to go to waste? I couldn't."

Nicholas laughed. "Sleep on the bed, love. It may be a while before you have another one."

"I shudder to think," she muttered, but she suspected that she would indeed sleep on the bed and be grateful for it.

The remainder of the afternoon passed almost pleasantly. Morgan managed to ignore the book open behind her on Nicholas's desk, as well as the knife lying wrapped next to it. She forced herself to taste the rest of her meal, managed nods in response to Nicholas's questions, and endured the arrival of the lads and the tale they were treated to. By the time the evening ended and she had sought her bed, she thought she might have herself back under control.

She would take the blade to Tor Neroche, hand it to the king, then turn right around and head for home. She would only have to touch it long enough to hand it off, then she would be free of it and back to herself. Surely she had that much discipline within her.

She fell asleep without trouble, but she did dream.

She dreamed of a slim, elegant sword.

Covered with a tracery of leaves and flowers, all the things that Queen Mehar loved . . .

Three

Miach, archmage of the realm and sufferer of a kingdom-sized headache, closed the manuscript he'd been reading and rubbed his eyes. When he opened them, things were no better. His chamber was an untidy, hazy blur. Perhaps that had to do with too much poring over manuscripts that had provided him with too few answers. He yawned, but that hurt his head, so he stopped. He couldn't remember the last time he'd slept. He couldn't remember the last time he'd eaten.

He could, however, remember the last time he had felt a shudder in his spells.

It had been a fortnight ago.

A slow, almost imperceptible tremble in his spells of defense along the northern border.

He'd wondered at first if he'd just imagined it. He'd paid special attention to the border for the fortnight following, but he'd sensed nothing else.

And then, yesterday, he realized that his spells were being eroded from beneath their underpinnings, much like sand being pulled out from a bather's feet as he stood upon the shore. It was a very gentle tide, but a relentless one.

Miach's first thought had been Lothar.

But the tide didn't have that stench of rottenness that permeated all that Lothar did. Indeed, there was nothing but a faint smell of evil, as if it were nothing but tainted water that washed away at his spells. It had made him wonder . . .

So he'd brought up to his tower all the manuscripts and scrolls he could find describing any of the black mages who'd ever troubled the Nine Kingdoms. He was fairly certain he'd been reading almost constantly since yesterday morning. At least he thought it had been just that long and no longer. His head was so full of names and terrible deeds that he could hardly tell for sure.

Lothar of Wychweald, Gair of Ceangail, Wehr of Wrekin: that was only the beginning of the list, and the most powerful of them. There were dozens of other nasty little mages lurking in the histories of the Nine Kingdoms. Determining who the offender might be would take a great deal of time.

Miach knew he did not have the luxury of too much time.

But perhaps he had time for a brief nap. He rubbed his eyes a final time as he rose, then he made his way around his long table and went to cast himself down on the unobtrusive cot tucked into a darkened corner of the chamber. Even if all he had was an hour or two of sleep, it would serve him well. It was a certainty he was in no shape to do anyone any good in his present condition.

He closed his eyes. It seemed as if he fell asleep instantly. He was fairly certain he began to dream.

At least he thought so.

Suddenly, he realized his mother was sitting in a chair before the fire in the tower room. It had been her chamber in her time as archmage of the realm. He had, during his youth, passed a great deal of his time in it with her. He'd thought, then, that it was simply because he loved his mother and found her company delightful. Later, after she'd died, he had begun to wonder if he'd felt his calling from an early age and such was his preparation.

Suddenly, he found himself sitting across from her before that same fire, but this time he wore his score-and-eight years upon his shoulders. He couldn't decide if he was dreaming or awake. In truth, he didn't care. He was exceptionally grateful to see a friendly face.

"Mother," he said in relief.

"Miach, my love," she said, her tone laced with affection. "How do you fare?"

"I've had easier fortnights," he admitted.

"Son, your burden is heavy," she said gravely. "Unfortunately, it will grow more heavy still."

She'd said as much to him before she died. She was descended from the Wizardess Nimheil, and because of that blood, had the gift of foresight. Miach had it as well, but he suspected that it was not so strong in him. Then again, who knew? Perhaps his time to be tested had not yet come.

Miach sighed. "Adhémar has lost his magic, Mother. Worse still, the Sword of Neroche retains none of its power." He looked at her bleakly. "I fear for the safety of the realm."

She considered for but a moment before she spoke. "Remember the prophecy of Uisdean the Wise: *'The king must sit upon his throne with his sword sheathed and laid across his knees before the tide of darkness will be stemmed.'*"

Miach considered. He knew the prophecy, of course, but it had been some time since he'd tried to unravel its meaning. He'd wondered at times if it meant that the kingdom would only be safe when there was no use for the king's sword. What he suspected, though, was that perhaps there would need to come a king to the throne of Neroche who had power to give *to* the sword, instead of taking power from it.

None of which was possible at present, what with Adhémar possessing no magic and the Sword of Neroche existing as nothing more than a well-designed but unmagical bit of metal.

He looked at his mother. "Any suggestions?"

She smiled at him in that way she had, looking supremely confident that he would find the solution on his own. "I imagine you already have an idea."

"The Sword of Angesand."

She nodded. "That and time is what you need, love. Time . . ."

Miach nodded and rubbed his eyes, wishing they didn't burn so badly. He was going to have to sleep more at some point. Maybe after he'd resolved the current crisis. He opened his eyes, then flinched in surprise.

He was standing in the great hall, and he was alone.

He stared stupidly up at the Sword of Angesand for several moments before he got hold of himself sufficiently to think. He had no idea how he'd come to be in the great hall instead of in his tower chamber, but perhaps he would learn the truth of it later. For now, there was something else he needed to do. He walked around the high table and looked for something to stand on. He pushed Adhémar's chair back toward the hearth, then stood up on it and took the sword down off the wall.

It did not whisper his name back to him as he called it.

It was as any other blade would have been: cold, remote, naught but steel.

He admired it just the same. It was light in his hand, perilously sharp, painfully bright. The blade was adorned with leaves and flowers, the hilt with the same in colors of gold, rose, and green, interlaced with silver.

It was the answer. He knew it, just as surely as he'd known it two months earlier. Someone who could call on that power would give him the added time he needed to determine what was amiss on the border. And if war came to Tor Neroche, at least someone would be able to raise an enspelled sword in defense—

"Miach?"

Miach turned around on the king's chair. Cathar stood there on the other side of the table, looking at him in surprise. For a moment, Miach couldn't decide if he was still asleep or not. He frowned at his brother. "Am I dreaming?"

"I don't think so." Cathar looked more than a bit worried. "What were you doing?" He gestured to the sword in Miach's hand. "Why do you have that sword?"

Miach looked at the sword in his hand. "It was part of my dream." He looked at Cathar. "I think I'm awake now, though."

"You're worrying me."

"I'm worrying *me*."

Cathar walked around the table and held out his hand for the sword. Miach stepped down off the chair, then handed it to his brother. Cathar gingerly took the sword and hung it back up on the wall. He put Adhémar's chair back in its place, then looked back at Miach. "It is the middle of the night. You should go back to bed."

"I *was* in bed."

Cathar's frown deepened. "I'm beginning to think, my lord Archmage, that you need a keeper."

Miach sighed and rubbed the back of his neck. "I'm not sleeping well."

"Apparently not." He slung his arm around Miach's shoulders and pulled him past the table and toward the doorway. "What's your pleasure? A handsome wench, or a hot fire and brotherly conversation?"

Miach smiled faintly. "The latter, surely. I hesitate to think upon how the former might ruin my reputation when I walk away without good reason."

Cathar laughed heartily. "I daresay. Come then, brother, and we'll talk away the night. What there is left of it."

Miach nodded and walked with his brother back to his tower chamber, trying not to show how unsettled he was. He didn't remember having descended the steps he was now walking up, but in truth, he had to admit that everything seemed to be something of a waking dream these days. There were times he wasn't even sure the days were actually passing.

Though he knew they were. He'd been counting the days since Adhémar had left, and the number of times he'd heard from his eldest brother. The latter was the easier number because it totaled none.

He'd sent out birds to search, but they had returned with no tidings. He'd sent messages with discreet messengers, but heard nothing in return. He'd had no sense of his brother himself, but perhaps that was not unheard of, considering how little magic, if any at all, Adhémar retained. But two months had passed, and then some, and Miach knew he had to act. Soon.

He sat down across from Cathar in front of his fire and accepted a cup of ale. It tasted flat and unappealing and he had to set it aside.

"Good heavens, Miach," Cathar said, sounding genuinely concerned, "what ails you?"

"I'm not certain," Miach said.

"Your eyes are red."

"I said I wasn't sleeping."

"Are you drinking?"

"Not that either."

Cathar let out a low whistle. "This isn't good. What is troubling you?"

"Besides the obvious?"

"Besides that," Cathar agreed.

Miach considered. If there was a soul he trusted with his innermost thoughts, it was Cathar. They had been close for as long as Miach could remember. Cathar had saved him from all manner of bullying from other brothers until Miach could stand up for himself, then he'd remained there, steady and solid, since that time. His brother was a vault, a silent repository of things that Miach never would have dared tell anyone else. If he could tell anyone what ailed him, it would be Cathar.

"Very well," Miach said seriously, "I will confide in you." He took a deep breath and let it out slowly before he spoke. "My spells are fading."

"Which ones?"

"The ones of defense," Miach said.

Cathar's mouth fell open. "You jest."

"I don't."

Cathar had a very long pull from his ale. "Defense? You mean those wee bits of magic that keep our border from being overrun by all manner of beasties and evil things sent from black mages we might know?"

"Those bits of magic are not so wee," Miach said dryly, "but aye, those are the spells I fear are being affected. An effect, I might remind you, that I did not author."

Cathar cradled his mug in his hands. "So? What have you decided to do? Are you going to go find what is wreaking this havoc, or merely wait it out and hope it goes away?"

"I daresay it won't go away. I have the strength to shore up the spells, but it will drain even me eventually." He paused. "I fear this is just the beginning of the assault. And if we are assaulted and it is only my magic we can call on . . ." He almost couldn't bring himself to voice his next words. "I am concerned about the outcome of that."

"Is it Lothar behind the mischief, do you think?"

Miach paused. "I suspected so, at first, but there is something different about this magic. A faint whiff of a something that is not Lothar's." Miach paused. "Now that I think about it,

Adhémar carried that same smell about him after he lost his magic in that battle."

Cathar shook his head. "Impossible."

"Is it?" Miach mused. "I daresay not."

"Who is doing this?" Cathar asked, stunned. "Who would dare? Who has the power?"

Miach shrugged. "All very good questions I wish I had the answers to. All I know is that I cannot watch the kingdom, maintain my spells, and solve this mystery at the same time. Not without some sort of aid. Even just the smallest bit of it." He looked at Cathar and smiled wryly. "I am stretched rather thin at the moment."

"You look terrible."

"I imagine I do."

Cathar paused and considered. "What will you do, then?"

"We need the Sword of Angesand and the power it will bring. Once that power is seated again here in the kingdom, I will have a bit of leeway to investigate. I must go and hurry Adhémar along. I've heard nothing from him since he left." He scowled. "I wonder if he's actually making a search, or simply searching out all the alehouses between here and Melksham Island."

Cathar laughed. "Aye, I wonder as well. Surely he should have sent some sort of message by now."

"My thought as well."

"So," Cathar said, taking a final drink of his ale, "when will you go?"

"Tonight."

"Tonight is almost over, little brother."

"Then I'd best hurry," Miach said with a smile. "You'll hold things together while I'm gone, won't you?"

"Me?" Cathar asked in surprise. "But Adhémar left Turah on the throne."

"So he did," Miach said.

Cathar looked at him evenly. "That would be treason, Miach."

Miach returned his look. "Clap me in irons, then."

"I imagine I can't."

"I imagine you can't either," Miach agreed.

Cathar frowned. "You know, in the hands of the unscrupulous, this power you have could be a very dangerous thing."

"Hence the refining fire that makes a mage into an archmage," Miach said easily. "I would be nothing but ashes if I hadn't passed the test."

"Then your heart is pure?"

"I wouldn't go that far," Miach said dryly, "but I am loyal to the crown."

"To the crown, or the king?"

Miach paused for several moments before he could manage a reply. "I think you wouldn't care for the answer."

"Treason," Cathar breathed. "And this time I'm serious."

Miach shook his head. "Nay, Cathar, I will be loyal to the king, the crown, and the realm, and I certainly have no plans to undermine any of the three. Regardless of what I think personally."

Cathar shook his head slowly. "Miach, it is no wonder Adhémar does not sleep well. I think you worry him."

"I likely should," Miach said with a sigh. "I think I should go now. You will see to things while I'm gone? If Turah makes a poor decision, go behind him and remedy it, won't you?"

"And find my head on a pike outside the gate when Adhémar finds out what I've done."

"He won't find out because neither you nor I will tell him. You'll make certain the kingdom stays safe and I'll make haste."

"You do that," Cathar said. He paused, then looked at Miach seriously. "Be careful."

"I always am." He rose and stretched. "I'll continue to watch the borders while I'm away. I think I can manage that, at least." He put his hand on Cathar's shoulder. "Put the fire out before you leave, would you?"

Cathar blinked in surprise. "You're going *now*?"

"Is there a better time?"

"But supplies . . . a horse . . ."

"I won't need them."

"Miach, you'll need food. At least take a bow and arrow for hunting."

"I won't need those either. I'll just use my talons."

Cathar shuddered. "I detest it when you shapechange. How can you bear it?"

"Flying is faster than riding," Miach said. He walked to the door. "I'll return as quickly as I can."

"How will I reach you?" Cathar called after him.

"You won't."

Miach pulled the door closed behind him, then loped down a single flight of his twisting stairs. He exited through a doorway that led him out onto the battlements. He paused to make certain all his spells were as intact as they were going to be for the moment, then he jumped up on top of the wall.

"Miach!"

Cathar's voice almost startled him badly enough to make him fall off. He glared over his shoulder at his brother standing below him.

"What?"

Cathar held out Miach's cloak. "I thought you might get cold."

Miach rolled his eyes, but he reached down to take the cloak just the same. He swung it around his shoulders, then looked at his brother. "Satisfied?"

"Only marginally."

Miach snorted out a small laugh, then turned and dove off the wall.

"I hate it when you do this!" Cathar bellowed after him.

Miach had used the shapechanging spell so often that he hardly had to do more than think about becoming a hawk before the change was wrought in him. He continued his downward swoop, then pulled up before he hit the ground. He beat his wings hard against the air and rose up through the dawn. He saw Cathar standing against the wall, shaking his fist and cursing him. Miach cried out in a hawk's voice, then continued his upward climb. He had no idea where to start, so he flew east. He hoped he would find his quarry quickly.

He needed the wielder of the Sword of Angesand.

He suspected that the safety of the realm might depend upon it.

Four

M organ kicked aside the rotting leaves to make certain she'd left nothing behind in the roots of the tree. She stretched, ignoring her muscles that protested the motion. It had been a most uncomfortable night's sleep, one of many recently, and she blamed Nicholas for it. If she hadn't passed an entire se'nnight at Lismòr, she wouldn't have been so soft. As it was, she would probably spend the rest of her life regretting those days of perilous comfort.

She shouldered her pack, trying not to think about the blade lounging in the bottom of it, no doubt waiting for a most inopportune moment to make its presence known. She'd already decided that the best thing to do would be to pretend it just wasn't there. Of course, that might not be as easy as it sounded, considering it was the reason for her journey.

She took a deep, calming breath, put her troubling thoughts behind her, and set out on her day's walk.

She walked for several hours, paused briefly for a hasty meal made from things Nicholas's cook had packed, then continued on her way. She was only a pair of days out of Bere and that spoke well of the quickness of her pace. Unfortunately, it meant that she would be getting on a ship that much sooner, but that was something she didn't dare dwell on—

She stopped suddenly, her ear catching something amiss. A

single step sounded behind her, then there was silence. Morgan didn't have to hear more. She cursed herself for thinking so deeply that she hadn't been paying heed to her surroundings. She started forward again, keeping to the near side of the road where the shadows of the trees gave some cover.

Twice more she stopped and twice more the footsteps stopped a scant moment later. The third time, the maker of the sounds was not so careful and she heard them distinctly. That was enough for her. With skill born of years of practice under Weger's less-than-gentle tutelage, she slipped off the road and doubled back until her pursuer was before her.

The man in front of her carried a sword; she could see the point of his scabbard hanging down below his long, travel-stained cloak. No scholar, that one, nor a pampered lord. Then who was he? And why was he following her? Was he looking for a traveling companion, or did he have a more sinister motive?

No matter. She had no desire for the former and no fear of the latter. She would merely keep him in her sights until an opportunity to choose a different path presented itself.

The man hesitated at one point, likely realizing that his quarry was no longer in front of him. He hesitated, then eased into the shadows of the wood to the right of the road. Morgan raised her eyebrows. So he was not unskilled. Interesting. She continued down the road, all her senses tuned to what was going on in the woods beside her, and allowed events to unfold as they would.

In truth, she likely should have been more careful, but she'd had a rather tedious journey so far, it was dusk, and she was in the mood for something to do besides walk. But not too much sport. She was, after all, in a fair bit of haste. Best that she merely take the fool and render him unconscious, then be on her way.

She was prepared when she heard a footstep behind her and felt a hand clap her on the shoulder. Morgan stomped back on the arch of his foot, elbowed him in the gut when he bellowed in pain. She drew her sword, then spun around and clunked him heartily on the side of his head with the hilt.

He fell to the ground like a mature tree, slowly and ending with a great thump.

Morgan waited an appropriate amount of time before she

attempted to roll him over, her sword still in her hand. She managed it with difficulty, but once she had him on his back, she could see that he breathed still.

Perhaps unfortunately.

She looked, in surprise, at the most handsome man she had ever clapped her poor eyes on. Not pretty, as many lords' sons she'd known were, but noble. Indeed, the first thought that came to mind was that he belonged as a statue in the Hall of Kings in Tor Neroche, not trailing her to do heaven only knew what. His hair was dark, his features perfectly fashioned, and his form enviable.

Of course, he was drooling, but that might have had something to do with her tender ministrations.

Morgan took an unsteady step backward. It took her three tries to replace her sword in its sheath. The man had been following her, likely with her death on his mind. Or worse. She hadn't killed him, for pity's sake.

Still, it was difficult to look away from him. She felt like she had the first time she'd laid eyes on the sword Nicholas had had made for her. It had been so beautiful, she'd done nothing but stare at it, hardly able to believe such a thing existed. And considering the undeniable beauty of the man before her, perhaps she could be forgiven her moment of weakness.

Weger wouldn't have agreed, but he wasn't there to witness her witlessness and she certainly wouldn't tell him when next they met.

She gave herself a good shake, reminded herself that she was not an empty-headed tavern wench, and attempted to turn her mind to other things. Usually at this point in a skirmish she would have been looking for spoils. She set herself to that task, almost certain it would make her feel more herself.

It was one of the rules of engagement. When one bested his enemy, the victor was entitled to the conquered's goods. If one was feeling particularly generous, he left the vanquished his boots and cloak. All weapons were fair game, though it was generally considered bad form not to leave the fallen at least something with which to defend himself.

She would first look for weapons. It would serve a dual purpose: he wouldn't be able to use them against her and she could perhaps fall upon them if she didn't regain her wits soon. She reached for his sword. Somehow, though, she could not bring herself to touch it. She gaped at her own hand as if she'd never seen it before.

With a curse, she reached again for the sword, only to find herself still unable to even put her hand to it.

Good heavens, what next? Would she take up stitching? She snorted and promised herself a good run later to clear her head. For now, she would settle for the man's purse, which she cut from his belt without a twinge of remorse, and a rummage through his pack.

She helped herself to a pair of socks so fine they had to have been stolen from someone else and a scarf made of the same stuff. These things she put into her own pack, then she examined the contents of his purse.

She was surprised to find the coins were not all of a Melksham strike. Half of them she did not recognize; she wondered if she might have pilfered fakes. They bit like gold, though, so she supposed they would do in a pinch. She hesitated, muttered in disgust under her breath, then deposited a bit of his gold back into his purse and put his purse into his pack. No doubt he would find himself robbed of it just the same, but she would sleep with a clear conscience knowing she hadn't been the one to leave him penniless. She had been far kinder to him than any of her mates would have been. They would have thought her mad.

She suspected she should have agreed with them.

With a sigh, she squatted down, put her hands under the man's shoulders and dragged him off the road under the trees. She retrieved his pack and dumped it down next to him.

She walked away before she did anything else foolish.

She had done enough already.

An hour later it was dark and Morgan was leaning against a tree twenty paces from the man she had felled, unable to explain to herself why she was there or what she hoped to accomplish by returning.

She had traveled for half an hour, then come to an unwilling stop, unable to go on. She had touched the mark on her brow, reminded herself that it had been earned at the expense of any emotion and any pity. She didn't pity the man. She certainly hadn't fallen prey to the fairness of his face.

Perhaps it had been the fineness of his socks. She'd paused to put them on, unable to resist their softness. It was possible that they had been what had dealt the killing blow to her common sense.

Or perhaps it had been instinct that had forced her to retrace her steps. Weger had never discounted instinct. Indeed, that was the one thing about her he had found to praise, if a single lifting of one eyebrow on one lone occasion could be taken as praise. Few earned even that.

But as she stood leaning against the tree, she discounted instinct and socks, and credited her return to too much rich food at Nicholas's table. She would have to remedy that with a large number of very meager meals on her journey.

The man in front of her stirred. Morgan saw him sit up, then clutch his head in his hands. He lay back down with a selection of curses that had even her raising her eyebrows in appreciation.

It was likely those curses that distracted her from the true peril—the one that had put the point of his sword on her shoulder and given her a brisk tap or two.

Morgan spun around. She had her sword halfway from its sheath before she stopped and stared in surprise.

"Paien?" she said.

Paien of Allerdale made her a low bow. "Morgan, you are not yourself," he said. "Didn't you recognize me?"

She should have. He was one of a trio of companions she had kept company with since her release from Gobhann. "I did. I just didn't expect to see you here."

"Actually, neither did I," Paien said with a half laugh, "but things change when you least expect them to." He nodded toward the road where vociferous complaints were still being made. "Who is that?"

Morgan shrugged. "I have no idea. He was silent enough after I felled him."

"No doubt," Paien said. "Well, we'd best go shut him up, or

we'll have every ruffian for miles joining us for supper." He looked at her calculatingly. "Why were you watching over him?"

"I wasn't watching over him," she said with a scowl. "I was . . . well, I was making certain he didn't attack me. You see, he came up behind me with untoward intent—"

"You attacked *me*!" the man said, suddenly struggling to his feet. He staggered about for a moment, clutching his head, then he stopped, swayed, and glared at her. "I thought you were a man!"

Apparently looks and sweetness of tongue didn't always go together. Morgan frowned. "You were mistaken—"

"And you're a girl!" the man exclaimed. "I've never been bested by a girl—and I'm not admitting to being bested now, of course. I was taken by surprise and in a most unchivalrous manner."

Morgan looked at Paien, who seemed to be struggling not to laugh. He reached down and handed the man his pack.

"We've all had our share of surprises with Morgan here," he said easily. "I'm Paien of Allerdale. Who are you?"

"Adhémar," the man said with a scowl.

Morgan rolled her eyes. Adhémar? Yet *another* fool bearing the current king's name? Why couldn't men name their sons after mountains or famous makers of swords? If she'd had a son, she would have named him Buck.

But thinking about Adhémar the king reminded her of what she carried in her pack.

Her pack that she had left by a tree far too far away for her comfort.

"I'll be back," she said to Paien as she strode past him.

"Come, Adhémar," Paien said, "and let us see to a fire. I heard nothing following me, but we've made enough noise here recently to be attacked by all manner of unpleasant things. You know, I'm for Bere. What of you?"

Morgan left them to their speech. If something had happened to that blade . . .

It was with a very unwholesome sense of relief that she found her pack just exactly where she had set it down, twenty paces into the forest. She picked it up, then hesitated. It seemed untouched, but who was to say? She closed her eyes briefly, opened the drawcords, then thrust her hand down inside. She felt around until she found a long, slim wallet of leather. She didn't have to pull it from her pack, or unwrap it, to know it contained the blade.

She could feel the whisper of magic, even through the leather.

She jerked her hand out, yanked the drawcords, then slung the strap over her shoulder. She wiped her hand against her leg, but her hand continued to tingle just the same.

She had not had a very good day so far. A poor night's sleep, a long and tedious walk, a handsome man, and magic. Could it get any worse than that?

She hoped not.

In time, she turned and walked back through the woods until she found Paien in a little clearing, feeding a cheery fire by himself. She dropped her pack on the ground and sat down. "Where's Adhémar?"

"He went to collect what gear you left him with." Paien looked at her knowingly. "Turned your head, did he?"

"He most certainly did not," she said.

"You left the lad with most of his gear."

"An altruistic impulse."

Paien only laughed. "I daresay." He chuckled again as he tended his fire. "He's of a finer quality than we grow here in Melksham. Perhaps it is that you have a discerning eye."

"I was impressed at first," she admitted. "But I feel more myself now. Besides, I have no time for that sort of thing."

"Don't you?" Paien looked at her with interest. "What are you about?"

She hesitated. It wasn't that she didn't trust Paien, for she did. Though he was old enough to be her sire, he fought with the strength and agility of one much younger. He was a giant of a man with hands as big as serving platters and a heart equally as large. Aye, she could say she trusted him. For her, there was no higher praise.

But she hadn't decided exactly what she would tell anyone who asked about her journey. Nicholas had not sworn her to secrecy, but then again, he hadn't needed to. She wasn't one to say more than she needed to about anything she was doing. But perhaps she could trust Paien with her destination at least.

She opened her mouth to speak, but closed it when Adhémar walked into the circle of firelight.

"Is supper ready?" he asked imperiously. "I'm starving."

Morgan frowned. How was it a man could be so handsome when he was unconscious, yet not so handsome when he was awake?

Perhaps she had hit him harder than she'd intended. He spent a good deal of his time wincing, as if his head truly pained him. If that was the case, perhaps he could be forgiven his bad manners.

Then again, truth be told she wouldn't have offered to help Paien with supper either. He was a much better cook than she and she repaid him for his efforts by always taking the first watch so he could savor the last bites of his meal in peace. Morgan let Paien cobble together a passable supper and avoided looking at Adhémar. It was likely the safest thing to do. Bere was close and perhaps she would make very good time on the morrow. Perhaps Adhémar would go his way at dawn and no longer be of concern to her.

She suspected that would be a very good turn of events.

Two days later Morgan followed Paien through the congested streets of the port of Bere, not enjoying the crowds in the least. Too many people jostling her, too many smells distracting her, too much noise making it difficult for her to concentrate.

She looked behind her briefly to see how Adhémar was managing. He still seemed to be following them, and she wasn't all that pleased about it. His face was beautiful, but every time he opened his mouth, she wanted to clunk him over the head again with her sword.

She and Paien had passed their brief journey to Bere in companionable silence, reliving past escapades, and reveling in past triumphs—of which there were many. Adhémar had offered more than his share of impossible tales of battle, simply saturated with delusions of grandeur. He seemed to think he'd had men at his command, then remembered in the midst of a glorious tale that he'd had none but himself.

Perhaps that bump on his head had done more damage than he cared to admit.

Running into Paien's back startled her from her thoughts. She opened her mouth to curse him, then peered around him.

There, before her, bobbing quite innocently in the water, was a ship.

She stared at it, openmouthed. She hadn't realized they were so close to the water.

"What a beauty," Paien said admiringly.

Morgan decided it might be best to refrain from comment.

"Morgan!" came a call from nearby. "Paien!"

"Ah, look who's come," Paien said. "Friendly faces, indeed."

Morgan pursed her lips. It was becoming a reunion of sorts; before her now stood the other mercenary companions she'd left behind. Apparently their business had been concluded successfully, for they seemed quite happy to be in Bere instead of camped out in a muddy field.

Glines of Balfour came to halt in front of her, bowed low, then straightened and smiled. He was a tall, fair-haired man who wore thirty winters on his shoulders and many pouches on his belt filled with gold he'd won from souls with lesser skill at dice than he. Glines was the youngest son of a minor lord who reportedly had a bastard elf lurking somewhere amongst his progenitors. Whether that was true or not, she couldn't have said. What she did know was that Glines vanquished his foes with elegance and a bit of distaste, as if he would have preferred to be discussing politics at dinner.

Next to him stood a red-haired dwarf, short in stature and sharp in feature, who fought with less elegance than Glines but quite a bit more enjoyment. Camid of Carr had traveled the Nine Kingdoms extensively, hiring out to the highest bidder and forever seeking to improve his résumé of escapades in order to impress potential employers.

"Who are these?" Adhémar asked.

Morgan introduced them all briskly. She would have said more, but Glines was staring at Adhémar as if he'd just seen a ghost. She could have sworn he started to bow, but Adhémar reached out and clutched him by the shoulder. Perhaps Glines had been preparing to swoon at the sight of Adhémar's admittedly very fine boots. She couldn't credit him with being impressed by Adhémar's face.

"Glines," she warned, "Adhémar has little left in his purse. Find some other mark for your afternoon's entertainment."

Adhémar glared at her. "How would you—*aha*! I wondered where my gold had gone." He drew himself up. "No matter. I will win more anyway. I am quite skilled in cards. Indeed, it might be said that there is not a better player in all of Neroche—"

Morgan didn't bother to comment. Far be it from her to bruise his ego along with his head. If he wanted to endow himself with qualities that were not his own, he was free to do so. That didn't mean she had to listen, though.

"Boast elsewhere," she said shortly. "Indeed, I'm certain you have other business to see to—out of earshot, hopefully. Don't you?"

Adhémar pursed his lips. "I didn't find what I was looking for on the island. I will begin again in Istaur."

"Is that where you're off to, gel?" Camid asked her.

"That is what we heard," Glines agreed, still looking at Adhémar with wide eyes. "When word was sent for us to meet you here."

"Word was sent?" she echoed. "By whom?"

"Lord Nicholas, of course," Paien said with a slight smile. "He sent a message to me as well. Didn't you know?"

Morgan wasn't sure if she should have been furious or relieved. What she knew, quite suddenly, was that Nicholas considered the blade to be quite a dangerous thing if he had entrusted it to her but then enlisted three of the most deadly men she knew to accompany her. She felt a little weak in the knees, and she never felt weak in the knees.

Of course, that could have had something to do with the ship in front of her.

Camid rubbed his hands together enthusiastically. "I understand you're taking this ship today."

Morgan nodded confidently, far more confidently than she felt.

"Where to?" Camid asked. "Or do we discuss it in a more private setting?"

"Best to do that," Morgan agreed, thinking that discussing it at all was a bad idea.

"Then let us find somewhere to eat and make our plans," Glines said. "Somewhere comfortable, of course, for His—"

Morgan watched Adhémar stumble into Glines. Clumsy oaf. He seemed to have quite a bit to say to Glines—in a low whisper—and Glines seemed to somehow know him. Either Adhémar was consorting with minor nobility, which she couldn't imagine, or he had encountered Glines in some tavern, already lost a goodly sum to him, and wanted it back, which she could readily believe. It was a mystery she would have to discover later. For now, it was best that she keep herself on her feet and not think overmuch on what she would be doing after the sun had set.

She followed the men into a tavern, only slightly surprised when Adhémar held the door open for her. "Are you still here?"

"Morgan!" Glines gasped.

Morgan pushed past Adhémar and took Glines by the arm. "Why are you so friendly with him?" she whispered fiercely. "I know he is fair to look upon, but I warn you, Glines, that his bad manners more than make up for it. Do not encourage him."

"Ah, uh, I thought I recognized him," Glines said, looking unaccountably nervous.

"And I thought he was a mark you intended to fleece at cards," she said. "I will admit that he would make a good one."

"Well," Glines said thoughtfully, "that would pass the afternoon quite nicely, wouldn't it?" He looked over her head. "Cards, my—"

"Certainly," Adhémar interrupted. "Of course, the wench here will have to give me back the rest of my gold before I can wager anything."

Morgan looked up at him, placidly. "Why would I have any of your gold?"

"You're wearing my socks."

"I keep telling you, lad," Paien said with a laugh, "to be grateful the damage was limited to that. Camid, I think we've finally found a lad to turn her head. Can you believe she left him alive?"

"But robbed," Adhémar said distinctly.

Paien only smiled over his shoulder. "It could have been worse."

Morgan agreed, but she didn't bother to say as much. She allowed Glines to pull out her chair. After two years of trying to convince him she did not need such courtesies, she had given up. She did scowl at him, though.

"You will never make a true mercenary," she said.

"So you say," he said, sitting down next to her, "and yet I manage to brandish my sword and do damage with it."

"You do more damage with your gaming."

"I game, you fight." He smiled at her. "I think we should wed and live our lives happily on our strengths."

Morgan was grateful there was no cup of ale in her hand, for then she would have already drunk and she would have wasted a mouthful by spewing it out. To her surprise, Adhémar was making the same sound of disbelief.

"Wed with her?" Adhémar said. "A man wouldn't dare!"

Camid's look would have felled a lesser man. "Careful, lad," he said quietly. "An insult would need to be repaid."

"By me," Morgan put in pointedly.

Adhémar ignored her. "You are very protective of a wench who obviously needs no protection."

"Don't mind him," Paien said, waving expansively. "Camid would be just as protective of Glines."

Paien looked at Adhémar with a friendly smile, but Morgan saw the steel beneath it. No doubt Adhémar didn't.

"You're a close group," Adhémar remarked.

"Loyal to the end," Paien agreed.

"Where did you meet?"

"Ah, now that's a tale," Paien said, rubbing his hands together with relish. "I'll tell it as we eat." He looked at the food that had been set down before Morgan, then at her. "Eat, gel."

She thought not. "I ate this morning."

"Very well, I'll eat yours. Now, Adhémar, our meeting was on this wise . . ."

Morgan listened with only half an ear as Paien described a rainy, miserable evening two years earlier when he had stumbled upon a young lass who'd reminded him of one of his daughters. Feeling protective of her, he'd made certain that she was not accosted in the tavern. When she left to go to the stables, he had followed her, just to make certain she would be safe, but he found there was no need. A group of men surrounded her with evil intent, but they had been dispatched, all four of them, with minimal effort on the girl's part. Paien had bought her a refreshing cup of ale afterward and their friendship had been born.

Camid had been added to that soon after, and Glines as well, once he had bested them all in a game or two of chance. Now they noised themselves about as a group, worked when it suited them, and returned to their homes when it didn't.

Morgan didn't mention that she generally took on other, less palatable assignments when the others had gone to their various homes and were putting their feet up in front of their own fires. Of course, now she could say nothing, for the luxuries of the university far exceeded anything any of the others could boast of, including Glines, and she had certainly partaken of them fully in the past se'nnight.

She noticed, as the others ate and recounted tales of glory, that they were being spied upon. There was a young man, likely not a score, sitting on the far side of the chamber, watching them nervously. Morgan looked at him openly and he turned away. She lifted her eyebrow, then shrugged to herself. He looked vaguely familiar, but she couldn't place him. Perhaps it was one of Nicholas's lads, come to make certain she was safe. She sighed. Judging by the number of escorts he'd sent her in the form of her usual companions, she shouldn't have been surprised to find that was the case.

The platters were taken away and they settled down to an afternoon with mugs of ale and conversation. There came a time, of course, when Glines pulled out his cards and smiled pleasantly. Adhémar grumbled as he investigated the depths of his plundered purse.

Paien leaned over. "He's tolerable," he murmured behind his cup.

"Are you thinking for yourself, or for one of your girls?" she whispered back.

He looked at her with wide eyes, then laughed. "Hard-hearted wench," he said, reaching out to ruffle her hair affectionately. "Someday you will fall."

"Pray you are alive to see it," she grumbled.

"I do, lovey, every night." He chuckled a bit more and turned his attentions to Glines's sleight of hand.

Morgan did the same, marking Glines's quite passable-looking face and his breathtaking cheating, Adhémar's breathtaking face and his less-than-passable gaming—and the lad in the corner who was having a very difficult time blending in with rough company. It was taxing and required her full attention. That was just as well, for it took her mind off what was to come.

Would she be able to get on that ship?

She was beginning to wonder.

Camid finished his ale eventually and set his cup down firmly. "Morgan, where are we off to?"

"Istaur," she said shortly.

"And then where?"

She chewed on her words, considered, then chewed a bit more. "North," she said finally.

"North?" Camid said, his ears perking up. "What mischief are we about?"

"Mischief of mine," she offered, giving them all a very pointed opportunity to thank her for a pleasant afternoon and be on their way, Nicholas's message aside.

"Mischief of yours is trouble of ours," Camid said without hesitation. He stroked his long beard thoughtfully. "North, eh? I can think of many things to do on the way north."

"Aye, well, don't give it so much thought it sours your pleasant humor," Paien said in a friendly fashion. "There will be time enough to discover what Morgan's about and plan your own adventures as well. I daresay Morgan isn't going to tell us until she's ready."

"North?" Adhémar said with a frown. "There is quite a bit of north available after you land in Istaur."

Morgan shrugged. "I'll find my way to it, I'm sure. Don't feel obligated to travel with us."

Adhémar shrugged. "There is safety in traveling with other souls."

"It is more difficult to find yourself robbed thusly," she agreed.

Or perhaps not.

Morgan looked at Glines, who was leaning back in his chair, holding his cards in plain sight, and looking at Adhémar from under half-closed eyelids. Glines, at his most dangerous. Adhémar would not emerge from this encounter unscathed.

"I'll come along as well," Adhémar said, hefting his further-lightened purse. "You might need me."

Morgan couldn't imagine it, but instinct reared its ugly head again and she found she couldn't discourage him. She hadn't left him for dead and now she wasn't stopping him from joining her crew.

Unbelievable.

Eventually, the afternoon waned and Morgan knew she could put off the inevitable no longer. She pushed her cup away and put her hands on the table—because she looked more in charge that way, not because she needed something to steady herself.

Not entirely.

"I must take the ship," she announced.

Camid, Paien, and Glines pushed their cups away immediately and rose. Adhémar drained his, then rose as well.

"Lead on, shieldmaiden."

Morgan did, though she would have given much to have plunked down Adhémar's gold for a comfortable chamber and taken her ease for a fortnight or two and avoided setting foot on that boat.

Unfortunately, she was no coward, no matter what she faced. She nodded briskly, then turned and led her little company from the tavern.

A man near the door leered at her. Adhémar immediately stepped in front of her, but Morgan pushed him aside. She looked at the man and smiled pleasantly. Ah, something to take her mind off her coming journey.

"Did you say something?" she asked.

"Aye," he said, "I asked if you were occupied tonight, but I can see you have a collection of lads here to keep you busy—"

Adhémar apparently couldn't control his chivalry. He took the man by the front of the shirt and threw him out the door. The man crawled to his feet and started bellowing. Adhémar planted his fist into the man's face.

The stranger slumped to the ground, senseless. Morgan glared at Adhémar.

"You owe me a brawl," she said.

"What?" he asked incredulously.

"A brawl," Morgan said. "And it had best be a good one."

"With me?" he asked, blinking in surprise.

"I'd prefer someone with more skill, that I might not sleep through it, but you'll do."

Paien laughed out loud and pulled him away.

"Adhémar, my friend, you cannot win this one. Next time, allow Morgan her little pleasures. She cannot help the attention her face attracts, and thus she has opportunities to teach men manners. In truth, it is a service she offers, bettering our kind wherever she goes."

Morgan would have corrected him on quite a few points, but Glines stopped her with a hand on her arm. He looked at her earnestly.

"Morgan, any man with eyes could not help but offer his life for yours."

"Daft, the lot of you," she said darkly. "I have no beauty but what lies in my skill."

"Hmmm," Glines said, unconvinced. "If you say so, then I must agree. Now, lest you skewer me for heaping more praise upon your lovely head, let us move on to another subject. Did you notice our young shadow inside?"

"I did."

"That's Fletcher of Harding, you know."

"Is it?" she asked in surprise. "I wonder why he's here."

"Who knows? We'll find out if he follows us aboard."

She nodded. "I'm surprised you noticed, though. I assumed you were fixed on your game."

"Your skill lies with the sword, mine with the cards." He yawned. "I had to keep myself from falling into my cups somehow."

She smiled in spite of herself. "You are really a terrible man, Glines."

"Stop," he begged, "I may blush soon."

"Then I will stop, lest the praise be too much for you. Oh, look," she said uneasily, "here we are."

And there they were. She had come to the point where to walk any farther would have meant she was walking into the water. Bad enough that she should have to get onto something that would be *on* the water.

"I'll book us passage," Paien said. He held out his hand and everyone filled his palm.

Morgan watched him go, concentrating on swallowing and breathing. She thought of the knife in the bottom of her pack, the knife that Nicholas had kept for years and entrusted to her. The knife that might have magic that the king was lacking.

It might mean the difference between victory and defeat, he had said.

Morgan continued to take deep breaths. She put her hand on her sword. It didn't help.

Paien returned, all smiles. "He'll even feed us."

"How long a journey?" Morgan croaked.

Adhémar frowned. "Haven't you made the journey before?"

"A very long time ago." She had, when she'd been ten. It had been with her mercenary guardians and she'd vowed if she survived it that she would never again set foot on another boat.

She took a deep breath to still her churning stomach.

It did no good.

"Time to board," Camid said, his long nose quivering in excitement. "I love boats," he said enthusiastically. "Not many where I come from, of course, but I've never not enjoyed a journey on one. I say we take a boat north while we're about our business—"

Morgan continued to breathe. In fact, there came a point where she almost felt better. The sea air was bracing and her stomach was settling quite nicely. She breathed a time or two more and thought that perhaps her fear of boats, or rather what would happen once she set foot on one, was perhaps ungrounded and unreasonable. Had she spent years avoiding something she should have enjoyed?

"Let us be off," she said cheerfully. She nodded to her companions, glared just on principle at Adhémar, then shouldered her pack more securely and followed her companions onto the ship.

She was well.

All was well.

She stood on the deck of the ship. It began to rock. Her belly began to rock with it.

She knew, with a sense of finality that wasn't at all unexpected, that she was in deep trouble.

Five

Adhémar almost went sprawling from the force of the shove. He turned, his hand on his sword, only to see a blur as Morgan bolted past him. He would have tried to stop her, but he couldn't catch her. Was she about to fling herself overboard?

Ah . . . apparently not.

Adhémar was bumped again as Paien of Allerdale hurried to aid his puking comrade. Unfortunately, he seemed to have an abundance of sympathy because he hardly had time to put his pack on the deck next to him before he was leaning over the railing as well, joining Morgan in her, er, business.

Adhémar found himself standing next to the dwarf. He looked down. "You too?"

Camid shook his head slowly. "Never." He patted his stomach. "Sturdy. Reliable. Unfailing."

Adhémar had to admit that he didn't have much to do with dwarves, as a rule, though Neroche did border their country of Durial on the east—and there was a dwarf on the Council of Kings. He thought he might perhaps have judged them as a group too hastily. Compared with the rather unsettling noises coming from the railing, the solid dependability of the dwarf next to him was rather comforting.

"I'll see to their gear," Camid said, then moved off to do just that.

"Your Majesty," whispered a voice at his ear.

"Glines, cease," Adhémar growled. "I'm traveling in disguise."

Glines made him the slightest of bows. "As you wish."

"What I wish is to have the gold back you pocketed from me not two hours ago."

"My cards are always at your service, Your—" He broke off, then smiled. "Perhaps you might suggest what I should call you."

"*Adhémar* will do. *Dolt* will not."

Glines smiled briefly. "Don't mind Morgan. She doesn't suffer fools gladly."

Adhémar glared at him.

"I mean," Glines stammered, "she doesn't suffer anyone gladly. Anyone who isn't her. Actually, she doesn't have much respect for anyone who can't best her in a swordfight and since there isn't anyone I know who can . . . well, you understand."

Adhémar pursed his lips. "I doubt that's the case, but we'll leave that be for the moment." He looked over his shoulder at the young lad who slipped onto the ship and went hastily below. Well, that one bore watching, but later, when he had seen how bad this situation here in front of him was going to get. He crossed the deck and stood next to Camid as the dwarf watched the indisposed pair.

"This does not bode well," Camid said mildly. "We haven't even left the dock."

Adhémar gritted his teeth. The entire venture had been doomed from the start. Traveling without magic had been bad enough; trying to travel without his identity had been worse. He'd been insulted countless times, listened to numerous tavern stories of the king of Neroche who sat upon his fat arse upon his even more comfortable throne and did nothing for the common man, and been cheated in cards and dice more times than he cared to admit.

Add to that being bested by a slip of a girl, and it had been more or less a perfect autumn. He supposed he would have been well within his rights to have heaved Morgan overboard for the slight and spared them all the misery of listening to any more of her . . . well, heaving.

He dropped his pack next to the collection that Camid was guarding. He looked at Glines. "Keep watch over that and over them."

"High and mighty, isn't he," Camid said to Glines with a snort.

Adhémar ignored the slur and walked over to the captain, where he inquired as to comfortable accommodations and the true length of the journey. The answer was, unsurprisingly, none available and longer than he would enjoy since he was the companion of the two fools hanging their heads over the railing. After promising to consider the captain's suggestion to check their pockets for valuables and heave them overboard—and declining to mention that he'd already thought of that—Adhémar returned to see if things had improved.

All sound indicated that they had not.

The ship moved out into the harbor. Adhémar stood idly by and tried to concentrate on the cries of the seagulls and the slap of the waves against the side of the boat. In time, as the land fell away and the sea became rougher, Paien finally seemed to find his legs. He turned, then sank down against the side of the deck.

He looked at Adhémar blearily. "I don't sail well."

Adhémar sighed deeply. He likely should do what he could to aid them. He looked at Glines. "I don't suppose there is a decent galley on this ship."

"Why?"

"I need hot water. I have herbs that will ease them, but they must be steeped."

"Of course." Glines stopped himself just before he bowed, then he went off in search of what was requested.

Camid moved to stand next to Morgan and do the honors of holding her hair back away from her face. "Herbs?" he said doubtfully.

Adhémar pursed his lips. "My brother procured them for me." He paused. "Likely from the local village witch." Adhémar generally didn't lie well, but he'd told so many over the past two months that he'd become quite proficient at it. And it served Miach right, being reduced to trafficking with local old women. It was Miach's fault he was where he was and wallowing in his current condition. A slander, even if it could only be enjoyed by him alone, was satisfying.

"Well, I'm not opposed to an herb or two," Camid said with a nod.

"Aye, what you can put in your pipe and smoke," Paien said hoarsely. "Adhémar, brew 'em up quick as may be. I think I'm—"

He leaped to his feet and turned just in time. Camid shifted against the railing, Morgan's hair still in his hand, and looked at Adhémar placidly.

"Let's hope the galley lads are quick."

Adhémar grunted in answer, then rummaged about in his pack and unearthed the herbs Miach had sent with him. He pulled things out of the large pouch, sniffing until he found something that smelled soothing. Adhémar supposed it was laced with magic, but neither Morgan nor Paien would be the wiser and he certainly couldn't tell himself. He would just use a little and hope for the best.

Glines returned with a large mug. Adhémar accepted it, sloshed a bit on his leg and bellowed until he realized the water wasn't nearly as hot as he would have liked, then dropped the herbs into it anyway and stirred with his dagger. Straining it properly was out of the question, so he scooped out what he could and flung that dross over the railing. He knelt next to Paien, who had resumed his place on the deck.

"Drink," Adhémar commanded.

Paien did, a healthy swig. He pushed the cup away, frowned, tested his stomach's resolve, then smiled. His eyes grew suddenly heavy, but he didn't seem to mind. "Better," he said happily, then tipped over and landed with his head on his own pack.

He began to snore.

Glines looked at Adhémar in admiration. "Well done."

"One down, the wench to go. Camid?"

Camid turned Morgan around and bodily put her down in a sitting position on the deck. Adhémar put his hand behind her head and the cup to her lips.

"Drink," he commanded.

She did, a large gulp that she couldn't seem to help. Adhémar held her nose until she swallowed. Somehow he wasn't surprised that she spewed out what she hadn't managed to get down. He looked with irritation at the front of his tunic. He started to censure her for it, but her words stopped him.

"Magic," she gasped.

Adhémar looked at her in astonishment. How in the bloody hell could she tell that? She was a shieldmaiden whose only magic came from the fairness of her face. That she should be able to sense Miach's spells when he couldn't even detect the faintest hint of them—

Morgan groped for what Adhémar could only surmise was a weapon. Camid managed to relieve her of several knives as she produced them from various places upon her person. "Damn you," she slurred, then her eyes rolled back in her head and she slumped over, using Paien as a pillow.

Camid organized her various knives and dirks, then paused, considered, and then did her the favor of stowing them in her pack. Adhémar frowned at him.

"Don't you want to help yourself to any of those?" he asked.

Camid almost looked startled, if such a thing was possible for the dwarf who looked as if nothing came as a surprise. "I suppose I could try, but I would pay for it later, when she's more herself." He looked at Adhémar evenly. "If you knew her as I do, you would treat her differently."

"More kindly?" Adhémar asked sourly.

"With more respect," Camid said. He arranged Morgan's pack on the deck, then beckoned to Glines.

Adhémar moved out of the way as they situated Morgan so she was as comfortable as possible. Well, perhaps familiarity bred fondness and for that he couldn't blame them.

But for himself, he could only judge her by what he'd seen of her. She had stolen his extra pair of socks, the ones he was wearing had holes, and she was carrying on her person the bulk of his funds.

He paused. He supposed that might be a boon. Less to lose to Glines.

At least she hadn't stolen his sword. Though given the number of weapons Camid had packed away for her, she likely had no need for it.

He sighed and looked at Camid. "We'll watch in shifts."

Camid only nodded, apparently not questioning the decision or the fact that Adhémar was making it. Adhémar took that as his due, then looked at Glines.

"I have a mystery to solve. Did you see the lad who followed us on board?"

"I did."

"Let us be about discovering his identity. I've no mind to find out who he is as he plunges a knife into my back."

"I know him," Glines said. "He's Fletcher of Harding. Why he is following us is worthy of our time, though."

"Then let us be about it."

It took little time to find young Fletcher and even less to intimidate his entire tale from him. Apparently he was an eavesdropper extraordinaire who had decided to follow Glines from a siege his father had been paying for.

"Siege?" Adhémar echoed, looking at Glines. "Over what?"

"Water rights," Glines said with a faint smile.

Of course. Water, sheep, and bickering farmers. Was there anything else on Melksham? Adhémar had wondered, over the years, why Neroche had never gone so far during any of her king's reigns to claim the island and its rich farmland.

Now, he understood.

"And what did you plan to do once you reached Istaur?" Glines asked the boy sternly.

"Follow you," Fletcher said, his teeth chattering. "I heard that Lord Nicholas of Lismòr had sent you on a quest." He attempted to puff out his chest. "I happened to be looking for a quest myself and thought I would see if yours suited me."

Glines snorted. "Fletcher, my lad, your quest will be to survive the journey to Istaur, then return home again before your father discovers you've gone and disinherits you. Go have a seat over there. I'll help you book your return passage once we dock at Istaur."

The lad looked primed to argue, but Glines shot him a look that had him backing down immediately. He gave in and went to sit down against a wall in the common room below.

Adhémar followed Glines back onto the upper deck. "The boy did not agree."

"We'll give him no choice," Glines said. "He would be a burden on the journey and Morgan will have no patience for it."

"What journey is she making, do you suppose?" Adhémar asked. "Not that I care, of course."

Glines gave him a look Adhémar couldn't quite decipher, then shrugged. "We'll know soon enough, I suppose. North is a very large place." He nodded politely, then turned and walked across the deck.

Adhémar frowned and wondered if that blow Morgan had dealt to the side of his head had rendered him witless as well as unconscious. Why he should care about the destination of one feisty shieldmaiden was beyond him. Shieldmaidens did not interest him, either for themselves or their skill. His mother had been a powerful mage, but she tended to cut herself even whilst laboring in the kitchen with any sort of blade. Swords were man's work and he had no interest in a woman wielding them.

But he was not beyond rendering aid where necessary, so he crossed the deck as well to see how things were progressing with the incapacitated ones.

Paien was still snoring peacefully. Morgan was heaving, even in her sleep. Adhémar looked at Camid.

"More brew," he said with a sigh.

Camid studied him for a moment or two. "You know," he said finally, "she cannot bear magic."

"I'm quite certain these are just plain herbs," Adhémar said. "If there is any magic involved, I certainly can't feel it." And that was the truth.

"We'll try mine this time," Camid said, then rose and patted a little pouch at his belt. He went in search of more hot water, then returned with something in a cup that smelled simply vile.

He managed to get it in Morgan's mouth by force. Adhémar was slightly satisfied to see that in the end it didn't do any more good than Miach's brew had. The only improvement was that Camid was wearing it, not him.

"We'll try mine again," Adhémar said, sending Camid off for another cup of hot water. He tossed in a few extra things and managed to get Morgan to drink most of it.

She fell immediately into a deep, if not restless, sleep.

He waited and watched with Camid, but the invalids seemed to be resting comfortably. Adhémar considered supper, then declined. There was no sense in tempting fate.

He went to stand against the railing, facing away from the sun sinking behind them into the west. He blew out his breath and examined the unhappy results of his journey so far.

He'd started in Ainneamh, despite Miach's warning, and had had absolutely no success. Miach was far better suited to treating with elves than he himself was. He hadn't purposely set out to offend King Ehrne. To be sure, Erhne had spent enough of his centuries dealing with mortals that he should have been less prickly, but somehow that had not been the case.

He would send Miach to do repairs after he returned to Tor Neroche. Perhaps he would send Nemed along as well, and between the two of them they could soothe the delicate, affronted elvish feelings.

But really, what else could he have said? Telling Ehrne that Ainneamh was the last place on earth he'd expected to find someone to wield the Sword of Angesand had been meant as a compliment, not an insult.

Elves.

Impossible creatures.

He had then worked his way south. Melksham had been his last resort and he had hoped to find something useful there. All he'd come away with was a sore head and an irritating shield-maiden. He grunted. She would have made a perfect match for Cathar. He was half tempted to take her home and introduce her to him, but that would potentially put her in line for a seat next to the throne and he didn't think he could bring himself to subject his land to her bad temper.

He drew his sword. He looked at the runes of power and might that had been carved upon it centuries ago. It was still bright, that sword, as if it had been newly forged.

Unfortunately it was bright with nothing but a bit of daylight. There was nothing in him that called to the power within the blade. He resheathed the sword with a curse and shoved away from himself the despair that threatened to engulf him. He was a man full grown and past that sort of self-doubt. Even though he was forced to admit that he never could have, at any point, claimed Miach's power, he did claim his sword and there was power in that.

He could not say how it had been done, or by whom, but his magecraft was gone, and he suspected it would not return to him until Lothar was dead and his spells unraveled. Perhaps it was for the best. The Sword of Angesand had been weighing on his mind. He was not anxious to admit to bullheadedness, but it was possible that he might not have done anything about it if he had been in full control of his powers.

But where to go now? He'd looked in the unlikely places. Perhaps now it was his task to look for unlikely souls in likely places. He cursed as he considered. Angesand, aye; or perhaps a less social visit to Penrhyn. There was nothing in him that whispered of a direction except *home* and that was not useful.

He cast his mind in farther circles than he had before. The schools of wizardry? He stepped back from that thought as if it stood to bite him. He hadn't been able to bear it there longer than necessary when he'd been a lad, and his sojourn had been cut mercifully short by his father's death. The wizards could likely be grateful for that, for if he'd had to listen to them pontificate one more time on the proper way to weave a spell, there would have been bloodshed.

Morgan stirred. He watched but saw that she only shifted, then passed into a deep, more peaceful slumber. Miach's brew seemed to work.

A pity Miach hadn't had an herb to restore Adhémar's magic.

Adhémar set his face forward and considered his route. He would perhaps travel with Morgan's company for a bit and continue north. After all, who knew but keeping company with unlikely souls might lead to the unlikeliest soul of all.

He had no other choice.

Sıx

Morgan woke. The deck was no longer heaving beneath her. She was no longer heaving either, which she took to be a very promising sign. She was somewhere that smelled of rich earth and a smoking fire. She remained still, trying to work out where that somewhere might be and where her weapons were. She had no knives up her sleeves, which was disconcerting, but the usual suspects were still stuck down her boots. The comforting coldness against her anklebones told her that much. Well, no matter. If she had to do damage, she could do so with her hands alone. That was assuming, however, that she could get to her feet and stay there long enough to do so.

She was having grave and unwholesome doubts on that score.

Twigs snapped and popped near her ear. She opened one eye a slit and saw that it was night; stars were clear in the sky above her. She was lying in a glade surrounded by trees. She was on bare ground, save that uncomfortable rock near her lower spine, and she was not alone.

"I'm running perilously short on gold," Adhémar was saying with a grumble.

"Then cease passing the time with Glines and his cards," Camid suggested.

"I cannot believe there won't come a time when I won't win," Adhémar returned.

Camid chuckled. "So say all his victims."

"I'm convinced the wench poached much of my coin," Adhémar said pointedly. "I should go through her pack whilst she sleeps."

"She's not sleeping," Glines said absently, shuffling his cards. "And, no disrespect intended, you wouldn't have been able to go through her pack."

"Why is it you are so protective of her and so unfeeling about my purse?" Adhémar groused.

"Save our lives a time or two as she has, then we'll think about it," Camid said.

"Don't bother about his gold," Morgan croaked, turning her head. She had to wait several minutes until the world stopped spinning and she could focus on the little group sitting on the far side of the fire. "He'll just spend it unwisely."

"Unwisely?" Adhémar said sharply. "How so?"

"Those herbs," she said, clearing her throat. "Where did you get them?"

"Here and there."

She closed her eyes. It was better that way, for then the world ceased to spin quite so violently. "Then it was either here or there where you were robbed. Some village witch slipped some of her wares into what you bought."

Adhémar snorted. "Your imagination has gotten the better of you."

Morgan let that pass. She was far more concerned with getting herself to her feet where she could argue more persuasively. Perhaps she would even have a look at those herbs and see if they looked as disgusting as they tasted.

She sat up slowly, appalled at how unstable she was. She looked briefly at Camid. His axe was lying next to him on the ground and he was sharpening his favorite dagger with a slow, careful motion. He looked at her and winked. Well, at least someone was concentrating on their safety.

She frowned. "Where's Paien?"

Camid pointed to her right with his dagger.

Morgan looked next to her. Paien was snoring in an alarmingly loud manner. He sounded dreadful. "Is he dying?" she asked in surprise.

"He likely wishes it so," Camid said with a small smile, "but nay, he's merely weary. We carried you both here, but with him it was a most unpleasant journey. I suppose he will remember bits and pieces of it in time."

"Likely all the times we dropped him," Glines remarked as he studied his cards.

Camid snorted out a small laugh. "One would think a few days without food would have lightened his bulk, but it was not so." He stood. "I'll stand watch. Glines, tend Morgan. We'll set off at first light." He looked at her. "Where are we going again?"

She closed her eyes briefly to recover from the sight of Camid leaping so spryly to his feet. "North," she managed thickly.

"*That* north?" he asked, rubbing his hands together in anticipation. "Wouldn't that look fine on my list of conquests? Let us go very far north and see what sort of sport we find—"

"Not *that* north," Morgan said, sounding appallingly weak even to her own ears. "Souther north."

"On foot?"

"How else?" she said, gritting her teeth.

"Not by boat, I suppose," he said, sounding rather disappointed.

Glines laughed. "Leave her be. We'll go on foot and be pleased with the journey."

Camid made sounds of disgust and tromped off.

Morgan didn't dare watch him go, but she determined that she would have speech with him, Paien, and Glines later, when Adhémar was not about. They would discuss their direction and she would tell them . . . well, she would tell them nothing. How could she reveal that she was carrying a weapon that was so slathered with magic that she could hear it singing from the depths of her pack?

They would think her mad.

She realized, with a start, that she probably should be considering the same thing. Was the blade calling to her? She hadn't realized until that moment that indeed it was.

Glines came to squat down next to her. "Are you feeling better? You look pale."

Morgan swallowed with difficulty. "I am well," she managed. She would have to keep thoughts of the knife out of her head or she would go mad in truth.

"Can you eat?"

"I daren't," she said honestly. "I think I might have a little walk, though, just to see what's left of me."

"Do you wish for company?"

"Nay, Glines, thank you just the same," she said, but she let him help her up to her feet. She swayed in an appalling manner and it took her far longer than she would have liked to feel steady. She managed, finally, to look at him without her eyes crossing of their own accord. "I will be well," she said firmly.

"I suggest you stay off boats in the future," he said.

Morgan couldn't have agreed more, but now was not the time to think on it. She leaned in toward him. "I suggest you be careful with Adhémar," she said under her breath.

"Why?"

"Did you smell those herbs? The man can't tell decent ones from enspelled ones; who knows what else he can't tell."

"I'll remember that," Glines said. Then he paused. "Morgan, about those herbs . . ."

"Aye?"

"How did you know they were more than they seemed?" He paused and looked at her warily, as if he expected her to draw a dagger and poke him with it at any moment. "That they were . . . magical?"

"I just did," she said, but she was beginning to wonder herself. First Nicholas's blade, then the herbs.

These were very unsettling events.

"I just did," she repeated, "but it was nothing. I need to go." She brushed unsteadily past Glines, ignoring his offer of an arm. She managed to make it to a tree at the edge of the firelight before she had to stop and take hold of something to steady herself.

No more boats.

The next one might just do her in.

B y the next morning she was not much more herself, but she had no more time to devote to lying about uselessly. She heaved herself upright and remained there through sheer willpower alone.

Paien leaped to his feet, looking years younger than his normal self, and greeted the world by ingesting a breakfast that just the sight of made her ill. She contented herself with tea she made from things Nicholas's very unmagical cook had very unmagically stowed in her pack.

"North?" Camid asked as they prepared to break camp.

"North," she repeated firmly.

"Skirt the edge of Istaur," Paien advised. "It isn't a friendly place and we would be well off to avoid any unnecessary encounters with the locals in our present states."

"I feel fine," Morgan said, hoping they would mistake the weakness of her tone for discretionary quiet.

Camid grunted, and shouldered his pack. "Well, we have to make at least a brief detour to the docks."

"Why?" Morgan asked.

"We've baggage to put on a ship back to Bere," he said, pointing at the baggage.

Morgan recognized the uncomfortable lad who had been shadowing them at the tavern in Bere, only now he looked different. Perhaps that had something to do with the fact that he was bound hand and foot and gagged as well. "Who is that?"

Glines pulled back the lad's hood and Morgan lifted an eyebrow in surprise.

"One of Harding's sons," she noted. "Not the youngest, for he is at the university. Which one is this?"

"Fletcher," Glines said. "He is the eighth, I believe."

The boy would have answered, but again, he was wearing cloth tied about his mouth that prevented him from expressing any opinion on the matter.

Morgan looked at him and for some reason she hesitated. She wasn't one to have pity on souls who should have been safely tucked into bed each night, but she did feel for the lad and his desire for adventure.

"Can he wield a sword?" she asked.

Fletcher nodded enthusiastically.

"Not well, if memory serves," Paien said. "Don't you remember him, gel? He snuck into our camp that one night and spent half an hour trying to merely draw it as he begged us to take him on?"

Morgan looked at the lad. She recognized the desperation in his eye. If she'd had a heart, it would have gone out to him. To be eighth in a line of eleven lads belonging to a man who seemed determined to live forever and spend all his gold so his sons saw none of it—perhaps he was merely burning to escape his unpromising destiny.

"Well," she said, "why not?"

Camid looked at her blankly. "Why not what?"

"Why not take him along?" she clarified. Then she frowned. Had she said that, or had something unruly taken over her mouth? Things were going downhill for her rapidly. First her fine form, then her wits. "Perhaps he deserves a chance."

Camid looked as surprised as she'd ever seen him. "But," he spluttered, "what will we do with him?"

"Train him," she said, then she looked at Camid, open-mouthed. If she could have turned around to look at herself, she would have.

Paien laughed heartily. "What did you put in those herbs, Adhémar? She's gone soft."

Morgan would have agreed, but she was distracted by the sight of Fletcher suddenly freed of his bonds by Glines and kneeling at her feet.

"Thank you, my lady," he said, clasping his hands and looking up at her with tears streaming down his face. "You will have my everlasting gratitude and I vow I will do all you tell me—"

"Then stand up and cease blubbering," Morgan said in irritation. She wasn't altogether certain at whom she was more irritated: herself for being a soft-hearted fool or Fletcher for looking at her as if she'd saved him from a life of torment.

He leaped to his feet enthusiastically. "Now?" he asked, in a fashion not unlike an over-friendly pup. "Now what shall I do?"

Morgan looked at Camid, but he shook his head. She turned to Glines. He managed to find something quite interesting about the sky. Adhémar only folded his arms over his chest and scowled. She turned to Paien.

"Oh, nay," he said, holding out his hands. "If you want him, you must train him."

"I wouldn't know where to start."

"Try beginning with obedience," Paien suggested.

"If I whip him like a disobedient pup often enough, will he learn, do you suppose?" she asked.

Fletcher gulped, but did not flinch.

Not overmuch.

Paien looked at her, no doubt to try to discover where she'd stowed her wits, then sighed and put his hand around the back of Fletcher's neck. "I will take him for a few days and teach him how not to aggravate you. You can work on his training then."

"I'm saving us a trip to the docks," Morgan reminded him.

Paien snorted. "Considering how just the sight of a boat might render you useless for the day, I daresay that is a self-serving sacrifice. What you have saddled us with, though, may turn out to be more trouble."

"Perhaps," Morgan said, but she could not erase the memory of the desperate look in the lad's eye. It wasn't her habit to aid lads who should have known better than to mix with mercenaries, but that look . . .

She cursed and shouldered her pack, stumbling to catch her balance as she did so. She glared at Fletcher.

"Keep up or we'll leave you behind," she snapped.

The lad nodded vigorously.

Morgan forced herself to walk away without swaying. She took each step carefully and did all she could to not do anything besides look at the ground in front of her.

She did pause, only once, to look back over her shoulder as they traveled along the road that rose up out of Istaur. It was easy to see the quay with the ships bobbing there so innocently.

Nay, there was no return there.

She spared a brief thought for Nicholas and ignored the pang that stabbed into her heart when she realized that she would never see him again. Perhaps after she accomplished the delivery of the blade to the king she would find someone traveling to Melksham and have word sent to him. It was all she could do.

She resolutely refused to think of that blissfully soft bed and those delightfully warm coverings.

Or of the generous man who had provided them for her.

The next afternoon Morgan found herself walking along wearily behind Adhémar, struggling to focus on her surroundings. Each footstep was an effort and she felt as if she were wading through deep water. A pity the physical effort wasn't enough to keep her mind from wandering to topics it should have left alone.

How did you know those herbs were magical?

How indeed. She wanted to believe it came from her years with Weger during which she learned to shun at all costs anything to do with finger waggling and spells muttered under the breath. She wanted to believe that such training had made her especially sensitive to anything that might resemble in the slightest that unmanly art.

She suspected, with growing horror, that it might rather have something to do with something untoward perched in her family tree.

It wasn't possible, was it?

She considered that for a time. Perhaps she would, after her present task was finished, contemplate searching for the mercenaries who had taken her in as a wee girl. Nicholas had said they hadn't given him any tidings of substance in regard to her parentage, but she supposed the lads hadn't been all that interested in chitchat while they'd been trying to force a furious, spitting, snarling gel of twelve summers inside Nicholas's gates against her will.

Nay, she would have to make a search and hope that some of those lads were still alive. It was for certain that she couldn't brave another sea voyage in order to question Nicholas on the matter—

The *twang* of a bowstring broke the relative silence of the late afternoon.

Morgan heard Fletcher cry out. She hardly had the wherewithal to get the boy behind her, an arrow sticking out of his upper arm, before a wave of something came crashing out from the trees. Morgan fumbled with her sword as she drew it, which cost her a moment or two but she managed to kill several things before she realized they weren't precisely men. They died like men, though, and that was enough for her.

The battle was not brief, for the enemies were numerous and she was not at her best. She fought, but not well. Added to her burden was the responsibility she felt toward Fletcher. He was not doing poorly, but it was quite obvious to her that this was his first battle that didn't involve his brothers and pretend

harm. A brief glance at his face told her that he was sick with
fear. She imagined he would be quite sick with his own gorge
later. That he managed to keep it where it should have been for
the moment was a promising sign.

She found it necessary to rest several times. At one point,
she drove her sword into the ground and leaned heavily upon
it, panting in a manner that made her wish that all the events
around her could be frozen until she had regained her strength.
She watched, gasping for breath, as Camid, Paien, and Glines
went about their own work.

Camid was, as usual, an enthusiastic wielder of his very
lethal axe. Paien was very vocal in his taunts, but his sword
spoke just as forcefully. Glines said little but killed with a very
businesslike efficiency that Morgan generally admired, but
now envied.

Fletcher made little squeaks of terror, as if he hoped to do
nothing more than survive. Morgan looked briefly at the arrow.
Was it poisoned? She considered that for a time, allowing herself the unheard of luxury of a bit more rest. When Fletcher
began to look faint, though, she knew her respite was over. She
turned him about to face her and looked at him sternly.

"This will hurt."

"What—"

She jerked the arrow out of his shoulder. Predictably, he
shrieked. She slapped him smartly across the face. "Put your
hand over the wound and stay behind me."

He did so. Silently.

Finding that to be something of an improvement, Morgan
turned to see what was left for her to do. A brief and unfamiliar
wish that all would be taken care of washed over her, but that
was quickly replaced by astonishment over what she was seeing.
Suddenly rising up before her were two creatures who looked as
if they had been spat up from the depths of hell. Misshapen,
drooling, limping but rushing toward her as if they had come for
just such a purpose.

She fought the first one, because he left her no choice. While
that might have been welcome on any normal day, today it was
not. It took an alarming amount of energy to stay on her feet
and continue to fight. She found that when she finally managed

to get her sword thrust into the creature's chest, she simply did not have the energy to pull it back out. Either that, or it was embedded in a body that was not made of the usual stuff.

She stood there with her hands hanging down at her sides and watched, breathing hard, as Adhémar took on the other, a creature even larger and faster, if possible, than the one she'd fought. Camid, Paien, and Glines stood to one side, watching impassively, though Camid was rubbing his nose thoughtfully as if he contemplated why these creatures should find themselves anywhere but tucked safely in a nightmare where they belonged.

Adhémar did not fight poorly; even she had to admit that. He had obviously had some sort of training. He was strong, which helped him, and determined, which aided him as well. But somehow, he seemed to be counting on an extra bit of skill that simply was not there. She was almost unsurprised when the creature reached out, grasped Adhémar by his tunic, and flung him across the glade.

"Damn it," Adhémar bellowed. "Not again!"

Morgan watched him dispassionately. Well, at least he managed to hold on to his sword. Or, rather, he did until he dashed his head against a rock.

He groaned, then slumped sideways, senseless.

Morgan stumbled across the twenty paces that separated them. It was too late to try to rouse him. The best she could do was protect him. She grasped his sword that lay on the ground, ignored the fact that the sword did not seem to want to be in her hand, then swung it up in an arc as she spun to face the creature bearing down on her.

The world made a great rending noise as she did so.

And then the sword blazed with a bloodred light.

She would have dropped it in surprise, but she didn't have a chance. The creature behind her shrieked in rage and leaped toward her. Its eyes locked on the sword.

It fell upon it as if forced.

It died with a gurgle.

Morgan wrenched the sword out of the creature's chest and looked at it in complete astonishment. It glowed with an unworldly light, a fiery red that seemed to pulse right along with her own heartbeat. For a moment she wasn't sure what ap-

palled her more, that the sword was magical or that she hadn't
wielded it past just holding it in the right place and watching
her enemy impale himself on it of his own volition.

She decided she would think about that later, when her heart
had stopped beating at such an appalling rate and her head had
stopped spinning. She turned to Adhémar.

He was unconscious and drooling. Apparently that was his
usual state of being where she and swords were concerned.
She jammed his sword into the ground at his side and released
it as if it burned her.

The red light disappeared, as if it had been a candle suddenly snuffed out.

Morgan backed away until she tripped over a body behind
her. She turned to catch her balance, then found herself facing
her comrades. They were looking at her with varying degrees
of astonishment.

Well, except Fletcher, who was leaning back against a tree,
clutching his arm and looking very pasty.

Paien was the first to break the silence.

"There's an inn ahead," he said briskly. "Let us be about
getting ourselves there." He paused. "Morgan?"

She wondered if she looked as horrified as she felt. "Do not
speak of this," she begged. "Not to anyone."

Paien, Camid, and Glines nodded as one. She didn't bother
with Fletcher. He had now begun to retch and she suspected
that he hadn't seen the business with Adhémar's sword.

She wished she hadn't seen it either. "I'll return for my
sword," she said hoarsely, then she turned and stumbled away.
She had no intention of losing the pitiful meal she'd had that
day, but she had every intention of trying to escape what she'd
just seen.

She flung herself into a stumbling run. It was Weger's favorite way to clear the head.

She suspected she might have to run all the way to Tor
Neroche before she managed to clear hers.

Dusk had fallen by the time she returned from her run to
the scene of the battle. There was a mound of the slain,
which she fell into almost before she realized what she was

doing, and the ground was soaked and unsteady beneath her feet.

Her sword was still buried to the hilt in the chest of that something that wasn't at all human. The creature was, however, quite dead, which was somehow very reassuring. Morgan pulled her blade free, after a ferocious struggle and an enormous amount of energy expended. She frowned. What had she killed? And why had Adhémar's sword thrust in so easily where hers had not?

She could still see that damned sword glowing with a red that burned like hellfire. Yet it had been a glow that was not evil, that much she could say with certainty. Indeed, now that she could look at it with a bit of detachment, she could say that it had been a rather welcoming light—much like a campfire after a hard day's march.

Unfortunately, it had been fire she had apparently called.

She jerked herself away from her thoughts and resheathed her sword. It was an aberration, it was behind her, it was forgotten. She would move on.

She slowly and wearily limped onto the road. She wanted to credit the weakness to aftereffects of sea travel. She wanted to believe it would pass. She almost couldn't bring herself to consider what her future might hold if it didn't.

How would she deliver Nicholas's blade to the king if she couldn't bear up under the simple strain of an easy battle?

For the first time in her life, she gave serious thought to the possibility that she might not succeed at what was set before her.

She dragged herself toward where she knew the inn to be. It was an ill thing indeed to not be in control of her faculties. She shuddered to think what Weger would have had her doing. Likely a fortnight's hard labor to burn out of her whatever illness might be lingering.

He would have been appalled to watch her draw her sword and lean on it periodically as she made her way slowly and feebly toward the inn.

Weger had been, she could admit now with a bit of distance, a difficult taskmaster.

The inn turned out to be quite a bit farther up the road than Paien had claimed. She could only assume that his ability to smell roast pig at ridiculous distances had led him astray. Then again, he was one for traveling, so perhaps he had been here before but merely forgotten the precise location.

She reached it, eventually, and paused at the door. She could hear the full-bellied laughter of Paien, well fed and no doubt happily nursing a large mug of ale. She shook her head. She could not face their merriment now, nor the looks on their faces when they saw her so undone. Perhaps there would be room in the stables.

She paused there next, but there were too many voices inside to suit her there as well, so she continued to walk. Perhaps in that little clearing up ahead. She knew there was someone in that clearing because she could hear the swearing from where she stood. Perhaps he wouldn't mind company. She attempted a quiet approach, but found that it was all she could do to get there.

She paused in the shadows. Damnation, it was Adhémar. Fortunately, he hadn't noticed her. Perhaps that had something to do with his being busy trying without success to light a fire. It was as if he had never before set flint to tinder.

The chill intensified. Morgan looked up, listening to the wind in the trees, and smelling the sweet, sharp scent of pine that enveloped her like a pleasant memory. There were pines in the high mountains of Melksham and she had spent an agreeable summer there once, tracking things as part of Weger's curriculum. The smell was equally pleasing now, accompanied as it was by the breeze and the cursing.

And then she realized that the breeze was not exactly what it seemed to be. It was the sound of wings. The wings belonged to a very large bird, perhaps an eagle or a great hawk. A hawk, she decided, as it circled the glade, then came to rest on the ground. It stood there for a moment or two, then hopped over to the well-laid pile of wood.

It opened its beak and spewed forth fire.

Morgan rubbed her eyes and wondered if now her descent into madness was complete. The boat had obviously done more harm than she'd dared suppose. The question now was, was it permanent?

She looked again at the cheerfully blazing fire and saw that Adhémar squatted next to it, warming his hands against it, but now he had been joined by another man.

Another man?

Morgan took a step forward and looked at them both. They looked so much alike, she could scarce tell them apart, though the newcomer was younger and seemed a bit raw, as if he had traveled a great distance in terrible haste.

Adhémar seemed to have no pity for him. He began to babble at the newcomer with great irritation. Morgan did not consider herself unlearned, but this was a tongue she had never heard before.

She leaned heavily upon her sword. Could the day worsen? First had been a battle with things from her nightmares, then the sword that blazed with a bloodred light, and now these words that were being spoken in front of her but swirled in her head as if she'd dreamed them long ago but forgotten them until just this moment.

She realized her knees were not going to hold her the split second before she went down upon them. Adhémar jumped to his feet and looked at her in surprise, but he made no move to help her.

The other man rose, shook himself like a wet dog, then walked around the fire and held down his hand to her.

"Don't bother," Adhémar said. "She won't take it."

"But I'll offer just the same," said the second man.

Morgan was not herself; it was the only reason she allowed him to pull her to her feet. Perhaps *pull* was not the right word for it. It was as if she had been floated back to her feet. That had everything and nothing to do with the man in front of her. She pulled her hand out of his immediately and clutched her sword as if it was the only thing holding her upright.

Which, as it happened, it was.

The second man coughed suddenly. She supposed it was from his long journey as an eagle. Nay, hawk. She looked at him with a frown.

"Who are you?" she asked.

"Does it matter?" he rasped.

She supposed it did not. "Are you a shapechanger?" she asked, feeling things around her beginning to spin. Shapechanger. How was it a word she had never considered before came so easily to her tongue?

"Who's to say? You know, you don't look well."

"I don't feel well." She paused. "I was seasick."

"That can be draining," he said, reaching out to lay his hand lightly on her shoulder. "Let me help you back to the inn."

"Nay . . ."

"I think you're going to fall."

"Never . . ."

She felt herself pitching forward.

She supposed the ground would hurt when she met it, but blackness descended before she knew for certain.

Seven

Miach stood with the woman in his arms and tried not to hurt her as he clutched her to him. He had been traveling as a hawk far longer than he likely should have and the wildness was still coursing through his veins. It was an effort to speak instead of scream, to use his arms for carrying instead of beating against the night sky.

And that was only part of the problem. He looked down into the woman's face and caught his breath. She was, without a doubt, one of the most beautiful women he'd ever laid eyes on. Not pampered and coiffed and painted like the princesses and their ilk who came to Tor Neroche singly and in packs, hunting for a prince or better. Nay, she was beautiful in an almost painful way, like air in the winter that shimmered with frost and hurt to breathe in, or icy water that rushed and cascaded over stones in a stream and was breath-catching to swim through.

Just looking at her hurt him.

He looked at his brother, intending to ask who she was, then thought better of it. Adhémar was definitely worse for the wear of the previous months and seemed eager to dispense a bit of blame for that. Miach suspected that if he asked for the woman's name, Adhémar would give him the wrong one out of spite.

He took a deep breath and focused with an effort.

"I should see to her," he said, "then I'll return and listen to what you've said. I'm sure you'll have still more to stay."

"Aye, I will," Adhémar growled.

"Where can I take her?"

Adhémar jerked his head to his left. "The inn is there. Didn't you notice it when you flew over?"

"I was concentrating on you," Miach said.

"Well, it's over there; you can take her there, but don't look to me to pay for a room for her there. I have no coin left."

Miach frowned. "And why is that?"

"The wench poached most of it; I lost the rest of it humoring one of my more vocal subjects in cards."

Miach decided he would learn the truth of all that in good time and probably at a higher volume than he would care for. He started toward the inn.

"Be careful," Adhémar threw after him.

Miach turned and looked at his brother expressionlessly. "Why?"

"She nearly killed me on Melksham when I was just trying to make sure she was safe. One moment I was following her at a discreet distance, the next she was attacking me as if I intended to do her harm."

Miach took note of her sword, standing there impaled in the ground. He could feel several more weapons strapped to her arms and waist. "Is she skilled, then?"

"Lucky, more like," Adhémar huffed. "But she fights with no chivalry. I have no idea where she trained—perhaps she trained herself."

"What is her name?" Miach asked.

"Morgan," Adhémar said. "Morgan from that backward island where there's nothing to eat but mutton and nothing to discuss in taverns but irrigation rights. She's uneducated and dangerous."

Miach looked down at her. "She looks quite harmless to me."

Harmless and lovely. Miach found it quite difficult to look away from her.

"She's unconscious," Adhémar said. "Wait until she's back to herself and you'll find quite a few surprises. Put her down and return. Immediately."

Miach turned and made his way to the inn. He hadn't paid
it any heed before, but he could hear voices coming from it
now. He felt more himself with every step, but it was still uncomfortable to go inside the common room with so much
noise and so many people.

He hadn't crossed the threshold before he was confronted
by two men and a dwarf, all of whom wore looks that bespoke
serious concern—and not a little promise. He caught the looks
they cast toward Morgan.

"She fell," Miach said simply. "I caught her. Where can I
take her?"

The older of the men assessed him briefly, then went to
speak with the innkeeper. Miach looked at the dwarf and the
younger of the two men who remained. The dwarf regarded
him steadily, but without any sign of recognition. The other,
fair-haired man gaped at him as if he'd seen a ghost.

Miach frowned. "A problem, friend?"

"I thought, ah, I thought we might have met—"

"I doubt it," Miach said, his voice sounding rough in his own
ears. The blond man might possibly be quite right, but now was
not the time to find out. He was relieved when the older man
returned.

"Follow me," he said briskly.

Miach did, leaving the dwarf and the younger man behind.
He cradled Morgan carefully in his arms and followed the older
man down a passageway. They entered what was obviously one
of the inn's finest chambers, as it was well away from the common area and relatively well furnished.

Miach laid her down on a soft bed, then stepped back and
looked at the other man. "Are you her father to care for her so
well?"

"I am not," the other man said easily, "but I will protect her
as if I were."

"You can see to her hurts?"

"I can. *You* can be on your way now."

Miach lifted his eyebrows briefly, then nodded. "As you
will, then." Not her father and not likely to divulge any details.
Then how did Adhémar know her? Were all these souls traveling in a group? Miach shrugged to himself. No doubt he would

have all the details, and more, from Adhémar sooner than he cared for.

He nodded politely to the older man then made his way out of the inn and back to the clearing. Adhémar was sitting on a fallen log near the fire, staring morosely into the flames. He looked up as Miach approached.

"It took you long enough," Adhémar groused.

"To settle Morgan, or to find you?"

"To find me," Adhémar said crossly.

"That was hardly my fault. Why did you wait so long to use your magic so I could? At least you have it back—"

"I don't have it back!"

Miach went to squat down next to the fire. He was suddenly and quite unaccountably cold. "You don't? But I saw your sword—"

"What are you babbling about?" Adhémar demanded. "There was a battle today, aye, and I'm a little foggy on it, particularly the end, though I'm sure I fought well. I'm also sure I used my sword, but it most certainly did not display anything magical except my skill in killing." He scowled. "All this does not explain why it took you so long to find me."

Miach wanted to stop the conversation until he'd had a chance to digest that. Adhémar had not called to the magic of his sword?

But Miach was certain he'd seen the magelight.

"Miach!"

Miach blinked. "Sorry. I'm not quite myself yet. I've been flying about looking for you for almost a month. And then today—"

"Today we are fortunate you have such a vivid imagination and a great deal of luck," Adhémar said, "else you would *still* be flying about looking for me."

"Of course," Miach said, but in truth he was completely baffled. He *had* seen the Sword of Neroche. It was unmistakable. It wasn't possible that Adhémar had called to the sword's power and not realized it. But if not he, then who?

Questions for later, he decided quickly. His brother was scowling fiercely and babbling just as furiously. Miach suspected he wasn't missing much, but perhaps he should listen just the same. He would think on the mystery of the Sword of Neroche later, when he had the peace for it.

"She's rumored to be a good swordsman but I wouldn't know because those companions of hers coddle her so thoroughly I've never been able to lift a finger against her."

Miach blinked. "Who?"

"Morgan!"

"She's a good swordsman?"

Adhémar glared at him. "Are you listening to me?"

"Intently."

"It doesn't sound like you are," Adhémar grumbled.

"Too much flying," Miach said promptly. "So, she's a shield-maiden and you don't care for her. Why do you continue to travel with her, if she irritates you so?"

"Did you hear nothing I said? The wench felled me with subterfuge, stole most of my gold and half my belongings, and won't give them back! I can't leave until I've had a chance to at least cross swords with her and intimidate her into returning my socks."

Miach would be the last not to offer credit for embellishment where it was due, but if any of Adhémar's claim was actually true, Miach could scarce wait to see Morgan the Fair and Deadly when she was awake.

"I'd command her to admit to her crimes," Adhémar continued grimly, "but I don't dare. I wouldn't want to ruin my disguise as a common traveling man."

Miach yawned to cover his smile. "This hasn't been easy for you, has it?"

Adhémar snorted. "You have no idea. The only justice on the entire journey was that the wench puked almost the entire voyage from Bere, save those several hours when your herbs rendered her blissfully unconscious, but she complained about the magic on them once she was unfortunately lucid enough to speak." Adhémar shook his head. "Cold comfort, indeed."

"How trying. How has the rest of your journey proceeded?"

"About the same," Adhémar said grimly.

"Insults?"

"Too numerous to relate."

"Complaints?"

"I could fill volumes."

"And now being bested by a beautiful wench," Miach said. "And all without your magic. Where have you been so far, by the way?"

"Where *haven't* I been?" Adhémar countered. "Oh, you'll need to make a visit to Ainneamh soon."

"Why?"

"Ehrne is touchy."

Miach rolled his eyes. He could only imagine the various feathers he would be called upon to unruffle by the time Adhémar returned home. "And in all these delicate parleys with rulers of other realms you found no wielder?"

"Not a one."

"Not even any decent mages?"

"There is a distressing lack of them. I suppose I'll have to look farther afield." He shivered lightly. "I do not relish a journey to the east. Only wizards and criminals there."

"You'll survive," Miach said. He rose wearily to his feet. "I'll let you be about it then—"

"Sit down," Adhémar commanded. "I did not give you leave to go."

"I wasn't planning to go far," Miach said and as he said the words, he realized it was true. "I was going to find something to eat."

And then find Morgan and see how she fared.

"Why did you even start out to look for me?" Adhémar asked sharply.

Miach hesitated, then sighed and squatted back down by the fire. He might as well give Adhémar tidings. He would have no peace otherwise. "I worried."

"About me?"

"Among other things."

Adhémar scowled at him. "Who is seeing to the borders?"

Miach forced himself not to hesitate. "Turah sits the throne, as you commanded," he said.

"I hope he can see to the borders," Adhémar said.

Miach refrained from comment—quite wisely to his mind. Cathar was minding the borders and most everything else. No doubt Turah would have quite a tale to tell when Adhémar returned home, but Miach would sort that all out later. For now, there was no sense in upsetting his brother.

"And you?" Adhémar asked. "Did you leave someone to mind things?"

"The realm will survive my absence. I hadn't intended to stay away long."

Adhémar grunted. "Neither had I. I'm telling you, Miach, that I have no more time for this wild hare of yours. I'll look for another fortnight, but then I'm turning for home."

"Perhaps you'll have good fortune," Miach said. "For now, I'm hoping for a good meal." He rose and stretched. "Are you coming?"

Adhémar pursed his lips. "I'll be in later. Pay for mine for me, if you managed to bring coin with you."

Miach picked up a rock, tossed it high into the air and changed it into a purse full of gold on the way down.

"Damn you," Adhémar complained.

"I'll buy you supper," Miach said, then he walked away. He pulled Morgan's sword out of the ground and took it with him back to the inn.

He ordered a meal for himself, paid for one to be taken to Adhémar, then went to sit down next to the fire. He drew a veil of disinterest over himself—not so strong that his supper wouldn't find him, but strong enough to discourage too many studious looks from the other patrons—and sat back to think.

He was not mad; he had seen the Sword of Neroche blaze to life. He'd been twenty leagues to the south, true, but he'd seen it just the same. Perhaps there was magic in the blade yet . . .

He looked at Morgan's sword. It was a simple, elegant blade, very well fashioned and adorned with a handful of gems on the hilt. It was not an inexpensive blade and Miach wondered how she had come by it.

Perhaps he would learn of it later. He sighed deeply, then set the blade aside as his supper arrived.

He tipped the serving wench handsomely and settled down to the simple fare with the gusto of a man who had been eating raw game for far too many weeks. It was only after he'd satisfied himself far past where he was comfortable that he leaned back in his chair and considered his next move.

He could return to Neroche and leave Adhémar to come in his own good time. Indeed, the situation at the border came close to demanding it. Even as he had traveled the Nine Kingdoms, searching for his brother, his mind had ever been on his spells. It had needed to be, for the erosion had continued. His ability to see to that constant drain on his defenses had not diminished, but he would eventually need the power of the Sword of Angesand.

He looked up from his cup when he saw Morgan's watchman heading back toward the bedchambers, dragging an obviously wounded lad with him. Miach found himself on his feet and following them before he knew he intended to do so.

He was being altruistic.

It was one of his finer characteristics.

He followed the men down the passageway, then paused at the doorway as the older man ushered the young man inside and bid him sit down upon a stool and not make any noise.

"She needs sleep," the man was saying. "I'll find a stitcher for you and we'll have your arm seen to. I suppose we should have done it earlier, but I thought food would serve you better. Now, sit you here and watch over Morgan until I return."

The lad looked at him with wide eyes and nodded. "As you will, Paien."

"Draw your sword, Fletcher my lad, and lay it across your knees. You'll look fiercer that way."

It would take more than that, but Miach forbore offering any comment. He continued to lean against the doorway as the man called Paien turned to leave. Then Paien froze. His hand didn't stray toward his sword, but even so, Miach had no doubt of his intent. Miach nodded to himself. A seasoned fighter, if he was that sure of his skill.

"Well, friend," Paien said slowly, "you returned."

Miach handed Morgan's sword to Paien and smiled in his most reassuring fashion. "I thought I might be useful," he said easily.

"And how useful might you be?"

"I do have some small skill in healing."

Paien studied him for quite some time in silence. Miach allowed it, given that he was doing a bit of the same. Finally Paien relaxed.

"You look like Adhémar."

"We're kin," Miach allowed.

"Brothers," Paien stated.

"Surprisingly enough."

Paien laughed. "What's your name, lad?"

Miach considered quickly. Many had named their sons after Adhémar, but none after him. Then again, Mochriadhemiach was quite a mouthful. He would just give the shortened version his family used and attach a small spell of insignificance to it. That would be anonymity enough for his purposes, as he didn't plan to be there all that long.

"Miach," he said, smiling and extending his hand.

"Paien of Allerdale," the other man said, taking Miach's hand and shaking it firmly. "The resemblance truly is strong between you and Adhémar."

"To my everlasting shame," Miach said with a smile.

"Your brother is not completely without virtues."

"So it is rumored, but I rarely believe it," Miach said. He looked at Morgan. She was pale, but she did not look ill beyond saving. He then looked at the lad Fletcher, who on the other hand did not look well at all.

"Arrow wound," Paien said with a nod. "From a band of unwholesome creatures. I was going to look for someone to sew it up for him."

"I can see to it," Miach said.

Paien considered only briefly before he stepped back and waved Miach inside. "Your brother apparently has no judgment when it comes to herbs, so I hope you'll acquit yourself in a more promising fashion. Do you require anything?"

"A mug of hot water," Miach said, producing a small purse from beneath his shirt. "And I *am* a better judge of herbs than my brother."

"Morgan will certainly appreciate that," Paien said. He propped her sword up against the wall. "I'll return quickly. That's Fletcher of Harding, by the way. He's on a quest."

Miach would have asked him what he meant by that, but he was already gone. Miach turned to Fletcher, who looked simply terrible. He pulled up another stool, sat down, and smiled at the young man.

"How did you earn this?" he asked.

The boy, who couldn't have been ten-and-eight though he was struggling to look as if he were, shivered miserably. "I was shot unawares. I should have been looking about me to check for enemies."

"You know," Miach said, unwrapping the bloody rag covering the wound, "many seasoned warriors are caught unawares."

"Not Morgan. Not any of the men with her."

"Well, perhaps they are especially canny. I wouldn't worry. You're young, yet."

"Not too young for an important quest," Fletcher said importantly. Then he seemed to reconsider. "At least I had hoped for an important quest. It was either that or remain on Melksham Island to till my father's fields and fade into obscurity."

"Many notable quests are begun with much less reason than that," Miach said. He looked at the wound and maintained a neutral expression. It was not so much that it was deep, nor that it looked as if the arrow had been ripped out without care; it was that it stank of a vile magic.

Interesting.

"A fierce battle, was it?" Miach asked conversationally.

Fletcher shivered. "I've never seen anything like it. The creatures—" He shivered again. "Never seen anything like it."

"Hmmm," Miach murmured noncommittally. He hadn't seen anything like that magic either, not on this side of the northern border. Was Lothar sending his creatures so far south?

If so, how were they crossing the border without Miach sensing their presence? And if they were circumventing the kingdom of Neroche, then why were they coming here? Istaur was nothing but a port town and there was nothing else in the area worth a visit. Why would Lothar care about it?

Unless that wasn't what Lothar had been seeking.

"If Morgan hadn't made the sword light up," Fletcher said faintly, "I think we would have been all overcome."

Miach froze. He turned slowly and looked at Fletcher full in the face. "What did you say?"

Fletcher looked rather frightened, so Miach softened his expression.

"Go on, Fletcher. What sword?"

"Adhémar's sword," Fletcher said, relaxing visibly. "I didn't feel very well, so I might have imagined it, but I'm almost certain I saw that sword flash red." He paused. "I began puking soon thereafter, so perhaps I was just seeing things."

Miach smiled. "Perhaps. It is easy to imagine things when you're ill, and that was no simple wound you earned. Perhaps you were momentarily overcome."

Or not.

Miach desperately wanted time to consider the possibilities of what Fletcher had just told him, but he was interrupted by Paien entering the chamber.

"Here you are, Miach."

Miach accepted the steaming cup from Paien, and dropped a pinch of herb into it, mixing it liberally with a spell designed to drive the poison from Fletcher's arm. He handed it to the lad.

"Drink it all," he instructed.

Fletcher did his best, wrinkling his nose at the taste. Miach didn't encourage him to drink faster because he needed the time to get his feet back under himself.

Morgan had called to the power of Adhémar's sword?

He could hardly believe it.

"What about Morgan?" Paien asked.

What about Morgan, indeed. Miach looked at Paien. "I'll finish with the lad, then see to her as well."

Paien nodded, left the chamber, then returned almost immediately with a stool of his own. He sat down next to Miach. "I'll help," he said, helpfully.

Miach smiled to himself, then nodded and set to work on Fletcher's arm with a needle and thread he managed to produce from thin air without drawing attention to it. He made quick work of the wound, then bound it securely.

Then he rose and crossed the chamber to sit on the edge of the bed.

Morgan was no less lovely than she had been the first time he'd clapped eyes on her. She was, however, considerably paler. Miach decided that the first thing to do was make her comfortable. He set to his task without hesitation. Paien squawked when

Miach began to remove her weapons from their secreted locations on her person, but Miach only held them out to Paien without comment.

When he had removed them all, he took her hand in his and stilled his mind. He sensed no serious hurt, just the aftereffects of a terrible bout of seasickness and a dreadful battle that afternoon.

And the bloodred magelight of the Sword of Neroche that troubled her even in her dreams.

Miach opened his eyes and stared at her in amazement. So, it was true. He could hardly believe that this woman, slender, lovely, and apparently unmagical, could have called forth the power of the king's sword when the king himself could not.

Astonishing.

Could she do it again or had it been an aberration?

Miach rethought his plan to look at her once more and then leave. Perhaps remaining with their company for a few more days would yield the truth of the matter. Something had happened that day, something he'd seen from twenty leagues away. Something that Morgan had been responsible for. All the more reason to find a reason to travel with her for a while and see for himself what the truth was.

He whispered two spells; one of healing and another of peace. Then he rose, stretched, and went to sit upon his stool. Fletcher was already asleep, leaning back against the wall and snoring happily. Miach looked to his right. Paien had joined the lad in blissful slumber, though he was quite a bit louder about his sojourning there.

Miach was tempted to get up and leave them to their snores, but he made the mistake of looking at Morgan again.

And once he looked, he found he couldn't look away.

He stared at her by the light of a pair of candles in the chamber and nodded to himself. Aye, it would be sensible to remain nearby for a while.

To make certain Adhémar didn't lose his way.

To see to Morgan if she needed aid.

To find the answers to his riddles.

"She's a vile wench."

Miach blinked and looked at the doorway. Adhémar stood there, scowling.

"I wonder how vile can she be with that visage," Miach mused.

"Aye, well, don't wonder too closely or she'll give *you* a lump on your head you won't soon forget."

"Interesting." He looked at his brother casually. "I believe I'll travel with her for a bit, just to make certain she's well."

"Why?" Adhémar demanded.

"Chivalric duty. Mother would have approved."

"I was going to travel with them too," Adhémar said with a grumble. "At least for a bit. I think, however, that *you* should return home as the crow flies."

"I don't like crows."

"I don't care. Go home. Morgan will be fine. I'll look for your wielder for another fortnight, then I'm for home as well." Adhémar looked down at him archly. "I, at least, am staying on task."

"And if she is y—" He shut his mouth before he said any more, but it was likely too late. *And if she is your task?* Miach watched the idea as it hung there in the stillness of the chilly air, brittle and fragile, so fragile that a single sigh would have shattered it beyond repair.

And then Adhémar snorted. "Impossible."

"Quite right," Miach said promptly, quickly waving the words away and leaving no trace of their passing. "I don't think I can take any shape but my own for a bit." He shivered. "Too much raw meat, you know."

Adhémar shivered in distaste. "Stay, then, but not overlong. I'm going to find a bed and sleep off my headache. I have another lump, but I can't fathom where I earned it."

He turned and walked off, gingerly touching the back of his head.

Miach looked at his companions. They were still snoring in a duet that he was certain would eventually give *him* a headache. He sighed and rose, collected all Morgan's weapons and piled them into a corner, then removed his stool from between his sleeping companions. He wrapped himself in the cloak Cathar had pressed upon him, sent a happy thought his brother's way, and sat down in a corner to try to find his own rest.

He found it difficult. Too many questions, too many possibilities, too much noise.

And too much beauty lying before him.

He supposed it would be a very long night.

Eight

Morgan woke. She shifted, and a thrill went through her, as if she'd had a great sickness and its vestiges were still coursing through her veins. It was not unlike what she'd felt after the sea journey from Bere. Magic? Not unless Adhémar had been pouring his foul brew down her; she suspected she would have remembered that.

Well, whatever it was, it would no doubt fade in time. The best thing for it would be to sit up and face the day. She managed to get herself upright with a minimum of effort, dragged her hand through her hair, then froze.

There was a man sitting on a stool in the corner of the chamber, watching her.

She reached for her sword, and found nothing. She could tell without moving that the rest of her daggers were missing as well. She glanced about her casually but with deadly purpose for the rest of her weapons. They were, as fate would have it, all propped up about the man who was sitting on the stool in the corner, watching her.

He looked briefly at her gear, then back at her. "Everything is here," he said calmly. "I kept watch."

"Good of you," she said. She could defend herself with her hands alone, but that was generally a messy business and she was resting on a quite nice mattress in what looked to be a decent chamber. It would be a pity to ruin all that. But she would, if she had to. She suspected by the way the man did not move that he realized the same thing.

Then she remembered who he was.

He was the man from the night before, the one who had flown into the clearing as a hawk, spewed forth fire, then changed himself into himself.

Hadn't he?

She frowned, then rubbed the spot between her eyes that had begun to pound. Sea travel was harder on the body than she had feared. First it was magical herbs, now it was shapechanging men. What next? Swords that sprang to life with magelight—

Oh. But that had already happened.

Heaven help her.

Morgan immediately shunned that memory and swung her legs to the floor. She waited until the tingling subsided, then forced herself to attempt a bit of politeness.

"Thank you for guarding my gear . . ." She reached for his name, but found she did not know it.

"Miach," he supplied helpfully.

"Miach," she repeated.

"Aye."

She looked at him. Once she managed to get her eyes uncrossed and could actually see him, she felt her jaw drop.

Nay, not another one!

He had to be Adhémar's brother. Indeed, he might have been Adhémar's twin, but he was obviously several years younger. And, she had to admit, he was handsome in a different way. He had the same dark hair, the same handsome features, but a leaner build. He was also not sitting there, puffing out his chest, demanding by his very presence that any and all in the area drop to their knees and shower him with accolades. Could it be that he was actually tolerable?

Well, the only way to know for sure was to listen to him talk.

"Are you his brother? Adhémar's?"

"So my mother claimed."

Morgan lifted one eyebrow. "And how does that set with you?"

He leaned forward with his elbows on his knees and

smiled a very small smile. "A bit like a rash that I cannot scratch but that burns like hellfire just the same and never goes away."

Morgan almost smiled. "That I can understand—"

"Morgan! You're awake!"

She whipped her head around to see Glines standing just inside the doorway. She had to put her hands over her eyes to make the chamber cease with its spinning as Glines leaped into the chamber. He put his hand on her forehead.

"You're not feverish," he said, sounding vastly relieved.

It was testimony enough of her weakness of form that she allowed it without thinking. It was obvious Glines had done the like before. Perhaps she had been out of her head with fever. She brushed Glines's hand away in annoyance. "I am well."

"We worried. You've slept for two days."

Morgan scowled at Glines. "Did Adhémar give me more herbs? I daresay I feel as if he did."

"Nay," Glines said. He shot Miach an uncomfortable look. "At least I don't think so."

Morgan frowned at Miach. So, he was not without his faults. "*You* didn't give me any of Adhémar's brew, did you?"

He shook his head slowly. "I didn't."

"Fortunately for you," Morgan said. She studied him for another moment or two. "You poor man. I vow you are the mirror of Adhémar."

"Morgan," Glines said, sounding slightly aghast. He looked at Miach. "I'm sure she meant no offense."

"Of course I meant offense," Morgan said. "Adhémar is a dolt and every time he opens his mouth, he confirms it. I'll reserve judgment on this brother until I've seen him with a sword in his hands. A sword of his *own*," she said, casting a pointed look at the collection of her weapons he was surrounded by.

"Oh, Morgan, please stop," Glines said miserably.

Morgan was on the verge of telling Glines to go soak his head until it became useful to him again, but she was interrupted in giving that instruction by the arrival of Paien, Camid, and Fletcher. Even Adhémar came to stand in the doorway. Her comrades seemed very interested in making certain that she was well, which was cheering, but it got in the way of her comparing Miach to his elder brother. Not that she didn't have better things to do, but she wasn't feeling fully herself. An excuse for a little extra time to get her feet under her was a welcome thing.

"She looks well, doesn't she?" Paien was saying. "Much better than last night."

"Or the night before that," Camid added. "There was an unwholesome pallor to her face then."

"A gel with a weaker constitution might still be senseless," Paien said, "but not this one. Glines, go fetch her something to eat. She could use it."

Morgan thought that while there might be many things she could use, food was likely not one of them.

Then again, perhaps she was being too hasty. She shifted on the bed. Her stomach remained quite steady. She frowned thoughtfully. She did not feel any overwhelming evidence of magic in her system, but she also did not feel completely herself. Perhaps a meal would serve her well.

"We'll wait for you in the great room," Camid said, shoving Adhémar out of the chamber before him. The rest of the men followed, dragging Fletcher with them. Morgan opened her mouth to thank Miach for tending to her blades, while of course taking the opportunity to chastise him for apparently removing them from her person, but the chamber was empty. She looked over at the corner. At least nothing appeared to have been filched.

But what of Nicholas's blade?

Her heart beat with uncomfortable swiftness and she found herself on her feet without really knowing how she'd gotten there. She crossed the chamber in two quick strides, grabbed her pack, and opened it with hands that shook far more than she would have liked.

It was unnecessary.

The blade still whispered to her.

She set her pack down with trembling hands and cursed softly. She could not continue this way, unsure of her next step, faced at every turn with magic and creatures from nightmares—

No more boats. They were just too hard on her.

"Morgan? Breakfast."

Morgan looked over at Glines. "I thought it was supper."

"It's morning."

Morgan nodded as if she'd known it all along, then began to methodically replace her weapons. Once they were all residing where they should have been, she buckled her sword about her hips and shouldered her pack. That Glines only waited and didn't offer to help was reassuring. Perhaps she looked more herself than she dared hope.

She followed him out of the chamber and into the gathering room, realizing as she did so that she had no memory of ever coming through there in the first place.

That was not a pleasant realization.

She continued to follow Glines over to a table where a place had been saved for her. She sat, applied herself briskly to her breakfast, and hoped it would remain where it was supposed to. It was only after she held a mug of ale in her hand and sat back to test her stomach's resiliency that she looked around her. She blinked in surprise to see that Miach was indeed still with the company. He sat over in a corner, very far apart from them, staring off into the distance as if he saw something no one else did.

"Adhémar," Paien said, tapping his fingers in an annoying fashion on the table, "where is your brother? I thought he would remain for a day or two."

Adhémar shrugged. "I told him to go home, but unfortunately I imagine he's somewhere hereabouts."

"Of course he is," Morgan said. "He's sitting over there."

Her companions looked to where she was pointing, then began to shift uncomfortably. All save Fletcher, who looked at her as if she'd lost her mind.

She frowned. "What?"

"Morgan," Glines said carefully, "there's no one over there."

"Of course there is, you fool," she said. "I can see him as plainly as I can see you."

Glines and Paien exchanged a look. The look was then exchanged between Paien and Camid. Then Paien turned back to her. "Let's have a bit of fresh air, shall we? It will clear our heads."

"I'm telling you, he's right there," she said, pointing toward the corner. "I'll go get him."

She got up, only to find that the corner was now empty. She came to a stumbling halt and rubbed her eyes. There was indeed no one sitting at that little table there.

But there had been a moment ago.

She would have sworn it.

The front door opened and she spun around to see who it was. She was somehow quite unsurprised to find it was Miach. Had he snuck out the back and come around to the front? She was certain, quite certain, that she had seen him in the darkened corner.

But why had no one else been able to?

"See?" Paien said, putting a hand briefly on her shoulder. "There he is."

"He was in that corner but a heartbeat ago," Morgan muttered under her breath.

Paien looked at her with a frown, then led the company from the inn, shepherding Miach out the door as he did so. Morgan walked along behind the group, daring Miach to meet her eyes and admit the truth. Unfortunately, Adhémar seemed determined to monopolize him.

"You're still here?" Adhémar said, sounding less than pleased by those tidings. "I told you to return home."

"You're returning home as well," Miach said calmly. "I'll go with you."

Adhémar glared, but Miach seemed unimpressed. Morgan could understand that, for she was not terribly impressed by any of Adhémar's fierce looks, but that didn't answer why they were having this argument in the first place.

"I don't see a horse," Miach continued. "Did you lose yours?"

"I had to sell it to eat," Adhémar grumbled. "I suppose we'll have to find something else. I see you have acquired a pack. How, I wonder, did you do that?"

Miach shrugged. "I picked it up somewhere."

"Speaking of somewhere," Paien said, taking up a position

and motioning for them to gather around, "we need to decide upon a destination." He looked at Morgan. "Well?"

Morgan refused to shift uncomfortably. She could not reveal her real destination to the gaggle of loose-lipped idiots surrounding her, her earlier deliberations aside. Perhaps when the time came, she would merely slip off and be about her business, leaving behind a note and a location where they might rejoin forces at a later time.

"Morgan?" Paien prompted.

"North," Morgan said, wrenching her gaze back to him.

"North and east?" Camid said, looking as if he might have a destination or two in mind already. "More east than north? North and a wee bit west? Which is it?"

Perhaps this wouldn't be as easy as she thought. She frowned. "Just north," she said.

"And how will we get there?" Paien asked.

"We'll walk," she said confidently.

He frowned. "On foot?"

"Aye, on foot," she said pointedly. "You know, with your feet. You've done it quite often in the past."

"On foot," Paien repeated doubtfully. "Well, if you say so."

"I do," she said. "You go first."

Paien shouldered his pack and turned himself around. "North it is, then, lads. Off we go."

Morgan followed, bringing up the rear only because she preferred to. It gave her a better vantage point for when trouble arose. She also didn't care to be followed, for who knew what someone behind her might be plotting?

She paused in mid-step. When had she become so suspicious?

Likely on the first day she'd entered Gobhann when one of Weger's finest students hadn't even given her a chance to set her gear down before he'd bellowed a war cry a hand's breadth from her ear. It had not been a good start to that day, but it had been a lesson learned.

She followed. It was more efficient that way.

The day wore on. Morgan was still not at her best, but the walking helped. It also helped to distract herself by watching the men in front of her as they marched easily on.

Paien and Camid walked together, chatting amicably; no

doubt they discussed activities they might engage in on their way north. Morgan suspected Camid already had a list of things to accomplish and she was quite certain many items would involve the odd but very visible job that might burnish his already sterling reputation. Paien would no doubt be happy to get to wherever he thought they were going, do the job, and return to Melksham. He had a family, but most were already wed and off on their own. His wife was used to his long absences, but Morgan knew she missed him. Paien returned home gladly each chance he had. There were times Morgan thought she might envy him.

Glines walked with Fletcher. The boy was watching him with wide eyes, so Morgan wondered what the poor lad's head was being filled with. As long as it had something to do with the need to be obedient and quiet, she was all for it.

She looked at the final pair of men and frowned thoughtfully. They were much alike in looks, similar in build, but it was obvious to her even now that they were completely different in temperament. Adhémar was handsome in a showy sort of way, like a demanding horse that needed to be brushed often and exercised twice a day. Morgan imagined him with all manner of bells and frippery on his gear, prancing and displaying for anyone who would watch.

She paused. Well, perhaps Adhémar would draw the line at bells.

She turned a jaundiced eye on Miach. He was quieter than his brother, not nearly so mesmerizing, and likely did not require so much attention. She had the feeling, however, that there was more to him than he let on.

Miach reminded her of Nicholas.

The realization came to her quite suddenly and with a settling somewhere in the vicinity of her heart. Perhaps she would never see Nicholas again, but perhaps she might find parts of him in the souls around her. That was reason enough to have not unkind feelings toward Adhémar's younger brother.

Miach looked back over his shoulder at her with one eyebrow lifted. She glared at him. He smiled briefly and turned back to listening to his brother complain in a language that Morgan didn't understand but found unsettlingly familiar.

She spared an unkind thought for Nicholas. Her life had been so simple before she'd touched that magical blade that hummed in her pack. Now, look at where she was.

On an endless road where the surrounding countryside never changed and magic hounded her.

She sighed, put her head down, and kept walking.

T wo days later, she realized things were not going to improve in the near future. They had left a landscape of rolling hills and beautiful forests and come face-to-face with an endless plain.

Endless.

Her companions were standing in a line next to her, staring out across that flat land with varying degrees of surprise. Well, actually only she and Fletcher were surprised. The others looked as if they were viewing nothing out of the ordinary. Paien sighed lightly and began to study the sky. The others, save Miach, avoided looking at her. Miach simply stared at her as if he waited for her to come to some sort of conclusion.

She sighed. The conclusion was reached far sooner than she would have liked.

She cleared her throat and went to stand in front of them. This was a decision that had been quite difficult to arrive at, but she could see no other choice. She had looked at a map at the university, but somehow the continent had not seemed so, well, vast. She had little liking for it, but she knew she would have to find some other means to reach Neroche besides her feet. She looked at her comrades.

"This is a great distance to cross on foot," she said finally.

"I told you so," Paien said, looking at her from under bushy eyebrows.

"You did not!"

"You said 'north.' I asked 'on foot?'" he said. "That was an expression of grave doubt and a suggestion that you look for other means of travel."

She scowled at him.

Adhémar folded his arms over his chest. "You didn't truly think to cross all of Neroche on foot, did you?"

"What makes you think I want to cross it all?" she demanded. "I only said 'north.'"

"Have you ever *looked* at a map?" he asked.

"Map reading is not my strong suit," she said unwillingly. She shot Paien a look of disgust. "I shouldn't have assumed someone would help me in that."

"I didn't dare," Paien said, holding up his hands. "Besides, you didn't say how far north. You could have been going north and a bit east and heading for Angesand."

"Why would you want to go to Tor Neroche?" Miach asked.

"I never said I did," she said. And she hadn't said as much. Never mind what she'd been thinking.

"You would need a horse, no matter how far north you intended to go," Miach advised. "And someone to call you foolish if you did not obtain one."

She pursed her lips. "Are you that man?"

"I might be."

Morgan watched out of the corner of her eye as everyone backed away. Even Adhémar deserted his brother without hesitation. Morgan took a step back and drew her sword.

"My honor is at stake."

"And your map-reading skills," Miach said solemnly.

She had the feeling he was laughing at her and that irritated her enough to make her feel justified in having already drawn her blade. It was enough that he had bamboozled her in the inn two days earlier by disappearing from his corner; now he was poking fun at her and enjoying it.

She looked at him pointedly. He patted himself for a moment or two, then drew forth from beneath his cloak a completely inadequate dagger.

Paien burst out in hearty laughter.

"You insult me," she said, feeling not a little foolish and quite a bit like she had started something she could not back away from without losing a great deal of her pride.

"He would bore you," Adhémar said. "He never goes to the lists."

"How would he know what they are?" she asked, turning to Adhémar. "Or you, for that matter? Do you venture in your lord's secretly when his garrison is away?"

Adhémar drew his sword with a growl. Morgan shot Miach a look of promise, which he accepted by promptly resheathing his dagger and going to look for somewhere to sit. Fortunately for her pride, Morgan found Adhémar to be almost worthy of that very bright sword he carried. Of course, he was no match for her, even after the weakness of that unsettlingly long convalescence, but there were few men who were—and that wasn't pride that spoke but experience.

She dragged the affair out much longer than was needful, more for the exercise than anything else. She finally caught the hilt of Adhémar's blade with the crossbar of hers and sent it flying.

Miach reached up without looking and caught the sword by the hilt. He stabbed it into the ground and went back to drawing in the dirt.

"Luck," Adhémar said, his chest heaving.

Morgan didn't dignify that with a comment. She resheathed her sword, then walked over to see what Adhémar's brother was doing. He had drawn a rather decent map with his very pitiful dagger.

"Here we are," he said, pointing to the southwest corner of a continent. "Here is Angesand," he said, drawing a line north and east. "Farther east is Ainneamh where the elves dwell, north for the dwarves, and farther north for the wild men of Gairn, but you must pass through Wychweald to reach them. That is quite a ways east, though, and perhaps not your destination. If you want north," he said, drawing a line that bent north and west toward Tor Neroche, "you must have a horse. Unless you've months to spend walking the distance."

"Nay," she said, finally, "I do not have months. I am in a fair bit of haste."

"But you will not say to where you are in haste?" Miach asked.

"I cannot," she said. "Not until I must." She looked at Paien. "What do you think?"

"I do not care overmuch for horses," Paien said slowly, "but I cannot deny young Master Miach has a point. The question now becomes, where we will go to procure them?"

"Angesand," Miach answered promptly.

Adhémar snorted. "You jest! Hearn of Angesand would not sell one of his prized mounts to a king for less than a king's ransom. He will not sell any at all to an unknown company such as this—for any money."

"How would you know that, lad?" Paien asked in a friendly fashion.

"Rumor," Adhémar said. "Have you not heard the same in your travels?"

"Aye," Paien said, "but I have traveled much."

"As have I," Adhémar returned. He looked at Morgan. "Search in another place."

She looked at Paien, who nodded his agreement.

"Hearn of Angesand is notoriously choosey about his buyers," he agreed. "You would have to offer him more gold than you'd see in a lifetime, and then some. In return you might get one of his nags."

Morgan looked out over the plain that spread before them like a brown cloth. She saw nothing of settlements, but that did not mean there were none. What she did see was an enormous distance that she couldn't hope to cross in a pair of fortnights, even if she ran.

"We'll see what we can come by," she said, turning back to look at her company. "And hope for the best." She looked down at Miach's map, then looked at him briefly before she smudged it with her boot. It was one thing to look at a map hung on Nicholas's wall; it was another thing entirely to be faced with the reality of what it represented. "I will remember that."

"My pleasure."

"You should find a sword."

"I might cut myself."

Camid laughed and reached out to pull Miach to his feet by the back of his tunic. "Don't torment her. It puts her in a foul humor and she can be quite unpleasant when she's in a foul humor. Now, you aren't serious about not having a sword, are you?"

They walked off together, deep in discussion about things Morgan imagined would include remedying Miach's lack of weaponry.

Adhémar resheathed his blade and looked at her. "You are a passable swordsman," he conceded.

"Thank you," she said simply. She would have said quite a bit more, but Glines was seemingly on the verge of choking to death and friendship demanded that she at least whack him firmly on the back a time or two. Adhémar and Fletcher fell in behind Miach and Paien, so she didn't have the opportunity for any more instruction or enlightenment.

"He doesn't know you," Glines said quietly.

"I'm not offended," Morgan said.

He looked at her in astonishment. "You would have destroyed any other man for saying such a thing."

"I know," she said with a sigh. She shook her head slowly. Her wits were returning, but not swiftly enough. She looked up at Glines. "I will be more myself tomorrow."

"One can hope," he said, slinging an arm around her shoulders.

She elbowed him sharply in the ribs and he laughed with a gasp.

"Better already, I see," he said with a grin.

"I was never *that* indisposed," she returned. But she did not feel totally herself either. There was something about looking over that lifeless brown plain that woke a terrible sense of foreboding in her.

"I am well," she said aloud, but Glines had already walked away.

Horses it would have to be, before it was too late. The knife in her pack seemed to concur because it whispered its assent.

She reshouldered her pack and followed her companions.

T hat night she dreamed.
   She was walking through a forest, a forest full of dense underbrush that forced her to struggle along. She made slow progress, but progress was made.
   She was alone.
   She continued to struggle, feeling a sudden urgency, as if there was an appointed place and a certain time set aside for something to happen that she must be a witness to. Something

dreadful was going to happen. She had to reach her journey's end before it did.

She pushed herself harder. The branches, thorns, and stickers tore at her clothing and her skin.

But she could not stop.

She could not or it would be too late.

Nine

Miach stood on the edge of camp, looking north as the sun began to set to his left. It had been a very long day so far and he suspected he would not go to his rest anytime soon. He stared, unseeing, into the distance and began to methodically test his spells for weakness.

Fortunately, or perhaps not, there was no change in what he'd become accustomed to as a normal level of erosion. That he had grown used to it was unsettling. That the deterioration continued despite his renewing and reweaving was perhaps even more disturbing. Was this truly part of a larger plan of attack, or was it nothing more than a concentrated effort by some evil mage to drive him mad?

He wasn't sure he wanted to know.

But what he did want to know was more about the circumstances surrounding the awakening of Adhémar's sword. Was it the sword itself that had decided to spring to life for that instant, or had Morgan called to the magic? Interesting questions, both of them, but ones he feared he would never have an answer to. He knew Adhémar wouldn't allow him to have a decent look at his sword and he suspected Morgan would likely skewer him if he suggested she had called any magic. If five days spent traveling with her had taught him nothing else, it had taught him that she despised magic in all its forms.

"Idle thoughts?"

Miach came back to himself with a snap that sounded audible even to his ears. He turned to find Morgan standing next to him. He focused on her with difficulty, then shook his head. "Nay," he said. "I was just thinking about home."

"Hmmm," she said. "And where would home be for you?"

"North."

"How far north?" She looked at him suspiciously. "*Very* far north?"

He smiled. "I thank you for the vote of confidence in my mighty power, but nay. I am not of Lothar's ilk."

"I was not suggesting that. I daresay you have delusions of grandeur enough on your own. But, now we come to it. I have something to discuss with you, something about our last morning at the inn—"

"I think I hear Adhémar calling me."

She grabbed him by the arm. Miach watched her frown as she felt around a bit. "You're not as weak as you look."

Miach had to laugh. "Thank you, I think."

"This is not the arm of a man who is unaccustomed to swordplay, yet you seem so incapable of it."

"Well—"

"No matter," she said briskly. "Now that I have you here, I have several questions to ask you. Actually, just a single question."

He could just imagine. He looked around him and wondered where he might escape, but she had a very firm grip on him. It was a not unpleasant sensation and he vowed to bear up bravely for another moment or two.

"That last morning at the inn," she began, "you were sitting in the corner. Why could I see you when no one else could?"

"Was I sitting in the corner?"

She shot him a look of impatience. "You know you were."

"Perhaps you were imagining it," he said.

"Perhaps I wasn't."

"Perhaps you just have very clear sight."

"Was it a spell?" she asked severely.

"Ah—"

"The truth, Miach."

He smiled to himself. He couldn't remember the last time

anyone had spoken to him so impertinently. Well, other than Adhémar, but that was to be expected. It was astonishingly refreshing. He tried to muster an appropriately contrite expression.

"Well," he admitted, "I might know a spell or two. Why you saw through that one I don't know—"

"I'm also not convinced I didn't see you shapechange," she added. "That night before."

He should have been more careful. That he hadn't been said much about his worry and weariness. "Do I look like a shapechanger?" he asked mildly.

"I've never met one, so I wouldn't know."

"If I were you," he said, "I would blame it on a fever and let that be that."

She frowned. "Aye, or I could blame it on bad herbs. Adhémar gave me some that were positively vile. You should have him throw them out."

"Why did you not care for them? I can't imagine there was anything truly odious about them, save their taste."

"They were drenched in magic," Morgan said, "and I'm not one for noticing magic. I couldn't help it with those." She shivered. "I vow I'm still feeling the ill effects."

Miach wanted to feel surprised, but somehow he just wasn't. This was part of what had kept him with the company for five days of stopping at inns and farmhouses and finding naught but nags and ancient plough horses. She had sensed the magic in the herbs Adhémar had given her. She had wielded the Sword of Neroche when his brother the king had been unable to. She had seen through his spell of concealment at the inn. His spells were not weak, yet there she stood, a shieldmaiden from a backwoods island where magic was shunned and strength of arm prized, and she had managed those feats?

"I don't care for it," she added suddenly.

"Care for what?" he asked, wrenching his thoughts away from those compelling observations.

"Magic," she said promptly. "In any form. I avoid it at all costs."

"You have none of your own?" he asked.

She looked at him as if he'd given mortal offense. "Death first," she said, quite seriously. "I would not wish such a fate on my worst enemy."

Interesting. Perhaps she had an ancestor at some point in her lineage who'd had a bit of magic and passed it on. Her sight might be clearer than most because of it. She might possess just enough to have awakened the sleeping sword of Neroche. It might be nothing more than that.

Or it might be something else entirely.

Finding out the truth of that was reason enough to remain with the company longer than was sensible. Because his magic was very strong and no one saw through his spells unless he wished it. Because the Sword of Neroche had been dead steel when he'd touched it last.

Because she was frowning at him as if she would have preferred to be getting her answers by means of a sword pointed threateningly at his gut.

Aye, he would stay a bit longer. If nothing else, he would solve the mystery of Morgan of Melksham and her brushes with several things magical.

She turned suddenly toward the darkening plain. "This is so much more vast than I imagined." She looked at him. "I have never been very good with maps."

"How have you gotten around Melksham?"

"Camid navigates for us," she admitted. "He's fond of a good map."

"Dwarves generally are," Miach said. "There is no shame in allowing him his enjoyment of it."

"Aye," she agreed. "I should have asked his opinion on this matter, but . . ."

"But?"

She looked up at him. "My errand is private."

"And urgent?"

"That too."

"Then you'll need horses, and ones built for speed."

She sighed. "I know nothing of Angesand and his horses save vague rumor."

"Do you not ride?"

"It isn't a quiet way of traveling."

"But it is swift."

"Melksham is not overly large," she said, "and I never had need of haste before." She looked at him. "Can you bargain with this Hearn of Angesand? You and Glines?"

"Why me?" he asked, turning to look at her with his arms folded over his chest. "Why not Adhémar?"

"We want horses, don't we? Forgive me since he is your kin, bastard brother perhaps, but he has not a sweet word in his mouth. He will flatter this lord of Angesand with his pretty face, then open his mouth and ruin the bargain."

Miach put his hand over his mouth to cover his smile. Poor Adhémar. "He is not overly diplomatic," he conceded.

"But you are," she said. "At least you do not bray on like the jackass who is your brother. Can you not take Glines and speak sweetly to this lord of Angesand and win us steeds? If nothing else, Glines can gamble for them and leave this Hearn feeling as if he'd had a fair bargain."

"I daresay he couldn't. Hearn loves his horses more than his children."

"Then what will we do?"

Miach looked off into the distance and gave it thought for several minutes. He could, of course, walk into Hearn's keep and trade magic for all sorts of things. After all, Hearn was his cousin, several times removed.

Then another idea struck him. He smiled at Morgan.

"We will attempt a bargain," he said.

"We?"

"You and I."

Both of her eyebrows went up. "You and I?"

It was terribly selfish, but Miach didn't care. He would have a handful of days with a woman he couldn't look away from and in return she would perhaps win a useful horse or two. Perhaps it wasn't all that selfish after all.

He smiled. "You have sword skill. Hearn will value that. I know a charm or two. I'll see if he has a patch of nettles he wants gone, or an ugly serving maid made beautiful." He shrugged. "Something small."

Morgan looked north, then turned back to him. "I fear I have no choice."

Not a stunning endorsement of his company, but it would do for now. "We should leave before dawn," he said, "on the morrow. We'll catch the man before his morning stables. He'll have a full belly and be thinking of what all those oats cost him."

She pursed her lips. "Are you any less devious than Glines?"

"I will win the horses fairly, if that's what you're asking. If we manage to win them at all." He looked at her thoughtfully. "I daresay Glines has a bit of magecraft at his disposal, at least when it comes to cards."

"Has he bested you yet?"

"No, indeed," Miach said with a half laugh, "but I see very clearly."

"Aye, but you cast a spell very poorly. If it was a spell you cast over yourself," she added under her breath.

Miach let that pass. "I wouldn't think on it overmuch."

She pursed her lips. "I will go fix our plans with Paien and discuss a meeting place. He won't want to remain in the area overlong."

"I imagine he won't," he agreed.

"Before first light, then," she said, then walked away.

Miach watched her go, then turned himself back to the north. Aye, his spells would do for another few days. He would aid Morgan in getting her horses from Hearn of Angesand and see if an opportunity to speak to her about Adhémar's sword arose. His spells would hold that long.

"Miach, supper! Morgan, where is that dratted boy? Go find him, will you, before this goes cold."

Miach smiled at Paien's bellows and turned away from his contemplation of the north before Morgan was forced to come and fetch him. Though he supposed if he'd had any sense, he would have waited for her.

Nay, that was a pleasure he would enjoy on the morrow. He went happily back to camp, setting aside the more serious matters of the realm for the less serious but more pressing matter of supper.

Ten

It was mid-morning when Morgan walked with Miach up to Hearn's keep. Aherin was an impressive stronghold and she supposed she could understand why. Hearn of Angesand obviously valued his horseflesh. Her heart sank within her. She wasn't one to give in to discouragement, but she suspected that twenty gold sovereigns would not buy her a ride on one of Angesand's horses, much less allow her to take even the worst nag away.

"Not to worry," Miach said cheerfully.

"I wasn't worrying."

"You were muttering threats under your breath."

"I was preparing."

He laughed shortly. "Keep those threats to yourself, please, lest we not see the inside of the gates. I will negotiate for us."

He would have to have a golden tongue far more skilled than Glines's to get them in the door, but he seemed to be sure he would manage. She had no choice but to trust him, so she turned her mind to other things in an effort to distract herself.

She looked about as they made their way through a village. If she'd been planning an assault, she wouldn't have relied on a siege. The castle walls were too high and the space they enclosed too large. She wouldn't have been surprised to know

Hearn had a vast quantity of things stored for such a possibility. Oats, at least. She wondered, absently, how hungry he would have to be before he began to eat any of his animals. Probably very, if ever. If that was the case, she suspected Miach would be hard-pressed to convince Hearn to part with any of his horses.

Well, at least he looked the part of a decently funded lord. She was appalled to find that her first inclination with either of these two brothers was to ascertain their handsomeness. Then again, there wasn't much to recommend them as far as their skill with weapons went, so perhaps it was natural. She had to have something with which to occupy her mind, especially since she wasn't feeling overly confident in the outcome of their current undertaking. She continued to observe Miach out of the corner of her eye.

He was, she had to admit upon further inspection, easily as fair to look upon as Adhémar. But his eyes were different. In this light, they were a blue so pale they made her shiver. What sorts of things had he looked at with those eyes that had rendered them so ageless?

She wasn't sure she wanted to know. What she did know, however, was that Miach was much better company than his brother. If she was going to choose a traveling companion, it would surely be him.

She could only hope his honeyed words would serve them here.

She dragged herself back to the present with an effort. "Have you met this man before?"

Miach only hesitated briefly, but that was enough.

"Did you mistreat one of his beasts?" she asked sternly.

"I didn't," he said, "and I am a fair horseman so Hearn will have no complaints on that score." He paused. "I have had speech with him before, and while it was not unpleasant, I would prefer that he not think on it overmuch."

Morgan came to a stop and looked at him. "Why are you here at all, traveling with us?" she asked. "You said you were from the north, and if so you are very far from your home."

"I came to find Adhémar."

"Why is he here? Did he flee from your lord?"

"He"—and here he paused for quite some time—"he was about an errand and it was taking overlong for him to return home."

"He is a grown man. Surely he did not need you to come fetch him. Unless your lord grew weary of waiting for him."

"Hmmm," Miach said noncommittally. "Nevertheless, I worried that something had befallen him and came to see what that was." He smiled briefly. "I daresay it was you."

"I felled him, 'tis true," she agreed, "and it was easily done. You would think that he would be a better swordsman, but he is all bluster."

Miach laughed. "Poor Adhémar. I daresay his pride suffers from your tender assessments of his skill."

"At least he had a sword to fight with," she said, looking at him down her nose. "You haven't even that."

"And you think I should?"

She frowned. "Don't you think so?"

"I have one at home. Perhaps I could purchase another from Hearn."

She shook her head and started walking again. "I can't imagine not having some sort of protection. Your dagger is not up to a serious fight. Then again, I suppose if you're going to shapechange, you don't exactly want to take a sword with you."

"Shapechange?" Miach echoed. "What an extraordinary idea."

"I saw you," she reminded him.

"We've discussed this before, haven't we?"

"I was dissatisfied with your answer."

He smiled. "You were dreaming, Morgan. Out of your head with fever."

Why was it her name could sound so very ordinary when Glines said it, but something far different when a stranger did? And this wasn't even a stranger she had given more thought to than to wonder how he'd gotten this far without losing his head to any number of ruffians. She shook her head and sighed. She hardly recognized herself anymore and she could lay the blame for that at Nicholas's feet. She would have to write him and tell him in what a sorry state she found herself.

"Besides," he said with a smile, "do I look like a shape-changer?"

"You look like a village brat who hasn't the sense to even use his eating dagger as a weapon. How have you managed thus far?"

"I try to avoid battles."

"That's a very unmanly attitude, Miach."

He only shrugged, seemingly unoffended. "So it is."

"I had more sword skill than you when I was ten."

"Did you?" he asked, looking interested. "That is a tale I would like to hear. But perhaps later. Here are the gates."

He pulled his hood over his head, which left his face in shadows even under the flat gray of the winter morning. "Leave me to do the talking, if you would."

She nodded, resigned. Her first instinct would have been to draw her sword and demand to see Hearn, but perhaps diplomacy would be the better course of action.

They were stopped at the gates. Miach was polite, but not overly. Perhaps he did not look like a lord who had the money to purchase an Angesand steed, but he certainly carried himself like one. It took only a handful of moments before a message was dispatched to Hearn, a message returned, and they were being escorted into the courtyard. There, they were bid await the lord's pleasure.

Morgan had no trouble recognizing Hearn when he arrived. He was dressed no differently than his men, nor was he the largest or strongest of them, yet he carried himself in a way that left her with no doubt that he was lord and master there.

He stopped in front of them and looked them over. It was a very long look, but Miach did not shift and neither did she. He finally returned his gaze to Miach.

"My man said there were a pair of travelers at my door—"

"I am . . . Buck," Miach interrupted. "Buck, um, Bucksson."

Morgan snorted before she could stop herself. Finally, someone without delusions of grandeur.

"Buck Bucksson," Hearn drawled. "Is that so? Well, *Buck*, what are you here for?"

"A horse, my lord. Actually seven horses, if they are to be had."

"Seven," Hearn said, raising an eyebrow. "But there are only two of you."

"Our company waits without," Miach said easily.

"Why did they send you?"

"We have the gold."

Hearn grunted. "I don't sell my horses to just anyone." He looked at Morgan. "What skill have you with beasts?"

"I prefer my feet," Morgan answered without hesitation, "but, er, Buck assures me that if there is a horse worth riding, it comes from your stables."

"Does he indeed? Then Buck has a keen eye and a good ear to have harkened to those tales. But the question is, do I want to let you up on one of those wonderful beasts?"

Morgan had never owned a horse. Indeed, if the truth were to be told, she'd never ridden one. But over her long and illustrious career as a mercenary, she had seen beasts well cared for and ones mistreated. She knew what sort of mistress she would be and she told Hearn as much.

He studied her, then looked at Miach. "What are you willing to offer for these seven steeds?"

"I have twenty gold sovereigns for each horse."

Hearn blinked, then laughed heartily. "You jest. One beast is worth all of that several times over. Still, let us not be overly hasty here." He folded his arms over his chest. "What else have you to offer? Have you any magic, either of you?" He paused. "Buck?"

Miach folded his arms over his chest as well. "A little."

"A little," Hearn repeated. "Well, perhaps it will be enough. I have a well needing a bit of sweetening."

"It would then be my pleasure, my lord, to attempt the deed," Miach said, inclining his head.

Hearn turned to Morgan. "And what of you, wench? Do you have anything to offer?"

Well, magic was certainly out. Morgan looked at him steadily. "I could improve the state of your garrison."

"Whoo-hoo," Hearn said with a grin. "Do you think? And just how will you do that, missy? Sing for them? Dance for them? Instruct them in the wifely arts?"

Morgan was accustomed to that sort of thing. Her usual

response was to leave the fool lying on the ground moaning in agony, but she could not do the like here. The speed of her journey lay in this man's hands. She bit back a tart reply, content to let her skill speak for itself.

"Let me see your second-fiercest guardsman," she said. "If I can best him on the field, perhaps you will see that I have something to offer your garrison besides a tuneful bit of singing and lessons in stitchery."

"My second fiercest?" he asked. "Why not the fiercest?"

"I prefer to leave myself something to look forward to after a long day of training those less skilled," she said smoothly.

Hearn stared at her in surprise for a moment or two, then laughed out loud. "Indeed. Well, lassie, I'll have the second fiercest fetched posthaste." He looked at the man who had brought Miach's message to him. "Athol, take our young gel here to the lists and have Rupert fetched. Don't let them begin, though, until I'm there to watch." His eyes twinkled. "I wouldn't miss this." Then he turned to Miach and rubbed his hands together. "Now, you, my little friend Buck, come with me. I have work for you. And then," he said with a pointed look at both of them, "and only then will I decide if it is enough to purchase a partially lame nag or two."

"Do you have any nags, my lord?" Morgan asked politely.

Hearn looked at her, then laughed again. He clapped Miach on the shoulder and walked off with him.

Morgan was not reassured. Indeed, though she had what would no doubt be a decent morning of deeds ahead of her, she was not at all hopeful that she and Miach would come away with what they needed. And if they did not, she had no idea what she would do. The burden of her quest demanded that she continue on, no matter how.

She watched until Miach and Hearn disappeared into another part of the castle, then turned to whom she assumed was a member of Hearn's guard. He was still staring at her as if he couldn't quite believe he was being asked to take her to his domain.

"A woman, no less," he said doubtfully.

"Amazing, isn't it?" she asked. "Now, if you'll lead me to your lists, we'll be about our business."

"Hearn's lads are not unskilled."

"I daresay not, but I need several of Hearn's horses and this is the purchase price. Lead on."

The man frowned at her, then led her away, grumbling.

T he rest of the morning passed quite pleasantly. Morgan made quick work of Angesand's second-best guardsman, entertained herself with the rest of the garrison singly or in pairs as they desired, then paused for a small bite of luncheon with Hearn. She contentedly saw to the rest of his men that afternoon. The sun was low in the sky when the fiercest of the lot stepped onto the field and grinned a most unpleasant grin.

Morgan paused to rebraid her hair.

She took another look at the man and asked him if his wife had any pins she might use to get it completely off her neck.

The garrison roared with laughter.

Pins were fetched posthaste from some obliging miss. Once her hair was seen to, she politely invited the man to begin. He did and she felt the first crossing of their swords clear to her center.

She smiled.

The sun soon began to sink. Morgan regretted that, as she regretted the last lingering bit of weakness she had. In the end, she had to dig deep for stores of strength she usually left dormant. In truth, that was not such an ill thing. It was seldom that she was called upon to test even the beginning of the end of what she could do.

The man cried peace, eventually, and offered her a sweaty hand in friendship.

"I want to know who trained ye, gel," he said, his face dripping and his chest heaving. "I would pay much to be so fortunate."

"I'm not inclined to speak of it now," she said easily, "but I will perhaps tell you before we leave the keep."

The man looked at her closely for a moment or two, then he nodded. "I'll ask ye again, then, 'afore ye go. But if you're intending to stay another day or two, I'd like to have another go."

"My pleasure," Morgan said, then looked about her. Finding the garrison in more or less of a shambles, she considered her duty done for the day and happily retreated to the great hall to look for supper.

Miach was sitting at one of the low tables and motioned for her to join him. She sat down and accepted a cup of ale gladly.

"How was the garrison?" he asked.

"Much as I expected, *Buck*. How did your labors go?"

He smiled a small smile. "Exhausting. I told you Hearn was a ferocious bargainer. He is taxing the very limits of what I can do."

"Magic," she said, shaking her head. "A most unmanly pursuit. What else is it you do, by the way?"

"I farm," he said. "Grow things. Do good."

"And your brother?" she asked. "Does he do anything useful? He is certainly full of tales of glory, though I don't know how they are possible given his lack of skill."

Miach smiled. "He is not completely useless."

"Nay," she conceded, "but he always seems to think he has more skill at his command than he really does. It is as if he counts on something else that is simply not there. He would do better to rely only on his strength of arm. Now, what does he do to earn his bread?"

Miach paused for a moment or two. "He has a landhold," he said finally.

"I am surprised he is not wed if that is the case."

"So is he," Miach said dryly, "though it is not for a lack of opportunities."

"Perhaps he frightens the wenches off when he opens his mouth," Morgan mused. "Does he travel often?"

"When pressed."

"Why did he go to Melksham?" she asked. "Did he hope to find a willing wench there?"

Miach shifted. Morgan frowned to herself. He was not a good liar and she was fairly certain he was preparing to lie now.

"The question is not difficult," she said, fingering her knife.

"It is when you have a blade in your hand." He drained his cup, then answered. "Something was stolen from him and I'm not free to say what. He set off in the fall to search for it. When he did not return when I thought he should, I set out to look for him. And now here we are at Angesand's table working off the price of several of his finest horses. Quite a journey, isn't it?"

"Hmmm," she said skeptically. There was more to the tale than he was telling. Perhaps she would take him out to the lists on the morrow and see if she couldn't wring a few answers from him then. "You have a reprieve now, but I will have my answers yet," she warned him.

He only smiled. "I wouldn't doubt it."

Aye, an early morning in the lists at her first opportunity. She nodded knowingly at him, then turned back to her supper.

She finished her meal eventually, then looked over the occupants of the great hall. Hearn's men, for the most part. The only guests, actually, were Miach and her. She looked at him.

"A close-knit group."

"Hearn does not care for strangers. One of them might say a cross word to one of his horses."

She nodded. "I daresay." She fingered her dagger for a moment or two, then looked at him. "I am not usually given to worry, but I do here. It is obvious to me that the situation here was as you said. Hearn is very fond of his horses."

"No reason to worry yet. You seem to have intimidated the garrison. Perhaps you can intimidate Hearn tomorrow."

"That won't win us any horses," she said with a snort. "I can't even imagine flattery serving us."

"Nay," he agreed. "Skill and skill alone will win the day." He smiled briefly. "I suppose then, that 'tis up to you to see to it."

She pursed her lips, then turned back to her contemplation of the great hall. It was a fine place indeed, but the stables even from the outside appeared finer. She knew she shouldn't have been surprised.

After supper was finished, they were offered beds in the hayloft. Morgan saw that her suspicions were correct. She had never in her life seen such fine accommodations for horses. Indeed, Hearn prized his steeds greatly.

Miach waited until their guides had departed before he spoke.

"This is a very great honor," he whispered. "To trust anyone near his horses says much of his esteem for us."

"Think you?" she whispered in return.

"Kings have no doubt longed to sleep in the hayloft. I daresay a very few have, and many more have wished to but been denied the pleasure."

"Miach, I have no intention of complaining," she said, feeling a little overwhelmed by the tidings.

"You might when I snore."

"I might," she agreed, "but if it is the price I pay for this honor, so be it."

She stretched out in the hay next to him and stared up at the ceiling. He lay down as well, then turned toward her. She could sense he was studying her by the faint light from a lantern below. Heaven only knew what he thought of her, but she found that whatever it was, it didn't trouble her.

But in time it did begin to annoy her. She turned her head to look at him.

"What?"

"You said you could wield a sword at ten summers," he said. "How did that happen?"

"If I tell you," she said, "will you shut up and sleep?"

He laughed. "Aye, I might."

She found that she enjoyed his laugh. It was full of sunshine and good humor, much like Nicholas's. It occurred to her, quite suddenly, that she had known few who laughed.

Well, perhaps that wasn't completely true. Paien laughed. Camid chortled evilly when the mood was upon him. Glines managed the odd snort of humor when he wasn't watching her with sad, longing eyes. But a man chuckling with simple delight? Nay, she knew few of those.

It was the laugh that disarmed her. To her surprise, she found herself hardly hesitating before she began spewing out details of her past that she had not seen fit to share even with Paien.

"I have few memories of my parents," she said slowly. "I think I had siblings, though I cannot say for certain." Indeed, she remembered little; what she did remember was dark and she did not like to dwell on it. "I suppose my earliest true memories are of the mercenaries who took me in."

"How old were you?"

"Six, I think."

"A scrawny, feisty slip of a girl?" he asked.

"How did you know?"

"You haven't changed much."

She looked at him coolly. "I daresay you haven't nearly enough respect for my skill."

"I'm relying on your mercy instead," he said solemnly. "So, these altruistic lads took you in and then what? Trained you to be the terrifying warrior you are today?"

"Nay, they taught me to steal whatever I could, lie whenever I spoke, and portray myself as a helpless child before I killed whomever they told me to."

Miach's mouth fell open. He leaned up on one elbow. "You jest."

"I do not."

"But that is not who you are today."

"Are you so certain?"

He smiled briefly. "I may be helpless with a sword, but I read men's hearts very well. What happened to make you change your ways?"

"I began my courses and they deposited me on the steps of an orphanage. The cowards fled without a backward glance."

Miach laughed softly. "That would do it, I suppose. Where was the orphanage?"

"At Lismòr, on the southern shore of Melksham."

Miach frowned thoughtfully. "Isn't there a university there as well?"

"There is."

"But I thought it was only for men," he said. "Was not the orphanage the same?"

Morgan nodded solemnly. "Aye, but they thought I was a lad, at first. At least the headmaster of the lads did. I suspect now, looking back on it, that the lord of Lismòr, Nicholas, knew from the start what I was." She sighed deeply at the memory. "He was kind to me when I did not deserve it. Then again, he has a tender heart."

"Surely his lady wife was there as well, was she not?" Miach asked. "To oversee, um, womanly things?"

Morgan shook her head. "I think 'tis common knowledge, so I'm not telling you something you couldn't hear at a local tavern, but his wife and children were slain in a terrible accident. He does not speak of it often, but I know it grieves him even to this day."

Miach winced. "I pity him, then."

"Aye, perhaps you should, because he lost all his sons. On the other hand, there are dozens of lads whom he raised to be good men because of his loss, so perhaps it was not in vain."

"Many lads and one lass," Miach said with a faint smile.

"Aye," Morgan agreed.

"So, how did you fare amongst all these lads and away from your mercenary ways?"

"Terribly at first," she admitted. "I almost cut Lord Nicholas's cook to ribbons for not allowing me extra salt for my stew and I ruined Nicholas's flower garden that first year by beating off all the heads of his blossoms with a stick whilst pretending that they were my training partners."

"Poor man," Miach said with a laugh. "What did he do to save his subsequent blooms?"

"Had a sword made for me and acquired a garrison for himself."

"What an interesting addition for an orphanage."

"He was desperate."

Miach smiled. "He must have cared for you a good deal."

Morgan rubbed her eyes, not because she was weary but they burned suddenly. Damned tears. She'd been plagued with them since she first touched that terrible blade. She rolled onto her back and looked up at the ceiling. "It is late," she said briskly. "I think I am overtired."

"Of course," Miach said quietly. He fell silent for quite some time. "Thank you for trusting me with your tale."

"Don't babble it about," she said, turning to look at him severely.

"I am the keeper of many secrets," he said simply. "I will keep yours as well."

I am the keeper of many secrets. Morgan had to think about that for quite some time, but she realized finally that Nicholas had said the same thing to her. She frowned. She could only hope that Miach wouldn't present her with something he needed taken to Neroche. At least it wouldn't be slathered with magic. She considered her memory of him changing out of a hawk's shape and decided she had imagined it. Perhaps a hawk had been there, then flown away as Miach had walked into the clearing. That was possible and quite a bit more likely.

She settled herself more comfortably, breathed deeply of the good, earthy stable smells, then put her hand on her sword.

She fell asleep as easily as if she'd been on that comfortable goose-feather bed in Lismòr.

Eleven

Miach reached in a dipper and tasted the water from Hearn of Angesand's well. He'd tasted worse. He had also tasted quite a bit better. It would have helped if he'd had something to work with initially.

It had taken him all of the morning the day before to find out which source of the well was making it so sour. He'd uncovered a very old spell laid by a not-unskilled wizard who had apparently been quite a bit fonder of Angesand's horses than he had been of the mortals there. Perhaps the wizard had borne a grudge toward Angesand's lord.

Once Miach had unraveled that spell, which had caused the humans' water to sour more with each passing year, he'd had to determine all the streams, all the inlets, all the points of moisture that ran together to make up the well water, as well as tending to the stones of the well. That had been his task that morning. He was making good progress, but even a spell to last a decade took time.

And Hearn wanted this enchantment to last a thousand years.

Miach had immediately agreed to the bargain. After all, Angesand's horses were without peer.

"So, my lord Archmage," said a low voice from behind him, "how does it taste?"

Miach turned to face Hearn. "Terrible."

"Hence my boundless enthusiasm at the thought of your seeing to it," Hearn said with a grin.

Miach smiled briefly. "It's clear to me now." He paused. "I appreciate the anonymity."

"I assumed you had reason."

"I do."

"Does the wench know?"

Miach shook his head. "She doesn't. And I don't wish her to."

"Why not?"

Miach paused and considered. He had several reasons, but he could give voice to none of them. "I'm not certain yet. I think it best for the moment to be just another lad."

"You'd best have a good reason for the secrecy and be very, very far away when she learns the truth. If it angers her, you are in trouble."

"You've seen her in the lists."

Hearn shivered. "There's something unwholesome about the way she fights. I've never seen anything like it." He paused. "Well, that isn't precisely true. I have seen a man of her ilk. Once."

Miach sat on the edge of the well. "And?"

Hearn considered, looked at Miach for a moment or two in silence, then sat down beside him. "What do you know of Melksham Island?"

Miach shrugged. "It is a minor tributary of Neroche. It would be a tributary of Angesand if the lord there had his way."

Hearn smiled pleasantly. "Aye, it would be if I had any ambition—or a lack of feed for my beasts. What else do you know?"

"There is abundant farmland and quite a few sheep if memory serves. Little magic and no wish for any."

"You learned your lessons well, my lord, but you're missing one of the most interesting things about it. Have you never heard of Scrymgeour Weger?"

"Weger?" Miach echoed. "Aye. He is a sword master of sorts, isn't he?"

Hearn looked astonished. "A sword master only? Surely you jest."

Miach shrugged. "A very skilled sword master?"

"Know you nothing of him, truly?"

Miach looked off into the distance for a moment or two. He thought back to rumors and tales borne on gossiping tongues, idle speculation in councils of wizards, table conversation during meals with visiting royalty. He looked at Hearn. "He trains assassins," he said finally.

Hearn smiled. "You could put it that way, I suppose, but I wouldn't. He trains men in the art of swordplay, but to a level that most can scarce imagine, much less attain."

"Indeed," Miach said, folding his arms over his chest. "Tell me more."

"I can only repeat rumor," Hearn said, "but I've heard that most who enter his gates are flawed in some way. You know, the sort of lad who has nothing to lose and is willing to grind himself into the dust to numb his pain."

"Aye, I've met a few of those," Miach said. "Go on. What other kind of man does Weger take?"

"Those with an abhorrence of magic and mages," Hearn said with an unholy twinkle in his eye. "I don't suppose you know any of *those* kinds of lads. Or lassies."

Miach pursed his lips, but refrained from comment.

"Whatever the state of the lad, it is still not a place for the faint of heart," Hearn continued. "Few manage to get inside his gates; fewer still leave with Weger's mark upon their brow."

"He marks them?"

"I understand they consider it a high honor, those who are so marked. It is a very exclusive band of those who have managed to leave his tower at all. Perhaps every time they touch their foreheads, they feel a rush of gratitude for their lives."

"What does he do with the failures? Toss them over the wall?"

"I imagine he does," Hearn said seriously. "You know, his keep is on the coast. I wouldn't be surprised to learn he feeds the sharks with those who cannot keep up."

Miach shivered in spite of himself. "What has this to do with Morgan?"

Hearn considered, then shrugged. "Perhaps nothing. I was

merely thinking of a man I knew briefly who bore Weger's mark. There is something about the way your woman wields a sword that reminds me of him." He shrugged. "I find it merely curious that a woman should fight so well."

"Many women fight well. And she is not my woman."

Though he had to admit, the thought was not an unpleasant one.

Hearn looked at him. "No woman I've ever met could fight *that* well. Hell, I don't know any *men* who can fight that well. And I daresay we haven't seen what she can truly do. Did you watch her last eve with Carney?"

Miach could still see Morgan in the lists, engaging Hearn's most skilled guardsman and making him look as if he were a page with no training at all. And then she had battled pairs and trios of other men in much the same fashion, seemingly making little effort to either keep them at bay or best them.

Yet somehow, it had not been an insulting thrashing. She was simply doing what she apparently did best and doing it at a level none of her opponents could possibly hope to match. She hadn't boasted loudly as she had been about her work, as Adhémar would have done, she had simply done.

It had been spectacular and terrifying, all at the same time.

"Aye," Miach said finally. "I saw."

"She was not sweating, my lord Mochriadhemiach. She might as well have been picking flowers for the effort she made. And my men are not unskilled."

Miach sighed. "Perhaps your men were afeared to truly engage her."

Hearn looked at him with pursed lips. "Think you?"

"In this matter, I try not to," Miach said dryly. He shook his head. "I cannot believe that a woman of her beauty would subject herself to whatever tortures Weger perpetrates in his keep."

"Believe what you like," Hearn said easily, "but I would think twice about irritating her. You will pay, and dearly I'd say."

"I'm hoping to have befriended her by the time she learns the truth."

"Ha," Hearn said with a snort. "You'd have more success

taming an asp, my lord." He stared off into the distance for a moment or two, then turned back to Miach. "I would speak to you of something else."

Miach could just imagine what that might be, but he nodded just the same. "Go on."

"I've heard rumors. Rumors of darkness, rumors of magic lost, rumors of someone being sought."

Unsurprising. "Has everyone heard these rumors, or is it just you?"

"I have ears in many places, so take that as you will."

Miach studied the older man. "It is rumored that your horses spy for you and that you can understand their speech."

"Fanciful imaginings," Hearn said dismissively. "But," he added in a conspiratorial whisper, "do not mistreat any of my beasts, or I'll hear of it."

Miach laughed. "I'll keep that in mind, my lord." Then he sobered. "As to what you've heard . . . aye, there is some truth to it."

"Which is why you are here and not at Tor Neroche, minding your spells," Hearn noted. "You're attempting to find someone to wield a particular piece of metal?"

Miach looked at him evenly. "I don't need to be at Tor Neroche to mind my spells. And aye, that other reason is why I am here."

Hearn grinned. "I was teasing you, lad. I never doubted you could be about your business at any location while beleaguered by any type of distraction. And speaking of that distraction, why is she here?"

"Morgan?" Miach asked dryly. "Well, she is here merely for a horse. Not that there are any mere horses here, of course."

"Nay, there are not," Hearn agreed. "And I suspect there is much more to it than that, but I'll not press you. To your work, Buck." Hearn shot Miach a look, then laughed heartily and rose and walked away. "Buck, indeed."

Miach pursed his lips. He might have seen humor in it, but that was obscured by the fact that he was tired, moving further away from the comfort of breakfast as he breathed, and it was beginning to rain.

He hoped that was not indicative of any future success.

* * *

He spent most of the day at his enchantment. There was a part of him that suspected that Hearn of Angesand had purposely ordered an enchantment of bitterness laid upon that water to torment him, for despite all his work of unraveling the day before, the water was still almost undrinkable. Progress was made slowly but there were times when he despaired of having any lasting success. He was bone weary when the sun set, too weary for supper. He limped directly to his luxurious place in the hayloft. Morgan was already there, stacking her blades in a particular order next to her.

Not on the side of her where he would be lying, if anyone was interested.

He sat down and looked as she considered a particularly small but lethal-looking dagger.

"A successful day in the lists?" he asked.

"The lads are improving," she said simply. "I cannot make them over in a pair of days."

He studied her long enough that she finally looked up at him. He wanted to shake his head in disbelief, but he didn't dare. What drove a woman of her beauty to take up the sword as her life's work? She could have had any man she wanted, surely, and enjoyed any number of comforts of home and hearth. Why had she chosen a life of discomfort, cold, and death?

And what of Hearn's other tidings . . . was it possible Morgan had actually trained with Scrymgeour Weger? He could hardly believe it, but he also could not deny that she fought in a manner that left chills coursing down his spine—and he was not unskilled nor afraid. Was she so without hope, then? Or was it just that she detested magic?

If it was the latter, it did not bode well for him.

It also did not bode well for the possibility of her having wielded Adhémar's sword. Perhaps, then, it had been nothing but necessity that had forced the blade to reveal itself. Miach supposed he should be grateful and just move on.

But he couldn't bring himself to. Not yet. Just a day or two more with this woman who had a collection of blades that Cathar would have salivated over.

Just another day or two.

"Have I grown horns?"

Miach blinked, then smiled. "My apologies. I was just thinking."

"Apparently too hard."

"It was a perplexing subject."

"Do I want to know what it is?"

He smiled. "Likely not. But I will tell you some of it, if you like."

"I feared you would."

He laughed. "Do not stick me with any of your very sharp daggers there, but I wondered what it was that made you choose your profession."

She shrugged. "I know nothing else."

"Yet you lived at the university for several years, did you not?"

"Aye. I was there from my twelfth summer until I turned ten-and-eight."

"Was the scholar's life not for you?"

"What, scribbling, scratching, reading, and nothing else? Nay," she said, shaking her head, "it was too tedious a life for me. I love a good tale by the fireside as well as the next soul, but I would prefer my days to be full of activity and purpose."

"I can believe that. So, you left Lismòr at ten-and-eight. Did you begin your mercenary endeavors then, or . . . ?" He looked at her questioningly.

She looked at him, clear-eyed and unconcerned. "I chose 'or.'"

He waited.

She only stared back at him, perfectly comfortable in her silence and apparently waiting for him to squirm first.

He did, finally, and laughed in appreciation of her technique. It was something he used quite often as well, his favorite way to make nosy souls regret their prying questions. "Very well, I understand. You've no mind to divulge any of your secrets."

"I've divulged an appalling number of my secrets to you already," she grumbled, "and I'm not sure why. You remind me a little of Lord Nicholas."

A compliment. Miach decided that he would happily trade that for any more of her secrets. "Thank you."

"You're comfortable," she mused, tilting her head to look at him.

"Indeed," he said, feeling more pleased than he should have, no doubt.

"Much like a favorite pair of boots."

He blinked. "Boots?"

"Boots," she agreed placidly, then turned back to her daggers.

Miach couldn't credit her with teasing—he had never seen her anything but straightforward and painfully blunt—so he had to assume that she spoke the truth.

Boots were better than the dung on the bottom of them, perhaps.

"How did you meet your companions?" he asked, casting about for another subject. "You seem to be quite loyal to each other."

"Aye, we are," she said.

"Have you traveled together long?"

"A pair of years," she said. "Fletcher is a more recent acquisition."

"And Adhémar?"

"He follows us like a bad smell," she said without hesitation. "I would rid myself of him, but he seems determined to follow along." She frowned thoughtfully. "Perhaps I shouldn't have said that, him being your kin and all."

"I am not blind to his faults."

"I don't know how you could be."

Miach laughed and wondered to himself if she was this cheeky with Adhémar. He suspected she was and the thought of it amused him greatly.

"I will admit, though it pains me to do this," she said slowly, "that he is quite a showy, attractive sort of man." She paused and looked at him. "Don't you think?"

What he thought wasn't fit to say. He cleared his throat. "What do you mean?"

She shrugged helplessly. "I can hardly believe I'm saying this, but when I first saw him, I thought him terribly handsome. I could not bring myself to look away. He was a bit like a bright sword that you cannot resist. Like a handful of gems that blind you with their beauty."

Like a shovelful of dung you find suddenly tossed upon your boots, Miach thought sourly. Boots. He should have known it would end there.

"And then?" Miach asked, against his better judgment.

"He came to and opened his mouth."

Miach laughed in spite of himself. "I understand, believe me."

Morgan made herself more comfortable on the hay and began to examine one of her daggers. "Have you ever found yourself in those straits? Seeing something you know you shouldn't want and cannot have, but yet finding that you are powerless to resist it?"

"Oh, aye," Miach said, with feeling. And that something was sitting not two paces from him.

"It was a most unsettling bit of weakness on my part," she said, sticking her dagger into the hay. "I may have to fight three at a time tomorrow. If the lads can bear it."

"You could help me if you'd rather," he said, listening to the words come out of his mouth and wondering what in the hell he was thinking. Oh, aye, that was what he wanted—to be close to this woman during the day as well. Was the nighttime not torture enough?

She looked at him pityingly. "Trouble?"

"The well is a difficult case."

Her look of pity turned to one of faint alarm. "Will you manage it, or do you lack the skill?"

"Ah—"

"We can find other horses," she said, though it sounded as if that might be a last resort in her mind. "We must have steeds, I daresay, but perhaps these are too far above us."

Miach wanted to tell her that he could have sweetened every spring within a hundred leagues of Angesand with a single spell, sweetened them so that everyone would look for bitter greens to soak in their cups before they dared sip the water. All it would have taken was one spell.

But it would have been a mighty spell and anyone with any magic in their veins would have felt tremors from it and known he was responsible for it.

It also might have put him in bed for a week.

And that would have meant he couldn't drag out those days that led to nights sleeping—and generally not sleeping—next to a woman whom he couldn't seem to stop looking at even when the light was so poor it was painful to attempt.

"I'll manage it," he said roughly.

"You're fretting overmuch," she said, peering at him. "Your eyes are quite red. Are you not sleeping?"

"I'm sleeping." And he was. After he had spent most of each night filling in the breaching of his spells.

"Stop worrying," she said. "Do your best. I'll expend more effort in the lists and woo Hearn with the improvement in his garrison."

"If you expend more effort in the lists," Miach said faintly, "you'll kill his garrison and then he most certainly will not give us any horses."

She looked at him in shock, then a faint smile crossed her features.

"Is that a compliment?"

"It might be."

She frowned. "Your brother is not so free with them. Did your mother teach him nothing?"

"My brother is not a good learner," Miach said, still struggling with the sight of Morgan's smile.

She yawned. "Perhaps you can advise him."

To what? Fall upon his sword? Return home by the swiftest route? Hold his breath while Miach turned him into a mushroom? The possibilities were so endless and so appealing to contemplate that he hadn't finished examining but the beginning of them before he realized that Morgan had put her head down on her cloak as her pillow and fallen asleep.

A clear conscience aided one in that endeavor, obviously.

Miach spread his cloak over her, then sat and watched her in the faintness of the light from below. He wondered why in the world he was bothering to work for a horse for himself. He had no intention of remaining with the company. There was no reason to do so, certainly no reason that might include a fierce shieldmaiden with eyes as green as Lake Camanaë and a smile as rare and lovely as the *kíla* who sang only in the bows of the rowans that encircled the elven palace of Ainneamh.

He was the Archmage of Tor Neroche; she was a shieldmaiden. If ever there were two souls who were not at all suited for each other, it was they two.

He had told Adhémar to go and look for the unlikely; how ironic was it that he should be felled by what he'd told his brother to find?

He would go. Soon.

Because his duty was in the north. Because she was unsuitable. Because he was the archmage and his duty was to wed someone with magic.

Damn it anyway.

He eased over to the ladder and climbed down. He passed through the stables quietly and walked out into the night. He cast a veil of illusion over himself that no one might mark him.

He began to run.

It was almost without thought that the spell of shapechanging whispered through his mind. Soon he was beating his wings against the chill of the night air, lifting himself over the castle walls and high into the starlit sky.

He quite happily lost himself in thoughts of flight.

D awn was still an hour or two off when he climbed back up the ladder and cast himself down on the hay next to Morgan.

She stirred.

Miach froze.

"You smell like the wind," she said with a yawn.

"A night on the battlements," he lied.

"Hmmm," she said, then she rolled over and fell back asleep.

Miach would have pitied himself, but it was his own fault. He should have left that night, that first night before he sat five paces from her bed and watched her sleep. He should have gone home before he spoke with her, before he had watched her wield her sword with the flashing gems, before he watched her look at Hearn's horses with a longing that smote him in the heart.

Aye, he should have gone.

More the fool was he for not having done so.

Twelve

Morgan walked through the lists. The garrison had already been exercised that morning and had begged, in not so many words, for a respite. Morgan had obliged them, though it had left her without anything to do but wander aimlessly about, trying not to look as if she wandered aimlessly about.

Lest Hearn of Angesand think her efforts were less than sufficient for one of his magnificent horses.

Her wanderings left her standing in the humans' inner courtyard. The well stood in a corner of this courtyard and upon the edge of that well sat a man who looked as if he'd passed the last four days with the garrison, not waggling his fingers in a more unmanly pursuit.

Morgan crossed over and sat down next to him, but he did not move. Surely this business of magic could not be this taxing. Unless he was *that* unskilled and even a task that looked as simple as this was beyond the extent of his art. Was he sleeping? In the middle of a spell? Wondering how he might flee the keep with his pride intact and his torso unpierced by her disappointed sword?

Miach rubbed his face and sighed. "Finished with the men so soon?" he asked.

"They needed a rest," she said gravely. "It does me no good to grind them so far into the dust that they cannot recover."

"True enough."

"So I came to see about you. Do you need aid?"

He reached behind him and drew out a dipper of water. He handed it to her and watched expectantly.

Morgan tasted. She froze, unsure if she was tasting water or dew from heaven. She sipped again, hesitantly. Nay, she had not been mistaken. She couldn't remember the last time she'd drunk something that tasted as if it had been made with sunshine and green things and clear blue skies. She looked at Miach in astonishment.

"It is . . ." She struggled for the right word.

"Adequate?"

"Oh, nay. It is worth at least four horses."

He smiled. "Generous of you."

"There is no shame in admitting that you have done the greater part of the work." She dipped more water for herself, drank, and shook her head in wonder. "I can scarce believe this came from a well. Honestly, I don't know how you managed it. I didn't think farmers had spells of this potency."

"A farmer has to drink too," he said.

"Then I envy your family if this is what you've done at home." She looked up to see Hearn striding toward them, rubbing his hands in anticipation. "I wonder what he will think?"

"We'll soon know," Miach murmured.

Hearn came to a halt before them. "Well?"

"It's drinkable," Miach said blandly.

Morgan refrained from comment, but she did stand up and move out of Hearn's way. There was no sense in preventing the man from tasting the purchase price of his steeds.

Hearn dipped, tasted, then froze. He tasted again, then shook his head, as if he couldn't quite believe it. Morgan looked at Miach and nodded knowingly. Miach only smiled faintly and continued to watch Hearn drink his fill.

The man set the dipper down on the rock of the well, folded his arms over his chest and stood there for a moment or two, then looked at Miach.

"My horses will enjoy that," he said finally.

Miach smiled. "I sense a shifting of your courtyards."

Hearn snorted. " 'Tis for damned sure my men won't be drinking this elixir." He reached out and clapped a hand on Miach's shoulder. "Well done, my little friend. Well done indeed." He looked at Morgan. "And my garrison overwhelmed as well. Is there any other miracle you two wish to fashion before I send you off?"

Morgan looked back at him unflinchingly. "I suppose that depends on whether or not we'll be leaving on our feet."

Hearn laughed. "Oh, nay, missy, you'll be riding." He had himself another long drink, dragged his sleeve across his mouth with a smack of satisfaction, then walked away. "Meet me in the lists."

Morgan felt an overwhelming sense of relief course through her. Had she been a lesser woman, she might have been forced to sit down. She settled for another drink and a gusty sigh.

"Let's make for the lists," Miach said, "before he changes his mind."

Morgan strode after him. "Miach?"

"Aye?"

"What kind of spell was that?"

He looked at her with faint amusement. "Just a little something I picked up somewhere. Water can be quite nasty when it comes from the wrong source."

"That tasted like sunshine."

He laughed and reached out to tug on her braid. "Thoughts of an Angesand steed have gone to your head, gel, and rendered you a poet. It was just water."

"Damned tasty, though."

"Perhaps," he said modestly. "It served our purpose and I cannot ask for more than that. Let's try not to look too eager to get our hands on that horseflesh. It might frighten Hearn."

Morgan nodded and walked with him out to the lists. She struggled not to look overly interested in the beasts that were being brought out before them.

"You're gaping," Miach murmured.

"I can't help myself," she managed. And she couldn't. A selection of the most amazing horses she had ever seen were being placed in a line before them.

"The number and kind of your riders," Hearn said, coming to stand next to Miach. "I will select the proper mount for each."

Miach nodded. "We are seven, including Morgan and me.

My elder brother Adhémar rides with us as well." He looked quickly at Hearn. "He's a fair rider."

Hearn called out to one of his lads who brought forward a horse that even Morgan had to judge as superior. She looked at Hearn with a frown.

" 'Tis fit for a king. Adhémar is a bumbling oaf. I would settle him on something less fine, were I you, and save this for someone who can ride."

Hearn choked. He finally had to lean over with his hands on his thighs and cough until he had apparently recovered from some sort of fit. He straightened eventually, put a hand on Miach's shoulder to steady himself, then he laughed heartily. "Well, Mistress Morgan, I just might. Or perhaps I'll make certain that young Buck here can teach his brother what he needs to know to ride such a beast." He drew his sleeve across his tearing eyes and chuckled a final time. "Ah, me. Oaf, indeed. Now, Buck, continue on with your company and we'll see what suits."

Morgan allowed Miach to discuss the needs of the rest; she spent her time admiring a line of horseflesh that men likely would have killed for. She suspected murder might have been the least of what a man might have done to have an Angesand steed. To think something of this quality might be hers . . .

Hearn put his hand on her shoulder in a friendly fashion. "Well, we've settled the rest of the company. What of you, missy? Is there something there that catches your eye?"

Morgan didn't dare say. There was a beautiful horse standing there, somewhat apart, of a mahogany color with a streak of white down his nose and little white socks on his feet. He stood next to a horse that matched him except that he was black. Both beasts seemed to be flying even as they stood there, perfectly still and perfectly mannered. Outside of the flashy horse that Morgan couldn't imagine Adhémar managing to ride, those looked to be the finest of the lot.

And that was saying a great deal.

But she didn't dare voice her desire. Miach's water had been sweet and her swordplay superior, but even those things could not possibly manage to win what stood before her.

Hearn studied her for a moment or two, then motioned to

one of his lads. Morgan watched in astonishment as the mahogany horse was brought forward. To her everlasting horror, she felt her eyes begin to burn.

Hearn met his lad halfway and brought the horse back to Morgan. "His name is Reannag," he said. He held out the reins. "He's yours."

She looked up at him. She could hardly see for the tears in her eyes. "How did you know?"

"Some things are destined to be, my girl," he said with a grave smile.

Morgan blinked, hard, then accepted the reins with a gingerliness she might have used with a legendary sword. Reannag didn't seem to mind, though. He merely stared at her in friendly horse fashion, as if he waited for her to come to terms with the magnitude of his splendidness.

Morgan thought that might take quite some time.

Hearn turned to Miach. "You'll have the black next to him, won't you?"

"Gratefully," Miach said. "What is he called?"

"Rèaltan. Do you care to try him?"

"Desperately," Miach said frankly.

Hearn laughed. "Saddle or none?"

"I'll manage without, thank you."

Morgan stood next to Hearn and watched with concern. "Are you certain he shouldn't have a lesson or two?"

Hearn shrugged. "If he's bucked off and breaks his neck, you may have his horse."

"Well, that's fair enough, I suppose," she conceded.

But to her surprise, Miach swung up onto that horse as if he'd done it all his life. Then again, he was a farmer. That would explain his proficiency on horseback, which even she could see was considerable. He rode the horse around the lists several times, then slid off its back in front of Hearn. He made Hearn a very low bow.

"My gratitude. He is a magnificent beast."

"Keep him well."

"I will."

"I'll know if you do not."

Miach smiled. "I imagine you will." He looked at Morgan. "What of you? Saddle or not?"

Morgan shifted. It wasn't in her nature to shift, or to display discomfort, or to doubt herself. Then again, everything that had happened to her in the past month had been out of the ordinary, so perhaps this was not unexpected. She looked at Hearn.

"Perhaps a saddle," she said, trying to sound more confident than she felt.

"Perhaps a gentler mount," Hearn offered. "Just until you feel secure."

Morgan chewed on her next words for a moment or two. "For me to feel secure might take longer than a pair of circles around your lists."

Hearn studied her for a moment, then turned and called for another of his lads. A sturdier-looking beast was brought in, saddled and apparently ready for a lesson.

Not a lesson for him, but a lesson for her.

Hearn took Reannag's reins from her. "You'll learn quickly," he stated.

"I had better."

"I wasn't going to say that," Hearn said with a twinkle in his eye, "but that would be best. Here, lass, come over here and I'll give you a leg up."

Morgan took a deep breath, then considered her weapons. She decided finally that perhaps it was best not to bring them all on board at first. She handed off her sword and a clutch of daggers to Miach, then walked over and let Hearn boost her up into the saddle.

The horse only shifted slightly.

She took a moment or two to get used to the idea, then smiled. Perhaps it would not be as difficult as she feared—

The horse, unaccountably, reared as if he realized he had something atop his back he did not care for. Before she could find the words to convince him that she meant him no harm, he was bucking wildly beneath her. She was not graceless, but this was completely beyond her experience.

She fell off, but landed on one leg, feeling quite confident that she would manage to at least hop briefly in an undignified fashion before she got both feet back under her.

There was a horrendously loud crack.

Morgan only realized that it had been her leg to make that sound the moment before her world went black.

*   *   *

S he felt as if she were swimming in deep water. It was similar to the feeling she'd had during her time aboard the
ship, but this was easier. Perhaps she was not seasick. Perhaps
there was no magic involved.

Perhaps she'd landed finally on her head and lost all sense.

She kept her eyes closed and tried to understand where she
was. She smelled hay and horse. She sensed Miach nearby and
heard Hearn making noises of concern and worry.

"At least the stable is cleaner than the house," Hearn said
gruffly. "Smells better too."

"She will be well."

"I've never seen a break this severe."

"My lord Hearn, she will be well."

Hearn sighed. "I feel responsible."

"I daresay she won't hold you so. Now, if you would be so
good as to let me think for a minute."

"I suppose there is no need to call in a physick, is there,
with you about—"

Miach must have glared at him, for Hearn sighed.

"I'll say no more."

"Thank you. That would be quite helpful."

Morgan felt Miach put his hand on her leg. Both hands.
Then he began to speak. She didn't recognize the language, but
even so, somehow the words seemed to sink into her very flesh
and become part of her.

Then the words started to sound familiar. She puzzled
mightily as to how that might be so, but before she could begin
to figure it out, a strange, sweet sleep crept over her.

She allowed it.

S he dreamed.
    *She watched a mother with her child. The mother kept
the child close, speaking to her in the same words that Miach
used. A strange, sweet peace surrounded the pair; it was
strong enough that it enveloped Morgan as well.*

    Morgan followed the pair as they wandered through the

forest. The underbrush didn't tear at her skin this time. The little girl was with her mother and all was well.

The mother left the girl at the edge of a clearing. Morgan didn't care for this, and neither did the girl, but the child didn't protest. The mother walked out from under the trees and approached a man. Morgan tried to see more clearly, but she couldn't tell in the end if the man was dressed in black or if it was that he was simply so dark in his soul that he appeared that way.

It didn't matter, though, because he began to speak in some horrible tongue that sounded dark and void. He stood over a well, raising his hands and speaking loudly and quickly. The longer he went on, the more nervous Morgan became. She wanted to leap forward and stop him, but she could not.

She knew something dreadful was set to happen.

Something she would not be able to stop.

M organ woke. She woke without moving, as usual, only today there were several things to determine before she gave any sign of being conscious. One was why her leg tingled so abominably. Another was why her hand felt the same way. The third was why she felt so completely unsettled.

She addressed the last first. She considered several alternatives before she realized it had been a dream to leave her so unnerved. She thought on it for quite some time but could remember nothing but a terrible sense of foreboding and a feeling of futility that she could not stop something that needed to be stopped.

She pushed that feeling aside with an effort. No doubt all would return to her at some point and she would face it then. For now, she would deal with easier things.

She wiggled her toes. She felt as if she'd had her leg cut off, but despite the pain it worked quite well. Her hand was another thing entirely. She turned her head ever so slightly to find that that hand was being held in both Miach's own. He was sound asleep, his face peaceful and quite beautiful in repose, and his damned long eyelashes fanned out against his cheek in a manner that was simply wrong. Why was it men had such pretties while women did not?

She debated as to whether or not she should move her hand. What stopped her, primarily, was the fact that she wasn't sure she could. It tingled in a manner that tempted her to cut it off and spare herself any more pain. And she had to admit that there was something unwholesomely comforting about warm hands around her own. As if Miach protected her.

Preposterous, but true.

"You had a nightmare."

She looked at him in surprise, but his eyes were still closed and he gave every appearance of sleeping. And then he opened his eyes and looked at her.

"You were crying out."

"I never cry out."

"It frightened the horses. I had to do something."

"But you don't have to do anything now," she said with a pointed look at his hands around hers.

But as soon as she said the words, she regretted them. Regret made her angry and that led to several curses that she directed at herself, at Miach, and at the fact that now that he had released her hand, it tingled so badly that it felt as if it might fall off her wrist of its own accord.

Miach sat up and dragged his hand through his hair. He yawned hugely, paused, then flopped back against the hay.

"I'll get up tomorrow."

There was hay in his hair. That might have had something to do with the fact that his cloak was covering her, not residing under him where it could have served him. He had comforted her without her even knowing it.

Or deserving it.

She regretted her ungracious words. She wouldn't even have said something that nasty to Glines.

Well, she would have said worse to Glines, but he was accustomed to it. Miach was simply doing her a good turn. He deserved better. She was mustering the courage to tell him so, when memory flooded back.

She had broken her leg. She sat up and looked at it in astonishment. The only mark on her leggings was a large, dark patch of what she assumed was blood. But when she moved it, it worked as it should. It ached dreadfully, but it worked.

"Did you mend my leg?" she asked Miach.

He looked at her, clear-eyed and calm. "Might have."

"It still hurts."

"It wasn't a very good spell."

She wiggled her toes, bent her leg, pushed against it with her hands. "It seems like a good spell."

"Well, it works on pigs."

She felt her mouth fall open, then she glared at him. "And there I was thinking about apologizing for being ungracious."

"I accept," he said solemnly.

"I changed my mind."

"I still accept."

She frowned. "I wonder if Hearn will give me a horse now."

Miach sat up. "I daresay he'll have no choice. Your mount put up such a fuss when we tried to get him to stop standing over you so we could move you off the field that I had to carry you here with his nose pressed up against my back."

Morgan could hardly believe it. "And he is below?"

"In the box below this loft. He demanded it."

"Astonishing," she murmured.

"Try not to fall off again. I don't know if I can muster up two spells in two days. It may take me weeks to recover from the exertion."

"I'll tie you to your horse and you can sleep there," she offered.

"Good of you."

"It goes along with the apology I changed my mind about."

He smiled. "I'll take what I can get."

She nodded. After all, he had healed her leg and her hand wasn't tingling anymore. And her dream was a distant memory that did not haunt her as she feared.

For the most part, at least.

"Will you tell me of it?" he asked.

She looked at him without surprise. "What? My dream?"

"Aye."

"I've forgotten it," she lied.

"You're still shivering."

"I don't like magic," was what came out of her mouth before she thought. And it was true; she didn't. But whatever magic Miach had wrought on her did not leave her ill or terrified. That in itself was alarming enough. She looked at him. "Perhaps it is only serious magic that troubles me. Yours does not seem to. Perhaps it is that you do not have very much."

"Perhaps."

She considered him severely. "Can you do any of that finger-waggling magic?"

"Finger-waggling?"

"You know," she said. "Like the wizards do. They mutter and waggle and sit upon their sorry arses and meddle with things better left to others."

"I try never to meddle," he said solemnly. "And I never waggle."

"Could you, if you wanted to?"

He wiggled his fingers and muttered. Then he smiled and shrugged. "Apparently not."

She reached out briefly and put her hand on his shoulder. "Then be content with your limitations, Miach."

"I'll try."

She looked at the edge of the hayloft and wondered if she dared approach. She scooted forward until she sat with her legs dangling over the edge of the loft. The horse beneath whinnied in greeting. Morgan's eyes began to burn again.

She glared at Miach. "It has to be the spell."

"What?" he asked, looking at her blankly.

Morgan gestured in irritation at the horse below. "Now, I'm weeping over a bloody horse!"

"He's quite a horse."

She would have thrown a dagger at him, but she found that they were once again not on her person. Miach pointed. She followed his arm and found them all in a tidy row, actually in the order she preferred, well within reach of where she'd lain. She would have reached for one, but she wasn't certain she dared move again. Morgan looked down at the floor of the barn and wondered if she dared that either.

"It will hold."

Morgan looked at him. "What?"

"Your leg. The break is mended."

"Then why does it still hurt so badly?"

"I didn't mend it *that* well. I didn't want you walking on it overmuch. Pain is a good thing, sometimes."

She paused and considered. "Miach, you can admit to me

if the spell was too difficult. I'm grateful for what you were able to do. The pain is nothing."

Miach crawled over, ruffled her hair, and was halfway down the ladder before she managed to get her hand in position to cuff him for the liberty. A moment later, he was looking up at her from the stable floor.

It was possible that he chuckled.

"You will regret that laugh," she said.

"It was meant to stir your blood so you weren't afraid to come down the ladder."

"I am," she said, turning around and backing down the ladder carefully before stepping even more carefully on the ground and turning back around to look at him, "never afraid."

He looked at her with a faint smile for a moment or two. "Then you are fortunate," he said finally. "Now, will you walk a bit, or take a ride on your magnificent horse?"

"I'll try to walk first. Perhaps I'll make it to the hall and Hearn will feed us."

"He might even give you a drink out of the good well."

"I'll ask for two cups and share the other with you."

"You are too kind."

"Consider it a poor repayment for your spell."

He nodded and waited for her to take a step or two before he walked on.

She left the stables with him, feeling more herself with every step. She even managed to cross the courtyard. Hearn was standing on the steps leading into his great hall, looking at her as if he'd seen a ghost.

"I wouldn't believe it if I weren't seeing it for myself," he said. He looked at Miach. "Very well done, indeed."

Miach shrugged depreciatingly.

"Will you have breakfast," Hearn asked, "or saddlebags packed with something for the journey?"

Miach looked briefly at Morgan, then made Hearn a low bow. "Perhaps we should be on our way before too much of the day passes and Morgan's leg begins to pain her further."

"As you will," Hearn said. He frowned briefly. "Make certain your companions are conscientious and careful with their steeds. I'll know it otherwise."

"I will warn them," Miach said.

"As will I," Morgan added, patting her sword pointedly only to realize she wasn't carrying her sword. It was up in the hayloft.

Truly, it had been a trying month.

"Are you ready to ride?" Hearn asked her.

A wave of unease swept over her. "I would prefer to stay for a lesson or two," she said finally, "but I have not the time."

Hearn shrugged. "I imagine you won't be comfortable, but I'll have a quiet word with your mount. He'll do what he can for you."

"I wish I had time to learn his language."

"Come again, when you can, and I'll teach you," Hearn offered. "For now, take the horses, treat them well, and be about your business. My stable doors are always open to you." He patted her on the shoulder and started past her. "I'll go prepare your horses."

Morgan watched him walk away before she looked at Miach.

"A generous offer."

"An historic offer," Miach said faintly. "You know, I've never heard of any lord of Angesand offering to teach any who weren't close kin the horse speech."

"He liked your water."

"He liked your swordplay."

Morgan nodded absently. "I should go back for my gear."

"Wait here and I'll fetch it for you."

Morgan couldn't deny that she was grateful for that. She paced gingerly in front of the hall until Miach returned. He was relieved of their things by Hearn's lads, who then packed them in fine saddlebags.

Hearn brought forth their horses and had a final word with each, particularly her horse, then he stood back and waited for her. Morgan wasn't one for long good-byes. Fortunately, it seemed that Hearn wasn't either. He boosted her up into the saddle, handed her the reins, and patted her booted foot.

"Ride well," he said simply.

She nodded her thanks. Words seemed quite inadequate.

Hearn looked at Miach as he swung up into the saddle. "I'll hold you accountable for any mistreatment of these beasts by any in your party. Best keep a close eye on them."

"I will, my lord," Miach said gravely.

Hearn grunted. "I'll expect you back here at some point, I imagine, the both of you. Perhaps, *Buck*, you'll consider working on my other well."

"It cannot be half as bitter as the first."

"My horses have been drinking from it," Hearn said, with a twinkle in his eye, "so that tells you something. A speedy journey to you, lad." He took a step backward. "My lady Morgan."

Morgan didn't feel at all as if she merited that sort of title, but then again, she was riding an Angesand steed. If anything was going to make her feel important, it was that.

They left the keep in grander style than they'd entered, riding ahead with five obedient horses trotting along behind. Morgan looked at Miach once they were clear of the village.

"Will they follow us, do you think?"

"I certainly hope so," he said, with feeling. "I daresay I couldn't catch them, could you?"

"I could not indeed," she said, feeling somewhat alarmed.

But the alarm proved to be ill placed. The five riderless horses followed unquestioningly, their gear jangling merrily, as if they merely rode off for a lark, not into darkness.

Morgan frowned thoughtfully at that. Perhaps she would do well to look at the journey from a horse's point of view.

Then again, she suspected the horses weren't dreaming her dreams.

I t took them several hours to find their comrades. Morgan would have taken pleasure in their astonished looks, but her leg ached and her dreams nagged at her. She was very grateful to stand on solid ground and allow Miach to tell their tale. She unsaddled her horse and turned him loose, accepted a plate of what Paien had on the fire, then excused herself and walked off across part of the plain that seemed to be uninhabited.

Reannag followed her.

She was a little unsettled by how long it took her to notice that. At first she noticed the breathing, then the footfalls that came in fours and not twos. She looked behind her.

Reannag came to a halt and returned her look.

"I'm off for a walk," she said.

He snorted at her.

Morgan almost smiled. She turned completely around and very slowly and carefully walked back to the horse. She reached out a hand and stroked his nose.

He made more snorting noises.

"Well," Morgan said, almost at a loss. "Indeed."

Reannag offered no opinion on the matter, but he did bump her hand. Then he followed her when she walked back toward camp.

Morgan wasn't sure how she felt about the responsibility of a horse, especially a horse that seemed to have taken a liking to her, but it was too late to complain now. Besides, it would allow her to take the blade to the king in good time. There had been a moment or two when she thought she might not manage that. Reannag would allow her to succeed and for that she would be grateful.

Perhaps it spelled a turn in the tide of events.

Unfortunately, that turning of tides did not last.

T hat night she dreamed.
It was the same dream she'd had the night before. She was comforted at first by the presence of the girl's mother, but that comfort did not last, for she knew what was to come. She followed them very reluctantly to the glade, then watched with dread certainty as events unfolded as they had before.

The little girl hid under the eaves of the forest. The mother went forward to argue with the man who was so full of darkness. Only this time Morgan noticed that they were not alone. There were others there, lads by the look of them. She would have stopped to count their number, but she didn't have time. She listened to the man lift his arms, speak his words of horror, then watched in astonishment as evil gushed up from the well before him, as if it had been a geyser of water.

It surged upward, then crashed down upon the glade. It rushed toward her in a wave of blackness and horror.

Her first instinct was to protect the little girl standing next to her, but she knew she couldn't. She was not there in truth. Even so, she leaped toward the girl, to cover her with her own

body if necessary. As she put her arms around the girl, she
heard the girl whispering words.

Words she recognized, but did not understand.

And still the evil rushed toward her with horrifying
swiftness.

S he woke, her heart pounding in her chest, her eyes full of
darkness. She would have moved, but her dream held her
captive. All she could do was lie there and struggle to suck in
breath.

She looked around her desperately. All her companions
slept peacefully. Camid was not there; he was obviously on
guard. Not that he could have helped her anyway.

Miach, however, sat across the fire from her, awake and
watching her. Without saying a word, he rose and silently came
around to where she lay. He sat down at her head, then stuck
his feet out toward the fire.

"Was it bad?" he asked quietly.

"Very."

He paused for quite some time. "I'll stay here with you, if
you like."

She was appalled by how comforting a thought that was. It
was quite a while before she managed to say anything at all.

"My thanks."

"My pleasure."

"Wake me in an hour or two and I'll watch."

He put his hand briefly on her head. "Morgan, I have much
to think on this night. I have no need of sleep."

"Wake me," she commanded.

"Hmmm," he said. "Go to sleep."

She didn't think she would, but somehow his presence was
far more comforting than she wanted to admit.

She fell asleep without trouble and did not dream.

Thirteen

M iach yawned. He didn't like to admit to weakness, but he was fast coming to the conclusion that he would have to sleep eventually or he would be of no use at all. He wondered if anyone would notice if he slipped off to the deserted barn they were using to shelter the horses. Surely there was a scrap of floor there he could use without being trampled.

Besides, he suspected that Morgan might be there, seeing to the horses, and in spite of his instincts for self-preservation, he wanted to see her. Just to make sure she was well, of course. It was the least he could do. He had no selfish motives.

None at all.

He looked at Paien. "I'll go check on the horses."

Paien lifted one eyebrow, but didn't argue. He merely waved Miach away and returned to listening to Camid recount an adventure that involved a handful of brave dwarves and a disgruntled troll. It was difficult to leave that engaging tale, but Miach forced himself.

He left the fire and walked to the barn, considering the spectacular steeds housed therein that had cost him that thousand-year enchantment of sweetness and Morgan several days of her own particular sort of magic. Though his bit had drained him and left him feeling a little sour, it had been worth it. He would have done it again in a moment, for it had given him a handful of days with Morgan of Melksham all to himself.

He came to a sudden halt.

He might have skidded. One tended to do that, he supposed, when one came to such a stop on the hay-strewn floor of a barn. He had, he had to admit, expected to find Morgan here, brushing her horse's mane.

He hadn't, in all honesty, expected to find her here brushing her own.

He should have turned right then and walked away. He should have walked from the barn, bid his brother good fortune, changed himself into a hawk of uncommon swiftness, and fled for home. He would have been safe there, in his cold tower of stone, surrounded by books and potions and herbs drying in bunches that only he knew the purpose for. It would have been the most intelligent thing he could have done. It would have been the safest.

Instead, he found himself walking forward.

Fool that he was.

Morgan looked over her shoulder at him. "Fretting over the horses?" she asked.

"I don't fret," he managed.

"Hmmm," she said wisely. "Well, I did. But I saw to them all."

"Then since you took on my task, I'll take on yours," he said, taking her brush away from her. He might as well have clutched a pile of nettles for all the sense it made. He dragged a bale of hay behind where she sat. "I think your mane will take longer."

She shrugged. "I don't have time for it."

"I'm surprised you keep it long," he said, finding it difficult to breathe all of a sudden. He gritted his teeth and set himself manfully to his task.

"I cut it after I left Lismòr," she said without inflection. "I'd grown it long to please Nicholas, but then I cut it." She paused. "Later."

"After you left the orphanage?"

She was still. "Hmmm."

Miach paused. Perhaps now wasn't the time, but if not now, he didn't know when. He put the brush down and rose. He walked around to squat down in front of her. It was a guess, he supposed, and likely none of his business, but since she seemed to view him not unkindly, she likely wouldn't stick him for the familiarity. He reached up and brushed her hair off her forehead. There, over her left brow, was a small mark.

A sword.

But it pointed neither up nor down. It pointed sideways, as if it neither rested nor was raised for constant use.

Or perhaps that meant that it was never sheathed.

"Interesting," he said.

"Is it?" she asked.

He thought that perhaps he might have been better off never to have started this, but it was too late now. He met her eyes. "It's Weger's mark, isn't it?"

She looked at him for several minutes in silence. "And what would you know of it?" she asked finally.

"Ah," he stalled, "word gets round."

"Does it, indeed?"

He curled his fingers into a fist to keep himself from reaching up and touching the mark again. "Why does it point that way?"

"Perhaps you'll learn that in time," she returned. "When word gets round again."

He looked at her and couldn't help himself; he laughed. "I imagine so."

She frowned at him. "I think you enjoy poking fun at me. You know, I have skewered men for less."

"Have you?" he asked, with another smile.

"Well, not for exactly that, but I do not like to be teased."

"Did you go straight to Gobhann after you left the orphanage?"

She blew her bangs out of her face in frustration. "Miach, I do not want to discuss it."

He tried not to enjoy the pleasure of hearing his name from her lips overmuch. "You really don't?" he asked. "In truth?"

"You aren't going to stop, are you?"

He smiled gravely. "I will, if you want me to."

"Nay, you will not. You'll be like the drip, drip, drip of an endless string of fall rainstorms, wearing away at me until I relent."

"What a flattering description," he said. It beat boots.

She sighed deeply. "Very well, I will spew even more of my secrets to you. But just a few," she warned.

"Wonderful." He sat down next to her on her bale of hay. "Go right ahead. Spew away."

"I see I have no choice," she grumbled. "Very well, I left the orphanage at ten-and-eight. I went straightway to Gobhann—"

"Where you cut your hair," he put in.

She glared at him. "Actually, I cut it just before I left the orphanage."

"Just curious."

"Are you going to let me finish?"

"I'll try."

She almost smiled. Miach was almost sure of it.

"I left Gobhann at a score-and-four. I could have left earlier, but I was invited to stay and teach."

"That *is* flattering," he murmured.

"Terribly," she agreed. "But as to the particulars of any of it, I will say no more."

Miach supposed that was far more answer than he deserved. Perhaps in time she might give him the entire tale so he wasn't forced to resorting to rumor and innuendo for his information.

He sighed lightly, then moved to resume his place on his bale of hay. "So," he said conversationally as he began to brush the tangles and prickles from her hair, "you cut it at some point before you went to Gobhann and earned that bit of business on your brow that I'm certain you will tell me all about someday."

"You are irritating."

"But very good with a curry comb. You're welcome. So, at some point you grew your hair long again. It is a perfect disguise. Who would think a woman with locks so fine would be so skilled with a sword?"

She looked over her shoulder at him with a frown. "Did you think that up on your own?"

"I may have poor sword skill, but I do have a brain."

"Poor sword skill? Miach, you have *no* sword skill."

"Untrue," he managed. "I hold my own against Adhémar."

"He has no sword skill either," she said promptly. "Even Glines shows better than you."

"Does he?"

"He can occasionally see to an enemy," she conceded. "If he manages to get his sword pointed in the right direction and the enemy does him the favor of falling upon it in precisely the right way."

Miach laughed again, then fell silent. Soon the only sounds were the whickers of the horses and the noise of the brush going through Morgan's long hair.

Soon, even that ceased. Miach stopped only because he felt her go quite still. It didn't take a mage's perception to know she was considering something serious.

Miach dropped his hand and fingered the brush. "Morgan?"

She sat for several minutes in silence, then turned and looked at him.

Miach would have blanched at the distraught look on her face, but he was the archmage and an archmage was made of sterner stuff than that. He did take a deep breath, though. This was something serious indeed.

"I've been dreaming," she said flatly.

"I know."

She considered for a moment or two, then stood up and took the brush from him. She set it down on the bale of hay where she had been sitting. Then she said a few appropriate words of un-noticing over the brush.

The brush disappeared under her spell.

Miach tried not to look as surprised as he felt.

Morgan shivered. "Well? What say you?"

"Interesting."

"It isn't the first thing I hid," Morgan said. She gestured across the passageway between the stalls. "I tried it on another pair of curry combs."

Miach thought that if she didn't sit, she would fall, so he took her hand and pulled her over to sit down next to him. He considered the brush lying directly before them. The spell was woven well, if not a little untidily. What surprised him, though, was that the spell was of Camanaë. He could see that magic shimmering in the threads of the spell that covered the comb. That was a beautiful magic, like a cloth woven of soft and lovely colors, shot through with a silver as hard as steel.

It was not his magic of choice. As archmage, he was free to choose what magic to use and he tended to use a combination of Wexham and Croxteth. He knew that in his own veins there ran Eulasaid of Camanaë's blood, because of his mother. He was, he conceded, also Camanaë sorceress Mehar of Angesand's descendant, which he supposed Hearn knew very well. Perhaps that had been a mark in his favor.

Which was neither here nor there. Camanaë was a gentler magic, but he supposed that was no reflection of the women who used that magic. Womanly they might have been, but with wills of steel and ferocious in their defense of their land and their children.

He turned to study Morgan. Perhaps he shouldn't have been surprised that such a magic would come from her. She was as adamant as polished steel, but even so, there was beauty there.

And then he felt his mouth fall open.

Morgan? Magic?

Perhaps that blazing of the Sword of Neroche hadn't been a fluke after all.

But fluke or not, she did not look at all as if she relished what she'd just done. Miach promised himself a good think on what that might mean later on. For now, he would do what he could to ease her mind.

He rested his chin on his fist and looked at her. "Well," he said, finally, "that's something."

She looked at him so earnestly, he almost winced.

"Can you see the brush?"

"Um," he said, wondering what he could say that wouldn't reveal more than he cared to, "well, I *know* it is there, of course. You've done a very good job of hiding it."

"I know," she said grimly. "But what of the others?"

Well, aye, he could see them as well, but there was even less sense in telling her that. He smiled faintly. "You'll have to show me where they are, of course. Now, tell me again how you knew the spell?"

"I dreamt it."

"Did you?" he said. It wasn't unheard of, but it certainly wasn't common. "Will you tell me of that particular dream?"

She took a deep breath. "I've been having it for days now. Bits and pieces of it." She patted herself for a weapon, drew a dagger from some bit of her person, and fingered it. "It has troubled me greatly."

Miach looked at her dagger. "Don't stab me by mistake."

She frowned at him. "Miach, I try not to be overly critical, but you need to work on your manliness."

He only smiled. "I'll be about it right after you finish."

She put her dagger away, clutched the edge of the hay bale, and looked down at the floor of the stable. "It started with dreams of running."

"Were you running?"

"I thought so, at first. Now I think I'm dreaming of a little girl and she's the one running. The forest was full of thorns and underbrush that could not be bested."

He waited.

"Then I had another dream. I stood near the edge of a clearing, under the trees." She stopped and stared off into the distance, as if she saw it afresh. She stared so long and so quietly that Miach finally took his life in his hands and covered one of her hands with his.

"And?"

She looked at him and there was a look in her eye he'd never seen before.

It was fear.

"There was evil there," she whispered. "A well of it."

"In the clearing?"

"In the clearing, aye," she said. "A man stood there. Tall. Dressed in black." She took a deep breath. "There was a woman as well. Children too, I think. I'm not clear on how many, though I think they were all lads."

He waited for quite a while as she shook. He squeezed her hand. "Did you recognize any of them, Morgan?"

She shook her head. "I didn't," she said finally. "But I did recognize some of the things the mother said, or at least I think so. For all I know, it was just the words you were saying when you healed my leg."

Miach blinked. "What?"

"I wasn't awake, not fully, but I heard the words you used for the spell. Soon I dreamed and those words were in the dream. The mother of the girl used words like those." She looked at him, obviously distraught. "The mother was there with the little girl, but she left her at the edge of the woods. Next to me."

"Did she," Miach said, frowning. "What happened then?"

She swallowed convulsively. "The man said words. He uncapped the well. Evil erupted from it. It fountained up, then came down and washed over the people like a black wave." She paused. "It killed them all."

Miach closed his eyes briefly. "Even the little girl?"

"Nay, not the little girl."

"Why not?"

Morgan took a deep breath. She had to take several. She was clutching his hand so tightly, it was starting to become a little painful. But he didn't move.

Morgan looked at the brush. "The little girl said those words, the ones I used on that brush." She looked at him. "The evil swept by her without seeing her."

Miach looked into her eyes as time slowed to a halt. A thousand questions clamored for answers, but they were naught but noise that distracted him from what he truly needed to know.

How had a shieldmaiden from a backward island famous for bickering peasants and too many sheep dreamed a spell that she managed to weave without possessing any magic at all?

Unless she had magic.

Unless she dreamed memories.

He looked away first, released her hand, and rubbed his hands over his face. Then he turned back and smiled at her. "We'll find answers."

"Are there answers?"

"There are always answers. The difficulty lies in knowing where to look." He nodded toward the brush. "Can you undo that?"

She shuddered. "I haven't the faintest idea how."

He waited. He could have unwoven the spell, of course, but he wasn't going to do it without her permission. He wasn't even sure he wanted her to know that he could. Her distaste for mages was clear.

Heaven help him if she ever found out who he was.

She frowned thoughtfully. "You wouldn't know how, would you? I mean," she said quickly, "being a farmer and all."

It was what he had told her, of course. And he was a farmer—of sorts. He grew all kinds of things in his garden, things that made his brothers uneasy and terrified the servants. And those were just the flowers. Aye, he farmed. He planted spells all over the kingdom and watched them grow and flower into enchantments of beauty and ward and defense.

"Well," he said finally, "a spell of un-noticing is a handy thing for anyone to know. When you have tender radishes growing that you don't want the pigs to find. When you have a particularly tasty cluster of grapes that you'd prefer to save for yourself after a long day of harvesting. That kind of thing. But you also have to know how to undo it or fairly soon your entire garden is invisible."

"Then you know the spell?"

"Aye." Several of them, actually, in several languages of wizardry. But he had to admit, he liked the one from Camanaë the best.

"Well," she said, "spit it out!"

He hoped he could pretend a look of concentration mixed with a little doubt well enough to convince her. "You wove it thusly. You unweave it this way."

He gave her the words. She took them from him as if he'd handed her a bowl of steaming dung, then spat them back out as quickly as possible in the direction of the brush.

There was a substantial rending sound as the spell tore itself apart.

The brush was revealed, in all its dusty glory.

Actually, all three brushes were uncovered. The others lay in the dirt across from them.

Morgan leaped to her feet. "Let's run."

Miach found himself taken by the hand and pulled from the stables. He was long since past the time where the mere touch of a woman's hand was enough to bring him to his knees, but somehow, his poor self had seemingly forgotten that.

"Doesn't your leg hurt?" he managed.

"Not enough to stop me."

Unfortunately, or fortunately perhaps, he soon found himself running alongside Morgan as she fled across a farmer's field. He counted himself fortunate that he had passed so much of his life outrunning his demons in the same way she had, else she would have left him on his knees, panting, leagues behind her. It did, however, take all his self-control not to whisper a few of his favorite words and exchange legs for wings and so he could outfly what troubled him.

He wondered if Morgan could change her shape.

He suspected he would do well not to ask.

There came a time, after the moon had risen, peaked, then begun to sink, that he suspected he might simply fall over if she did not stop. He took her arm and pulled her back as he stumbled into a walk.

"You have bested me," he said, gasping for breath. "I can go no farther."

She was breathing deeply as well, but it was a very even, measured bit of business. "We have doubled back. The barn is just ahead."

"Good. You can carry me there."

She looked at him in surprise for a moment, then she laughed. It was not a loud laugh, nor a long one, but it finished him as the run had not. He hung his head and prayed for sanity.

"You're killing me," he wheezed.

She patted him quite firmly on the back. "You're soft, Miach. Pick up a sword now and then along with your ploughshare."

He heaved himself upright and caught up with her as she started toward the barn. "I'll remember that."

She was silent until the barn was within reach. Then she stopped and looked at him. "How did you know those spells—really?"

He shrugged. "I heard them somewhere." And that somewhere was the schools of wizardry at Beinn òrain. Actually, it might have been earlier than that. He suspected his mother might have taught them to him. "From my mother, perhaps."

"Did she have magic?"

"A little."

"I do not care for magic."

"I know."

"I have not said it strongly enough. I loathe it. It is a weak, foolish, unmanly way to conduct a body's business. I prefer steel."

"I know," he said again.

She seemed to have more to say, but it was long in coming. She chewed on her words, sighed, cursed, then glared at him.

"This was not in my plans."

"I imagine it wasn't," he said dryly.

"It might just be a little magic, this business that troubles me," she said, sounding as if she didn't dare hope the same might be true.

"It might be."

"Indeed," she said, apparently warming to the idea, "it's possible that there is merely some village witch lurking amongst my ancestors. Perhaps she passed this weakness down through the generations to me." She put her shoulders back. "An aberration. That's all it is."

"Very likely," he said, though he didn't exactly agree.

She shot him a sharp look. "Weger would be disgusted."

"Hmmm."

"He would likely take back his mark."

"Does he do that?" Miach asked in surprise.

"There's always a first time," she said darkly.

"Well," he said, putting his hand briefly on her shoulder, "we'll try not to let him know. Perhaps the magic only comes when you've had too little sleep."

"Think you?" she asked, without hope.

Miach patted her shoulder, then took his hand back before she cut it off. "Stranger things have happened."

"I suppose," she muttered, then she hesitated. "It looks as if your brother is looking for you."

"Or you," Miach said under his breath. For all he knew, that was true. After all, what man with eyes could not look at Morgan and not find her lovely?

Would it be unsporting to place a hex of thorough ugliness upon her?

Miach thought not.

Adhémar glared at him as he approached. "Where have you been?"

"Out for a run," Miach said easily.

Adhémar grunted, then looked at Morgan. "And you? What is your excuse?"

"Do I need one?" she asked tartly.

"You'll fall off your very expensive horse if you do not sleep." He nodded toward camp. "Take my spot. I'll go watch the horses."

Miach watched as Morgan nodded a little unsteadily. She did pause, however, at the edge of camp and look at him.

"Thank you," she said simply.

"Thank you," Adhémar echoed. He looked after her as she walked away, then turned to Miach. "Thank you for what? What did you do for her?"

"Why do you care?"

Adhémar drew himself up. "I like to know what's going on."

Miach opened his mouth, then shut it. There was no place to begin that Adhémar would have the patience for and even if he did have the patience for it, Miach wasn't certain he wanted his brother to know anything about the direction in which his thoughts were going.

"Nothing," Miach said, pushing past his brother. "Go see to the horses, would you?"

"How dare—"

Miach didn't stay to hear the diatribe. He walked into camp, found his pack and a bit of ground that was relatively free of rocks, and rolled up in a blanket.

It was an extremely odd dream, that dream of Morgan's. It was obviously vivid enough that she could recall spells from it. The possibility of her dream actually being memories was a tantalizing one, but one he couldn't begin to take seriously until he had more information. But where to find it—

The chamber of scrolls at Chagailt. Aye, that was the answer. Chagailt was not far. He could slip in, do a bit of searching in the musty manuscripts, then rejoin the company before they went much farther north.

He considered north for a moment or two. There was only so much country before north ended in Lothar's land, or the sea. Just where was Morgan planning to go anyway? And why had she chosen such a journey?

Miach sighed deeply and closed his eyes. Too many questions and not enough answers.

Morgan had magic.

It was an astonishing turn of events.

Fourteen

Morgan rode slowly with her company, realizing that she was going to have to make a course decision soon. She thought about Miach's map and knew that though Angesand was large enough and Neroche substantially larger, she would eventually have to bear west to reach Tor Neroche. Her route would bypass most of the places Camid and Paien were looking forward to.

They would not be pleased.

She sighed and looked down at her hands. They were the same hands she had possessed the whole of her life. Sure. Steady. Comfortable with a blade. Then how was it that after six-and-twenty years of life, her hands should suddenly be capable of something so completely foreign and abhorrent to her?

She had woven a spell of un-noticing.

She had undone that spell as well.

She touched the mark over her brow. It had burned like hellfire when it had been made, and continued to burn for days afterward, as if there had been something put into the wound to make it so. But during those days of discomfort, she had not resisted the pain, knowing that it would burn not only into her flesh but into her soul just exactly what she had become and what she was capable of.

How was it, then, that this magic should catch her so unawares and slip into her being with such little fanfare?

She thought back over the past several months. Her mercenary activities were nothing notable. Her journey to Lismòr was unremarkable—

She froze. Unremarkable?

She realized with a start that it was her journey to Nicholas's orphanage that had started it all. Actually, it was touching the blade at Nicholas's orphanage that started it all. It was then that she had begun to dream, dreams of swords and spells and darkness.

But mostly darkness.

But why? Why would something that was entrusted to her by a man who she *knew* beyond all doubt loved her and never would have wished her ill cause her such grief?

She couldn't fathom it.

The knife in her pack was silent now, but that wasn't always the case. Indeed, as she gave it more thought, she realized that it tended to sing to her when all else was quiet—when she was preparing to sleep. Likely while she was asleep as well.

But what was she to do? Leave it behind? She could not. Though it was tempting to fling it as far away from her as possible, she knew she could not. She had been charged with protecting and delivering something to the king of Neroche that was obviously quite powerful. She could do nothing less than her duty where it was concerned.

No matter the personal cost.

She suspected that the personal cost might be quite high.

Unless she could find out more about it. Perhaps if she knew whose blade it was, or how it fought, she might be able to fight it in turn. She wished for another visit to the chamber of records below Nicholas's university.

A pity that was impossible.

By the time her company had made camp, she had almost convinced herself that she had passed too much of the day thinking idle thoughts. Her heart was heavy and her head hurt from too much speculation on things she didn't understand. Apparently she wasn't the only one who had a temper shortened by the journey. She watched Adhémar and Miach walk off into the forest, arguing already. While that wasn't new, there was an edge to Adhémar's voice that was more than simply an elder brother taking his younger to task.

She made meaningless conversation with Glines until the brothers had traveled out of earshot, then she turned and followed them.

"Morgan!" Glines exclaimed.

Morgan waved him off and continued on her way.

She walked into the shadows of the forest quietly enough, then eased into deeper shadows. It was an easy thing to track Adhémar and Miach. What surprised her, though, was that she hadn't been able to hear them bellowing from where she'd been sitting.

"Chagailt?" Adhémar was saying incredulously. "Have you lost your wits?"

"I don't think so—"

"What can you possibly hope to accomplish in a pile of dusty old manuscripts?"

"I'll let you know when I return."

"Fairy tales, Miach?" Adhémar said curtly. "You're taking time out of our journey to go read fairy tales?"

"I'm looking for something in particular," Miach said calmly. "Nothing that concerns you—"

Adhémar began to curse. Morgan admired the depth and breadth of them, but she found herself quite a bit more interested in where Miach was going that had riled his brother so thoroughly. She had to admit there was a part of her that was feeling almost a little protective of him.

Poor, helpless farmer that he was.

She considered the topic of conversation. A pile of dusty old manuscripts? Who knew what she might find there herself?

"When will you go?" Adhémar growled.

"Now. I'll return in a day or two. Take my horse and see if you can linger in the area. I'll hurry."

Adhémar cursed and stomped about in a circle before coming back to stand in front of his brother and curse him a bit more. Morgan took that opportunity to slip back to camp. She would ask Paien to take care of her mount, then follow Miach and see where he went.

She squatted down behind Paien, who was sitting apart

from the others, watching Glines teach Fletcher how to game while being corrected in the finer points of cheating by Camid. An otherwise quite unremarkable evening. She put her hand on Paien's shoulder.

"I'm off for a day or two," she said quietly. "See to Reannag, will you?"

"Where're you off to, gel?" Paien asked, looking up from his supper.

"Nowhere important," she said with a yawn. "I'm tired of sitting."

"You were tired of riding an hour ago," he pointed out.

She pursed her lips. "If you must know, I'm off to shadow Miach."

"Are you?" he asked. "Why?"

"I don't know."

Paien looked over his shoulder at her. "I thought you liked Adhémar."

"I can't stand Adhémar. Where did you get any other idea about it?"

"I have a vivid imagination. So, do you like Miach now?"

Morgan suppressed the urge to cuff him briskly on the back of the head. "I can't believe we're having this conversation." She frowned. "Am I dreaming?"

Paien shrugged. "I'm awake, but maybe you aren't."

"It was the boat."

"Avoid them in the future."

"I fully intend to."

He smiled and winked. "Adhémar is a fine lad. Miach is a finer. You could do worse."

"I don't intend to *do* at all."

"It was merely a thought."

"Aye, and a poor one." She shook her head. "Why I talk to you, I don't know." She rose. "Watch over my horse."

He nodded. He didn't ask her why she wasn't taking the beast, which pleased her somehow. Perhaps he hadn't completely given her up for lost. Besides, she was a better tracker on foot.

She turned and walked back to the place where she had last seen the brothers. Adhémar was still arguing with Miach. Miach simply and quite suddenly turned and walked away while his brother was still at it. Adhémar bellowed after him for a moment or two, then gave up. Morgan stood in the shadow of a tree as Adhémar stomped past her, completely oblivious to her presence.

Adhémar continued to crash through the undergrowth as he headed away from her. Morgan waited until he was gone before she set out to track Miach. He was walking quickly, then he hesitated. Morgan stopped as well. He started up again, then stopped a time or two more. Morgan had no trouble anticipating his halts, but she gathered after a time that he suspected someone was following him. She waited until he'd started up again and gone quite a distance before she took up his trail.

He was a very fast runner and keeping up with him was surprisingly difficult. There were times she half expected he would begin to fly.

An appalling thought, to be sure.

She had to push herself to keep up with him. She was quite grateful that she'd had that time at Angesand to recover her strength else she would have been hard-pressed indeed to have matched his pace.

She ran through the night, stopping to eat and drink only when Miach stopped. Fortunately he seemed to have the good sense to never be too far from a trickle of a stream.

It was barely dawn when the forest suddenly ended. Miach slowed his pace, but he didn't stop. Morgan couldn't help herself. She skidded to a halt at the edge of the forest and gaped at the sight before her.

Well, it was Chagailt, obviously. And without meaning to slight anything on Melksham, she could freely say that she'd never seen anything so large or so fine in all her life. The battlements soared into the sky, the long wings of apartments were flung out grandly from the main part of the palace, and everything was surrounded by glorious gardens. It was spectacularly elegant and she could hardly believe she intended to enter it with her mud-encrusted boots.

Miach, however, seemed to feel no such hesitation. Morgan wrenched her attention away from the palace and back to him to find that he was far ahead of her.

She had to sprint to keep him in her sights. As an afterthought and almost before she knew what she was doing, she whispered the spell of un-noticing over herself.

That was appalling enough to almost make her stop.

Almost.

That she continued on as easily as if she'd indulged in magery her whole life said much about the state of her wits and the shocking lack of self-discipline she had currently at her command.

More running was obviously called for.

She heard Miach whisper something as well. Obviously the other spell he knew, which she suspected was the same one she'd just used. He wasn't doing it very well, though, because she could still see him plain as day.

And daylight was coming. She hugged the wall of the enormous palace and slunk along behind Miach, trying not to breathe loudly. He never looked behind him, so she assumed she was safe and un-noticed.

Then he walked up to the front door and knocked.

Morgan watched, openmouthed, as the door opened. A servant looked out, then started to close the door. Miach threw a small stone over the poor man's head into the palace and when the guard turned to see what the noise was about, Miach slipped inside. Morgan leaped forward to do the same thing. The only trouble was, she was not quite quick enough and the guard shut her cloak in the door. She would have merely opened the door and liberated it, but the man leaned back against the door, apparently waiting for something else untoward to happen.

Miach was disappearing down the hallway.

Morgan felt she had no choice. It was either rip her cloak or leave it behind.

She pulled. Her cloak tore with a horrible rending sound. The guard squeaked in surprise, but Morgan didn't stay to apologize. She bolted down the passageway after Miach.

She took the time to get her bearings, lest Miach lose them both and they not be able to find the front door again, then she continued to follow him. Perhaps his spell was better than she thought, for even though she could still see him, he passed by other souls without their marking him. They didn't look at her either, but she knew her spell was working. Her experiences with the brush in the barn told her that much.

Miach paused several times, as if he wasn't quite sure where he was going. He even scratched his head a time or two in a fashion that was so reminiscent of Adhémar, she almost snorted.

There were many turns and twists, however, and she came to a point where she stopped blaming Miach for his head scratching. She was completely turned about and wondered if she would ever escape the palace without aid.

It seemed like forever that she wandered the halls behind him, but in the end he stopped, looked about him, then opened a door and disappeared through it.

Morgan followed quickly and only caught herself before she fell down the steep steps because she was lucky. She was almost certain she had squawked in surprise, but Miach didn't stop his descent so perhaps she had imagined that. That she couldn't tell was a little unnerving.

She was beginning to suspect she needed a nap.

The steps seemed to descend into the very bowels of the palace. The passageway wasn't overly damp, but it was very cold. She drew her cloak about her, grateful she'd managed to pull most of it free of the front door.

The stairs ended eventually and Miach came to a stop before a doorway. He opened it and a weak light spilled out. She hung back in the shadows and waited until Miach had gone inside. Luck was with her again for he left the door open behind him. Morgan slipped into the chamber, but just barely. She clapped her hand over her mouth and flattened herself against the wall as Miach reached around her to shut the door. He was so close, she could feel his breath upon her hair.

But he said nothing. He only turned, dropped his pack onto a table, then began to poke about what she could now see was a library. Morgan found a chair and silently took off her pack and set it down on the floor beside her. She watched Miach as he perused manuscripts, much as she had done at Lismòr, though with far less fervor than she had used. If he was curious about something, he was certainly being nonchalant about it all.

Finally, he chose a pair of very dusty books and carried them over to the table. He fetched a pair of candles, lit them, sat down, and began to read.

Morgan watched.

In time, she felt her eyelids begin to grow heavy.

She fought the relentless march of weariness, but in the end she lost the battle. She started to sleep. She feared she might drool. She knew she had snorted.

She knew this because she snorted herself awake.

She clapped her hand over her mouth, wondering if she'd given herself away. She looked quickly at Miach, but found that she needn't have worried. He was sound asleep with his head down on one of the manuscripts, his face turned toward her, making snorts of his own.

He was also drooling.

Master Dominicus would have had his head for that.

Well, at least his snoring covered up what was a tremendous growl from her stomach. She put her hand over her quite empty belly and willed it to be quiet. Perhaps Miach would grow hungry as well and go off to seek something to eat so she could be about her own business.

She folded her arms over her chest and frowned at him, willing him to wake.

Fifteen

M iach suppressed a smile at the horrendous noises Morgan's stomach was making. He did his best to continue to snore, but he suspected she might not believe him for much longer. It had been a very long night and most of a very long morning. He wondered if the rest of the day would move as slowly. Hopefully not, for Morgan's sake.

He was quite impressed by her ability to track him, especially since he'd cast his own spell of invisibility over himself. That she could apparently see through it was astonishing.

Why had she chosen to follow him? Was she afraid he would get lost? Had Adhémar sent her after him?

He immediately dismissed the last. She wouldn't have done Adhémar's fetching for him. If anything, Adhémar could have asked and she would have said nay just to spite him. No doubt she had reasons of her own. Perhaps he would discover those in time. For now, it was enough to enjoy having Morgan and Chagailt together.

Chagailt was, as it happened, one of his favorite places. It had once been the center of Neroche, both governmentally and culturally. That had changed when Gilraehen the Fey had been king, courtesy of a particularly nasty battle with Lothar. The capital had been moved to Tor Neroche, which had once been the king's hunting lodge. Tor Neroche had been rebuilt in the ensuing years and fortified with magic that began at the foundations, rose to the tops of the towers, and left it impervious to all assaults. It was a safe place, but rather uninspiring when it came to the surrounding countryside.

The palace of Chagailt, on the other hand, was in a beautiful part of the country where it rained a great deal and everything was green. Flowers bloomed effortlessly, gardens grew enthusiastically, and trees were so thick that at times they were troublesome to the inhabitants of the area. The palace itself held a special place in Miach's heart. He had passed several summers here with his mother, tending the gardens, tending his magic. Adhémar didn't like it; he said it rained too much. Miach found the weather rather to his liking. There was something quite spectacular about seeing the sun, finally, after weeks of solid rain.

All of which didn't matter at present except that it was set to rain outside and he had come back to a place he knew as well as he knew Tor Neroche. It was magnificent still, in spite of the fact that it had been relegated to mere summer home status.

And Morgan was there with him.

Un-noticed in the corner, for the moment.

Miach sat up and rubbed his arms. Though there was light from the candles, that light did nothing to warm the chamber. Miach turned and kindled a fire in the hearth by mostly normal means. Once that was burning cheerily, he lit more candles and put them on the table.

Morgan was watching him, silently.

He admired her commitment. He would have to acknowledge her at some point, but he would give himself a few more minutes to see if he couldn't find what he was looking for. He'd read for hours already, but with no success. If he'd had a better idea of where to look, it would have helped. Many men were arrogant, many had children, and many were evil. Finding a man to match Morgan's dream was not an easy task.

But it gave him the unexpected pleasure of yet more of her company, away from the distraction of her comrades and the annoyance of his brother. He wouldn't purposely drag out his search, but he would relish the time it took him.

He pushed aside the manuscript he'd been reading, rose, and walked about the chamber. He stopped in front of Morgan simply to see what she would do. She was as still as death. He smiled to himself and continued on, then came to a sudden halt. He reached out and picked a heavy book off a shelf where it lay, dusty and unused.

Something that might have been termed unease went down his spine.

He took the book back over to the table and sat down. He touched the book and it fell open to a page he hadn't called.

Gair, the black mage of Ceangail, lived a thousand years before he wooed and wed a princess of Tòrr Dòrainn. Seven children were born to them, six sons and a daughter.

Miach stared off into the distance. He knew of Gair, of course. He'd considered him more than a month ago as he sat in his tower chamber at Tor Neroche and contemplated that rather populated list of black mages who might have been responsible for his troubles. But Gair was dead, so he had dismissed him. Odd that now he should come across his name again in such a serendipitous fashion.

Miach frowned and continued to read.

In time, his lady wife realized that she could not change Gair's nature and she sought a way for him to destroy himself. When he proposed a journey to a place where he could prove to her his power, she agreed, though she insisted that her children remain behind. He refused. After much argument, she allowed the children to be brought, feeling sure she could protect them from whatever spells he might unleash.

He brought them to a well of evil. Sarait sent her children into hiding before he began his spell to uncap the well and prove his ability to contain it.

It geysered forth and swept over everyone there. Sarait managed to cover her eldest son from its effects, but it was not completely done. The lad crawled off into the forest, lived long enough to find aid and tell his tale, then died.

Miach sat back, stunned. The similarities between that tale and Morgan's dream were too great to be dismissed. But why would Morgan be dreaming of Gair and his demise? And why would Gair's daughter know a spell of Camanaë, the spell that Morgan had heard the girl whisper?

Miach looked off into the darkness of the chamber's shadows. It didn't seem to him that the tale was that old. Rumors of Gair's evil, of his deeds and mischief were hundreds of years old, of course, but this tale of his ending . . . nay, it was much more recent.

Miach rested his hands on top of the manuscript. Gair's death was definitely during his lifetime. A pity the eldest lad had not survived longer than merely to tell his tale. He could have said much about his father and the circumstances surrounding his death, as well as a few other interesting details.

Such as whether or not his sister had survived.

Miach continued to leaf through the book, but found no listing of the names of the children. That wasn't a complete surprise. The records in Chagailt were of a broader stroke than might have been kept in other places.

He contemplated that for quite some time, idly turning pages, when his eyes fell upon something else.

> . . . *given to Nicholas, the wizard king of Diarmailt, whose wife and five sons were killed by Gair, for Nicholas was wed to Sarait's elder sister* . . .

Miach was startled by a terrific noise coming from the corner where Morgan was sitting. It took him a moment to pull himself back to the present. He blinked for a moment or two, then looked at Morgan.

"Hungry?"

Morgan swore. "Starving."

"You could come sit by the fire. Or we could go hunt for a meal in the kitchens."

She undid her spell with a shiver, then rubbed her face with her hands. "I don't know if I would make it to the kitchens. I'm not sure I'll make it to the fire." She groaned as she stood and limped over to sit down next to the hearth on a stool.

Miach shut the book. There was indeed more to Gair's tale than he'd remembered, but he set it aside for the moment. First he would feed Morgan, find out why she had followed him, then spend the day with her if she liked. There would be time enough that night to find out more about Gair and his doings.

"How long have you known I was there?" she asked.

"Not long," he lied.

She looked at him narrowly. "In truth?"

"You're very good."

She frowned. "I used the spell." She paused. "I was desperate for some kind of concealment."

He turned in his chair to look at her. "Were you? Why did you come? Were you worried about me?"

"Partly," she admitted. "But mostly because I am looking for something."

"Are you? What?"

"Luncheon," she said. "I don't suppose you could find some, could you?"

"Aye, I suppose I could. Do you want to come along?"

"I'd rather read, if you don't mind."

She looked more unnerved than he'd realized at first. He suspected that she'd come for much the same reason he had, hoping to find something to help her with her dream.

He started to turn, then paused. He had left the book on the table. It wasn't in his nature to be secretive—his current secrecy aside—and he also wasn't one to make decisions for others—his former desire to get Adhémar away from the border aside as well—but he suspected that if Morgan read anything about Gair and the circumstances of his demise, it might be too much for her.

At least for now.

He reached over the table and casually picked the book up. He reshelved it carelessly and covered it with a very strong spell of aversion. Then he started toward the door.

"I'll return soon," he said.

"Miach?"

He stopped and tried not to shiver. It was madness to think about sharing anything with this woman besides a loaf of bread. But there was something about the way she said his name . . .

"Aye?" he asked, not turning around.

"Will anyone come?"

He did turn then. "Surely you aren't afraid."

"Of course not. But I like to know what to expect." She paused. "Perhaps that is what I do not care for about magic."

Poor girl. "I think no one will come," he said slowly. "You could use your spell if you had to."

"I might." She looked at him thoughtfully. "How is it you knew about this place?"

"Chagailt is famous for its records."

"And lunch?"

"It is famous for that as well. I'll see what I can find."

She stood, rummaged about in her purse, then walked over to hand him a coin. "Pay them for it."

He took the coin. It was of Neroche strike. "Where did you come by this?"

"Your brother's purse," she said shortly. "We'll thank him when next we see him."

He smiled. "Is this not stealing?"

"Spoils," she said promptly. "I told you before, didn't I? He was following me, no doubt with evil intent. When I felled him, it was well within my rights to take everything save his weapons."

"Weger's rules?"

"Oh, nay," she said seriously, "those would suggest that I help myself to all his weapons and perhaps his boots if they fit. Of course, I left your brother with far more than I should have, which Weger would have found . . . unacceptable."

"I daresay," Miach said dryly, vowing to someday see what else the man found unacceptable. "Well, I'll go find something to eat."

"I appreciate it," Morgan said as she began to wander about the chamber.

Miach put Adhémar's coin in his purse and left the chamber. Answers later; food first.

He ran up the steps and walked swiftly toward the kitchens. He passed many souls, but none took any notice of him. He had already reached the kitchen before he realized that he'd undone his spell below and hadn't taken the time to reweave it. He was face-to-face with Finlay the cook before he further realized that it was too late.

"My lord Mochriadhemiach!" the man said, clapping his hands together joyfully. "Your visit is unexpected, but not unwelcome. Nor unprepared for, as you can see." He waved a sweeping arm over what he'd been cooking that day. "We are always ready here for any size entourage."

"My friend Finlay," Miach said with an answering smile, "I vow I haven't eaten a decent thing in months. Since I was here this past summer, at least."

"You are here for long, I can hope? No one appreciates my efforts as you do."

Miach laughed. "I will readily admit that the fare is far superior to what I put up with in the mountains."

Finlay pursed his lips. "No offense to the king, of course, but his only requirement is that the offerings are hot."

"True enough," Miach agreed. "So, I suppose I am reduced to hoping for a good meal only occasionally. Happily that occasion is today. As for the length of my stay, I imagine it will be only for the night." He leaned over the table and motioned for the cook to do the same. "I'm here in disguise," he whispered.

Finlay looked at him with one raised eyebrow. "But I saw through your disguise, my lord."

"You have special talents."

Finlay seemed to need to consider the import of that. "How can I best serve?" he asked in a loud whisper. "Food? Supplies? Aid in your mage-like endeavors?" He paused. "My silence?"

"That first of all," Miach agreed. "Perhaps a bit of lunch for two, then supplies on the morrow, if possible."

"For two?"

"Aye."

"Two?" Finlay asked, lifting one eyebrow questioningly.

"Two manly, hearty appetites."

"Oh," Finlay said, looking slightly disappointed. "I had hoped that perhaps you had . . . well . . . one does hope, you know . . ."

"My mother would have said much the same thing," Miach said with a laugh. "I'll wed eventually."

"And your brother?"

"Who knows? He doesn't discuss that with me. I am too far from the throne for it to concern me, you know," Miach said as he watched Finlay prepare a basket filled with enough food for several people.

"But, my lord," Finlay said, looking faintly horrified and terribly interested, "you are the *archmage*."

"Hmmm," Miach agreed. "You would think that would be inducement enough, wouldn't you?"

Finlay handed him the basket and a bottle of wine. "I would think so, my lord."

Miach paused. "You'll keep my presence here a secret?"

Finlay drew himself up. "Of course."

"I knew I could rely on you. A good day to you and many thanks for the meal."

He left Finlay bowing and scraping and promising all manner of magnificent delicacies upon Miach's return. He walked quietly through the mostly empty palace, imagining how it might have been in the days of its glory, with shimmering lights reflecting on the marble floor, sweet music filling the air, and elves and men both making up the court of Iolaire the Fair. He wondered why it was Adhémar had no stomach for any of that. Then again, Adhémar didn't have any more to do with elves than necessary. Miach supposed that was probably for the best. His brother was skilled with a sword, not with the delicacies of diplomacy.

Well, Adhémar was happy where he was and Miach was more than happy to have Chagailt to himself when it suited him to come south.

He made his way back down the stairs, then pushed his way into the chamber of records. He walked in, set the basket on the table, then looked at Morgan.

He wished he'd hurried.

She was standing in front of the book he'd put away, staring at it as if by so doing, she might uncover what was inside. She reached out a hand, but couldn't seem to bring herself to touch it. She looked at him.

"Is this not the book you were reading?" she asked.

"It might be."

"How could you bear to touch it?" she asked, rubbing her arms. "It is crawling with something I cannot name."

"I have a strong stomach," he said lightly. "There was nothing interesting in it anyway. Hardly worth the effort of dragging it off the shelf."

"In truth?"

"In truth," Miach lied.

He wondered, though, if that lie might cost him at some point.

There were answers he had to have before he dared discuss Gair of Ceangail with her. Answers about the man's magic, about his children, about things that might spawn dreams in a woman who could not possibly be related to him in any fashion.

She simply could not be.

Miach was almost certain of that.

Morgan stepped back from the book and looked at him. "I must find the truth."

"The truth?" he said, with only a slight pang of guilt.

"About my dreams." She shivered. "I think they will drive me mad soon." She looked at him. "Do you dream?"

"Aye."

"Of mages, and wells of evil, and death everywhere?" she asked.

Unbidden, memories came back to him. Of mages, and dungeons of evil, and death that had hung over his head for months as Lothar held him captive and his mother tried desperately to free him. He'd been ten-and-four at the time.

Aye, he had dreams enough of his own.

The next thing he knew, Morgan was standing a hand's breath from him, searching his face as if she looked for her own horror there.

"You do."

"I do," he agreed. "But they are not your dreams."

Morgan took him by the hand and started toward the door, dragging him with her. "I need to run."

He started to tell her that she couldn't outrun all her troubles, but the thought generally appealed to him as well, so he couldn't exactly tell her to stop.

"Is there a place where we might run freely?" she asked as she pulled him up the stairs.

"Lunch first?" he asked, hoping to distract her.

"Later."

He didn't argue. He suspected he would have followed her quite a long way before he asked her to stop.

She cast a spell of un-noticing over the both of them, shuddering as she did so, then opened the door out into the grand hallway. Miach walked with her without speaking as she wandered, finally finding her way out the side door and into the formal gardens. Miach was faintly relieved he had become accustomed to her habits else he would have found himself left behind quite quickly.

Was she merely dreaming?

He wondered.

Perhaps he would offer, when the time was fit, to teach her the few spells a poor farmer might know. It might show them both what she was capable of.

He thought again of Gair of Ceangail, his arrogance, his absolute stupidity in taking his precious wee ones to a place of such evil.

The man had deserved death.

He wondered, however, what he had left behind.

He would give that more thought later, when he'd lured Morgan back inside, fed her, and put her to sleep. For now it was all he could do simply to keep up with her.

Sixteen

M organ sat on a little stool near the hearth, shivering. She wondered when it would all stop, this appalling departure from her usual method of conducting her life. First it had been that unsettling bit of charity when she'd first encountered Adhémar, then that horrible seasickness, and then—

She shifted her stool closer to the fire. She didn't want to think about anything else, not Adhémar's sword, not Nicholas's blade, not her terrible dreams. She held her hands out toward the blaze, but it didn't help her. The chill had settled in her heart and there was nothing to be done about it. She looked over at the book that sat on the shelf on the far side of the chamber. Such an unassuming tome. There was nothing engraved upon the outer cover. If one could ignore the magic that blanketed it, one might have been able to read it easily.

Morgan wondered what was inside that book.

She'd wondered that since she'd first seen it yesterday. Knowing it was there while she tried to sleep the night before had only kept her awake.

She turned away. Whatever was in it would likely give her nightmares anyway—and possibly worse ones than she was having at present.

She'd hoped her dreams would pass and leave nothing behind as a new day had dawned.

Unfortunately, that had not been the case.

Her dreams were always at the edge of her mind, pulling and tugging at her, trying to intrude upon the activities of the day. She couldn't stop herself from wondering about that man who had spoken the words at the well, the words that had loosed such a terrible evil. Had he been a mage? Had the little girl survived? Had the evil ever been stemmed, or was it continuing to spew forth even now, simply because there was no one there to stop it? Was she the only one who dreamed this dream, or was the horror of it so terrible it leaped from dreamer to dreamer, troubling all in its wake?

She looked about her for a distraction and found Miach. He lay at her feet next to the fire with his head on his pack and watched her with tranquil eyes. To be sure he was by far the most handsome farmer she'd ever seen. Then again, most farmers she knew were wearing boots coated with dung and carrying swords coated with their neighbors' blood.

And none of them looked anything like Miach.

"What are you thinking?" he asked, looking for all the world as if the most pressing thing on his mind was what to have for breakfast.

"My dream."

He nodded slowly, as if that didn't surprise him. "It is a powerful dream."

"I think the man is a mage. Was a mage," she corrected. "What do you think?"

He seemed to consider. "'Tis possible, I suppose."

"Are there evil mages?" she asked, then she stopped. "Well, of course there are. Lothar, for one."

"Aye."

"Are there others, do you suppose?" She paused. "Others who might have . . . um . . . uncapped a well of evil?"

He winced. She was almost certain of it.

"I daresay there are," he said, finally.

"Do you know any?"

"Personally?"

She frowned at him. "Don't make me force you to be serious."

He sighed. "I am not treating your questions lightly. I suppose there are evil mages enough for any number of nightmares."

"Ones who did what that man did?"

Miach crossed his feet at the ankles. "Possibly. Lothar of Wychweald is, as you know, someone who could have done something like that, but I don't know that he was ever that interested in doing any magic that wasn't visible to everyone for leagues." He paused. "There was, of course, Gair—"

Morgan gasped. A terrible chill went down her spine. She opened her mouth and words came tumbling out. *"'Then came the black mage of Ceangail, Gair by name, who never aged and begat children after a thousand years—'"*

Miach sat bolt upright, suddenly not relaxed at all. "How did *you* know that?"

"I read it," she managed. "In Nicholas's study." She paused. "Do you know more about this, um, Gair?"

He closed his eyes briefly. "Aye." Then he looked up at her and the serious expression on his face chilled her.

"Do I want to know any more?" she whispered.

"Wanting and needing are often two different things," he said gravely. "You may not want to know, but perhaps you need to know."

She nodded.

Miach sighed. "Gair's history is a troubled one. The magic he made was not exactly of a wholesome sort."

"Is any magic wholesome?" she asked tartly.

He looked at her solemnly. "Aye, it is."

Morgan decided she would argue that point later. "Very well, so he was not a nice man. What else?"

"He lived a thousand years, then he wed. I know he had seven children. I do not know how many of them survived him." He paused and looked at her. "But 'tis said he uncapped a well of evil that slew everyone within the sound of his voice."

Morgan closed her eyes briefly. It could not be.

But it had to be.

"You know too many tales," she said faintly.

"It is possible that I passed too much of my time sitting before the fire listening to tales and not enough time training with my sword."

"Aye." She paused for several minutes, then slowly met his eyes. "I have the feeling I am dreaming of him."

Miach looked at her gravely. "I'm afraid so."

Morgan bowed her head and sighed deeply, feeling as if she'd been holding her breath for days. Perhaps she had her answer, but it raised another question she couldn't answer.

Why was she dreaming about Gair of Ceangail?

She pushed the name away. She would think about it later, perhaps while she was doing everything in her power to keep from falling asleep again.

She looked around for something else to discuss. Her gaze fell upon her pack and she thought about her blade. Perhaps Miach might know something about it. She looked at him hopefully.

"Do you know anything about swords?" she asked.

"I know which end of them to point away from me."

"One could hope," she said. "Actually, I'm thinking of daggers."

"I would recognize one as such, were I to see it."

She glared at him briefly, then went to fetch her pack. She could hardly believe her actions; she seemed powerless to keep herself from doing things with Miach she wouldn't have done with anyone else. There was something about him that inspired the telling of confidences. She suspected Nicholas would have liked him very much.

She began to unpack her gear. Miach laughed softly when he saw the scarf. Morgan looked at him.

"Spoils."

"I see you're wearing the socks that match."

"More spoils."

"Poor Adhémar. What a blow to his pride."

"He could use several more such blows," she groused, "until his ego was down to the level of his sword skill. But such is, happily, not my task."

"Nor mine," Miach said. "What else have you in there?"

Morgan pulled out the slim leather wallet that contained velvet wrappings that cushioned the blade as if it had been a priceless treasure. Morgan set her pack aside, then put the knife on her knees. She knew she was doing much the same thing that Nicholas had done and that gave her a queer feeling inside, something that felt quite a bit like Fate.

And she was, after all, a great believer in Fate.

She untied the leather closure, then began to unwrap the

velvet coverings. She kept an eye on Miach as she pulled out the cloth containing the blade. He suddenly went quite still.

She couldn't blame him. She had the same kind of unease come over her when she touched the blade. She continued to unwrap the cloth. Something fell to the stone hearth under her feet. She watched Miach pick it up.

It was a ring.

He looked just a little unsteady. "What is this?"

"I've no idea. It must have come with the knife. I don't remember agreeing to take it with me." She took it and put it on the table. Then she took the blade and held it up.

Magic shimmered along it, a silvery magic that connected with her in a manner she simply could not understand and did not want.

To her horror, she felt her eyes begin to burn with tears. She dragged her sleeve angrily across her face. "I loathe magic. And look you," she said, thrusting the blade at him. " 'Tis slathered with it!"

Miach took the blade from her. He looked at it as if he held either a great treasure or a live asp.

"Miach?"

"Where," he said hoarsely, "did you come by this?"

She supposed there was no harm in telling him. "Nicholas of Lismòr gave it to me."

"Nicholas of Lismòr," Miach repeated. "And where in the world did he come by it?"

She shrugged helplessly. "I have no idea." She paused. "What do you think?"

He seemed to be having trouble breathing. "I think," he said finally, "that leaves and flowers are a rather unusual thing to adorn a weapon with."

"A pity that isn't the end of the troubles with this dagger," Morgan said. "Can you not feel the magic? I can see it as well."

Miach twisted the blade this way and that as he examined it by the firelight. He slowly traced the engravings on the blade and the hilt with his finger. "Nay," he said finally, "the blade does not call to me."

She blinked. "What does that mean?"

He opened his mouth, then shut it and shook his head. He seemed to consider his next words quite carefully. "It can mean many things," he said slowly. "It is said that if a mage fashions a blade, ofttimes that blade will respond to another with magic in their blood." He paused and looked at her. "It seems to call to you."

"I have no magic in my blood," she protested.

"The knife seems to think you do."

She shivered. "You know, it sings to me as well."

"Does it, indeed?"

"It does," she said. "I did not ask for this and I have no idea what it means for me, but you are fortunate not to bear the burden. Stick to farming," she advised, "and be grateful you have so little magic."

"I daresay I should be," he said, handing the knife back to her.

She wrapped the blade back up and put it back in the bottom of her pack. She paused and looked at the ring sitting on the table. "I wonder whose this is."

"It seems to match the knife," Miach said.

"Aye, you're right," she said, dropping it into her pack. She packed up the rest of her gear, then set her pack beside her.

"Morgan?" Miach said suddenly.

She looked at him. "Aye?"

"Why did Lord Nicholas give you that blade?"

She started to speak, then hesitated. It was one thing to show him a knife and wonder if his apparently vast stores of lore might tell her where it had come from; it was another thing entirely to tell him of her plans. Then again, who better to tell than a farmer from the north? He might be able to aid her in finding the castle.

"I will trust you," she said slowly.

He nodded solemnly. "Thank you."

"You will keep my secrets," she stated.

"I will carry them to my grave."

She believed him. There was, she decided, much to like about him. She'd never had much use for farmers before, but that was perhaps that she had only known Melksham farmers and they were generally of a more bickering nature, limiting their conversations to who was due what amount of water and how that water was being filched by their neighbors.

She suspected Miach did not allow his water to be stolen, but that he never had to draw a sword to see to that.

Astonishing.

Morgan took a deep breath. Her announcement seemed to merit it. "I am on a quest," she said.

"I see," he said. "What sort of quest?"

"I am to carry that blade to the king of Neroche."

Miach choked.

Morgan frowned and looked about for drink. There was only a little left in the bottle from the night before, but she gave it to him without hesitation. He seemed to need it far more than she did.

"You have a weak constitution," she said disapprovingly.

"I don't," he gasped. "I just wasn't expecting to hear that."

"Why not?" she asked sharply. "Do you think me unequal to the task?"

"Morgan, I don't think you unequal to anything," he said frankly. "It's just I've never met anyone with that sort of quest before. It isn't something you hear every day."

"I was equally as surprised," she admitted.

He frowned thoughtfully. "I still don't understand why Lord Nicholas had this blade."

"I asked him the same thing, but he told me he had been its keeper for several years and now the time had come for it to go to the king of Neroche. He charged me with the doing of the deed."

"And you said him aye?"

"Of course," she returned. "How could I refuse?"

"You couldn't," he murmured. "He was very much like a father to you, I imagine. I daresay he wouldn't have asked you to do the like without a good reason."

"I suppose he considered me a fit carrier," she said. "I was not pleased, as you might imagine, for I felt the magic immediately. I instructed him to put it in my pack or I would not take it otherwise." She frowned. "You know, it was then that I began to dream. The second night I slept in that damned goose-feather bed."

"A goose-feather bed?" Miach echoed, his ears perking up. "Did you?"

"It was blissful."

"I envy you."

"Aye, well, you shouldn't. I'll likely spend the rest of my life dreaming about it without hope of ever using it again, for there is no way I will force myself on another boat to visit it again."

Miach smiled. "Poor girl. Well, it will live on as a pleasant memory, at least." He looked up at her. "What did you dream of that second night?" He raised the bottle of wine to his lips. "Of soft clouds and pleasant sunshine?"

She shook her head. "Nay. I dreamed of a sword that looked just like the knife."

Miach spewed out the wine—fortunately not all over her. It was a near thing, though. She took the bottle away from him, for all the good it did her being empty.

"Good heavens, Miach, you are excitable. Perhaps you should eschew conversation while you are about eating and drinking."

"I should," he agreed fervently, dragging his sleeve across his mouth. "A sword that looked like the knife? How interesting."

She shrugged. "I only dreamed of it once." She paused. "I daresay it resembled the ring as well, though the work on the ring is much finer."

"Aye, it is beautiful." He rose unsteadily to his feet. "I think we should break our fast and go."

"But I haven't found what I sought," she said. "I want to see if there might be a drawing of that blade. Surely there is a book here with that sort of thing."

"This is a small library," Miach said. "If I were you, I would search in the vaults at Tor Neroche."

"Would you?"

He nodded. "I've heard tell of their splendor."

"You hear tell of much," she said, looking up at him with a frown.

"My kin are always angling for a look inside the palace," he said, reaching for her pack and handing it to her. "Word gets round, you know."

Morgan had to agree that it likely did, but she wasn't ready to give in so easily. "I think I should have another look here."

He looked at her silently for a moment or two, then nodded. "As you will. I'll go fetch breakfast."

"Be careful," she said absently as he made for the door. "I don't want to have to liberate you from any dungeon."

"You're too kind."

"Too lazy," she said, finding that the lighthearted words came easily to her. It was almost as surprising as hearing herself blurt out words of magic. She looked at him in surprise. "I fear I am unwell."

"Too many dreams of goose feathers," he said with a smile, then disappeared out the door.

She would have put her hand to her head, but she knew she had no fever. She also, apparently, had no wits either. First she was trusting a complete stranger, next she was coming close to jesting with him. What next? Would she be offering to aid ruffians who sought to harm her instead of braining them as she should?

She shook her head in disgust and set to looking through the manuscripts and scrolls. In truth, she had little idea where to start and nothing she selected seemed to be of any aid. By the time Miach returned, she was cross and beginning to feel caged.

"Food?" he asked politely.

She sighed as she sat down next to him at the table. "Quickly, then we must be away."

"Did you not find anything useful?"

She shook her head. "I fear the chamber closes in on me in an unwholesome way."

"Tor Neroche," he advised. "A body can likely find just about anything there."

"You hesitate," she noted. "Why?"

He shook his head. " 'Tis nothing." He smiled gravely. "The journey north is perilous, but you are not afraid."

"Are you?"

"Quite," he said frankly.

"Then stay nearby," she advised. "I imagine I can see to you and Fletcher both."

He smiled, more sincerely this time. "I appreciate that."

They ate without haste, but without lingering. Morgan helped Miach put the chamber to rights, then made certain the fire was completely out. She turned away from the hearth to find Miach standing near the door, a ball of werelight floating gently above his head. Morgan gaped at him.

"How did you do that?"

"A spell," he said easily.

"How do you know so many spells?"

He only hesitated slightly. "I know many things. Knowing how to light things and hide them is very useful."

Morgan shouldered her pack and walked toward him. "Aye, I suppose so. It would be a poor thing indeed to stomp through the mire in the dark."

He snorted and shut the door behind her. "Indeed." He shifted his pack and led her up the stairs, the little ball of light bouncing up high to light the stairs as they ascended them.

"Have you ever been in Tor Neroche?" she asked as she followed him out into the hallway of the palace.

"Aye," he said simply.

But he didn't seem inclined to say more, so she didn't ask. Perhaps it was a poor memory for him. Perhaps it was so glorious that he couldn't bear to think on it for it compared poorly with his own life.

Perhaps she had spent far too much of the past fortnight dreaming and it had wrought a foul work upon her own poor thoughts.

She paused with him as he peeked out into the hallway. The light above his head vanished without his having to say anything. She did, however, hear him murmur a spell of un-noticing before he turned and looked at her.

"Shall we?"

"How did you make the light go out without saying anything?" she asked.

"Years of practice. You know, not wanting to stomp through the pigsty in thc dark."

"Hmmm," she said, following him out into the passageway.

He looked at her. "Would you care to learn a few?"

"Learn a few whats?"

"Spells."

She knew what he'd been going to say and had wished to avoid hearing it. It was quite some time before she could say anything. She took a cautious breath. "Spells?"

He nodded.

"I loathe magic," she whispered.

"I know." He paused. "But a spell or two is never a bad thing."

"I have a sword."

"So do I."

"I know how to use mine."

He laughed a little. "You have little faith in my skill."

"Miach, I've watched you train. If training it could be called—and with someone else's sword, no less."

"I'm fiercer in battle."

She snorted. She would have to see that.

"You know," he said slowly, "Adhémar could teach you a spell or two."

She looked at him in astonishment.

Oddly enough, he was looking at her in the same manner, as if he couldn't believe what he'd said.

"Did I say that?" he asked, sounding incredulous.

"Aye. Does he know any spells?"

"Not any interesting ones," Miach said. "But perhaps a useful one or two."

Morgan took him by the arm and started down the passageway. "I'll think on it," she said again. And unfortunately, she suspected she just might. She loathed magic, 'twas true, though she was beginning to find that spell of concealment tripping far too easily from her tongue. The werelight, as well, was something quite useful she couldn't create with her sword.

But anything else?

If it were taught by Adhémar?

She wondered if she would manage to listen to more than one spell before she grew so irritated with him that she would skewer him on the end of her sword. She likely should have done that the first time she'd seen him. She had been prepared to do damage to him without regret, but his visage had stopped her.

Was it a weakness that would be her downfall now?

She examined that as she allowed Miach to make a diversion to get them out the front door. Even Weger had been known on occasion to comment on the fairness of a wench's face.

Never hers, of course, but perhaps he had considered her unhandsome.

She walked down the palace's front steps, then stopped Miach at the bottom of those stairs.

"Am I fair to look upon?" she asked bluntly.

His eyes widened and a look of astonishment came upon his features.

She scowled at him. "You wear that look often."

"You catch me unawares often."

"Is the question so difficult, then?" she asked tartly.

He looked at her darkly, then turned and walked away, muttering under his breath. Morgan followed him, unsure why she felt so not herself. Indeed, her eyes began to burn and she suspected that had she had any feelings, they might be smarting as well.

"It was a ridiculous question," she announced, to save her pride.

Miach whirled on her. "You're bloody beautiful," he snarled. "Satisfied?"

Admittedly she hadn't known him very long, but she had never seen him so undone. Confused, aye; baffled, aye to that as well; astonished, aye, more than once. But angry?

It was her turn to be astonished.

"It was a simple question," she managed.

"And a simple answer. Let's go."

He strode away. Morgan followed him a little unsteadily. Well, it hadn't been very politely said, but the words were somewhat pleasing. Whether Weger had ever stopped to consider anything about her besides her sword skill was really beside the point. It wasn't Weger she was interested in. It was for damned sure she wasn't interested in Adhémar.

She was fairly certain she wasn't interested in Miach, either.

Fairly.

Paien would have waggled his brows at this point and begun to list all Miach's finer qualities. She would have, at that same point, reminded him that her quest, aye, her very choice of professions demanded that she not be interested in anyone.

Perhaps it was time she reminded herself yet again that she was most certainly not interested in anyone who had truck with magic.

Never mind that such a plague haunted her.

Miach looked over his shoulder, glared at her again, then strode swiftly ahead.

Still, there was much to like about Miach. He was frank and

clear-eyed. He was seemingly unafraid to acknowledge his limitations, he agreed with her that Nicholas's knife was unsettling, and he seemed as troubled by her dreams as she did.

And she liked his laugh.

She caught up to him and found it far too comfortable a thing. Despite the darkness that seemed to be swirling around her, she felt eased in her heart, somehow. It was almost as pleasant a feeling as a se'nnight on that goose-feather mattress at Lismòr.

Almost as much of a feeling of home.

Heaven help her.

Seventeen

M iach continued to walk away from the palace of Chagailt, cursing himself under his breath. What had he
been thinking? He'd had almost two days alone with Morgan
and what had he done? Had he wooed her? Had he sung lays
to her beauty, taken long walks with her in Iolaire's lovely
gardens, plied her with delicacies from Finlay's kitchens? Of
course not. He'd opened his mouth and suggested an activity
during which she could spend vast amounts of time with his
brother.

Adhémar could teach you a spell or two.

Ha!

It had either been the height of stupidity or a flash of bril-
liance. He latched on to the latter and examined what the potential benefits of such an arrangement might be.

First, if Adhémar taught her a few spells, she would continue to believe that he, Miach, didn't know them. Given her
substantial distaste for all things magical and their dispensers,
that could only be good for him and bad for his brother. Second, the more time she spent with Adhémar, the less she would
like him. Again, good for him, bad for his brother. Finally, if
Adhémar spent time with her, he would no doubt begin to see
her finer qualities and when she handed him that bloody knife
she carried, he might actually be kind to her.

Miach frowned. That was good for his brother, but he wasn't quite sure what it meant for him.

He blew out his breath and turned his thoughts away from the whole subject. It was certain that he had many more things to think on that were equally as troubling and perhaps more pertinent to the current situation.

He ignored the fact that all those things seemed to have Morgan of Melksham in the center of them.

So, Nicholas of Lismòr had given her a blade, a blade that so greatly resembled the Sword of Angesand that it had to have been made by Queen Mehar herself, to take to the king of Neroche. That was an extraordinary thing alone, but it was made even more so by knowing that Morgan had been dreaming of the sword itself.

When she had never seen it before.

More surprising still were her dreams of a situation that mirrored Gair of Ceangail's demise so perfectly that he could hardly call it dreaming. He revisited his earlier thoughts. Perhaps she wasn't dreaming after all.

Perhaps she was remembering.

Gair of Ceangail, of all people.

Gair of Ceangail, whose daughter had possibly cast a spell of un-noticing over herself and escaped drowning in evil.

But had the little girl escaped nothing more than that first wave of evil? Had she perished in the forest? Or had she been taken in by kindly souls and was now living out her life, blissfully ignorant of her parentage and what she was capable of?

Or was Gair's daughter walking next to him, remembering spells she'd learned as a child and dreaming memories?

There were just too many things that made his mind expand far beyond where it should have. Gair, Morgan, the Sword of Angesand, Weger . . . and he himself, who couldn't seem to stop finding ways to suggest to Morgan that she spend more time with Adhémar.

He wondered if he should just turn and invite Morgan to run him through. At least with the latter, he wouldn't have to watch his brother woo her—

Which he was sure Adhémar would do when he took a long enough look at her.

Miach cursed silently as he walked along. He had ample time to curse because he wasn't walking all that quickly. There was no sense in showing up at camp sooner than he had to. He supposed the others might have continued on their way and perhaps he and Morgan would have some running to do to catch up with them.

Perhaps while they were running, he would cast a spell of ugliness over Morgan that only Adhémar could see. It was possible, of course. After all, he was the bloody archmage of the realm. What good did all that power do him if he couldn't use it for good now and then?

He spent the better part of the morning thinking about that. In fact, the idea was so beguiling and he was concentrating so thoroughly on its implementation that he didn't see the trap laid before them until he'd walked into the middle of it.

Creatures came at them from all sides.

It took him a moment or two to regroup. Before he could manage it completely, Morgan had spun him around so they were standing back to back.

"Draw your sword, you idiot!" she shouted. She paused. "Do you even have a sword? Damnation—"

Miach pulled one out of thin air.

"Where did that come from?" she said, looking briefly over her shoulder.

"Found it on the ground—"

"Good," Morgan said. "Use it."

He wasn't a bad swordsman. In fact, if he'd taken the time to judge dispassionately, he would have said that he was a better swordsman than Adhémar and at least Cathar's equal—and that without the benefit of any finger-waggling.

He fought now with all the skill he had and he could hear Morgan behind him doing the same, but he knew almost instantly that it would not be enough. Had it been just men attacking them, aye, but not with these monsters. Miach continued to fight, but while he was doing so, he wove his spell of death.

It wasn't something that he did lightly. Indeed, it was something that he hadn't done since he'd inherited his mother's mantle. He certainly hadn't managed it with any success the one time he'd done it before that, which had been during his extended visit to Lothar's dungeon. There had come a point during that incarceration where he had been so desperate to see light, so desperate to be free, so desperate to be anywhere but where he was, standing in slime and knowing he would die anyway if he didn't act, that he had woven a spell of death to include everything in Lothar's keep save him.

The spell had dropped into the air of Lothar's keep like a coin into a bottomless well, silent and useless.

Fortunately for his sorry, shivering young self, his mother had felt what he hadn't realized had been a tremor in Lothar's fortress and that had been enough to convince her he was still alive.

Those were memories perhaps left for a better time.

He wove his spell of death now over the hearts of all who lay within the scope of the battle, taking care to make certain it didn't include him or Morgan. He also took care to make certain there were no others within the reach of the darkness he created who might innocently fall to his power.

He quietly spoke the final word.

All but three of the remaining creatures fell to the earth.

Miach staggered as his spell rebounded off the remaining three. He gathered it to himself and dissolved it, managing at the same time to kill one of the last three with his sword. What were these creatures covered with? It was a spell, surely, and one that seemed faintly familiar.

He realized why. It was the same magic Adhémar had smelled of after the battle in which he'd lost his power.

Miach promised himself a good moment of being startled later, when their lives were no longer in peril. He heard one of their remaining two foes bellow in fury. He would have turned to aid Morgan but he saw that she didn't need it. Sword skill alone would win the day with her, apparently. That left him with the final creature, a drooling troll who laughed maniacally as he strode across the glade.

Miach focused all the rest of his power at the creature, smashed through the spell that had been woven over him, and crushed his body with a single command.

The creature crumpled like a length of rough cloth.

Miach dropped to his knees, feeling half dead himself.

"Miach!"

He could only manage to shake his head. He felt Morgan's hands on his shoulders and found himself wrenched upright.

"Are you wounded?" she asked.

Miach knelt there, sucking in breath in an alarming fashion. He shook his head again, the only answer he could make. He was almost certain Morgan looked worried. Or he could have just been imagining that. He couldn't actually see her face anymore for all the spots dancing in front of his eyes.

"You don't appear to be bleeding," she said with a frown.

"I'm not," he managed. "Just spent."

"Miach, there weren't that many of them," she chided. "And look you there; it would appear that many of them simply died on their own."

Miach would have snorted out a laugh at that, but he was too busy trying to catch his breath.

She took hold of the sword at his side. "Where did you find this? Is it yours?"

"Nay," he gasped. "Leave it behind."

She rose easily and jammed it into the ground. "Have you ever been in a battle before, Miach?"

"Once or twice."

"Do you always react this way?" She looked down at him narrowly. "You aren't going to puke, are you?"

He shook his head.

"Good. Don't. Or if you're going to, don't do it on me."

"Won't," he agreed.

"Don't move."

"If you say so," he said faintly.

She shot him another look of thinly veiled concern, then cleaned her sword and resheathed it. She walked around the glade for several moments, looking down at the creatures slain there and shaking her head slowly.

Miach understood completely. He knelt there, wheezing, and managed to get his head upright where he could at least see what he'd killed. He wasn't surprised to see spells hanging in tatters around the trolls. Miach renewed his determination to have a closer look at Adhémar's sword. He suspected he might find the same thing there.

Morgan came to the last troll, the one he had felled with his magic. She stopped, looked at the creature for a moment or two in silence, then turned and strode over to Miach.

"Come," she said, hauling him to his feet. "I do not like this at all."

"Did you see something?" he asked.

"That creature," she said, shivering. "He is much like the one that came at Adhémar. If his sword hadn't come to life—" She stopped speaking. She looked at Miach with wide eyes. "I mean—"

"I already know," Miach said, struggling to get his feet under him.

"Who told you?" she demanded.

"Fletcher," Miach said. "Accidentally. Kill him later."

"I just might," she said, reaching out to steady him. "I suppose I will have to trust you with that secret as well. After the past two days, I daresay there are few still left between us."

Miach grunted. It was all he could do. Heaven help him if she found out any of his real secrets.

Morgan drew his arm over her shoulders. She was surprisingly strong for a woman. He was not given to fat, but he was tall and solid. He did, however, find it somewhat satisfying that she staggered just a bit while trying to keep him there. She looked about them once more, then shivered.

Miach understood. The stench of evil was overpowering.

"I don't like this," she said quietly. "There are three times the number who came against us at Istaur."

Miach nodded. Only this time, they had come against just him and Morgan.

Something foul was afoot.

He hated appearing weak, but he was desperately tempted to ask Morgan to either stop or carry him on her back. There was magic, of course, and then there was magic. Killing magic did not come without a desperately high cost, both in its execution and in the price it exacted from his soul. It was one thing to face an opponent with a sword and give him a fair chance. It was another thing to take his powers and destroy life when that life had no chance to defend itself.

Though he supposed Lothar's creatures, if these were actually Lothar's creatures, were better off being free of Lothar's influence.

It was cold comfort, indeed.

He stumbled along for miles, waiting for some of his strength to return to him. He finally pulled Morgan to a stop, leaned over, and took several deep breaths. Then he heaved himself upright.

"Let's run," he said.

Morgan opened her mouth, no doubt to ask him if he was up to the challenge, but then she shut it and nodded.

She made him run in front of her, which he supposed said quite a bit about her opinion of his recovery, but he didn't object. It took all his strength and determination just to put one foot in front of the other and fling himself forward.

It was afternoon before they could see the others and their camp. Morgan caught him and pulled him back. She motioned for him to follow her as she walked carefully and silently through the woods.

It was then that Miach realized they were still wearing his spell of un-noticing.

He stumbled and landed heavily on a stick that snapped as it broke in two. Morgan glared at him briefly before continuing even more carefully. Miach examined his spell and found it completely intact.

He followed Morgan back to camp. They walked past Paien without his even looking in their direction, so Miach knew the spell was good. Not that he would have doubted that anyway. Unfortunately, it raised a very unsettling question.

How had those creatures seen through it?

He dissolved the spell as they walked into camp. Well, Morgan walked into camp; he hobbled there. Everyone rose, wearing expressions of astonishment. He made it to the fire before he dropped to his knees. He could hardly keep his eyes open. He suspected he could have slept on a bed of sharp rocks and been grateful for it.

He listened to the conversings going on around him but could make no sense of them. This certainly wasn't what he would have preferred—to be looking like a feeble old man in front of Morgan, but he was past aiding himself. He knelt there and concentrated on breathing.

"Miach."

He couldn't even look up at Adhémar. "What?"

"What was it?"

"Fell things that attempted an ambush."

Adhémar squatted down in front of him. "Lothar?" he asked quietly.

"They were of the same sort that attacked you near Tor Neroche." He put his hands on his knees and straightened. "We must break camp. Keep moving."

"Why?"

"Did you not hear me? There were two score and ten of them, at least! Who knows what else lies in wait."

Adhémar drew himself up. "I'd like to see for myself."

"Very well then," Miach groaned. "An hour back, if you must go look."

"Whose lads were they?" Camid asked sharply.

"The same sort who attacked us before the inn outside Istaur," Morgan said.

"Let's all have a look, then," Camid said. "Morgan, are you coming?"

"Of course," she said. "Glines, look after Miach."

"Fletcher," Adhémar said, "you come as well. We'll collect Paien on our way. He should have been standing guard. I'm not sure why he didn't see you pass him."

Miach felt Morgan rest her hand on his head briefly before she tromped off with their companions. Miach thought he might have been able to get up before that, but her touch left him weak in a far different way.

He was truly in trouble.

There was silence for quite some time.

Miach was certain he hadn't fallen asleep, but then again perhaps he had. When the blackness receded, he lifted his head to find Glines of Balfour studying him. Glines smiled briefly.

"My lord Archmage."

Miach had avoided the youngest son of Graeme up until this point, mostly because he had demonstrated quite clearly that he was barely capable of stopping himself from bowing each time Adhémar walked near. Miach suspected he might like the man, however. He had a quick wit and a rather wry sense of humor.

"Are you sure of that?" Miach asked.

"Perfectly."

Miach grunted. "Today, I do not feel anything so lofty." He looked back over his shoulder. "Perhaps they will return with a count of the corpses."

"Were there many?"

"Too many."

Glines studied him until Miach actually began to feel uncomfortable—and there were few things in this world or the unseen one that made him so.

"What?" Miach asked. "What ails you?"

"I'm curious."

"A dangerous indulgence."

Glines smiled. "Why are you here?"

"Do you think I can tell you?"

"I'll wager that possibility on a game of chance, if you like."

Miach smiled dryly. "I've watched you lighten several purses on this journey, my friend. I dare not wager anything so serious."

Glines lifted one eyebrow, looking mildly surprised. "Not off on holiday, then."

Miach shrugged and managed to get himself upright. He supposed it might be several days before he was fully recovered. He resisted the almost overwhelming desire to throw himself into a se'nnight's sleep. "You never know."

"I suspect not."

Miach sighed deeply. "Nothing to worry over. I simply came to find my brother."

"Did he escape," Glines asked, "or was he merely off looking for something?"

Miach considered the other man. "I daresay you know more than you're telling. Has Adhémar been talking to you?"

Glines smiled briefly. "He mutters when he loses."

"Which I imagine is quite often. If that is the case then you know that I am not on holiday and my brother has not merely escaped for pleasure. He is searching for something in particular and I came to find out why it was taking so long for him to find it. I thought perhaps I should offer him my aid."

Glines produced wine and poured a cup. "And now you've found something *you* hadn't intended to find?"

"What would that be?" Miach asked.

"Morgan." Glines handed him wine. "You love her, don't you?"

Miach choked and grasped desperately for the wine Glines proffered. "What in the world are you talking about?"

"I recognize the symptoms, if not the illness," Glines said dryly.

"The illness of what?" Morgan asked from behind them.

Miach spewed the wine out of his mouth. He supposed it was better than choking on it, but neither was a good choice. When had Morgan and the lads returned? Had he napped for that long? Had she heard Glines's babbling?

"He's excitable," Morgan said, dropping her pack down next to the fire and squatting next to Miach. She looked at him. "Recovered?"

"Completely," he managed.

She pursed her lips. "You're optimistic."

"Always. How many were there?"

"Thirty," she said without expression. "I do not remember killing so many. I daresay you didn't either." She looked at him closely. "How did we manage that, do you suppose? Not a mark on many of them. It's as if they simply died of fright."

"Ah," Miach said, casting about desperately for a plausible reason, but finding that nothing came to mind. He was, he would be the first to admit, not in top form at present. A normal spell of that magnitude would have drained him for days and left him quite happily taking to his couch to rest and recover. But the spell he'd wrought against those creatures from one of Lothar's nightmares?

He wondered if he would manage to walk steadily in a se'nnight's time.

Unfortunately, he had no choice.

"It's Chagailt," Glines said.

Miach turned to look at him. "What?"

"Chagailt," Glines repeated. "There are spells laid upon the forests here around. Didn't you know?"

"I didn't," Miach said, "but I'll hear the tale." *Pray, make it believable.*

"What would you know of it?" Morgan asked skeptically.

"More than you, apparently," Glines said with a smile. "I

have traveled upon the continent before, you know. One picks up tales here and there while one is about his travels."

"Tales from men well into their cups do not generally count as truth," Morgan said dryly.

"There is a little truth in each cup of ale," Glines said.

Miach smiled. "Is there, indeed?"

"If not, there should be." Glines looked at Morgan. "I heard that there are spells of ward and protection laid about the palace of Chagailt. It was built, you know, for Iolaire of Ainneamh by her husband, Symon of Neroche, as a wedding present. What spells she did not weave into the surrounding countryside, he certainly did. I heard that the magic is still very much in force and will hinder any creature who comes upon unwary travelers with evil intent."

Miach stole a look at Morgan to see if she was going along with Glines's myth. She glanced at him; he fixed an expression of surprised relief on his face, as if he'd just heard the answer he'd been seeking. She shot him a look of faint skepticism before she turned back to Glines.

"What else did you hear?"

"Nothing that I remember," he said vaguely. "I'm merely suggesting that perhaps there were forces at work that you couldn't see. Forces that aided you when you needed it." He rose and stretched. "I wouldn't resent help in any form, were I you."

"You are not me," Morgan said, standing as well, "but I will not begrudge myself the aid either." She shivered. "I had counted, but not well apparently. I do not doubt my skill, but even I have to admit we are fortunate to be alive."

Miach nodded, trying to look as innocent and grateful as he could. It wasn't difficult to look grateful, because he was—for solid ground under his feet and no need to move anytime soon.

"We should press on," Morgan announced.

So much for rest. Miach nodded. "Aye, you're right."

"You sound unconvinced. Do you not fear meeting more of those?" Morgan asked.

He started to tell her that he sensed none of them, nor anything like them for miles, but he hadn't sensed the first lot either. A powerful spell had certainly concealed them.

He wished he had the energy to return and examine the corpses. He wished he had the opportunity to have a closer look at Adhémar's sword. Then again, he *had* managed a decent look at the lads near Tor Neroche and seen nothing that told him about the author of the evil. Perhaps here, the result would be the same.

He didn't want to give voice to the thought, but he suspected this would not be the last time he met this particular sort of magic.

He heaved himself to his feet, swayed, then found himself with Morgan's arm around his waist.

"You're pitiful," she said, turning him toward the horses. "Can you make it across the glade?"

"Possibly," Miach said, tossing Glines a brief smile before he turned back to Morgan. "With help, of course," he added.

Glines cursed.

"Glines, be useful," Morgan said. "Bring his pack and yours. I do not like the feeling here." She looked at Miach. "Can you manage a horse?"

"Um," he began.

"Likely not," she said. "We'll ride together on yours and mine will follow."

Miach decided at that point that silence was likely the wisest course of action. Besides, who knew but that he might fall off his horse, take a fatal blow to his head, and leave the mantle of archmage falling upon someone who wasn't expecting it? It wasn't unheard of, that.

Though it was true that most archmages were made from someone within the royal family, it was equally true that the calling had fallen upon the occasional unsuspecting wizard or even, in one particular case, a farmer with latent magic. The poor man had been out plowing his field, come close to being crushed by the power that had suddenly surged into him, then woken to find he had suddenly become responsible for quite a bit more than just his fields.

Miach could sympathize with him, actually.

So, lest he cause another soul such wrenching distress, silence was the order of the day. Perhaps if he was feeling particularly faint, he could ask Morgan to put her arms around him and hold on until he felt better.

"So, where are we going?" Glines asked as he followed along obediently.

"Still north."

Glines began to wheeze.

"Not *that* north," Morgan said.

"Well, if we're headed anywhere north, we should pause at Penrhyn," Glines supplied helpfully. "They make a delicious wine."

They did; one Adhémar was far too fond of. The kings of Neroche had, from time to time, bargained with the kings of Penrhyn for a particular type of gem they had periodically used to make their magic. The need for that had long since ceased, but the need for Penrhyn's sour wine had not. The entire history of trade relations was long and tedious, but what Miach could say was that the sour wine was potent and Adhémar's taste for it was legendary. He would be immediately recognized and his anonymity compromised.

"Better to avoid them," Miach put in. "Rumor has it they are a stingy lot. We would likely be forced to pay huge duties coming in and out of their country. Best we stay on lesser-known roads."

Morgan stopped next to his horse. "There is wisdom in that, no doubt." She gave him a leg up, then fixed his pack to her horse before she swung up behind him. Miach spent far too much time enjoying what he shouldn't have been enjoying. By the time he thought to look around, the rest of the company was mounted and Morgan and Paien were discussing a direction. Adhémar was balking. Apparently the lure of sour wine was far too strong.

"I vote for Penrhyn," Adhémar said firmly.

"We have another hard day's travel before we must needs make a decision," Miach said, casting his brother a pointed look. "Let us ride today and decide tomorrow. One way or another, today we must go north."

"North?" Paien said. "How far north?"

"We'll speak more of it later," Morgan promised, "when we're away from this accursed wood."

"Enspelled," Glines corrected her.

"I stand by accursed," she said. She put her arms around Miach. "Can you remain in the saddle this way?"

"I'll soldier on bravely," he promised. He supposed his

manliness would survive being coddled like a toothless dotard, but he wasn't sure his heart would.

"You aren't really going to fall off, are you?" Morgan asked sharply.

"I'll do my best not to," he promised, but it was too late for that. He had fallen into an abyss that opened up without warning before him, an abyss named Morgan. He suspected there was no way out. Worse yet, he wasn't certain he wanted to find a way out.

I dreamed of a sword that looked just like the knife.

Her words came back to him, but he shook his head. He hadn't truly considered the possibility before, but he did now and without hesitation decided that Morgan could not possibly be the wielder. She had one spell to her credit, a vile dream that haunted her, and a blade that was the twin of the Sword of Angesand. Those things did not a wielder make.

Yet, what if she were?

Miach couldn't stop his poor, overworked mind from considering that. If Morgan was the wielder, then he would have to watch Adhémar take her and do with her as he pleased.

He closed his eyes at the feel of her arms around him. He would wait and see. Maybe she didn't really have any magic. Maybe her dreams were just dreams and not memories. Maybe she dreamed of Mehar of Angesand's sword only because it resembled the knife in her pack.

He wasn't sure what he should hope for.

He was sure what he feared.

Eighteen

Three days later, Morgan rode atop her magnificent Angesand steed and examined her situation. Chagailt and her inhuman attackers were left far behind. Her leg was very much mended and had ceased to pain her. And, finally, Miach was upright in his own saddle. It was an improvement, but he still looked terrible, which was not. She wasn't sure if he had eaten something foul or if the battle with those nightmarish creatures had simply been too much for him. Perhaps she should have tried a few of Adhémar's herbs on him to see if they couldn't have aided him.

Though she had to admit that riding with him for all that time had not been unpleasant. He was good company. There was something about him that was very comfortable.

Far beyond her favorite pair of boots.

She shifted in the saddle, uncomfortable with the direction of her thoughts. Best she leave those be and concentrate on something less troubling to her heart.

If she could manage it.

The rest of her company seemed happily oblivious to her distress. They were passing the time discussing potential locales they might visit on their way north, locales that might provide a bit of entertainment in what for them had been a rather uneventful journey.

Uneventful? Morgan wished she could agree.

Her unease had grown with every league they traveled north. At first she'd thought it might have been uncertainty over what to expect once she reached Tor Neroche. What was she to do, exactly? Walk up to the king and simply hand the knife to him? What if he would not see her?

She could scarce bear to think about that possibility.

In time, though, she'd come to realize that her unease sprang from a different but unsurprising source. Her dream had not troubled her in a pair of nights, but that didn't matter because now it had begun to haunt all her waking hours. It didn't matter how often she sought distraction, it was still with her.

She could hear the words the mother whispered to the girl. She could hear the words the man shouted at the well. She could hear the names that the man and woman called each other.

Gair.

Sarait.

She knew the number of the children and she knew some of their names. There were seven. Six lads and a wee lass. The eldest son's name was Keir.

The wee lassie's name was Mhorghain.

By now, she knew the way through the woods so well, she supposed she might have been able to walk them herself while awake. She knew the words that the mother had spoken to the little girl.

Words of warning.

A reminder about the spell of un-noticing and another spell of comfort and protection.

Morgan could have said the words aloud if she'd dared—or if she'd had the stomach for them. But she couldn't. Not the second spell. That she'd used the first at all was enough to set her to shivering.

She had come to the point where she wasn't sure anymore sometimes whether she was awake or asleep. She could smell the sweet scent that clung to the mother. It was lavender and a faint hint of rose.

She could feel the mother's hand as well, around the little girl's. The little girl seemed wrapped in a feeling of deep love and great affection. Morgan found herself wrapped in those same feelings—as if she had been that little girl and that woman her mother.

It was, oddly enough, the same feeling she had each time Miach touched her.

She had seen the glade with the well so many times in her dreams, she had no doubt she would recognize it immediately. She had relived the argument between the man and the woman so many times, she could repeat it word for word, though it was in a language she had not learned on Melksham.

She dug the heels of her hands into her eyes. It didn't help clear her head, but she hadn't really expected it to. She wasn't quite sure what would. Perhaps a very long, very difficult siege that would require for its ending a piece of daring business that would tax the very limits of what she could do. Or perhaps she could just ask Miach to clunk her over the head with her own sword. That might buy her a few minutes of peace.

She paused. Would Miach know a spell to drive away dreams?

She was almost afraid to ask.

She decided abruptly that she would not, but she would see if he could be prevailed upon for a bit of conversation. He was weary, she was anxious; it might be a good distraction for both of them.

"Miach," she said.

He seemed to struggle to focus on her. "Aye?"

"Who was Sarait?" was the first thing out of her mouth. She almost swore. Would this damned dream never cease to plague her?

"She was youngest of the five daughters of Sìle, king of Tòrr Dòrainn," he said with a yawn. "Why?"

"She was Gair's wife, was she not?"

He shut his mouth with a snap and looked at her in surprise. "Aye, she was. How do you know?"

"How do you think I know?" she asked crossly.

A look of profound pity came over his face. "Ah, Morgan," he said quietly. "Poor gel."

She cursed. It made her feel a little better. "I'll wager you know more about Gair and his doings than you're telling."

"I'll wager I don't," he said with a grave smile. "I've told you everything I've heard, or read."

"Know you nothing of his children?" she asked, pained.

"I don't," he said. "But we'll find the answers. Perhaps when we reach your destination."

"Will you come that far?" she asked in surprise.

He seemed to consider for a minute or two. "I will, if you like," he said quietly.

She found she could do nothing but nod. Her relief was so great, she almost cried. She didn't dare look at Miach for fear she would weep in truth, so she put her face forward and continued on.

Out of the corner of her eye, she saw Miach hold out his hand. She took it without thinking. He squeezed once, hard, then let go.

"Dreams are frightening, Morgan," he said. "Full of things we cannot understand."

She nodded as if she agreed, but she did not. Her dreams were full of things she understood all too clearly.

And she was beginning to suspect she was not dreaming.

T hey paused briefly for a meal, then continued on. Morgan couldn't decide if the pace was too swift, or if it chafed. What she did know was that she could not bear for night to come.

But it came anyway. There was no inn, no deserted outbuildings for them to borrow, only the sky above with its bitter stars shining coldly down upon them. Morgan volunteered for the first watch. She was more than happy to stand in the shadows and try to become invisible.

It did not help.

She heard Gair's words in her head, over and over again. She heard Sarait's spell of un-noticing, the one she had used a handful of times already.

Then she heard other words. It seemed that they came from other dreams that she could not quite remember. But the words were good ones and she wished they had been hers to use. She wondered if the words might have belonged to Sarait.

She was certain they were not Gair's.

It was well into the next watch when she realized she was not alone. She turned to slip back into the shadows only to find Miach not ten paces from her, leaning against a tree, watching her. She would have squeaked in surprise, but she never squeaked.

"How long have you been there?" she demanded.

"About an hour."

"I was concentrating," she lied.

He grunted, pushed off from the tree, and took her by the arm. "Come back to camp."

She dug her heels in and gave him no choice but to stop. She looked up at him seriously. "I cannot."

"Morgan, you cannot remain awake for the rest of your life. You must sleep."

"I daren't," she said.

"Then perhaps a pinch of herb in wine to help you along?"

She scowled. "Don't tell me you use those for the pigs as well."

"You would be surprised," he said dryly. "It would help you, I think."

"Miach, I don't think anything will help me sleep."

"You haven't tasted my brew."

"If it contains a magic spell, then no matter how lovely your pigs might find it, I will not enjoy it."

He smiled. "I should suggest a run, but I fear tonight you would soon leave me far behind."

"You are not fully yourself yet," she agreed.

He took her hand in both of his. Morgan suspected she should have pulled away, but it was so soothing she just couldn't bring herself to. It was something Nicholas would have done.

But Miach was not Nicholas.

Not at all.

"I could tell you a tale about something," Miach offered, rubbing her hand absently. "If you like."

She frowned thoughtfully. "What sort of something?"

"Something that would soothe you," he promised. "I'm sure there would be swords involved. Bloodshed. Peril. That kind of thing."

"Romance?" she asked skeptically.

"Do you *want* romance?"

She snorted. "I daresay it would ruin my sleep."

He put his arm around her shoulders and started back toward camp. "I know just the thing. I'll tell you of Catrìona of Croxteth. She was an ordinary gel, you know, who found herself thrust into quite extraordinary circumstances."

"Is there magic involved?" Morgan asked, putting her arm around Miach's waist when he stumbled.

"Only to make her sword sharper," he said. "A pity she died so long ago. You would have liked her very much, I think."

"Miach, how do you know all these tales?"

"I—"

"Never mind," Morgan interrupted. "I remember now. Too much time at the fire; not enough time in the lists."

"Something like that," he agreed.

Morgan walked with him back to the fire, nudged Glines ungently with her foot to wake him for his watch, then made herself a place by the fire and rolled up in her blanket. Miach did the same, stretching out with his head near hers. Morgan rolled onto her belly and rested her chin upon her folded hands.

"Well?" she said expectantly.

"It is a very *long* tale," he said, "but very necessary for those who might want to spend a great deal of their time not sleeping."

"That would be me," she said gratefully.

"So I suspected. Now, make yourself comfortable and give heed to the interesting facts I plan to lay out for you. The manner of Catrìona's birth is on this wise . . ."

Morgan watched him as he spoke, the firelight flickering softly on his face, his eyes alight with the enjoyment he obviously took in his words. And he did spin a fine tale, reminiscent of Nicholas, and Morgan listened with pleasure. She remembered finally having to rest her head on her pack because she grew sleepy. The singing of the blade did not trouble her, for a change. Catrìona of Croxteth had put a spell on her blade so it would sing to her in a different scale depending on what sort of trouble was near. Morgan wondered if she could teach her knife the same thing, then she remembered that it was the king's blade, not hers.

Perhaps after her task was done, she would take her marvelous horse and ride across the mountains to Durial where she might learn from the dwarves there the art of forging. Then she would make her own blade. And she just might teach it to sing as well.

The thought was pleasing and quite comforting. She fell asleep, to her great surprise, with the touch of Miach's hand on her hair and his voice whispering in her ear.

And she dreamed of blades that sung a song only she could hear.

Nineteen

Miach sighed as he sat on the edge of yet another well. It had been a very long se'nnight and it looked to be lengthening still. He remembered little of the journey from Chagailt save that he'd wanted desperately to sleep and he knew Morgan couldn't bear to. He pitied her the dreams that haunted her. He wished he had a good explanation for them save the one she wouldn't want to hear.

The more he thought about it, the more he realized that the suspicions he'd begun to have at Chagailt about the fate of Gair's daughter were but a foreshadowing of a truth he now realized he could no longer deny.

He was convinced Gair's youngest daughter had survived. He was equally sure she had been taken in by a band of traveling mercenaries. There she had learned to shun anything to do with magic. That distaste had been strengthened at an orphanage. It surely had been completely cemented into her at a particular tower on the coast of a backward island famous for sheep and feuds over water rights.

In short, he was positive Morgan was Gair's lost daughter.

There was simply no other explanation for Morgan's abilities, or her dreams.

And if she was Gair of Ceangail's daughter, she certainly

would have the power necessary to wield the Sword of Angesand. Was it possible that she dreamed of the sword not only because it resembled her blade, but because she was destined to wield it?

The Wielders of the Sword of Angesand will come, out of magic, out of obscurity, and out of darkness . . .

If there was a darkness out there, Gair had certainly been a master of it. And if Morgan sprang from that line, it would fit the prophecy. But what would Morgan say to it all?

He imagined he knew already, and her response wouldn't use very many polite words.

He dragged himself back to the present with great effort. He would think on it later. Now, he was working and needed to make certain he had earned their keep.

They had made camp at twilight near the barn of an obliging farmer. Miach had paid their price of supper by a quietly made promise of a sweetened well, which the farmer had enthusiastically agreed to. Miach had eaten briefly, then gone about his work. It had been nothing compared to what he'd done at Angesand, but still it had been wearying.

He was now finished, but he couldn't bring himself to do more than sit while their host prepared to taste the price of their stay.

The farmer drank suspiciously, but then his face broke out into a genuine smile of surprise. "Delicious," he said happily. He looked at Miach with sudden calculation. "Don't suppose you want to stay another night, would you?"

"Why?"

"I have a cow who gives sour milk. I've tried everything, but nothing helps." He paused. "She's the reddish one in the end stall there."

"Sorry," Miach said regretfully. "We cannot stay."

"The next time perhaps."

"Perhaps."

Miach watched the farmer walk away, then he quietly laid a charm of sweetness on that poor, sour cow in the end stall that would last the length of the beast's life. It took little of his energy, but that, combined with his brief work on the well, left him rather short-tempered. He supposed he should have saved a bit of sweetness for himself.

He was contemplating the irony of that when Adhémar walked out to the well. He had a long drink, dragged his sleeve across his mouth, and grunted.

"Good."

"Thank you."

Adhémar propped his foot up on the edge of the low brick wall. "Well?"

"Well, what?"

"What did you find on that useless jaunt to Chagailt save a clutch of nasties?"

"A fine meal or two," Miach said.

Adhémar grunted. "I daresay. Anything else?"

Miach paused, considered, then looked up at Adhémar calmly.

"I believe I found your wielder."

It was worth it. There was something tremendously satisfying about being able to say something that would so thoroughly undo his brother that Adhémar should lose his balance, flail about a bit, then plunge headfirst into a very cold, albeit sweet, bit of water. Fortunately for the very wet king of Neroche, the well was deep but rather large and he had no problem surfacing. Adhémar clung to the brick that enclosed the water.

"My *what*?"

Miach reached out a hand and pulled his brother out. Adhémar stood there, shivering and dripping. Miach almost felt sorry enough for him to dry him off with a bit of magic.

Almost.

That the tidings would, in effect, turn Morgan over to Adhémar's care and heaven only knew what else, was what kept him from it.

"You heard me," Miach said. "I think I have found your wielder."

"You *think*," Adhémar said, scowling fiercely. "How on earth would you be able to recognize him?"

Miach pretended to consider that. There was no sense in irritating Adhémar unnecessarily by telling him that he was just as capable as the king of recognizing the man—likely more so since he still had the ability to sense magic in another. That would lead to a discussion about why Adhémar had been sent when Miach could have gone. That was destined to finish poorly.

"Well," Miach began slowly, "I know the requirements. The wielder should have magic—"

"I knew that," Adhémar huffed.

"And perhaps something that shows an affinity for the sword," Miach continued thoughtfully. "Of course, there's no way to tell for sure until we take her to Tor Neroche and see if the Sword of Angesand calls to her."

"I knew that as well," Adhémar snapped. "Tell me something I don't know—her? What do you mean *her*?"

"Morgan."

Adhémar spluttered. He swore. He cursed Miach in five different languages and laid upon him spells that would have left him crawling in a garden in the form of an earthworm if he'd had the power for it.

Miach regarded him with his arms folded over his chest. "Are you finished?"

"Hardly," Adhémar spat. "Have you gone mad?"

"Hardly," Miach returned. "Aren't you at all curious?"

"Nay," Adhémar said shortly. "You've lost all wits and I'm uninterested in where they went." He paused. "But then again, just out of curiosity, why do you think she might be the one?"

"I can't say."

Adhémar growled and launched himself at Miach. Of course, having grown up in a hall with six brothers left Miach expecting something like it, but he was weary and didn't move quickly enough. He went down with a thump. There was a sickening crunch as something smacked against stone. Miach realized that that something had been his head. He waited a minute until his vision cleared and he was certain he wouldn't become senseless, then he changed himself into a man-sized scorpion.

"Arrgh!" Adhémar exclaimed, leaping up and backing away in revulsion. "Cowardly whelp," he spat. "Can you not fight me in the form of a man?"

Miach returned to his manly form with a smile.

"I daresay you won't have the guts to remain as you are," Adhémar muttered.

Miach crawled to his feet, looked at Adhémar for a moment in silence, then happily lived up to his brother's low expectations.

He was not at his best, which hampered his creativity, but he did manage several shapes that left Adhémar very unhappy. Miach almost took his brother's head off in the form of a great bear with glistening claws, tripped him and sent him sprawling thanks to a brief stint as a darting snake, and made him back up a pace involuntarily as he put on the trappings of an enormous, misshapen troll. He grabbed his brother and heaved him up high over his misshapen, drooling head.

Perhaps the last wasn't all that fair. Miach had come face-to-face with just such a creature at Chagailt and hadn't been able to stop his own recoiling. He started to say, or gurgle rather, that he had perhaps stepped over the line of gallant behavior, when he heard the unmistakable and unwelcome sound of Morgan's voice. He saw her standing at the edge of the little courtyard.

He hardly had the time to register that she'd told Adhémar to prepare to fall, and that such would happen because she had a dagger in her hand, before she was in process of flinging it with all her strength toward Miach's heart.

He managed to turn himself into nighttime dew and waft to the side before the blade struck, but just barely.

He had the feeling that when he managed to gather himself back to himself, he would find he had not escaped harm altogether.

He watched damply as Adhémar picked himself up, cursing loudly and vigorously. Adhémar drew his sword and sliced though all the air around him. Miach would have clucked his tongue if he'd had a tongue to cluck. Since he did not, he cast himself onto the first available breeze and floated well away from the farmer's barn.

It was tempting to continue to laze along, but he feared he was so weary that he might forget himself as he lay upon the hard crust of field, turn into frost before he knew it, and be crushed under the hooves of wandering cattle. Or his own Angesand steed. The irony of that would have done him in—if the hooves wouldn't have.

He resumed his proper form and stared in consternation at the bloody gash in his arm, visible through the rent in his cloak. Well, at least it wasn't a gash in his chest. He cursed nonetheless as he clutched his arm. Why was it he couldn't weave a spell of binding on his own self? It would have made things so much easier.

He trudged off with another curse toward the barn. Surely someone in the company would have a needle and some thread and some small bit of skill with both.

He walked into the circle of firelight and endured the gaping stare of Fletcher and the manly looks of comradely pity from Camid and Paien. Glines, however, jumped to his feet immediately.

"What did you do?"

"I cut myself," Miach said through gritted teeth.

"Got too close to someone else's sword, eh, lad?" Paien boomed.

"Something like that," Miach muttered. He looked at Glines. "Have you a needle?"

"The question is, do you want him to ply it?" Camid asked, getting to his feet. "And the answer is nay. Come sit over here, lad. I'll see to you."

Miach looked at him. "Do you have any skill with a needle?"

"Oh, aye," Camid said with a grin. "Haven't you seen me darning my socks?"

"I haven't and I don't want to, but I'll trust you anyway," Miach said, sitting down heavily. "Be gentle; I might scream."

Camid stroked his nose thoughtfully. "I could give you a wee tap under the chin first. You wouldn't feel a thing."

"I'll settle for a leather strap between my teeth, thank you just the same."

Camid laughed with far more delight than Miach was comfortable with, but dug about in his pack and came out with something that might have resembled a kit for the odd small job of putting things back together. Miach looked at it in alarm.

"Those look to be awfully thick needles," he said.

"Well, lad, aren't you thick-skinned?" Camid said, with twinkling eyes.

"Nay, I'm not," Miach answered promptly. "And when I look at your gear there, I think I might prefer to bleed to death."

"That's for my saddle," Camid said, setting aside one set of needles and pulling out another. "These are for flesh."

Miach honestly couldn't see how Camid could distinguish between the two, but he supposed it wouldn't make much difference. It especially didn't make any difference when he was treated to the spectacle of watching Morgan and Adhémar walk into camp. The sight of that, the sight of them actually *conversing* without blades drawn, was enough to have him gritting his teeth so hard, the cracking noise drowned out any grunts of pain he might have made.

"Easy, lad," Camid chuckled. "I haven't begun yet."

"Be about it then, friend," Miach said, still through gritted teeth, "while I am distracted."

Camid applied himself to the stitches. "Fond of her, are you?" he murmured.

"Is that really the kind of question"—Miach grunted—"you should be asking right now?" Miach grunted another time or two. It was a more manly noise than yelping. Camid was obviously more suited to stitching saddles than stitching men.

"Your brother is desirable, perhaps," Camid offered, "but he is not for Morgan. I wouldn't worry."

Miach met Camid's eyes. "Did you think I was?" he said. "Worrying?"

"I have two good eyes. And a fine nose for a romance."

Miach grunted. "Don't sniff too hard."

Camid cinched a stitch with enthusiasm. "I never smell amiss. Ah, Morgan, look at who I have here. Apparently he cut himself training."

Miach glared at Camid, who only smiled innocently, then looked up as Morgan came near. She bent down to look at his arm.

"You," she said, meeting his eyes, "need a keeper."

"He'll be fine on his own," Adhémar said smoothly. "Morgan, we should go check on those fine Angesand steeds. Shall we?"

Morgan looked at Adhémar as if he'd suggested a visit to a nearby dung heap. "Thank you, but nay. I'll wait until Camid has finished with Miach."

Adhémar looked wounded. "If you must."

Morgan hesitated, then frowned. "I suppose you can wait as well. If *you* must."

"I would like that very much."

Miach was torn between glaring at his brother, smiling at Morgan's lack of enthusiasm, and yelping over Camid's very businesslike attention to his arm. Camid finished the final stitch and packed up his gear. Miach thanked the dwarf kindly, then rose.

"Why don't I come to the barn with you," Miach said to Adhémar. "An extra pair of hands is always useful."

Adhémar, predictably, ignored him.

Miach was slightly gratified to find that Morgan was ignoring Adhémar in much the same fashion.

She took him by the arm and pulled him toward the barn. "Miach, how did you manage this? Did you run into some bit of the farmer's gear? I should think you'd be more careful than that, being a farmer yourself."

"I was distracted," Miach said under his breath.

He walked along with her and Adhémar as they inspected the horses. He wondered why in the hell he had bothered to say anything to his brother about her. Spite spawned spite, apparently. Unfortunately, he couldn't imagine that his brother was paying any attention to her out of fondness.

Morgan lingered in front of Reannag's stall. Then she looked at Miach. She seemed to consider her words quite carefully. She started to say something several times, then stopped; finally she cursed and spewed out what she'd obviously been chewing on.

"Will magic heal that?" she spat.

Miach was momentarily taken aback. "Aye, it might," he said.

"Do you know any more spells like the one you used on my leg?"

"Spells?" Adhémar echoed. "What spells?"

Miach threw him a warning look. "I disclosed, brother, that you have your own landhold and that I am a farmer. Morgan knows that our mother had a tiny bit of magic which she passed on to us. Useful magic, of the sort you might find on a farm."

"I have no magic," Adhémar growled. "Not anymore."

Morgan frowned. "What does that mean?"

"What it means is that he remembers a spell or two, but he hasn't used them in a while," Miach said. "But he could teach them to you just the same. As we discussed at Chagailt," he said, doing his best to ungrit his teeth. It was very difficult.

Morgan frowned at Adhémar. "I don't care for magic," she said shortly, "but I will do this thing. Your brother will slow us down if this plagues him. Let us be about fixing it."

Miach looked at Adhémar. "Perhaps a spell of binding," he suggested. "Like one would use with a harness, or a plough."

Adhémar considered calculatingly. Miach wished quite suddenly that he hadn't sent his brother plunging into that icy well. Adhémar smiled slowly, then turned to Morgan.

"Let's try this one," he said. "It's crude, but it might do for our purposes."

Miach sat down on a bale of hay. It seemed wise, as he simply couldn't unman himself yet again by showing Morgan any more weakness than she'd seen already. He listened, unsurprised, as his brother taught Morgan the most rudimentary of binding spells. It would bind the edges of the wound together, true, but leave a large, ugly scar. At least it wasn't being used on a slice down the side of his face. Things could have been worse.

Then again, perhaps worse was the touch of Morgan's hand on his arm as she said the words.

It burned like hellfire.

Miach looked down at his arm. The wound was closed, without a trace of it having been there. The stitches were gone as well, being unnecessary. What was left was the imprint of five fingers. Burned into his flesh as if they'd been a branding iron.

He gaped.

Adhémar gaped as well.

Morgan looked at the burns in consternation. "Oh," she said in a small voice. "Did I do that?"

Adhémar clapped his hands together, then rubbed them enthusiastically. "I say we should be abed early. We've a long ride before us. Perhaps tomorrow, Morgan, you would care to ride next to me? We'll travel quickly and stop early. I wouldn't mind training with you, if you have a spare moment. Then perhaps you might be interested in another spell or two. Just useful ones. The kind a swordsman of the finest mettle might find handy as he goes about his business."

Adhémar then made her a low bow, straightened, and favored her with his most dazzling smile.

Miach scowled. Adhémar, being charming. Truly, there was not a more unsettling sight in all the Nine Kingdoms.

Morgan only looked at him blankly. Adhémar tried again with much the same results. He cursed, then spun on his heel and strode from the stables. Miach watched him go, then sighed and leaned back against the stable wall. It wasn't as if he generally competed with his brother for women. His brother attracted those princesses of the realm who were stunningly beautiful, perfectly mannered, and elegantly begarbed in dresses requiring delicate washing so the jewels might not fall off into greedy servants' hands.

Miach, on the other hand, tended to find himself being presented with princesses who were coming his way thanks to their fathers' swords in their backs. There had been the occasional elvish maid admiring him at King Ehrne's court, but those had been rather adventuresome lassies more interested in his spells than in his person.

It did not surprise him that the one woman with whom he'd had a decent bit of conversation would find herself in his brother's sights—no matter Adhémar's true reason for his interest, which Miach suspected had very little to do with Morgan herself and very much to do with her potential as a wielder for Angesand's sword.

Morgan sat down on the hay next to him. "Well," she said finally.

"Well?" Miach asked crossly.

She looked at him, then frowned. "Your arm pains you," she said. She reached out and touched the burn marks.

Miach flinched.

"I'm sorry," she said, looking genuinely so. "I never meant—"

He couldn't tell her that he hadn't flinched from pain. He couldn't tell her that he was presently wasting a great deal of time and energy trying to convince himself that she had no magic. He couldn't say that he was wasting any further unused energy trying to convince himself that she could not possibly be the wielder.

Because if she was the wielder, that would put her in a kind of danger he couldn't bear to think on.

He leaned his head back against the wall and closed his eyes. He couldn't say anything.

Damn it anyway.

She touched his arm again.

Miach shivered.

"Can I fix that?" she asked. "Those marks I made?"

He looked at her. He cursed. He didn't mean to, but there were times a man was forced to take drastic measures to protect his vulnerable parts.

His heart, for instance.

"I'm fine," he said roughly.

He wasn't about to tell her that he would bear the marks of her fingers on his arm for the rest of his life and never regret it for an instant.

She looked at him for a moment or two in silence, then rose, just as silently. Miach sighed deeply after she left. This was his own doing. When would he learn to take his own advice? He should have made certain Adhémar was well, then returned immediately to the palace. He could have been standing in his own comfortable tower chamber, contemplating the affairs of the realm and looking over a list of terrified brides whose fathers were determined to see them wed to him. There was great appeal in that, truly. Who knew but that he might find a woman who would actually remain conscious when presented to him at court?

Stranger things had happened.

The sound of a soft footfall distracted him. He looked up from his contemplation of the hay beneath his feet to find Morgan standing next to him. She put her pack on the bale of hay and arranged it. She looked at Miach.

"Lie down."

"I beg your pardon?"

"Lie down, you fool, before you fall there."

Miach did so only because he was too startled not to. He put his head on her pack then watched in complete astonishment as she covered him with her cloak. She came close to patting him, he was almost certain of it. She did look down at him with something akin to concern in her eyes.

"The blade is still singing," she said. "Will it disturb you?"

Miach listened. He could hear it too, now that it was so

close to his ear, but it was a pleasant, soothing song, so it did not trouble him.

It was a song of Camanaë.

"I'll be fine," he said. "Thank you."

Morgan sat down on another bale of hay at his feet. "I'll keep watch."

"The horses will be fine."

"I wasn't talking about the horses," she said. "Go to sleep, Miach. I vow you need it. Your eyes are very red."

"I haven't been sleeping well."

"You will tonight." She rose, drew her sword, then sat and laid it over her knees. "Sleep in peace."

"Don't let Adhémar take a turn without waking me," he said. "I'll pay for it, else."

She smiled. He saw her do it. "I won't. Now, shut up and go to sleep. I have much to think on."

He imagined she did.

Acid-tongued, ruthless, unyielding girl.

Good heavens, he was lost.

Twenty

❧

M organ looked at her hands as they held Reannag's reins and wasn't sure she recognized them anymore. It wasn't the first time she'd thought that. Indeed, she'd spent an inordinate amount of time considering them over the past month.

But how could she not? She had gone from using them to hold a sword to using them to weave a bloody spell. Was it any wonder she could scarcely stop herself from looking at them?

Spells, swords, calluses, chipped nails—she had them all. And not that she cared, but no man in his right mind would want anything to do with her hands.

She paused. Perhaps that wasn't completely true. Miach didn't seem to be all that frightened of her or her hands. He'd held her hand in his in Hearn's stables when her dreams had troubled her; he'd squeezed it briefly now and again when she'd been overwhelmed by her dreaming; he'd held it the night he'd told her of Catrìona of Croxteth.

She wondered if he might ever do something so foolish as to ask for her hand in marriage.

"Morgan?"

She realized with a start that he was looking at her. "Aye?" she managed.

"You look unwell," he said with a frown.

Unwell? Daft, was more like it. She had a quest, for pity's

sake, then other adventures to pursue. She had no time for a marriage.

Especially to a man who could render her quite sensible self equally insensible by a simple touch of his hand on her hair.

She straightened. "I am well. Just distracted by the noise."

He nodded. "I agree."

The noise was, as fate would have it, the polite discussion going on in front of her. They sat at a crossroads and there was, from all accounts, a difference of opinion on which path might lead in a northerly direction. Well, apparently both would eventually lead one north, but the left-hand way was a straight shot and the right-hand way a more circuitous, interesting route that led past taverns frequented in the past.

Morgan suspected left was the way to go, but she was in unfamiliar country now. It was difficult to truly know which way was best when she had spent the whole of her life on a small island hundreds of miles to the south.

Well, almost all of her life.

The part of her life she remembered, the simple part that had nothing at all to do with her life now—that life that was full of dreams and darkness and wishing she need have no more part of either.

"I say a jaunt wouldn't be out of the question," Camid pointed out loudly. "It would be brief."

"It would have to be," Paien said with a grin. "I daresay you left quite an impression on the locals the last time you were there."

"And how would you know that?" Camid asked.

"They're still speaking of it," Paien said. "At least they were the last time I was here, oh, ten years ago. Deeds worthy of song, my friend. I vow I might be able to find the precise tavern where I first heard the most impressive tale. Shall we search for it?"

Camid stroked his beard and chortled modestly. "How could I refuse? They might want me to scratch out my mark for them. On the wall, or a table, or some such place."

"The keg behind the bar, no doubt," Glines said. "And after that tavern, we'll search out a more respectable part of town where I might replenish my funds. My purse is feeling quite light."

"How could that possibly be the case?" Adhémar asked crossly. "Given that so much of my gold finds home in it?"

"Some day I may find myself unable to game properly," Glines said earnestly. "I'm seeking to put a little away against such a time."

Morgan snorted. She hadn't meant to be involved in this conversation, but the thought of Glines not being able to lighten any and all purses within a five-league radius of himself at any moment and leave those bearing the lightened purses feeling as if they'd had a wonderful time at cards was almost more than she could bear.

"Glines," she said, "you could be drooling into your cups and still manage to pay for your ale. But go if you will and be quick about it. I, for one, grow weary of listening to the three of you complain." She looked at Miach. "What do you think?"

"I think we should continue on our road," Miach said quietly. "I do not like the feeling here—"

"You worry overmuch," Adhémar said. "Let us be about a bit of a lark. Penrhyn is a fine place and I've a mind for a little visit as well."

"Absolutely not," Miach said curtly.

Adhémar drew himself up and glared at his brother. "Who are you to tell me what to do?" he demanded.

"I am apparently the only one who is thinking clearly," Miach said patiently. "You shouldn't go to Penrhyn, brother, and you know why not."

"Trouble last time?" Camid asked. "Give us the tale, Adhémar, and we'll see if it matches any of my exploits."

"It won't," Miach said firmly. "Let the lads go, Adhémar. You remain behind with us."

Morgan watched Adhémar consider that. She could almost see his thoughts flitting across his face. They ended with something that she couldn't call anything but calculation.

"I suppose," he said, drawing his words out to an excessive length. "Who knows that Morgan might need protection while you take time to recover from that cut in your arm that still seems to pain you."

Morgan would have reminded him that she most definitely did not need any protection he could provide, but he looked at her and winked.

She recoiled as if she'd been struck. She looked swiftly at Miach. "Let him go. I'll protect you."

"Nay, I will remain," Adhémar said, smoothing the front of his tunic down over his chest. "Lads, you go on. Have your amusements then meet us a day's ride down this left-hand road. We'll dawdle. Besides," he added, "I was recently in Penrhyn and took care of my business there."

Morgan caught the smirk Adhémar threw Miach's way, but didn't bother to pursue what it might mean. She had enough to think on already. She would have much preferred to have seen Adhémar go off with the lads, but luck was apparently not with her today.

"We'll be off, then," Paien said promptly. "You take care, we'll return in three days' time with supplies, and then we'll continue on our way." He paused. "We might have to have a wee skirmish or two, but that won't add overmuch to the time that we'll be away."

"Are you taking Fletcher?" Morgan asked.

"He's a lad ready for an adventure," Paien said, grabbing the boy by the back of the neck and shaking him. "Aren't you?"

Fletcher only gulped.

Morgan understood. Surely he was not up to any of Paien's or Camid's adventures. She looked at Glines. He nodded slightly in response and she relaxed. Whatever mischief they combined, at least Glines would make sure that Harding's son came out of it with his head atop his shoulders.

Besides, what harm could come to any of them in three days? They certainly deserved a bit of their own amusement after having traipsed after her for so long. And as for her, she found the thought of a brief rest to be not unwelcome.

In truth, the farther north she went, the less haste she wanted to employ.

Perhaps if she'd been to Tor Neroche before, she would have ceased to fear the unknown. If she'd had any idea what to say when she met the king, she might have been less troubled. If she'd been confident that he would even see her, she would have ceased to fret.

Unfortunately, she knew none of the three and she was left to her own imaginings.

And those were not pleasant.

The lads soon rode off on their very expensive horses while Morgan watched them go, hoping it didn't turn out to be a foolish idea. She supposed, however, that she was no judge anymore. She could scarce tell daytime from nighttime; all was darkness and evil about her. When Miach suggested they find a more secure location to set up camp and wait, she could do nothing more than nod dumbly. It was pleasant, in a way that made her feel not at all herself, to allow someone else to make plans for her. She followed where Miach led and stopped when he suggested she do so. She dismounted and leaned against her horse's mane. He didn't seem to mind and she was very grateful for the chance to stop moving.

"Shall we train?" Adhémar asked enthusiastically. "I vow I'm in need of a bit of light exercise."

Morgan realized he was speaking to her only because he was bellowing his words into her ear. "Then seek it from your brother, not me," she said crossly.

"But I need *heavy* exercise," he amended. "Such as only a swordsman of your skill might provide."

Morgan sighed. She suspected that he would not give in, so she did with a weary nod.

"Miach, see to the horses," Adhémar ordered. "Morgan and I are going to train."

Morgan watched as Adhémar walked off, rolling his shoulders and swinging his arms about as if he prepared for heavy exercise indeed, and wished she had said him nay.

Miach took the reins out of her hands. "You needn't do this, if you'd rather not."

"I'll humor him," Morgan said, draping her cloak over her saddle and unfastening her sword from the same. "Perhaps it will shut him up."

"We couldn't be so fortunate," Miach muttered. "But if anyone can manage it, it will be you. Go to, gel, and earn us some peace."

He reached out and patted her shoulder, then led her horse away.

Morgan smiled inside, then turned and walked over to where Adhémar was boasting proudly of his accomplishments with the sword to no one in particular. Morgan couldn't bring herself to sort out truth from wishing anymore with this fool. She let his babbling wash over her and set to her labors.

She fought with him until the sun was well into the afternoon and he determined that to train any longer would put a strain on her. She sent him off, sweating and panting heavily, to find lunch. She went off to find Miach.

He was sitting on a fallen log, staring off into the distance as if he saw something she could not. She had wondered absently if he slept with his eyes open and unseeing. Now, she could see that he was most certainly awake, but very, very far away. She didn't dare disturb him. Something poured off him; the echo of something that she might have called magic if she hadn't known better. Perhaps he *was* dreaming and his nightmares were of the same stuff as hers. Whatever the case, she thought it best to leave him be.

But she couldn't bring herself to move away from him.

So she sat very quietly and found herself unwholesomely glad to have that place. Was it familial affection? She couldn't have said for certain, not having had a brother.

She suspected it was something far different.

She found herself wanting to be near him, to talk to him, to watch him smile to himself when something amused him. She liked it when he put his hand on her hair, or when he pulled her up by her hand and ran with her.

And why not? He was, she could admit quite objectively, rather more handsome than his brother, but in a quieter sort of way. She imagined that Adhémar would eventually go to fat. He would likely sit in his chair in his old age and tell his greatly embellished stories in a very loud voice. Miach would be harvesting turnips or something else useful until the day he died.

Besides, she liked the laughter that seemed to ever run beneath the surface of his eyes, even when they were bloodshot or serious.

"Spells, now?" Adhémar boomed.

Morgan was so startled, she jumped. Miach was so startled, he fell backward off the log and landed with his feet up in the air. Morgan glared at Adhémar but received a conspiratorial wink in return. She found nothing at all amusing or inviting about that wink, so she shot him another glare, then hauled Miach back upright. He looked quite dazed.

"Miach?" she asked. "Are you well?"

"Fine," he said promptly. "I'm fine. I should go."

"I'll come with you," Morgan said.

"But the spells," Adhémar protested. "Wouldn't you care to have another one or two at your command?"

"Later," she said, standing up and pulling Miach with her. She looked at him. "Walk or ride?"

"Ride."

She followed him because she feared not to. He looked almost fey, as if the slightest thing would have plunged him into a world where she would not have been able to call him back. He saddled both their horses before Morgan could gather her wits to help him. He boosted her up into her saddle and swung up into his.

"Where—" she began, but there was apparently no need to ask. Reannag seemed determined to follow his brother, leaving Morgan having nothing to do but hold on and hope she would manage it for as long as was needful.

Miach was, she could admit without shame, the far superior rider. Indeed, it seemed as if horse and rider were one, each knowing what the other intended so there was no need for commands. There came a time when Morgan suspected Miach would have given his horse wings if he'd been able to. Morgan envied him his skill. Perhaps when he was in a less frenzied state, he would be willing to teach her how he rode.

They rode until the sun was setting, though the horses were not winded and seemed fully prepared to continue on. She was, therefore, very grateful when they reached camp again, her horse stopped, and she was able to slide down to the ground. She rested her head against her horse's neck and sucked in great breaths full of horse and sweet night air.

Miach jumped down off his horse and held out his hand for her reins. "I'll walk the horses."

"So will I," she said, holding on to her reins. She absolutely refused to be subjected to the companionship of Adhémar alone by the fire. She shooed Miach on ahead. "Reannag and I will follow you. I'll do what you do."

Miach looked over her head at his brother, then looked at her and smiled faintly. "I see."

"He's boasting to himself," she grumbled. "I can hear him from here."

"You've no stomach for listening?"

"I'd rather listen to you blather on about pigs and magic."

He paused and looked at her quite seriously for a moment, then smiled and nodded for her to come with him. They walked the horses for another half hour, then tended them and their gear. It wasn't nearly delay enough, but it was something.

Once the horses were seen to, she sat down with Miach by the fire.

Adhémar was full of conversation and didn't seem to notice that both she and Miach were not. Morgan let his ramblings evaporate into the night air. It was actually more soothing than annoying, but then again, she wasn't paying any heed to what he was saying.

Until he began again to speak of magic.

"You know," Adhémar said, leaning forward with a gleam in his eyes, "a little magic can be quite a useful thing for a swordsman."

"Can it indeed?" she asked with a yawn. "I would prefer to rely on my skill."

"But skill can be augmented."

"Aye, by more time in the lists," Morgan said pointedly. "Magic is an unmanly pursuit."

"But—"

"Adhémar, enough," Miach said wearily. "Enough. We have heard enough of magic, and swordplay, and tales of your great prowess. *Enough*."

Morgan agreed heartily. Adhémar, not unsurprisingly, did not. He rose and started to fling himself toward Miach, but suddenly he changed his mind. She watched as he stood there, in a towering rage, seemingly unable to make himself leap over the fire and beat his brother senseless as he apparently very much wanted to do.

"Well," Morgan said, surprised, "I'm impressed. Most men don't have that much control over their tempers."

"I daresay Adhémar agrees," Miach said, looking up at his brother tranquilly. "Isn't that so, brother?"

Adhémar took several deep breaths, then took a step backward. He shook himself, as if he had shaken off restraining arms. He shot Miach a look that made Morgan flinch and she was not of unstern mettle. "You'll regret that."

But then he turned to Morgan and put on a pleasant smile. "I do have control over my temper," he agreed smoothly. "A trait many would admire."

"I agree," she said, but her first instinct was to draw her sword and sit closer to Miach. It was ridiculous, of course, for the man was full grown. He could look after himself. Besides, this was his brother. Just the same, Morgan thought that perhaps a bit of distraction might be useful at the moment.

"What were we discussing?" she asked.

"Spells," he said promptly. "And the need for them in a warrior's life."

Morgan frowned. "I do not agree."

"The king has magic," Adhémar said.

"I would like to believe he doesn't use it very often," Morgan said.

"And if your king asked you to learn a spell or two?" Adhémar asked archly.

"Morgan would tell him to go to hell," Miach said shortly. "Adhémar, shut up and let us have a bit of peace. It has been a very long day and you are only lengthening it. Why don't you go have a watch and let us have some quiet?"

Adhémar glared at him. "How dare—"

"Go!" Miach bellowed.

Adhémar rose with a curse, cuffed his brother so hard on the way by that the sound ricocheted in the stillness of the air, and stomped off into the darkness. Morgan looked at Miach, aghast.

"You allowed that?"

"I'm hoping he will bare his arse to the wind tonight and fall backward upon a patch of nettles," Miach said, rubbing his ear crossly.

Morgan laughed. The thought was so singularly appealing that she laughed again.

When she finally controlled her mirth, she dragged her sleeve across her tearing eyes and looked at Miach. He was staring at her as if he'd never seen her before, but a smile was playing about his mouth.

"What?" she asked.

"I've never heard you laugh before."

"Haven't you?" she asked. She smiled again, just for the pleasure of it. "You know, I can't remember the last time I did. But that was quite possibly the most fitting revenge I've ever heard of."

"I thought you liked him," Miach said mildly.

"You know, I don't. I never did. I was confused during our initial encounter, but then he sat up and began to bray." She looked at him and shrugged. "I can't say I'm surprised by my first thoughts about him. I have no experience with men. I mean, that kind of experience," she added. "Well, save Glines, of course, but he does not truly love me."

"I daresay he does," Miach said with a smile. "Hopelessly, no doubt, but he does."

"He is a fool." She looked down at her hands. "Your brother is a different kind of fool. I'm certain he does not want me for me." She looked at him. "Does he?"

Miach stared at her openmouthed. Then he shut his mouth and patted himself suddenly. "Why is it I never have a blade on hand to sharpen when I want to change the subject?"

"I could loan you one of mine."

"Yours are already too sharp." He looked at her. "Cards?"

"Are we changing the subject?"

"Aye, we are. Have you coin in that small purse of yours, or do we wager something else?"

"I have a coin or two," she said, "but that does not seem a very interesting wager."

Miach looked up thoughtfully into the night sky, then back at her. "I'll wager a useful spell against an hour of training with you."

"Miach, I'm dreaming spells even during the day. I'm not sure I want to know any more."

He reached out and covered her hand with his. "Poor girl," he said quietly. "I wish I could take this from you." He paused. "Do you want me to? Take the blade for you to Tor Neroche?"

She caught her breath. It was quite possibly the single most devastating temptation she had ever faced. Every league brought her closer to the end of her quest, but each league seemed to bring her closer as well to the end of her sanity. Darkness covered the journey before her.

But it also covered the distance behind her.

She squeezed his hand. He did not flinch, even though she quickly could not feel her fingers anymore.

"You cannot take this from me," she managed.

He looked at her for several moments in silence. Indeed, Morgan felt the world fall away until it was nothing for her but looking into those palest of blue eyes and wondering if she would ever find herself again.

And then Miach lifted her hand, kissed it roughly, and put it back in her lap.

"A useful spell, then," he said harshly. "Werelight, or some other such rot."

"The ability to cause nettles to grow in a short time?" she asked lightly.

He looked at her, then laughed suddenly. "Aye," he said, clearing his throat. "Aye, that one I might manage."

"All right, then," she said, "but it is absolutely the *last* spell I'm going to learn. I've learned more than I ever intended to and I'm weary of it."

"As you will," he said.

"I had best win this hand quickly," she said, "for I daresay I'll need that very last spell before the first watch is finished."

Miach looked at her from under his unreasonably long eyelashes, laughed again, and dug about in his pack for cards.

Morgan rubbed her arms and moved to sit closer to the fire. She waited until Miach had dealt out their hands before she spoke.

"Thank you," she said seriously.

"For what?"

She considered her cards for some time before she looked at him over them. "I don't sleep well. Somehow, every time I wake, you are not sleeping either. Instead, you are either sitting next to me, or watching me." She paused. "I appreciate the company."

"It is the very least I can do, Morgan," he said. He glanced down at his cards, then smiled. "I daresay you'll owe me an hour of training for this hand."

"Do you *want* to win?" she asked.

"Not really," he said, and he laughed again. "I think I would very much like to lose, that you might have the prize of that very useful spell for speeding the growing of a nasty herb or two."

Morgan smiled as well. In truth, she wanted no more of magic and spells, but the thought of a little something to give Adhémar a rash to concentrate on was welcome indeed.

Besides, Miach's mirth kept the darkness at bay yet a little longer.

She was very grateful for it.

Twenty-one

Miach stood in the pale morning sunlight and watched Adhémar train with Morgan. That did not trouble him. Morgan could have cut Adhémar to ribbons without an effort, but she seemed to be humoring him. Sadly enough, Adhémar had no idea. Miach enjoyed that. He shouldn't have, but he did.

It wasn't even what his brother was saying that troubled him. It would appear that Adhémar had finally become convinced, by some unfathomable leap of logic that Miach had been certain his brother could never make, that Morgan was indeed the wielder. Miach had warned him repeatedly not to overwhelm her with too many spells or she would bolt. Besides, how was he to explain to Morgan that a mere landholder such as Adhémar was purported to be should know so much about magic?

Adhémar ignored him.

Adhémar was also, predictably, suffering from a rather nasty rash. Nettles would do that to a body. Morgan had won the first hand of cards and proved to be quite adept at his nettle-growing spell.

Nay, it wasn't any of those things that troubled him.

It was that he loved her.

Miach paced, smiling, then found that his smile was fading. It was easy enough to consider Morgan, viewed by the light of the fire, and think of her as nothing more than a beautiful, if deadly, shieldmaiden. It was easy enough to look at Morgan, the pale winter sunlight shining down on her dark hair, and think of her as a beautiful woman. It was easy to think of her as a perfect comrade with a smile that would have made a lesser man's knees a little unsteady beneath him.

It was not so easy to think of her as the wielder.

Miach wondered when he'd first known—that he loved her, not that he might have found the answer to the kingdom's troubles. He cast back over the recent past and suspected that it might have been from that first night, when he had caught her in his arms and carried her back to the inn. She'd been lovely and remote, the image of a queen of old.

Then she had woken and looked at him.

Somewhere, somehow during the past endless succession of days, he'd lost his heart for good. His mother had warned him there would be peril in his future. Why hadn't she warned him of the potential for peril to his heart?

"Another spell," Adhémar commanded, shifting uncomfortably as the aftereffects of his sitting apparently caught up with him again. "I'm sure you'll find it useful."

Morgan yawned. "When you can best me," she said, "then I will think on it."

Miach watched his brother throw himself back into the fray with all his strength and force. Even Miach had to credit him with a valiant effort.

Unfortunately for him, king of Neroche or not, he was simply not Morgan's equal. Morgan finally rid him of his sword in disgust.

"I'm finished," she said, resheathing her sword with a scowl. "You be finished too."

"A spell, just the same," Adhémar cajoled.

Miach was on the verge of telling him to just be silent or he would find himself helped to silence when he caught wind of a change in the air. He turned and looked behind him to see the rest of their company riding as if the very demons of hell were after them. Morgan walked over to him.

"They look unsettled," she remarked.

"Is it Glines outrunning a disgruntled gambler?" Miach asked, trying for levity.

"I wonder," Morgan murmured.

Paien thundered up and jumped down off his horse with the energy of a man half his age. He ran up to Miach, panting hard.

"We must away."

Miach looked at him in surprise. "Why?" What had he missed? He'd been concentrating on the border, true, but surely he would have sensed something coming toward them with evil intent. Then again, given his experience near Chagailt, he knew he shouldn't have been surprised by anything. Apparently, there were things going on in the realm that he was not marking.

An unsettling trend, to be sure.

"Ghouls," Paien said succinctly. "Tales of them everywhere. We heard they were searching for something."

"Or someone," Glines said, coming to stand next to Paien. He looked at Miach seriously. "We saw a few. Not many, but terrifying just the same. We outrode them easily, but that safety will not last. I daresay we would do well not to camp in the open unless we are prepared to be assaulted."

Miach nodded, considering furiously. Someone was being stalked. He could only assume it was Adhémar. Lothar couldn't possibly know anything about Morgan. It was he and Adhémar who drew the evil to them. The sooner that they were away, the better it would be for Morgan.

The safer for Morgan.

The truth of it sank into his heart and refused to move. He tried to turn away, but found he couldn't. He wanted to walk away, but his feet remained rooted to the ground. The reality of it was as bracing as a blow across the face.

The farther north they rode, the more danger Morgan unwittingly rode into.

Perhaps Lothar did not seek him; it was a certainty Lothar sought Adhémar. That did not begin to reckon anything about the magic Miach still couldn't identify. It was a treacherous mire of danger Morgan walked into without any idea of what she faced. She thought she simply carried a blade to the king of Neroche.

Miach knew better.

He wrenched himself away from where his body seemed to want to remain and started to pace. Perhaps he was wrong about her, about all of it. Just because she had dreamed once of the Sword of Angesand didn't mean that she was destined to be the wielder of it. Just because she dreamed dreams of Gair of Ceangail that were so detailed she could repeat while awake the spells she'd heard while asleep did not mean she possessed magic enough to wield the Sword of Angesand. Just because he was certain that she was Gair's daughter didn't mean she was destined to wield that sword.

He could take Nicholas's knife for her.

He could send her far away from Tor Neroche.

What he could not do was send her to her death.

"Let us ride, then," Morgan was saying to Paien.

Paien didn't move. "Morgan, lass, you know I'll follow you anywhere, but don't you think 'tis time you told us where we're going?"

Morgan bowed her head for a moment, then lifted it and looked at him. "I'm going to the palace of Tor Neroche." She paused. "I can say no more."

Paien did not look all that surprised. The man was canny indeed. "No more needs to be said," he said briskly. "Let us be off."

"Are you too weary to ride?" Morgan asked.

"We aren't. And the horses will do as we ask." He shook his head in wonder. "Magnificent beasts."

"Great-hearted," Morgan agreed. "We'll break camp and be ready to ride immediately. Miach?"

Miach felt her touch on his arm. "Aye?" he croaked.

"Come," she said simply. "We must away."

"Aye," he agreed. He looked down at her and would have liked nothing more than to have taught her a spell of shape-changing and bid her fly off to safety with him.

Unfortunately, he was no place of refuge. He would have to send her off on her own. He would, however, need to find the proper time to do it. Perhaps when Adhémar wasn't looking. Perhaps when the rest of the company was asleep. Perhaps when they had ridden far enough from the danger Paien had spoken of for him to feel certain Morgan wouldn't encounter it on her way back to Melksham.

He nodded briskly and went to saddle his horse.

* * *

They rode north, the miles being consumed by the hooves of the marvelous Angesand horses. Miach finally forced the company to stop at an inn. He dismounted and waited for the rest of the company to do so as well. Miach studied the inn. He wasn't pleased with the look of it, and he wasn't without the resilience and stamina to keep going, but he had to stop. He was certain that they had far outridden whatever Paien had caught sight of. It would do no harm to rest here. Indeed, Miach suspected this might be a good place to stop for the night.

Giving him the perfect opportunity to convince Morgan that she should return home by the most direct route possible.

"I'll watch first," Camid offered. "Go ahead inside and eat. Just save me something."

"I'll stay as well," Paien said. "Glines, take Fletcher with you and make certain Morgan doesn't eat everything."

Morgan scowled at him before she walked into the inn. Miach followed her over to a table by the fire. He set his pack down, then went to find them something to eat. Once that was seen to, he sat down with her, Adhémar, Glines, and Fletcher, and was unashamedly grateful for a seat that didn't move.

It took some time, but soon the conversings of the men around him began to make sense to his ears. Miach suppressed the urge to look over his shoulder when he heard the king's name being mentioned. He did manage to not look at Glines, though that was something of an effort too.

"I've seen him fight," said a man behind Morgan. "Remarkable, and make no mistake about that. I've never seen a finer."

"Ah, but all his brothers are decent men of war," said another. "Each with his own strengths. 'Tis rumored the next down, Prince Cathar, is an even finer swordsman than the king."

"That isn't possible," said the first.

"Aye, it is."

An argument ensued. Miach paid little attention to it. Indeed, he could have ignored the rest of the conversation, but then another, more lucid-sounding voice cut through the arguing.

"But you've missed the most interesting of the princes," that clear voice said. "The Prince Archmage!"

"His name escapes me," someone slurred.

"Not pronounceable," said another. "And 'tis bad luck to do so."

"So I hear as well," said the strongest voice. "Though I don't know why. Perhaps it angers him."

Adhémar snorted. Miach didn't dare look at him, so he concentrated on his ale. Morgan looked with interest over her shoulder.

"You know," said one, "I've heard that the youngest—"

"The archmage—" put in another.

"Aye, the archmage," the man said impatiently. "I've heard that all the talents of all the brothers are manifest tenfold in him."

"In truth?"

Adhémar snorted so loudly that he choked. Morgan glared at him and turned her attention back to the conversation going on behind her. Miach exchanged a bland look with Glines.

Glines only smiled in return.

"He can outride the king, outfight Cathar the Fierce, weave melodies in the wind that would shame Nemed the Fair, and other things that normal men couldn't do even if they had magic—and the archmage can do all these things in spite of his magic."

"Is that so," said one of the men. "Then heaven preserve us if he intends to do any of that *with* his magic."

Miach buried his thoughts in his cup. He would have happily continued to do so, but Morgan leaned over toward him. "I wonder what it would be like to cross swords with *him*."

"You would likely leave him on his knees, weeping," Miach whispered back.

"There are limits to my skill."

"You jest," he said seriously. "I can't think of a man who can stand against you. And you need no finger-waggling to improve your swordplay."

"It doesn't sound as if this archmage does either," Morgan said.

"Oh, enough," Adhémar said crossly. He glared at them both, got to his feet with a curse, and walked out of the inn.

Morgan looked at Miach. "What ails him?"

"Envy," Miach said promptly. "No doubt you bested him once too often. Are you finished?"

"Not by half," she said, and applied herself to her meal.

Miach caught Glines still looking at him. Glines winked, then continued on with ingesting a substantial repast. Miach supposed he should probably do the same thing. Who knew when he next would have a decent meal?

He corrected himself. He might have a decent meal once he reached the castle, but would he manage to eat it?

He suspected not.

"How much farther?" Morgan asked, pushing her plate away finally. "Miach? Glines?"

"Three days, on the outside," Glines said. "If we ride hard."

Morgan leaned forward. "Will we get inside the gates, do you think?"

Fletcher leaned in as well. "Why wouldn't we?" he whisper-ed.

"They're guarded by magic," Morgan said seriously. "Didn't you know?"

"But, Morgan, you don't believe in magic," Fletcher breathed.

Miach found himself on the receiving end of a very pointed look from Morgan before she turned back to Fletcher.

"I don't *like* magic," she said, "but I must concede that it exists. Don't rely on it, though. It is fickle."

Fletcher nodded seriously. Miach counted that as one of Weger's rules that the boy would now emblazon upon his memory and carry with him for the rest of his days.

Miach sat back and looked at his companions sitting around that table. He was a little surprised by how much affection he'd grown to feel toward them in such a short time. They were good souls. Honest. Trustworthy.

And, in Morgan's case, too dear for his peace of mind.

He was tempted, almost beyond his ability to resist, to remain at the table and bask in the warmth of the fire and in the radiance that was Morgan of Melksham, but he knew he couldn't. He had to put his plan in action.

He had no choice.

"I think," he said suddenly, as if it had just occurred to him, "that we should stay the night."

Morgan looked at him in surprise. "Think you?"

"I do," he said firmly. "Rest the horses, and all that."

"But Miach," she said slowly, "what of those creatures? What of the rumors of them?"

He would see to them after she was safely away, but he didn't dare say as much. "I think we have lost them. After all, we will be safely ensconced in the inn. I imagine we won't have any trouble with them."

"If you say so," she said doubtfully.

Miach watched her exchange a look with Glines, who shrugged, then she nodded.

"Very well," she said. "Let us go guard the horses while the others eat, then we'll come back and inquire about chambers."

Miach rose when the rest of his dinner companions did, paid the serving girl extra, then left the common room. He waited with Morgan, Glines, and Fletcher as Paien and Camid had their turn. Of Adhémar, there was nothing to be seen. Miach didn't worry. He couldn't have been so fortunate as to have had his brother go ahead without them.

Time proved him right. Adhémar returned as Camid and Paien came outside. They gathered together for a moment to review their plans for traveling farther that night. Miach was just preparing to inform the others of his plan before the peace of the evening and the comfort of their full bellies was disturbed.

Hell broke loose.

Miach watched in astonishment as a half dozen creatures of the kind he had grown accustomed to seeing sprang out from the shadows of the inn. He wasn't sure if he was more surprised that he hadn't noticed them, or that they made straight for Morgan.

Morgan jerked Fletcher behind her and dispatched two with only a slight bit of effort. Miach didn't even have a chance to draw his sword before the others were seen to.

Morgan?

They had come for Morgan.

He could hardly believe it, but he knew he had to. It proved to him beyond doubt that he had to act.

"Convinced?" Adhémar panted, sheathing his sword and glaring at him. "There is no safety on the road."

"I never disagreed with that," Miach said. "I was thinking we should pass the night here—"

"You're mad," Adhémar said. "We must make for Tor Neroche as quickly as possible. It is our only hope of safety."

"And speaking of safety, there is something we must discuss." Miach nodded curtly at his companions, then took his brother by the arm. "Excuse us."

Adhémar tried to pull his arm away. "What do you mean, excuse us? I've business—"

"With me," Miach said shortly. He dragged the very resistive king of Neroche out of earshot, then turned on him. "I'm sending her home," he began without preamble.

"You're sending who home?" Adhémar said, jerking his arm away and rubbing it in annoyance.

"I'm sending Morgan home."

"You're *what*?" Adhémar said incredulously.

"I'm sending her back to Melksham. She'll be safe there."

Adhémar looked at him as if he'd never seen him before. "But she's the wielder!"

"We don't know that."

"You convinced me."

"My mistake," Miach said shortly. "I don't care what she's capable of. She's a target and I won't be responsible for putting her life in jeopardy."

"And I don't want to lose what might turn the tide," Adhémar snarled. "I want her in Tor Neroche and I want her hand on that blade. If it calls her name, I fully intend to use her to win the war."

"Adhémar, you fool, she might die!"

"And I don't take that risk with every sortie?" Adhémar retorted. "Perhaps you have yourself safely tucked inside your tower, but I do not enjoy such luxury—"

Miach punched his brother in the mouth before he thought better of it.

Matters did not improve from there.

When they finally pulled themselves apart, Miach was rapidly losing sight from one swollen eye and Adhémar was clutching his nose with his hand as blood gushed from it. Miach glared at his brother.

"I have been places you wouldn't dare dream about," he said coldly.

"And you have shown me the one person who might possibly spare my kingdom," Adhémar said, likewise quite chilly in his tone. "You have a *duty* to your liege lord to aid him in keeping that kingdom safe. Until I have my magic back, I'll use Morgan however I have to."

Miach folded his arms over his chest and suppressed the urge to break a few of his brother's bones. "I might be able to determine what's happened to your magic if you'd just let me look at that damned sword of yours."

Adhémar put his hand protectively over his blade. "I'm not convinced you don't want it for yourself. I'll do my own investigations. And until that time, your duty lies in doing what I tell you to do."

Miach had to clench his hands down by his sides to keep from throttling his brother. "My duty does not include sending a woman to her death."

"It certainly does, if that death happens while ensuring the safety of the realm."

"I—"

"Your *duty* is to the kingdom first, Mochriadhemiach," Adhémar snarled. "Surely you are old enough to understand that. Or perhaps the mantle was misplaced?"

And with that, he turned and walked away.

Miach couldn't have been more winded if Adhémar's horse had kicked him in the gut. He leaned over until he thought he could catch his breath.

Duty.

He remained where he was, hunched over with his hands on his thighs, sucking in breath until the nausea and the shock receded.

Adhémar was right. He had a duty to the kingdom, a duty that came before what he wanted or what Morgan wanted or even what Adhémar wanted. If the potential wielder had been anyone but Morgan, he would have strapped the lad to the back of his horse and thundered back to the palace without a second thought. If the wielder had been anyone but Morgan, he would have moved mountains to get the lad to Tor Neroche and slap that sword in his hands in order to stem the tide of erosion.

If it had been anyone but Morgan, he wouldn't have felt as if there was a hole in his gut that would gnaw at him through eternity because he would be responsible for making her life hell.

Damn it, he hated it when Adhémar was right.

It happened so seldom.

He looked up at the sparkling night sky and blew out his breath. What he wished, briefly, was that he had never touched the Sword of Angesand, that he had never left Tor Neroche, that he had never once clapped eyes on Morgan.

Salvation of the realm.

Destruction of his heart.

But what to do now? As Adhémar had so kindly pointed out, his duty dictated his actions, no matter how he might feel about it. He was duty bound to see that Morgan went to Tor Neroche. His position as archmage, demanded that he see that she at least held the Sword of Angesand. He had a responsibility to the inhabitants of not only Neroche, but the Nine Kingdoms, to use everything and everyone in his power to not only keep Lothar at bay, but destroy him if possible.

But Morgan . . .

"Miach?"

He closed his eyes briefly, then straightened and looked at her. "Aye?"

"We're ready."

"Of course." He swallowed with difficulty. "Of course."

"You look terrible." She paused. "But Adhémar looks worse."

He smiled in spite of himself. "A little disagreement."

"Hmmm," she said. "Well, disagreement or no, Adhémar says there is danger and we must ride."

Miach nodded. "Aye."

"Then let us be off. I do not fear danger, but I cannot see subjecting my comrades in it when flight would evade it."

If he hadn't been so numb already, he would have lost his breath with a whoosh. "You are a loyal companion," he said, finally.

"Loyalty is highly prized," she said quietly.

"As highly prized as magic is shunned?"

She smiled faintly. "Weger has a very unique code of conduct."

"I daresay," he said. "Perhaps you'll tell me more of his strictures someday."

"It would be a welcome reprieve from too much magic," she said quietly.

He looked down at her. "It troubles you?"

She took a deep breath. "I am no coward, but I vow, Miach, that if I had not given Nicholas my word to deliver this blade to the king at Tor Neroche, I would turn around, brave the ship, and return to Melksham." She paused for quite some time. "I don't know if I can carry these burdens much longer."

"It weighs upon you, doesn't it?" he asked softly. "The blade and your dreams?"

"More with every step we take north."

He nodded slowly.

"I want," she said finally, "*nothing* more to do with magic, mages, or my dreams. *Nothing*."

Miach nodded. "I can't blame you."

"I don't blame *you*," she said quickly. "Then again, I don't consider you a mage of any sort. You can't help what you can do." She paused. "I suppose neither can I. But I want no more of it than necessary."

And here he was on the verge of plunging her into magic she might never escape from.

"Duty is a difficult thing, at times," he offered finally.

"Hmmm," she said. She took his hand and pulled him along. "Let us be about it, then. Then perhaps we can move on to something else."

He walked with her back to the horses, then swung up into the saddle. Adhémar took the time to curse him, then wheeled his horse about and rode off into the dark. The rest of the company followed. Miach found himself riding next to Morgan, as had become their custom. Even in the dark, he could see the worry on her face.

"Paien was right," she said.

"Aye," Miach agreed.

"Will it grow worse, do you think?"

"I fear so," he admitted.

She was silent for quite a while. "I fear," she began hesitantly, "I fear they are coming for me."

Miach didn't dare disabuse her of the notion. "It is possible," he said.

Aye, that was indeed possible.

He couldn't count Adhémar's most recent battle on Neroche's northern border. That was a common occurrence. But Morgan had been at the first attack with Adhémar near Istaur. She had been at the second attack with him. She had been at the inn behind them.

But why would Lothar know anything of her?

He shook his head. It made no sense. Just because she could wield a Camanaë spell of un-noticing did not mean she was the possessor of that magic.

Surely there were many alive who could use the spells of Camanaë without having any of that magic flowing through their veins.

Though he couldn't bring a single bloody one of them to mind.

Was it possible that Lothar had been searching for Morgan all along?

"Miach?"

Miach looked at her. Perhaps Adhémar had a point. If Morgan was ensconced in Tor Neroche, she would be safe. Perhaps she would hold the Sword of Angesand and it would remain lifeless in her hand. Her potential to be the wielder would be proved wishful thinking, but she would be within the walls where Miach could guard her.

Perhaps his duty would be a good thing in the end.

"Nothing," he said finally.

"That wasn't what I said," she said. "I asked if you thought they were coming for me."

He shook his head. "I don't know, Morgan. But what I do know is the walls of Tor Neroche offer safety."

"Even to farmers?" she asked doubtfully.

"Even to farmers," he assured her. "But most assuredly to dutiful carriers of blades destined for kings."

She looked at him for a moment or two, then nodded. "I

will see if I can win a place for all of us," she said. "You have been very valiant as well."

He smiled, but it was a pained one. If she only knew . . .

He nodded his thanks and turned his face forward. The castle was three days' hard ride ahead. Three days before they would know the truth of her gifts. Three days before he would have to tell her the truth about himself.

Three days before he would fulfill his duty.

Duty.

What a bloody awful word.

Twenty-two

❧

Morgan rubbed her face with her free hand. It didn't aid overmuch with the weariness, but it was one of the ways she used to stay awake. What she wanted to do was sleep for a solid se'nnight. She wanted it so desperately, she was tempted to simply lean over, put her head on Reannag's neck, and close her eyes. Would the horse continue to carry her, or would he allow her to fall off? It was indication enough of her state that she didn't care which it would be.

She sat up straighter and pulled the hood back off her head. The chill brought some semblance of clarity back to her mind. It was little wonder she was tired; no doubt the entire company was tired. They had ridden north almost without ceasing from the battle at the inn. The weather had worsened. The road had worsened. Even her mood had worsened, for the closer she got to the king's palace, the more she wanted to bolt the other way.

The blade continued to sing from the bottom of her pack.

In fact, the song had begun to get in the way of her hearing the men around her.

That was just as well, for there had been much commentary on her choice of destinations from all corners.

"Halt," Adhémar said suddenly.

Morgan peered blearily into the distance and saw a company riding toward them. Outriders from Tor Neroche? She could scarce believe that she might have actually come this close to reaching her journey's end, but perhaps the impossible had actually become reality.

Adhémar swept them with a look. "I will go ahead and see if I can bargain for entrance. Remain here."

Morgan yawned hugely and gave in to temptation. She leaned over, wrapped her arms around Reannag's neck, and closed her eyes. It was so marvelous, so decadent, she feared she might never be able to straighten again. And bless the steed, he didn't complain. The only time she felt him move was when she realized she was truly falling asleep. Perhaps he sensed it too and wished to spare her an undignified tumble.

"Morgan."

She sat up suddenly, bleary-eyed. She rubbed her eyes and found that Miach was next to her. "Aye?"

"I thought you might fall off soon."

Morgan couldn't even manage a decent nod of agreement. She looked ahead of them and saw that Adhémar was still speaking with the outriders. She wasn't convinced he would win them entrance. Unfortunately, she could do nothing but wait behind, in the snow, shivering, and wonder if she had just given her chance to complete her quest into the hands of a fool. She should have gone ahead herself. But that would have meant yet more time in Adhémar's company and she simply couldn't bear the thought of that.

At least the journey with such terrible haste had rid her of Adhémar's constant harping on magic and its usefulness. She did not agree and she was tired of arguing with him. She had come to the point where she did her best to ignore him. That task was made much easier by the sounds of her blade singing.

She could scarce hear anything else.

Actually, that wasn't true. She suspected that the ring might have joined in with the blade.

If she hadn't made Nicholas a promise, she would have heaved her entire pack into the nearest patch of briars and been well rid of it.

"Well," she said finally, looking at Miach, "perhaps he will manage it."

"Aye," he said, his tone curiously flat.

"Will you not be relieved?"

He managed a wan smile. "I will be relieved when we are inside the walls and you are safe."

"I am safe out here," she reminded him. "As are you, with me to guard your back."

He smiled truly then. "Aye, you have that aright. I am grateful for it." He looked up. "Oh. It looks as if he managed it."

Morgan found herself somewhat relieved by the sight of Adhémar riding back their way. He seemed to be very pleased with himself. She supposed she couldn't blame him, but having to listen to him brag about it for the foreseeable future would make for a very tedious ride.

"Come," Adhémar boomed. "I have seen to it all."

Moran pursed her lips. Aye, here it came.

"I will ride ahead, of course, but you may all follow. Slowly," he added. "I will pave the way."

Well, that was something at least.

"Good of you," Morgan muttered.

Miach snorted, but said nothing else. He did smile briefly at her before he urged his horse forward. Slowly.

They made their way up a very long winding road. Morgan was too preoccupied with the blade in her pack and the damned ring as well to pay much heed to her surroundings. She was cold, tired, and nervous. It was work enough to keep her mount on the road.

The day went on endlessly. The snow was blinding in its brightness and the road ceaseless in its twisting and turning.

"Morgan."

Morgan looked at Miach in annoyance. He pointed upward.

Morgan humored him by looking.

She felt her mouth fall open. She didn't even manage to rein her horse in. She simply clutched the reins and gaped, feeling every inch the country miss who had never stepped out of her pigsty.

It was Tor Neroche, perched high above her on the edge of a cliff. Actually, it looked as though it had simply grown out of the rock, daring the unwary and the unwashed to venture beneath its mighty shadow. It was terrifying and beautiful all at once.

"Oh," she managed, finally. "It's magnificent."

He smiled. It seemed something of a sad smile, which only made sense if he wished such a place might have been his. Morgan shook her head.

"Do not envy the king this palace," she said, struggling to master her own surprise. "I imagine he longs for a garden such as yours and the peace with which to farm it."

"Think you?" Miach asked quietly.

"I daresay. Though this is a bloody impressive palace, isn't it?" she managed. "And these just the outer walls." She paused. "Are they guarded by magic in truth, or is that rumor, do you suppose?"

"I've heard that magic was woven into the foundations," he said slowly. "I imagine it finds itself everywhere here."

Morgan shivered. "Dreadful."

"Safe."

"But at what price?"

Miach nodded thoughtfully. "I suppose."

Morgan rode on for quite some time under the shadow of those enormous outer walls. She supposed there wasn't a ladder built tall enough to touch their crenelated tops, nor a lad born brave enough to try to scale them. The wall was made of massive granite blocks, held together with heaven only knew what, and tilting out at an alarming angle that gave those who rode under them the impression that they were about to be crushed beneath them.

At least she had that impression.

Paien looked equally as nervous.

Camid's nose was quivering, but he was made of very stern stuff.

The farther along they went, the more Morgan realized that she was a very, *very* small part of a much larger world. True, she bore in her pack a blade that Nicholas of Lismòr had bid her bring to the king, but what did that mean? For all she knew, the king wouldn't be bothered to see her. Perhaps she would only deposit the blade into the hands of a retainer, then be shown the front gates.

Assuming she made it inside the front gates to be shown back out of them.

"Morgan."

Morgan looked at Miach. Her mouth was appallingly dry and her eyes unsettlingly moist. Good heavens, was her form going to desert her fully now?

"Aye?" she croaked.

Miach tapped his finger meaningfully over his left eyebrow.

Morgan touched Weger's mark. It seemed a very small thing, somehow, when compared to what she was seeing now. "But—"

"The king would give his right arm to fight as you do. He would take you as his champion in less time than it takes me to say as much—and count himself more fortunate than any of the other eight kings."

She managed a frown. "You are a flatterer."

"Never," he said seriously. "Of all the things I am, a flatterer is not one."

"I will likely not even see the king."

Miach pursed his lips. "Then it will be his loss." He looked at her meaningfully. "Do not forget who you are."

She felt apprehension well up in her so suddenly and so strongly that she caught her breath. It took her quite some time to be able to draw a normal one again. When she could, she looked at him.

"Will you stay with me?" she croaked. She cleared her throat. "If you can?"

He smiled, but he looked a bit winded, as if he'd had his own brush with something devastating. "I will," he said finally. "I would count it an honor."

And then he looked at her for so long that she thought she might have blushed if her cheeks hadn't been so red already from the chill. There was something in his expression she simply could not understand.

Was it affection?

Was it resignation?

Was she losing what few wits she had left?

She couldn't say and didn't dare speculate. Perhaps later, when her task was finished and she could think clearly. Perhaps Miach would stay with her until then. Perhaps then he would be willing to speak of other things besides swords and magic.

Perhaps.

She found herself unsettled by something that annoyed her, only to realize it was the singing of the bladc. If nothing else, at least ridding herself of *that* might improve her mental state.

Morgan set her face forward. Damned goose-feather mattress. Bloody magic-slathered knife.

What was to become of her now?

She considered that until they crossed the massive drawbridge, rode underneath the terrifying spikes of the raised portcullis, and managed to get past the third defense of the massive iron gates. By that time Morgan had forgotten who she was, where she came from, and what she carried in her pack. She was clinging to consciousness by means of her pride alone. She would have given even her horse to have slunk off back through the gate, under the portcullis, and over the drawbridge to leap down into the snow and hide.

"The palace is made to impress," Glines said, dropping back to ride beside her. "It was once, if you can believe it, a hunting lodge."

Morgan blinked in surprise. "You jest."

"I do not," Glines said, looking far too comfortable.

Then again, he didn't have a damned blade in his pack, singing loudly and distracting him.

"How do you know?"

"I have been here before," Glines said. "With my father." He smiled. "I was shown about by one whose task that is."

"Surely not," she said.

"Surely, aye. They show visiting nobility about the palace to impress and intimidate them. I'll pretend to be one of the servants now and show you about."

"But I'm already intimidated," Morgan protested.

"I'm not," Miach said, "so you can show me the palace. What can you tell us now?"

"Well," Glines said importantly as they rode along through the outer bailey that looked as if it might have housed an entire country in a pinch, "Tor Neroche was actually Yngerame of Wychweald's hunting lodge. This was several generations ago."

"Several," Morgan repeated reverently.

"Aye," Glines said. "When Yngerame crowned his son Symon, he gave him his hunting lodge to use for a palace and Neroche to use for a country."

"But it wasn't this grand," Morgan said.

"I daresay not," Glines agreed. "So when Symon wed with Iolaire of Ainneamh, he simply could not have brought an elven princess to such a mean hall, so he built her the palace of Chagailt."

Morgan looked at Miach with raised eyebrows. "That was a handsome gift."

He nodded in response and Morgan suspected he was thinking of Queen Iolaire's gardens that they had run through so heedlessly.

"Aye, well, Chagailt was beautiful, but it was vulnerable to attack. It has been destroyed and rebuilt a time or two. When Gilraehen the Fey was king, he decided that for the safety of his family and the crown, he needed somewhere more defensible. He retreated here. Over the years it has been strengthened until it has become the palace you see today. Tor Neroche; Neroche of the Mountains."

"I think I like Chagailt better," Morgan murmured.

"You haven't seen the inside," Glines said. "Wait until you've seen the great hall before you pass judgment. For now, let us see if we can at least get ourselves inside the front doors." He looked at Morgan. "Are you going to tell us now why we are here?"

"I am not," Morgan said.

Glines shrugged. "Very well. Off we go then. There are the front doors. I suppose we'll see if Adhémar was able to talk his way inside and gain us entrance as well."

Morgan nodded, though she had acquired a knot in the pit of her stomach that seemed determined to remain there despite her best efforts to make it disperse. She kept her head down and followed the horses in front of her until they stopped. Then she looked up.

Well, those must have been the front doors. Morgan sat in her saddle, clutching her reins, and wondered what to do now. Miach dismounted, then looked up at her.

"Coming?"

"Of course," she croaked. She swung down out of the saddle with as much grace as possible. Her knees came close to knocking together. She credited that with the great amount of hard riding she'd done recently. It surely had nothing to do with trepidation over where she was.

A servant approached. Morgan wasn't one to hide, or to shrink back, but she found herself gladly standing behind Glines as he discussed their situation with the servant. Fletcher had tucked himself in behind her. Even Miach had pulled his hood up over his face and appeared to be trying to be unnoticed. Only Paien and Camid looked the same as they always did: alert and watchful, but not afraid.

Morgan was terrified.

There, she had admitted it. It hadn't been all that hard. Shameful, but not hard.

"'Tis big," Fletcher whispered.

"Very," Morgan agreed quietly.

"My father would wet himself at the sight."

Morgan looked over her shoulder at him, then laughed in spite of herself. "Ah, but you have that aright, lad. This is a far cry from anything on Melksham. And to think the Lord Nicholas thinks he has a luxurious life." She shook her head. "Astonishing."

Glines came back to stand by her. "The servant is expecting us. Apparently Adhémar talked them into giving us a chamber for our use." He paused. "You are going to have to state your business at some point, Morgan. To someone."

"I know her business," Miach said. He reached out and took Morgan by the hand. "Come, shieldmaiden. We'll find our chamber and then perhaps go for a little explore."

"Food," Paien suggested.

"Sleep," Glines sighed.

"Silence," Morgan whispered. She looked up at Miach. "The singing is starting to deafen me."

"The knife?" he asked in a low voice.

"And the ring as well, I think." She paused. "Am I going mad?"

He squeezed her hand. "I daresay not. Let's find this luxurious chamber we've been promised, then eat. I'm sure things will look a bit better after supper and a good rest."

Morgan looked at their horses. "And these?"

"They will be cared for in a manner befitting their breeding," Miach said.

"How do you know?"

"I watched Glines pay the head stable lad to see to it," he said.

"That would do it," Morgan murmured as she followed him in through the front doors. No one seemed to mark them as they passed. She walked with Miach, stunned and overwhelmed, for quite some time before something occurred to her. "Miach?"

"Aye?"

"Why didn't you go home?" she asked.

He pushed his hood back off his face and looked at her solemnly. His eyes were very pale in the torchlight that seemed to be everywhere in the passageway, driving back the shadows.

"I thought you might need me," he said quietly.

"Oh," she said. She took a deep breath. "Thank you."

"It was nothing."

"It is something to me."

He pulled his hood up again, squeezed her hand, and walked with her down the passageway. Morgan was grateful for that, somehow, and that her companions had encircled her, Paien and Camid leading, Miach and Glines on either side, and Fletcher walking behind. She looked over her shoulder at him.

"Don't lose yourself."

He shook his head vigorously. "Won't."

Morgan nodded and took comfort in their companionship. She would have to thank Nicholas for it at some point. She wondered if she would have managed to even walk upright instead of crawling if she'd been by herself.

It was, she conceded, difficult to remember you were an important person when your surroundings made you feel the size of a child. She wondered how Weger might fare.

Better than she, no doubt.

The servant stopped before a door, opened it, then stood back for them to enter.

Morgan walked inside and gaped. She wondered if that might possibly be her continual reaction to Tor Neroche. The chamber was nothing short of sumptuous.

It was also seemingly prepared just for them. There were low couches lining the walls to one side, seven in number. On the other side of the chamber was set a dining table and other chairs for relaxing and conversing after the meal. A fire blazed in a massive hearth. Food was being brought in and laid on a sideboard.

Morgan found herself wishing quite desperately for a bath.

The company was ushered in, then the servants withdrew and left them to themselves.

There was water at least for the washing of hands and faces and a prettily written note that promised more washing on the morrow if desired. Apparently food and sleep were what the masters of the castle had decided were most important. Morgan had to agree.

So she ate wondrous things with her companions, said fairly intelligent things after supper when they sat before the fire, then found that her only desire was to find a bed and make use of it. She put her pack on the floor but hardly dared crawl between such costly sheets. Miach seemed to have no compunction about the like. He pulled off his mud-encrusted boots and stretched out his filthy self upon a goose-feather quilt. He looked at her as she sat gingerly on the bed next to his.

"Well?" he asked. "Aren't you going to make use of that?"

"I don't dare."

"Dare. You need to sleep." He reached over and pulled her pack up to sit between their beds. "There. It will be safe here and you will be safe there. Sleep, Morgan, while you may. You can be about your business tomorrow."

She nodded numbly. Perhaps it was the length of the day. Perhaps it was the grandness of the surroundings. Perhaps it was a bit of disbelief that she should be in such a place. She lay down and found that tears were slipping from her eyes and dripping down to wet her hair.

Miach reached for her hand and held it. "All will be well," he said, very quietly.

She nodded, but she wondered. The knife in her pack had quieted down, so perhaps sleep was not so unreasonable an expectation for herself. She nodded again, closed her eyes, and knew she would never sleep.

"Miach?" she asked sleepily.

"Aye, love," he said softly.

"Where's Adhémar?"

He snorted. "Slumming with the servants, no doubt."

"Does he know many?"

"Aye."

Morgan nodded and allowed herself to relax. The feeling of Miach's hand around hers was comforting, the bed was nothing short of delicious, and the song of the blade and the ring had subsided to a pleasing echo of a whisper.

"Morgan?"

She would have opened her eyes to look at him, but she was simply too weary. "Aye?"

"I have something to tell you," he said softly. "Something important."

She wanted to ask him if he was going to ask her to marry him, chipped nails and callused hands aside, but she couldn't even manage that. Besides, that was too ridiculous, even for her, so she merely nodded. "If you like."

"First thing," he said. "We have to talk first thing tomorrow."

"Hmmm," Morgan said. She felt herself drifting off into the first safe, peaceful sleep she had had in days.

Miach had called her *love*.

That was worth a dozen pleasant dreams.

Twenty-three

❧

Miach wrapped himself in a spell of invisibility and walked swiftly through the midnight halls of Tor Neroche. He hadn't considered how grand a place it was until he had seen it through the eyes of an innocent, honest woman who had never been anywhere so fine. He supposed he might never look at the palace in the same way again.

He'd told her he had something to tell her. And he did. He would tell her who he really was. At least in that much, he would be honest with her.

He ran up the steps to his tower chamber. All was as he had left it. Indeed, a fire burned in the hearth, as if he had merely left to poach something from the kitchen, not flown all the way to Istaur to find his liege lord.

His liege lord that he would have cheerfully strangled if it wouldn't have meant his own neck in trade.

He slammed the door behind him, cast aside his spell as if it had been a cloak, and crossed over to the table still littered with books and sheaves of paper and other things he didn't need and couldn't bear to look at. What he wanted was to be back downstairs, holding the hand of a woman who trusted him; what he needed to do was be about his business quickly so he could—before she woke and found Adhémar right there, more than willing to show her the great hall and that interesting sword hanging over the fireplace.

He turned toward the fire only to find that one of the chairs before it was occupied. He hesitated, then walked over to sit in the vacant chair. He smiled. "Cathar."

Cathar handed Miach a cup of ale. "You look tired."

"I *am* tired," Miach said with a sigh. "Tired and heartsick."

Cathar's eyebrow went up. "Heartsick? That sounds promising."

"It wouldn't, if you knew the entire tale." Miach drank, then set the cup aside and looked at his brother. "Well? Anything interesting transpire during my absence?"

"Haven't you been watching?"

"Of course."

Cathar hesitated only slightly. "I meant, haven't you been watching the castle?"

"I assumed you would see to the castle. I've been watching the borders." He smiled. "What are you going to tell me? Has Rigaud made over the Chamber of the Throne in purple velvets? Or greens, to match his eyes?"

"He tried," Cathar admitted.

Miach managed a brief laugh. "I've no doubt he did. How did Turah fare?"

"As you might expect. He was nimble and canny and left the fighting up to me."

"Wise lad."

"Lad? He's older than you are, Miach."

"And yet so fresh and spry still," Miach said sourly.

"I can see it was a long journey," Cathar said. "Did you not find what you sought?"

"I found more than I sought," Miach said. "I found Adhémar, as well as a few creatures I thought were gifts from Lothar but now I suspect not." He opened his mouth to say more, then shut it.

"And?" Cathar prodded. "Come now, Miach, and tell Cathar all your sorry tidings."

Miach threw him a glare. "Very well. If you must know, I met a woman."

"A woman?" Cathar said in surprise. "You had time to meet a woman?"

"Surprisingly enough. Unfortunately, she's not one I can have."

"Wed?" Cathar asked sympathetically.

"Nay, not wed," Miach said.

Cathar smiled. "Are you going to tell all, or must I guess?"

Miach looked at him in silence for a moment or two. As usual, if there was anyone he trusted inside the walls of Tor Neroche, it was Cathar. He needed a ready ear—and a sensible one. He sighed and leaned forward with his elbows on his knees.

"I found a wielder for the Sword of Angesand."

"You're off topic, brother," Cathar said with a small laugh. "What has that to do with your woman?"

"I believe she is the wielder."

"A woman?" Cathar said, stunned.

"As fate would have it."

"A woman you like?"

"I wouldn't say *like*," Miach said grimly.

"Oh," Cathar said almost silently. "So, your problem is that she doesn't like you?"

"Does it matter?" Miach asked, pained. "I suspect she looks at me like a brother."

"Hmmm," Cathar murmured sympathetically.

"She also bears Weger's mark."

"Scrymgeour Weger?"

"The very same."

Cathar shivered. "She's dangerous then."

"Very. Let's also not forget that if she does prove to be the wielder, she will immediately join forces with Adhémar and I will be left forever looking at them together and wondering why it is I can't bring myself to fall upon the Sword of Angesand in a fit of despair."

"Well, that I might be able to spare you."

Miach blinked. "How?"

Cathar scrunched up his face, as if he thought he might have said too much.

"Cathar," Miach warned, "if you know something—"

"I don't know anything," Cathar said frankly. "You know Adhémar never talks to me."

"What has he done?"

"There's some sort of feast being planned," Cathar ventured carefully. "For a month hence."

"Of course," Miach said grimly. "He's probably set to celebrate finding his wielder and dooming her to being used as his weapon against Lothar."

"I don't think the feast is for that."

"Then what is it for? Yet another banquet to celebrate Adhémar's glorious reign that is devoid of disaster?"

Cathar shifted uncomfortably. "I don't know anything more than that. I suppose we'll find out. Now, what of your woman? Does she know what you think about her?"

"That I love her, or that I think she's the wielder?"

"Either. Both."

"She's ignorant of both, and that is my doing." Miach sighed deeply. "I'm not sure I want her to know either of the two."

"Why not?" Cathar asked. "If she's the wielder, don't you want her to use the Sword of Angesand?"

Miach sighed deeply. "Of course I want the wielder to use the sword. But that was before I knew who the wielder was. That was before I was complicit in bringing a woman here who has no idea what lies in wait for her, what her destiny is, how we intend to use her until her usefulness fails. Does that satisfy you?"

Cathar buried his response in his cup.

"You and I were born to this duty," Miach said. "We could renounce our birthrights at any moment. I could go be a farmer. You could go raise sheep."

"Not now," Cathar observed.

"Of course, not now," Miach returned, "but I could have. Before Mother's mantle fell upon me."

"Could you?" Cathar mused.

"I had a choice," Miach said flatly. "Before she died. I was old enough to understand exactly what my future would hold and I accepted the task."

"Did you understand truly?" Cathar asked. "Fully?"

"I never saw this, if that's what you're asking," Miach said. "And nay, I did not understand how that mantle would come close to crushing me beneath it before I found the strength to bear it properly. But I have been amply rewarded for taking a chance on something I perhaps didn't fully understand. You're missing the point. At some point, you and I understood. We made a choice. Morgan will not be given a choice."

"Won't she?"

Miach shook his head curtly. "She'll touch that damned sword, it will deafen us all with its singing and blind us with the flash of magelight, and then she will be pulled into a life she does not want and never asked for. How will she then say nay?"

"Then why did you bring her here?"

"Duty," Miach said wearily. "My duty to my king."

"Which comes before your duty to your heart."

"Exactly."

"Or to her."

"Damn it, that too."

"Poor lad," Cathar said sympathetically.

"Nay, poor Morgan," Miach said. He looked at his brother bleakly. "I cannot stop this thing now. It is too late. And I fear to tell her who I am. She will never look at me in the same way again."

Cathar was silent for quite some time. He looked into his cup. He drained his cup, then looked into it, as if it might provide him with better answers thusly. He fingered his cup, crossed and recrossed his legs, sighed, then put both feet on the floor and looked at Miach.

"You could send her away before she sees the sword."

"I tried that."

"Try harder."

"Treason," Miach said wearily.

"Aye."

"You're a bloody romantic."

"So, little brother, are you."

Miach rolled his eyes and wished he had a better response than to simply sigh. He finally looked at Cathar. "There is more."

"There always is."

Miach cursed him, then continued on. "I think she is Gair of Ceangail's daughter."

"Impossible," Cathar said promptly. "All his children were killed in that horrible bit of business with the well."

"Morgan dreams of him."

"I dream of him," Cathar said, "but only after bad beer."

"This is serious."

"So is bad beer."

Miach couldn't laugh, but he did smile. "Perhaps I will see humor in that someday, but not today. I have sat with her while she dreamed of him." He sighed. "It was not easy to watch."

Cathar set his cup down on the floor. "Miach, perhaps she heard fireside tales as a wee thing and she's dreaming a tale she once heard. It could be that being close to your magic has wrought a foul work upon her delicate senses. Perhaps she ate something vile and paid for it during the night. There are a dozen things it could be."

"They did not find the bones of the young girl in those woods," Miach countered. "The eldest boy died later from his wounds, after he finished telling the tale, but they never found the girl."

"But—"

"She knows Camanaë spells that I didn't teach her."

"Gair was not of Camanaë."

"Oh, but he was," Miach said quietly. "He was the youngest son of Sgath of Ainneamh and Eulasaid of Camanaë. It was the only reason he convinced Sarait to wed with him, for she never would have wed one without magic to equal her own."

"But Camanaë is a matriarchal magic," Cathar protested.

"Tell that to King Harold," Miach said promptly. "Tell it to Gair of Ceangail."

"I can't. They're dead."

"Tell it to me, then, for I have it from Mother in abundance. Matriarchal it may be, but not always. I tell you, Cathar, Morgan *is* the young girl she dreams of. They aren't dreams; they're memories."

"Very well," Cathar conceded, "let us suppose that is true. What does that mean for the sword?"

"It means she will not only have the power to wield it, but the right as well. It means she will never rest until she has fulfilled her place in the sword's history. It means that when she realizes what I've done, how I've brought her here without admitting who I was or what I wanted from her, she will never look at me again without wanting me dead."

"Perhaps she'll stab you with the blade right off and you won't have to see any of those looks."

"Thank you," Miach said shortly. "I knew there was a reason I trusted you with all my secrets."

Cathar only laughed gently. "Ah, Miach, all will be well. You'll see."

"Are you peeping into the future now as well?"

Cathar shook his head with a smile. "I am not. I'll leave the bloodshot eyes and sore head to you. I'm just thinking that you're a braw enough lad and if your Morgan has sense, she'll forgive you."

"I daresay her sense of vengeance is what she'll rely on."

"I doubt it," Cathar said easily, "else you wouldn't love her as you do."

"Why does everyone think I love her?" Miach asked crossly.

"You said so," Cathar pointed out.

Miach scowled. "Perhaps I'm confused. The woman is fiendishly proficient with everything sharp and she hates magic in general and mages in particular."

"And so a blissful union is begun," Cathar said with a wide smile. "May I live to see it bloom and flourish."

"Aye, I hope you do," Miach agreed with a half laugh. He smiled for a moment then felt it fade. "Aye, and I wish the same for myself."

Cathar collected the cups, rose, and walked toward the door. "I'll leave you to it, then. I'll go see what Adhémar's combining. I'm sure it can't be good."

"Likely not," Miach said. "I'll come find you later."

Cathar nodded and left the chamber. Miach rose, stretched, and wondered if he dared take the time for a bath. He looked toward the window and saw that it was still dark. He had time to see to his spells, have a bath, and return downstairs before Morgan was awake.

He went about his work with a single-minded determination that might have impressed even Weger.

Then he found something that brought him up short.

Was there an actual hole in his spells?

He cursed for quite a lengthy period of time, then started again from the beginning, rechecking each spell. He wasn't sure how much time had passed; all he knew was that he had indeed found a hole in one of his spells of defense.

Large enough for a single man, perhaps. Not large enough for a company of creatures. He sat back down in his chair and considered. There had been no sign of anything like that after Adhé-mar had been ambushed in the fall, which made Miach wonder how those creatures had come so near Tor Neroche. There had also been no disturbance in any of his spells that would explain how any of the other creatures had entered Neroche.

So, how had those nightmarish beasts come into Neroche without breaching his spells?

And who had come in after brazenly making such a rent in his defenses?

He turned his attentions to the gap and rewove the surrounding spells until there was no sign of any opening. He reexamined everything one last time to make certain he'd missed nothing.

Apparently that took him far longer than he'd suspected.

He came to himself to find that he was standing in the middle of the room. He had no idea how he'd gotten there.

Or how long he had been at his task.

But there was an evening sky visible through his window.

He bolted for the door, then leaped down the stairs, cursing as he did so. He ran through the passageways, up and down more steps, and burst into the chamber where the company was being housed.

Only Glines was there, pacing uneasily before the fire.

Miach came to a skidding halt. "Where are they?" he asked, feeling panic descend.

Glines crossed the chamber quickly. "I couldn't stop her."

"Where did she go?"

"I don't know, but I sent the other lads with her. I remained behind in case you came. She put all her weapons on the bed over there and left, holding a knife in one hand and a ring in the other." He paused again. "My lord, she was not herself."

"I daresay not," Miach said. Morgan had left her gear behind? He could only imagine what was going on inside her head. He turned and made for the door. "Follow me."

"Trouble?"

"That doesn't begin to describe it," Miach said grimly as he jerked the door open and strode out into the hallway. "How long ago did she leave?"

"Half an hour. I would have come for you, but—"

"My fault," Miach said unflinchingly. "I never should have left her."

"Do you know where she's going?" Glines asked.

Miach looked at him briefly. "The great hall."

"Why?"

"You'll see."

And he would. Miach cursed. The entire bloody castle would see and then the future would be changed forever.

Without his having told her who he really was.

He began to run.

Twenty-four

❧

Morgan clutched Nicholas's blade in one hand and the ring in the other. She had thought she might be able to drown out their singing that way, but it wasn't so. The blade not only sang, it glowed. The ring merely lay in her hand without any otherworldly manifestations. She slipped it onto her finger for safekeeping, then continued on her way.

She hadn't intended to go on any sort of exploration. She'd woken that morning to find Miach gone and the rest of the company tucking in to a substantial breakfast. She would have eaten, and indeed she did try, but the blade troubled her so greatly that she found she couldn't. She picked at her food, then spent the morning pacing and trying to ignore the buzzing in her head. She'd wondered what had become of Miach, but she'd had trouble even holding on to that thought.

She'd even gone so far as to send a message to the king through one of the servants. The reply had been that the king was busy and would see her later.

She would have been satisfied with that, but the blade was definitely not.

Finally, as evening had approached, she had surrendered. She had walked over to her couch and laid out all her weapons. She suspected they would not be welcome if she managed to see the king. She had then emptied her pack onto Miach's bed. The ring had fallen out and landed with a clink on the marble floor. She had picked it up, then unwrapped the knife.

It had blazed with a sudden light.

Its song had burst forth as well, briefly, then subsided into a calmer, more pleasant hum. Morgan had stared at it, feeling as if her life were no longer under her control.

She had risen and made for the door. Her companions followed her, or so she thought, though she really couldn't have said. Her eyes were full of the blade, her head so full of its song, and her heart so desperate to be free of both that she hadn't really noticed anything else.

She decided to go look for the king. She would find his audience chamber and shove the bloody things under the door if she had to.

The sooner, the better.

She wondered if that was Paien calling her name, or the knife. She tried to look behind her to see who was following her, but found that she couldn't. She could no longer tell the difference between dreaming and waking. This dream was not evil, but it was powerful. She was not running through thick underbrush, she was walking through magnificent passageways.

But still she could not wake.

The souls filling the hallways increased, but Morgan pushed through them and past them without stopping to converse. They were richly dressed, some were carrying food, some were looking at her in surprise and dismay. She didn't stop to ask them why.

Another song had begun.

One not sung by her knife.

She had to find it before she went mad. She had never considered madness before, not truly, though she began to consider it now. Was this how it felt? Slowly losing contact with the world you knew, being drawn into a dream where songs were sung that only you could hear and blades glowed in a way that only you could see?

She found herself suddenly standing in front of a set of doors that reached far up into the darkness of the ceiling above. Guards stood there, blocking her entrance. Morgan struggled to catch her breath.

"Open them," she managed.

The guards only stared back, silent and watchful.

"Open them!" she shouted.

"Morgan," Paien began miserably from behind her.

Morgan spoke a spell of opening. She had no idea where the words had come from, but they were there on her tongue and ready for her use. The doors responded with a great creaking sound. Guards leaped away in surprise and fear.

She heard Paien curse. She thought she might have heard Camid squeak. She wanted to weep, but she couldn't. She rubbed her eyes with the back of her wrist, then walked into the great hall. She walked until she found herself standing in front of a large table on a raised dais. She drew her sleeve across her eyes again, wishing the fog would dissipate—

"Morgan!"

Morgan turned and saw through a mist of song and dream that Miach was standing just inside the massive doors.

"Morgan," he said again. "Let me help you."

She couldn't answer. That new song had grown louder. She turned away from Miach and looked toward the back of the hall.

There, above a massive fireplace, hung a sword.

Covered with a tracery of leaves and flowers, all the things that Queen Mehar loved . . .

Morgan sucked in air desperately. The blade was terribly loud. In time, Morgan realized her name figured in its song. The sword and the knife created a melody that wove itself around her, through her, in and out of her thoughts, until she lost all sense of who she was. She knew she walked around the long table until she was standing in front of the hearth, looking up. She slipped the ring off her finger and set it with a fumbling motion upon the table behind her. She set the knife down as well, though it seemed reluctant to leave her hand. But the blade above her shimmered with a light that was so bright, so lovely, so compelling that she could do nothing else but look at it.

The song swelled into a crescendo that continued on until she was tempted to put her hands over her ears so she didn't have to listen to it anymore. But the song was part of her and covering her ears would not help. So Morgan waited, wanting to cower but unable to, until the song reached its height.

Then the blade leaped off the wall into her hand.

And the song ceased.

Morgan looked at the sword she held. The silence of it was as deafening as the noise had been before. The blade continued to glow with a soft light that was so exquisite she simply could not look away.

And then it too subsided, until Morgan could only see a faint glow. She realized that the song was still there, sung between the sword and the knife, but faint enough that it didn't trouble her. She took a deep breath, finding that she hadn't breathed in quite a while.

She held the sword in her hand and turned to look behind her for the first time.

The great hall was full of people who were all staring at her as if they'd seen either a miracle or a nightmare.

Morgan understood completely.

To her right stood Adhémar. He was watching with a look of satisfaction on his face. Her company was standing directly before her on the other side of the table. They were watching her with varying degrees of amazement.

And there, to her left, stood Miach. Alone. Apart. Watching her with an expression she couldn't identify. She wanted to walk around the table and fling herself into his arms, but she found she couldn't move. All she could do was stand there with her feet rooted to the ground and clutch the new sword in her hand.

But then a voice cut through the silence like a particularly sharp blade.

"And who, pray tell, is this?"

Morgan looked about the chamber, feeling a little drunken with what was going on inside her head, and searched feebly for the speaker of those words. She found, at length, a woman who had come to stand next to Adhémar.

The woman was, put simply, the most beautiful creature Morgan had ever seen. She was perfectly coiffed, perfectly dressed, perfectly mannered. Perfection embodied. She even spoke with perfect crispness; as if she could not have permitted anything less.

"Could no one find her a bath?" the woman demanded.

Morgan felt compelled to answer. She had to have some excuse for her filthy clothes, her boots that had tromped through mud, manure, and snow, and her hair, which she was quite certain she hadn't brushed since Miach had done it for her. Morgan took her free hand and pushed her hair, back from her face. "I was going to today," she managed. "Bathe, I mean." She paused and drew in a ragged breath. "I was distracted."

The woman raked her with a look that was perfectly callous. "One does not enter the king's great hall in such a state."

Morgan nodded dumbly. Of course not. But the song . . .

"Who are you?" the woman demanded. "Why are you here?"

Morgan would have asked the same thing, but she was not quite herself and this was not her hall. She took a deep breath. "I am Morgan. I have something for the king." She paused. "A blade. I was charged with its delivery."

"Well," the woman said shortly, "give it to him and be off with you before we have to clean the floor again."

Morgan looked around, wondering where the king might be hiding. She'd never seen him, save on his coins, and those could have been any man wearing a crown. There were no crowns to be seen in the hall at present, no robes trimmed in ermine, no cloaks of purple velvet. There was a man standing near Adhémar wearing quite nice clothes, but he had no crown, so Morgan continued to look.

"Um," she said finally, feeling very uncomfortable with everyone staring at her. She couldn't even bring herself to touch the mark over her brow. She was past that now. She was so far out of her usual existence, she couldn't have recited one of Weger's strictures if her life had depended on it. It was all she could do not to fall to her knees and weep. "I don't see the king," she whispered miserably.

"Is this possible?" the woman said with a humorless laugh. "Is it possible that this ragged country wench does not know who the king is?"

Morgan did not care for the slight, but could not bring herself to defend her honor. She was too desperate to get the sword out of her hand, the knife in the king's, and be on her way. She looked at the woman hopefully. "Do you know who he is?"

The woman looked at Adhémar in astonishment. "Adhémar?"

Morgan shrugged. She was not above asking Adhémar, though she couldn't imagine he knew any better than she did. "Very well," she said. "Adhémar, do *you* know the king?"

The woman's laughter was painful to listen to. It left bits of ice in the air as it wafted toward Morgan. "You foolish girl, he *is* the king."

Morgan blinked. "No, he isn't."

"Adhémar, you should perhaps improve your likeness on your coinage," the woman said scornfully.

"Likeness?" Morgan repeated, feeling that her feet were not stable beneath her.

"Perhaps after we are wed," the woman said smoothly.

"Wed?" Morgan repeated dumbly.

The woman looked down her nose. "Did you think you would have him, my little cabbage leaf?"

"He's an ass," Morgan said without thinking. "I wouldn't have him if he begged."

Gasps echoed throughout the chamber. Morgan suspected Adhémar's was the loudest.

Paien and Camid took a step backward. Morgan saw them do it but couldn't manage to tell them not to bother. She was still having too much trouble reconciling what the woman was saying with what she knew couldn't possibly be true.

Adhémar, the king?

Preposterous.

She looked at the men gathered in a neat row to one side of Adhémar. They looked enough like him that they could have been his brothers. There were five of them.

The king had brothers, didn't he?

Morgan clutched the sword in her hand and looked back at Adhémar. He had only folded his arms over his chest and was watching her expressionlessly. He was named after the king, true enough, though she had suspected his parents had indulged in too much wishful thinking while he was a baby and named him after the eldest prince. Was it possible? She thought back swiftly to all her encounters with him. He had been boastful, irritating, condescending, and autocratic in the extreme. She had thought it was just a bit of wishful thinking on *his* part.

Perhaps it had been something else.

She managed to swallow.

"Are you—" Her voice broke and she had to try again. "Are you the king?" she asked, but there was little sound to her words. She sounded faint, even to her own ears.

"Of course he is the king, you idiotic shieldmaiden," the woman in blue snapped.

Adhémar shot the woman a look of warning, then turned back to Morgan. "Aye," he said with a curt nod. "I am."

"But—" She could almost not find voice for her thoughts. "But why? Why did you say nothing? Why did you let me believe otherwise?"

"I need you to wield the Sword of Angesand."

Morgan looked at the sword in her hand. "This?" she asked. "This is the Sword of Angesand?"

The woman in blue threw up her hands in disgust.

Morgan looked at Adhémar. "Is it?"

"It is."

Morgan frowned. Well, if that was the case, then it was little wonder that he had tried to teach her spells. Perhaps he'd known all along that the sword would call to her. But how? She'd told no one about her errand to Tor Neroche. She'd told no one about the knife she carried. She'd told no one she had dreamed of a sword that perfectly matched that knife—a sword that even she could now see was the Sword of Angesand.

Then she froze.

That wasn't exactly true.

She looked at the men standing next to Adhémar. Five brothers. Now that she thought about it, she remembered that the king had six brothers.

She looked to her left. There, standing by himself silently, watching her with a very grave expression, was Miach.

Adhémar's youngest brother.

"Miach?" she said, but there was hardly any sound to her voice.

"Who does this wench think she is?" the woman asked shrilly. "He's the archmage of the realm and she addresses him so familiarly?"

Morgan felt the ground begin to sway beneath her. "Archmage?" she said, her breath nothing but a puff of sound that floated out before her and hung in the chill of the hall.

Miach closed his eyes briefly. "Aye," he said quietly.

She wanted to sit, but she didn't dare. Was it possible? Was it possible that he was who they said he was?

But why? Why would he have lied to her?

She stopped still. The cold steel in her hand was answer enough, she supposed. It was all very clear to her now. The charm and friendliness. The anxiousness to teach her spells. The gallant offer to see her all the way to Tor Neroche.

All only because they wanted her to put her hand on the damned Sword of Angesand and see if it called to her.

Perhaps that she could have borne, if that was all the betrayal there had been. But it went deeper than that—and it all had to do with Miach.

He was not Miach the bumbling farmer, he was Mochriadhemiach, the son of Desdhemar of Neroche. The archmage of the realm.

The archmage, not an inept weaver of spells.

The embodiment of everything she despised.

Her fingers tightened around the hilt of the sword—that beautiful sword that fit so perfectly in her hand—and she looked Miach full in the face.

"Who are you?" she rasped. "Tell me yourself, if you have the courage for it."

The woman laughed. "Goodness, Adhémar, is it possible she truly has no idea of who —"

"Shut up," Morgan said, whirling on the woman and pointing the sword at her. "Shut up, you shrill harpy, before I aid you in doing so by means of a dozen ways you won't care for in the least."

Adhémar's fiancée fell, blessedly, silent.

Morgan turned back to Miach and looked at him furiously. "Tell me. Say the words."

Miach paused only a heartbeat before he looked at her

gravely. "I am Mochriadhemiach," he said quietly. "And I am the archmage of the realm."

Morgan heard nothing but that. She saw the truth of it in Miach's eyes and knew he would not apologize for it. But to think of the lies, the deceit, the misleading he had done—

He had called her *love*.

A great anger welled up in her. It was so strong, she half feared it would consume her, but that it didn't was even more terrifying. It raged through her with a sound of rushing wind, white hot in its fierceness, leaving her blind to all but her fury. In that moment, she understood what fueled Gair of Ceangail. She understood how he could hate so fiercely that he would destroy everything in front of him without mercy.

She lifted the sword—

And brought it down with all her strength against the banquet table before her.

The blade splintered, shattered, sparked as it disintegrated into thousands of shards and bits that floated through the air before her like snow.

The table remained intact.

Morgan stared at the haft of the sword, that beautiful hilt that was worked with a tracery of flowers, and could not believe what she had just done. She looked about her. Adhémar was staring at her, openmouthed. Soon that would turn to anger, she was certain of that. She looked at Miach.

His expression of profound pity had not changed.

Where there had been hate inside her, now there was only a deathly chill. Morgan threw the hilt onto the table with a sob and bolted.

She wasn't certain where she intended to go. *Out of the great hall* seemed like a good start. Her cheeks were wet and she found she could hardly see where she was going. She realized, to her horror, that she was making horrendous sounds of pain that she supposed some unkind village bard would have termed weeping. She had never wept thusly before, so she wasn't quite sure what to call it. All she knew was that she was in a dark passageway and she could not go back.

She would go back to Melksham. Perhaps she would die of seasickness on the boat. If she had the misfortune of surviving the voyage, she would find a siege and throw herself into it.

Perhaps she would seek out Weger and see if he could drive whatever magic there was in her—and she now had to accept that it was a staggering amount—out of her. Whatever she did, she would at least become invisible.

Perhaps she would forget, in time, that once she had come to love the archmage of the realm. Perhaps, in time, she would cease to believe that she'd once thought he might have loved her in return—

She heard a crash and realized that she had upended a tray of fine crystal glasses. A servant stood there, having rescued one, apparently. The others lay in shards about his feet. Morgan dragged her sleeve across her eyes.

"My apologies," she said, starting to brush past him.

"Wait, lady," the old man said in a kindly fashion. "Perhaps this will ease you."

She looked at the man. He had a horrible scar down one cheek. That prompted her to stop and humor him where she wouldn't have otherwise.

"What have you there?" she asked, looking at the lone survivor from his tray of drink.

"Wine," he said dismissively. "A very fine vintage, I daresay, but not too high for the likes of us, eh?"

She wanted to tell him that she was the wielder of the Sword of Angesand, but what point would there have been in that? The sword was no more, and she was disgraced and shamed. Aye, she was little better than a servant indeed.

She took the glass, nodded her thanks, then drained it before she tasted it.

She heard more glass shatter against stone. It was only after she recognized that sound that she knew it had been her glass to fall from her fingers.

The bitterness of the poison spread through her like fire, though it was not fire, for it was cold. She looked at the man in surprise.

"Why?"

He shrugged. "Why not?" Then he smiled. "Actually, there is a good reason, but I daresay you'll never know it."

"Who are you?" she managed with her last thought. Darkness was hard upon her and she felt the flicker of flame that was herself becoming weaker.

"Lothar of Wychweald," the man said with another conspiratorial smile, "but don't tell anyone I'm here. I was planning to keep myself out of sight so I could serve at the king's wedding feast when it comes, but I thought I'd try out my brew on you first. How do you like it?"

Morgan had no strength to offer any opinion.

The flame flickered wildly.

Then went out.

Twenty-five

❧

M iach looked at the shards of the Sword of Angesand that
  lay scattered over the table and spilled onto the floor. A
thousand shards that would never be put together again. He
closed his eyes briefly. He'd known it would be terrible when
Morgan realized the truth, he just hadn't known how terrible.
He'd wanted to stop it. When keeping her from Tor Neroche
had failed, he'd wanted to at least soften the truth.

He had come too late.

He supposed he might never forget the sight of the Sword
of Angesand leaping down into her hand, as if it had waited
decades to do just that.

He supposed he would also never forget the sight of her
slamming it against the king's table and shattering it into pieces.

He ruthlessly put both visions behind him and strode forward. He snatched the knife off the table and shoved it into his
belt. He caught the ring up as well and shoved it into a pocket.
Adhémar wouldn't remember that the knife was intended for
him and Miach would make sure he continued to forget. The
ring was something he would think about later.

Then he reached out and carefully picked up the hilt of the
Sword of Angesand. He held it, then turned and looked at his
brother.

"You could have done that better," he said shortly.

"Me?" Adhémar said, stunned. "I didn't tell her to ruin the bloody sword!" He scowled. "Not only did she break the sword, she insulted the princess of Penrhyn."

Miach looked coldly at the woman standing to Adhémar's left. "Is that who you are?"

"I am Adaira," said the woman in question. She looked down her very aristocratic nose at him. "I am here, my lord Mochri-adhemiach, to become your queen. The wedding is in a month's time. Did my lord not see fit to tell you?"

Miach shot Adhémar a look of barely repressed fury. "Congratulations on your nuptials, my liege. A lovely surprise."

Adhémar shrugged. "I told you I'd had business in Penrhyn. Now you see what that business was."

"Indeed, I do. Now, if you will excuse me, I am going to find our very vital wielder and see if I can stop her before she throws herself off the battlements."

"Why bother?" Adhémar asked. "She's ruined the damned sword."

"Then she can use yours," Miach snapped. "You don't have the magic for it."

"What?" said Adaira, looking unpleasantly surprised. "Adhémar, what is he talking about?"

"Nothing," Adhémar said. "Mindless babbling. An aberration. My brother is a fool, on many accounts. Leave Morgan be, Miach. She's not worth the trouble."

Miach walked over and plowed his fist into his brother's face before he thought better of it. Adhémar went sprawling. Miach did not bother to help him up. He turned and tossed the hilt of the Sword of Angesand at Glines. "Guard that with your life."

"I will," Glines said faintly.

Miach looked at the rest of the companions he had grown quite fond of. They were all regarding him with various degrees of astonishment. "I apologize for the subterfuge. I will find Morgan, then we will all have speech together. Guard Glines and the hilt, if you will. I will return as soon as may be."

"Aye, to find yourself in the dungeon!" Adhémar bellowed, struggling to his feet.

Miach turned and looked at him. "Do you honestly believe you can manage that?" he asked. "In truth?"

Adhémar opened his mouth to say something, then apparently thought better of it. "I'll expect more courtesy from you at my wedding banquet."

"I imagine you will," Miach said, then he strode from the great hall.

He ran through the passageways, up and down half flights of stairs, and out toward the kitchens. There was a pair of souls standing at the end of the hallway.

Morgan.

There was someone with her.

Miach skidded to a halt, then forced himself to run even faster. He skidded again, through shards of glass and spells laid to tangle about the feet and entrap.

Miach caught Morgan as she fell.

Lothar made him a low, mocking bow, then straightened. "Kinsman. Or should I say great-nephew several generations removed? Or should I merely say *former guest in my dungeon?*"

Miach hardly had the wherewithal to block the spell of death Lothar threw over him like a dark cloak. He was no longer the child he'd been when Lothar had first captured him riding recklessly along the border. He was a man full grown, in full possession of his powers, and damned close to being Lothar's equal.

Lothar laughed with genuine humor. "Do you think so?" he asked. "Oh, I daresay not. But we'll find out eventually, I imagine." He yawned, patting his hand delicately over his mouth. "Unfortunately, my work is finished here for the day. I'll be back for you later."

And with that, he vanished.

Miach was torn between catching his enemy and caring for the woman in his arms. He took a step, then stopped, the glass crunching under his boots. He looked down. There were the spells of entrapment, which he wiped away easily. But covering them, as if it had been wine sloshed generously upon the floor, was something else.

Poison.

Miach countered that as well, but it took him a moment or two and left him a little light-headed.

Or perhaps that was the aftereffects of the look Morgan had given him.

He'd known she would be angry and he'd been sure she would feel betrayed. He hadn't expect to see naked hatred on her face. He certainly hadn't expected her to destroy a sword that had hung in the hall of Neroche for five hundred years.

Her power was staggering.

He suspected he had met his match—and then some.

He shook his head, realizing that he would never know just how much power she had if he didn't get her somewhere quiet where he could set to healing her. He turned, then found himself facing another man with a crown full of white hair and power roiling off him like heat from a raging fire.

Miach backed up a step in spite of himself.

"Outside," the man said, nodding toward the end of the passageway. "Follow me."

"What?" Miach demanded in astonishment. "Are you mad?"

"Do you want her to live?"

Miach continued to balk. He gathered his wits about him and readied a spell of defense. The man looked over his shoulder.

"Don't bother with that," he said. "Come along, Mochriadhemiach. There's a good lad."

Miach gaped at the older man as he walked toward the doorway leading out into the courtyard. "Who *are* you?"

The man stopped and looked back. "Nicholas of Lismòr. Are you coming?"

Miach found himself following, if for no other reason than to be free of the lingering stench of spilled wine. Perhaps if he walked out into the chill night air, his head would be clear. For all he knew, it might even aid Morgan.

Nicholas of Lismòr? How in the world had he gotten to Tor Neroche? How had he come to be here at this particular time? And just what in the hell did the man think Miach was using for wits? Did the man actually think he would simply hand Morgan over because he was ordered to?

He followed Nicholas until they stood out in the courtyard. He clutched Morgan to him.

"I will fight you—"

"Your battle, lad, is not with me," Nicholas said.

"Lothar is gone," Miach said flatly.

"Your fight with him will come later. You have hearts and loyalties to win inside. I will see to Morgan."

Miach did not ease his hold on her. "How did you get here?"

"I flew."

Miach blinked. "You what? But how . . ."

"I daresay you'll know in time."

"I want to know now." Miach cradled Morgan more closely to him.

"Would it make you feel better to know she is my niece?"

Miach frowned in spite of himself. "Your niece? How so? Gair had no brothers."

Nicholas smiled approvingly. "Then you know that much. If so, then you know that Sarait had a sister. Four sisters, actually."

Miach cast his mind quickly back through the histories he'd read until he latched on to a name that had never seemed important before.

Until now.

Nicholas of Lismòr.

Lismòrian of Tòrr Dòrainn.

Too close for coincidence.

"Lismòrian of Tòrr Dòrainn," Miach said in amazement. "She was Sarait's sister."

Nicholas nodded. "Very good. Lismòrian was my lady wife."

"You named your university after her."

"It seemed fitting."

"But that would make you . . ." Miach looked at the other man in profound surprise. "Nicholas, the wizard king of Diarmailt."

Nicholas smiled. "You're very well read, lad. No doubt you became so while you were recuperating from your time in Lothar's dungeon and learning to bear the weight of your new mantle."

"But you dropped out of tales two hundred years ago!"

"Did I?" Nicholas mused. "I suppose that might be true. But I have been here and there, doing what needed to be done. I tried to stop Sarait from marrying Gair, you know, but she thought he had changed his ways."

"Soft-hearted, was she?" Miach asked faintly.

"Aye," Nicholas said. "And Gair was charming, when he wanted to be. I know how she was deceived. He was my friend at one time as well."

"Indeed," Miach managed.

"Aye, indeed," Nicholas said. "But that is a tale for another time. My turn on the stage is over, but yours has just begun. You have made a good beginning."

"How do you know?"

"I've watched you for years."

Miach looked at him in surprise. "Why?"

"Why do you think?"

"I hesitate to ask," Miach said frankly.

Nicholas shrugged with a smile. "I always thought you and Morgan would make a fine match."

Miach wondered if he could possibly be surprised by anything else that happened that night.

"I doubt Morgan will agree," he said grimly. Then he frowned. "I wonder something, though. Did you know who Morgan was when she came to the university?"

Nicholas smiled. "Aye, I knew who she was. You see, Sarait had asked me to care for her children should anything have happened to her. I said I would, of course, never dreaming that she intended to risk her life by goading Gair into proving his power. By the time I realized what she'd done, the mercenaries had already taken Morgan in."

"Why didn't you tell Morgan the truth about her parents?"

Nicholas looked at him sideways. "Can't you imagine how she would have taken it? How have her dreams haunted her now? I shudder to think how it would have affected her then. Besides, I wanted her hid and there was no better place than in a mercenary camp. And then my orphanage. And then Weger's tower of terror." He smiled. "Aren't those the last places you would have looked for her?"

Miach wished for nothing more than a seat. "I suppose so." He paused. "But I fear all that safekeeping may have been undone tonight. I must return inside and tend her."

"You cannot heal her of this hurt."

"I could—"

"Perhaps," Nicholas conceded, "but it would take all your skill and leave you none for other things. Now, your task lies elsewhere and your land will lie in ruins if you do not see to it. That is your duty, if you will."

Miach wanted to stop time, so he could determine for himself if this was the right course. In truth, Tor Neroche could have fallen down around his ears and he wouldn't have cared. Not if it meant he could save Morgan.

"Duty," Miach said with a sigh. "I detest that word."

"Of course you don't, Mochriadhemiach," Nicholas said gently. "Now, give her to me and be about your business."

Miach couldn't bring himself to release her. "I do not doubt you are who you say you are, and I know the care you've taken of her over the years, but how can you possibly equal in that university of yours the herbs I have here?"

"You aren't the only one with a decent garden, lad."

"But healers—"

"Do you think I have only a selection of Harding's sons in my hall?" Nicholas asked.

"When will I see her again?" Miach asked, pained.

"If she lives—"

Miach clutched her to him. "I'm coming with you."

"You will be of no use to her now," Nicholas said calmly. "If she lives, you will know."

Miach closed his eyes briefly. "I want an assurance."

Nicholas looked at him with one raised eyebrow. "You're the archmage, lad. Stretch your vision. Surely you don't believe your duty lies within your own borders alone, do you? You can know of what happens in other countries besides your own." He smiled. "You'll know—without my sending word."

Miach found he had no response to that.

Apparently seizing that as his opportunity to be about his business, Nicholas took several steps backward. Miach didn't look away, he did not blink, but suddenly in the place of the man crouched a great dragon with scales of emerald and a breast so encrusted with gems that Miach couldn't begin to speculate on their worth. As it was, they dazzled him with their brightness and hue.

The dragon beat its great wings and rose, then stretched out its great talons. Miach found himself offering Morgan to the wizard king of Diarmailt as if he hadn't a useful thought in his head or the smallest bit of sense to go with that thought.

I will see to her, if seeing can be done.

And with that, the dragon rose into the air, its burden clutched delicately in its talons. Miach stood, gaping, until the wind from the creature's wings stopped blowing his hair into his eyes and he could finally see.

He watched until the creature from a dream ceased to sparkle in the night sky.

All that was left was stars. Those sparkled as well, but he supposed that might have been from the tears standing in his eyes.

Miach dragged his sleeve across his eyes and continued to watch until he knew he would be standing there forever if he didn't turn away.

He took a deep breath. He would secure the kingdom, then he would take his own journey to Melksham Island and he would do it as quickly as possible. Perhaps Nicholas was equal to the task of healing Morgan, but he couldn't possibly love the girl the same way Miach did. If nothing else, he would offer what aid he could . . . and an apology, if allowed.

He turned away from the courtyard and walked back into the castle.

The great hall was still in an uproar. The shards of sword had been swept up and were currently being contained in a brass ash bucket held rather uneasily by Cathar. Cathar and Paien were eyeing each other closely, as if they wondered who would draw the first blade. No doubt Cathar was wondering if he might be able to put the bucket down before blood was spilt.

Miach took the bucket away from his brother and handed it to Fletcher.

"Guard that with your life," he said briskly.

Fletcher edged closer to Glines.

Miach turned to Adhémar. "Get on with your wedding. I've other things to do."

Adhémar glared at him. "When I have my magic back, you will find yourself in a place you won't enjoy."

"Your magic *back*?" Adaira of Penrhyn screeched. "That keeps resurfacing, Adhémar. What do you *mean* by that?"

"I told you it was an aberration," Adhémar said dismissively. "I'm going to go dress. Perhaps you'll care to see to supper."

Miach watched his brother walk off in one direction, his suddenly quite furious betrothed stomp off in another, and found himself somewhat relieved that he was not in either's shoes. His brothers likewise departed for safer ground, leaving him there with Morgan's companions. He looked at them to find them still watching him with expressions ranging from astonishment to disapproval.

He faced disapproval first. He walked over to Paien and held out his hand.

"I'm Mochriadhemiach," he said. "Archmage of the realm. I've been traveling in disguise for a pair of fortnights for reasons I will give later. My friends call me Miach."

Paien looked at his hand for several moments, then studied him for several moments more before he finally took his hand and shook it in a crushing grip. "Where's Morgan?" he asked.

"That is a tale better reserved for my private chambers," Miach said. "She is safe."

Paien grunted and released his hand. "I wondered about you."

"Did you," Miach said dryly.

Camid came and clapped hands with him, looking up with a squint. "I didn't. I've no use for magic, outside of using it as a way to describe my skill with an axe, but I suppose I won't hold it against you. Sweet on her, are you?"

"Hmmm," Miach said.

"Then why in the bloody hell did you bring her here?" Camid asked, fingering his axe purposefully.

"Again, a conversation for another place."

"But the time will be now," Paien growled.

Miach looked about to see if he had any friends in the area. Fletcher was holding the bucket as if he feared it might come alive at any moment. Glines, however, was casually swinging the hilt around his finger and looking at Miach with a smile. Miach nodded at him and started toward the door of the great hall. Glines caught up with him easily, leaving the others to follow.

"Where's Morgan?" Glines asked.

"I sent her off with a dragon."

Glines choked. Miach smiled grimly.

"I wish I were jesting. She will be well."

"You'll see to it," Glines stated.

"If seeing can be done," Miach said. He sighed and walked quietly for several moments, out of the great hall, through passageways, up and down half flights of stairs, and then to the bottom of the twisting steps that went up to his tower chamber. He looked at Glines. "I hope she will be well."

"Could you not cure her?"

Miach put his hand on the wall and considered his words very carefully for some time. Finally, he looked at Glines. "I could have, perhaps," he began slowly, "but to do so would have required all my attention, all my skill, and perhaps all my strength." He paused. "A thousand years from now, I might have gained the fortitude to do that and see to the realm at the same time."

"A thousand years," Camid snorted. "Ridiculous. Who will be alive in a thousand years?"

Miach decided that perhaps that was a topic for a more private setting as well. He smiled at Glines. "I relinquished her to someone with the skill, the strength, and the age. He will see to her. I will see to the realm."

"And when she is whole?"

"Then I suppose you and I will battle for her hand," Miach said lightly.

"I would lay odds on myself, at this point," Glines said seriously.

"Unfortunately, so would I," Miach said. He swept them all with a look. "Come, friends, and ascend with me. We have plans to make and tales to tell."

"And a wedding feast to attend," Glines added helpfully.

Miach sighed, then climbed the stairs, leaving the others to follow along. He would tell his tales, they would make their plans, then he would set his spells and secure the borders. If he had time, he would see if he couldn't get a reasonable look at Adhémar's sword and determine if it had been enspelled or not. He would take a moment or two more and think about that strange magic that seemed to be cropping up in unexpected places.

And then he would put it all behind him and take his own journey south, to see what aid he could offer Nicholas.

And hope there would be a reason to.

Twenty-six

❧

Nicholas of Lismòr, brother-in-law to the fair Sarait and uncle to the lass lying in the bed before him, sat in a chair under a window in a peaceful, quiet chamber and stared out at the night sky. He'd been sitting in that chair for quite some time. He generally didn't rest overmuch, despite his years, but he had expended all his energy and he was weary.

If there were stars, he could not see them. It was indicative of the state of things. Darkness covered the land. Darkness covered the young woman lying in the bed nearby. Darkness covered even his own heart, and he wasn't one to give in to despair.

He fingered the ring he held. It was a man's ring, a jet-black stone set in silver. Nicholas did not shiver when he touched it, though he supposed he should have. The ring had belonged to Gair of Ceangail. It was a reflection of his power and the darkness of his heart.

Nicholas had received the ring when he'd received a wild, headstrong lass of twelve summers. The mercenaries who'd gifted him Morgan had also shoved the ring in his hands. They had warned him, though, never to show it to her. She'd been holding on to it when they'd found her wandering in the woods, dry-eyed and mute. A quick reconnaissance of the area had produced a darkness so complete that the men had fled in terror, taking the girl with them.

The ring, they had said, gave the girl nightmares, but they had feared to throw it away lest at some point it prove to be the only link to her parentage.

Of course, Nicholas had recognized the ring. He'd seen it thousands of times on Gair's hand, even before Gair had wed Sarait. When he'd received it from the mercenary lads, he'd put it away in a trunk and put the girl in a chamber.

The chamber he was sitting in, actually. The girl, who now lay in the bed, had grown up to be an astonishing young woman. Nicholas had had the privilege of watching over her during part of her youth. It had also been his privilege to exert all his power to do his best to call her back from the brink of death.

He wondered, wearily, if she would wake.

The poison had been strong, but Lothar's poisons always were. Nicholas had had herbs dried and prepared for just such an occasion as this and he'd had the energy to pour into his own spells of healing.

Perhaps Mochriadhemiach could have tended her well enough on his own. It was obvious the lad was desperately in love with her. Surely that had to count for something.

But he was also guardian of the realm and his duty lay there.

Nicholas fingered Gair's ring and considered a bit more. Lothar's spells were indeed strong and his hatred of Camanaë yet even stronger. There had been times, over the centuries, when Nicholas had wondered if that hatred might be too strong to overcome. Morgan had been their best hope.

Perhaps he had been wrong to send her to Tor Neroche.

But it had been her destiny . . .

The night began to fade. Nicholas leaned forward and looked at Morgan. Her breathing was shallow. There was an unwholesome pallor to her face. If he hadn't known better, he might have suspected she had already passed on. He cast about for something else he might do, some other concoction of herbs, some other spell of healing.

Unfortunately, he was forced to admit that he had done everything possible. His strength and his magic were spent.

He stared out the window and waited for a dawn that seemed long in coming.

He distracted himself by thinking back over Morgan's life. He'd known her, of course, from her birth, watched over her from afar during her childhood, then rejoiced the day her mercenary guardians had left her in his care. She had become everything, and more, her mother could have wished for. One day, if he had the chance, he would tell her so. And he would tell her how much Sarait had loved her.

He remembered Sarait's joy in her daughter and the foreknowledge she'd had of Morgan's place in the history of the Nine Kingdoms. She'd never given up hope for Morgan's future, despite Gair's evil. Indeed, hadn't she said as much by the name she'd given her daughter?

Mhorghain.

In the language of Camanaë, it meant *hope*.

He watched as the morning star began to rise. It shone forth, heedless of the darkness, heedless of the fear in one man's soul as he watched the daughter of his heart fight for her life.

The star continued to brighten.

And then, from the bed, there was a movement. It was not the last breath drawn before a soul's final departure. It was a deep breath of life. Morgan stirred, then sighed and turned over in her sleep.

Nicholas closed his eyes briefly, then looked at her. She slept, suddenly peacefully, as if she had merely been about a hard day's labor and was resting from it.

He let out a ragged breath. She would live.

He smiled to himself, then looked out the window at the bright star in the east.

The star of the morning.

He took a deep breath. One test successfully passed. No doubt there would be others and they would be more grave than this. But just as the star of the morning heralded dawn, Mhorghain would bring hope to a kingdom that desperately needed it.

And to a man who held that kingdom together by his magic alone.

Nicholas put Gair's ring in his pocket and stretched briefly before he sat back and closed his eyes.

Morgan would be well. And though he could not control the events that would swirl around her, he could steady her before she plunged into them. He would tell her of her mother. He would give her what strength he could and offer what aid she would allow.

He looked out at the dawn once more before he closed his eyes and smiled.

It was enough for now.

Turn the page for a sneak preview of the
newest release from Lynn Kurland

Spellweaver

Coming in January 2011 from
Berkley Sensation

To follow the adventures of Miach
and Morgan look for *The Mage's Daughter*,
on sale now!

*T*he magic was a mighty wave that rose with terrifying swiftness toward the sky, hovered there for an eternal moment, then crashed down again to earth, washing over everything in its path.

The lad who had been standing at the edge of a glade watched with horror as the wave rushed toward him. He started forward to save his mother from being washed away only to remember that he had another task laid to his charge. He took hold of his younger sister's hand only to feel her fingers slip through his grasp despite his efforts to hold on to her. He shouted for her, but his calls were lost in the roaring of the evil as it engulfed him, sending him tumbling along with it. He groped blindly for his sister in that uncontrollable wave—

Only to realize he wasn't a lad of ten winters, but a man of a score-and-ten, and it wasn't his younger sister Mhorghain he was so desperately seeking.

It was Sarah of Doìre.

And it wasn't a wave of evil from a well he was running from, it was a terrible storm washing down the hill from the castle that had collapsed in on itself, the castle at Ceangail where his sire had lived for centuries, endlessly honing spells that never should have been created . . .

* * *

R uith woke abruptly.
    He forced himself to remain motionless and breathe shallowly, simply because it was his habit. When one had to rely on more pedestrian means of protecting himself than magic, one learned early on to not give an attacker any more advantage than necessary.

It took him a moment or two to realize that he *was* awake, but somehow that didn't matter given that the memory flooding back in a rush was unpleasantly similar to the wave of spell that had overcome him in his dream—and, it would seem, in his waking life. He reached for Sarah only to realize that he couldn't.

But that could have been because he was sitting with his hands tied so tightly around the tree behind him that he couldn't move them.

He opened his eyes a slit, then fully when he found that no one was watching him. His companions were none but a trio of rough-looking lads standing in front of him, arguing not over the best way to put him to death, but the quality of his weapons and how they might reasonably poach the same without harm to themselves. He prayed their discussion might go on for quite some time so he might determine where he was and why he seemed to be the only one within earshot who wasn't talking about his knives. He took a slow, careful breath, then looked around himself.

There was no one else there.

Sarah.

He closed his eyes and forced himself to continue to breathe evenly. Anything could have happened to her. She could have been lying where he couldn't see her, senseless, or dead, or carried off beyond his reach. There were any number of mages infesting not only the keep but the woods surrounding the keep, mages who would have taken her and . . .

He let out his breath slowly. He couldn't rescue her if he were dead, so the most sensible thing to do would be make certain he remained alive.

Sensible sounded so much more reasonable than frankly terrified at the thought of what could have befallen her, which he was.

He quickly assessed his situation. His knives were both still down his boots and two others were still strapped to his back—not that he could have reached either set. The only bright spots in the gloom were that he still had all his magic, safely buried as it was inside himself in an impenetrable well capped with illusion and distraction and that the lads in front of him weren't paying him any heed.

He kept those lads in his sights as he focused on his hands, working the rope against the bark of the tree and finding the knots less secure than he would have dared hope. The hiring of his guards had been poorly done. If he had been in the market for the like, he would have invited his potential guardsmen to tie a knot or two and examined their work before entrusting them with anything more complicated than securing a bed-roll to a saddle—

The rope gave way without warning. He froze, partly because he didn't want to reveal what he'd just managed to accomplish and partly because the pain of blood rushing back into his hands was so intense, it rendered him immobile. He closed his eyes and concentrated on breathing evenly until his hands stopped throbbing enough that he could think again. And once he could, he turned his mind quickly to how best to escape.

Fortunately, luck was with him. The lads were so involved in their conversation, they still weren't paying him any heed. Then again, they hadn't paid heed to the mage standing just outside the circle of their torchlight either.

Damn it anyway.

It was Amitan of Ceangail who stood there, watching silently. Ruith held out no hope that his bastard brother hadn't seen him. He was only surprised Amitan hadn't already plunged a knife into his chest.

Then again, that might have been because it would have been deflected by the spell of protection Ruith suddenly realized he was covered by. It was, he had to admit, a rather elegant thing—and fashioned from Olc, if such grace were possible from that vile, unwholesome magic. Given that he certainly hadn't provided the like for himself, he had to wonder who *had*. Obviously someone wanted him alive and unharmed.

But who?

He supposed he could at least eliminate from the list his

half brother who swore at him before he strode out into the light cast by the fire. The men spun around, their hands on their swords.

"Oy, what do ye want?" the largest of the three demanded, with an admirable amount of fierceness.

"Tidings," Amitan said shortly, jerking his head in Ruith's direction. "Who captured that one?"

"Can't say," the first said stubbornly.

"Can't, or won't?" Amitan asked in a low, dangerous tone.

The second stepped up to stand shoulder to shoulder with the first. "I don't see as that matters, friend, do you?"

"It matters, *friend*, because I demand the answer. And if you have two wits to rub together, you'll give it to me before I reward you for your refusal, a reward you will find very unpleasant indeed."

The lads stood firm, but Ruith imagined they were beginning to regret having taken on such a task to begin with. He couldn't blame them. He had his own very vivid memories of countless encounters with his elder half brothers. They were, to a man, unpleasant and without mercy. He supposed he could concede that they were justified in their hatred of him and his siblings—given that he was certain they had looked upon them as usurpers—but he'd suffered enough as a child thanks to their abuse not to feel compelled to extend any undue understanding their way now.

"There was a woman with him earlier," Amitan pressed on relentlessly. "Where is she?"

The third elbowed his way to the front of the group. "Sold her to traders, did His Lordsh—"

Ruith watched as his companions jerked him backward and shouted him into silence. He wasn't sure if it was because Sarah's fate had been revealed or if the man had been on the verge of unwittingly revealing who had them.

He would have given much to have known both, truth be told.

He continued to keep his hands behind his back as he listened closely to Amitan and the men carrying on their discussion in increasingly belligerent tones. He quickly looked around him for a convenient escape route, then noticed something he hadn't before.

The spell he was covered with was sporting a great rent in itself, as if someone sliced through it.

Yet he was still breathing.

He would have considered that a bit longer, but he was distracted by Amitan beginning to lose his patience.

"I don't care about the traders from Malairt!" he shouted. "I want to know who hired *you* and why he wanted you to guard that *thing* over there."

The third of the group, the mouthiest by far, told Amitan in the most detailed of terms just what he could do with his questions.

That man crumpled to the ground quite suddenly, either dead or senseless. That seemed to bring the other two to a spirit of cooperation they hadn't enjoyed before.

"I don't know who the mage was," the second blurted out. "In truth. He just gave us orders to keep watch until he returned. Said that man there was a lord's brat who needed tending."

"What did this beneficent lord look like?" Amitan demanded.

"I couldn't look at him," the first answered promptly. "He was all darkness."

"But that could have been anyone!" Amitan thundered.

Ruith had to agree. Given the nature of every bloody soul inhabiting the keep up the way and the surrounding environs, the description could have applied to anyone within a thirty-league radius.

But why would darkness have wanted to keep him whole?

He considered that quickly as he watched the escalation of hostilities in front of him. Amitan was demanding that the guardsmen bring Ruith to him; the remaining two were refusing just as adamantly. It said something, perhaps, about the man who had hired them, that they were terrified enough of him to choose facing down an angry mage over facing his wrath later.

Amitan cursed them, then turned and flung a spell at Ruith.

Ruith rolled away from the mysterious rent in the spell of protection, more than willing to use something not of his own making to save his own sweet neck. Amitan's spell was absorbed easily, then it gathered itself into something quite different and hurtled back toward Amitan. It slammed into him with the force of a score of fists, then encompassed him from head to toe.

Amitan began to scream.

Ruith wasted no time in making his escape. He shoved apart the spell, dove through it, then rolled up to his feet, drawing his knives as he did so. The pain of that almost sent him to his knees. He looked at his palms in surprise only to find them covered with blisters.

He would have given that more thought, but he was too distracted by watching the spectacle of Amitan clawing at his face, trying to remove what had attached itself to him. Ruith winced as Amitan staggered about the glade, making altogether inhuman sounds of agony before he dropped to his knees. There was something about that spell, something he thought he likely should have a closer look at—

He shook off the thought. He had no time for anything but finding out where Sarah had been taken. He took a firmer grip on his knives, ignoring the pain of his ruined skin, then turned a fierce frown on the remaining guardsmen who were gaping at him as if he'd been the cause of Amitan's suffering.

"Where did the traders go with the woman?" he asked shortly.

They lifted their hands, then, as one, slowly pointed to the south.

"Fair enough," Ruith said, trying to sound calmer than he felt. "If I were you, I would hurry away and hide somewhere you think you won't be found. Because that," he tilted his head toward Amitan, "will be the least of what's coming."

The men looked at each other, then turned and bolted.

Ruith would have followed them in like manner, but it occurred to him that there might be answers to be had that would make his journey quicker. He resheathed his knives, then turned to his bastard brother who was now lying on the ground, panting.

"Who survived the fall of the keep?" he asked.

"I wouldn't tell you . . . if my life . . . depended on it," Amitan gasped.

Ruith was unsurprised. Though he would have much preferred to have had a tally of what had now been loosed into the world, he didn't have the time to wait until Amitan was in enough distress to unburden himself.

"Help . . . me," Amitan wheezed.

Ruith actually considered it, even though the little stinging things Amitan had tossed at him whilst he'd been captive in Ceangail's great hall were still quite fresh in his mind. Unfortunately, he possessed nothing—or, rather, nothing he would use—that would counter what had taken his half brother in its painful embrace.

"I think you'll need a mage for what ails you."

Amitan looked at him with naked hatred on his face. "I'll find you . . . and kill you."

"I imagine you'll try," Ruith agreed.

Amitan struggled against the spell that seemed to be wrapping itself ever more tightly around him. Ruith wasn't above seeing a black mage come to his own bad end, but he wasn't one to enjoy overmuch the watching that journey there. He started to walk away, then paused.

"There appears to be one end of the spell near your left boot, brother," he conceded. "I think if you could reach it, you might be able to unravel the whole thing."

Amitan wasted a goodly amount of energy condemning Ruith to a score of different deaths, each more painful than the last, before he apparently decided he would be better off saving his breath. Ruith left him to it.

He left the camp in a southerly direction, following the tracks of a handful of horses. He hadn't gone twenty paces before what had struck him as odd before presented itself as slightly more than odd.

Someone had made a rent in that spell of protection. He was willing to bet his knives that maker of the spell and the maker of the rent were not the same mage. But if that was the case, who had slit through that spell, and why?

He leaned down absently to adjust one of the knives stuck down the side of his boots only to find the answer.

The spells, pages from his father's book of spells, that he had rolled up and stuck down his boots were gone.

He turned immediately and strode back to the camp. It cost him precious time, but he forced himself to look methodically through everything. He ignored the continuing shrieks of his bastard brother as he rifled through the packs the guardsmen had left behind and searched all about the tree where he'd been bound.

The spells were gone.

He started to curse, then felt the hair on the back of his neck stand up.

Someone was watching him from the shadows.

He straightened his knives, furiously weighing his alternatives. Sarah was captured and carried off to who knew where, he was being stalked by something he might be able to name with enough time, and his magic was buried, which left him unable to address either problem easily. But if he released his magic and someone took it, he would be unquestionably powerless, which would leave Sarah alone, unprotected, unable to fight what he was quite sure would be hunting her.

Then again, perhaps the fact that he was still breathing said something about who was following him. Apparently he was worth more to that mage alive than dead, which led him to wonder if perhaps his unexpected benefactor intended to follow him and take his magic at a later time.

That left him with only one choice. He would find Sarah, then remain as attractive a prize as possible until he could get them both somewhere safe—hopefully before the mage in question tired of his sport.

He left Amitan trying to bring his foot up toward his face where he could presumably take hold of the end of the spell with his teeth, then walked off toward the south, looking for tracks. There were two sets: one made by horsemen and the other made by a single man.

That single set of tracks would eventually lead him all the way back to his own house where he could shut his door on things he didn't care to look at anymore. It was the road he had taken as a lad of ten winters when he'd had been seeking only refuge from the storm.

But he was no longer a lad of ten winters and he had taken on a quest willingly, knowing that it would lead him into a darkness he knew all too well. Only now that quest included a woman who had relied on him for protection and been repaid with harm.

He turned away from a path he wouldn't have seriously considered and started quickly down the other because the truth was, the quest was no longer just about finding Sarah's ridiculous brother and stopping him from trying to make magic far beyond his capabilities. He had himself loosed things in Cean-gail's keep that would need to be contained, he had lost spells that could wreak untold damage on the world, and he had failed to hold on to a woman whose only error in judgment had been desiring to do good.

And to trust him.

He would give her no reason to regret that trust in the future. Once she was found, he would seek out the closest safe haven for them both where they could hide until she was rested and he had unraveled a mystery or two. Perhaps by then he would have had the time to consider just who might have protected him with magic whose main purpose was to destroy.

He wasn't sure he would care for the answer.

But have it he would, then he would leave Sarah safely behind and follow the trail of his father's spells himself. There was naught but darkness in front of him and darkness following, and he would be damned if she would have any more of it.

He pushed aside his absolute dread that he would find her too late and concentrated on the tracks before him.

He could do nothing else.

**Enter the world of the Nine Kingdoms
from *New York Times* bestselling author**

Lynn Kurland

"[A] superb romantic fantasy trilogy."
—*Midwest Book Review*

"A fantasy world . . . too wonderful to miss"
—*Paranormal Romance*

Star of the Morning
The Mage's Daughter
Princess of the Sword

**And the first book in a brand-new trilogy set
in the Nine Kingdoms**

A Tapestry of Spells

M616AS1209

ALSO FROM *NEW YORK TIMES*
BESTSELLING AUTHOR

Lynn Kurland

With Every Breath

When medieval laird Robert Cameron pounds on Sunny Phillips's door, he isn't paying a social call. He's braved a trip onto enemy soil to fetch the MacLeod witch, a crone renowned for her healing powers. But the woman who opens her door to him is enchanting and young…and not from his century.

"[Kurland] consistently delivers the kind of stories readers dream about."
—THE OAKLAND PRESS

"I dare you to read a Kurland story and not enjoy it."
—HEARTLAND CRITIQUES

penguin.com

Also from *New York Times* bestselling author

LYNN KURLAND

Till There Was You

❦

Zachary Smith is finished with high-maintenance
women, impossible clients, and paranormal adventures. But when he walks through a doorway into a
different century—and meets Mary de Piaget—he
knows his life isn't going to turn out quite the way
he planned.

M620T1209